Georges Bank

A Novel

by

Bradley Bagshaw

D0974782

Published by Clyde Hill Publishing,
2011 89th Avenue NE, Bellevue, Washington 98004

In the United States of America

http://www.clydehillpublishing.com

Jacket design by Barbara Geisler

Photo by Donna Ardizzoni

The cover design incorporates a statue by Morgan
Faulds Pike for the Gloucester Fishermen's Wives
Association (GFWA).

ISBN-13: 978-0692110713 (Clyde Hill Publishing)
ISBN-10: 0692110712

This book is dedicated to Hope B. Bagshaw, whose roots were deep in Gloucester, and to James H. Bagshaw, who knew the difference between law and justice.

Law grinds the poor, and rich men rule the law.

Oliver Goldsmith

Chapter 1

Gloucester — February 1885

The windowpanes rattled in their muntins. The radiators, though too hot to touch, were no match for the cold northeast wind that invaded every loosely caulked seam. The congealing remains of fried eggs and bacon so soft you could almost see through the fat sat neglected on the dining room table. Maggie was not a delicate eater, but on this stormy morning she could not get any of it down.

She had never been out to sea on Georges Bank during a winter gale, or in any other weather for that matter. Yet she knew the danger there. All too well, she knew. Ten days ago, Ray had sailed a hundred miles offshore to Georges, that most dangerous of all fishing grounds, and he hadn't come back yet. She couldn't focus on anything else.

She walked through the swinging door to the kitchen to refill her coffee mug. No fine china for her, and despite the rooms set aside for them in this grand house, no servants either. She was back to doing domestic chores, much as she'd done decades before for William Hudson. But this was her house, with its cupola, its widow's walk, its slate roof, and all that gingerbread. No matter what people said, and despite how she earned the money to buy it, having this house proved to her that she had arrived. Filling it with servants would have proven too much, though; it would have made her house feel too much like his.

She returned to the dining room, and through the wind-whipped branches of a young chestnut she saw the frozen prow of a schooner slowly emerging from behind the Tarr and Wonson Paint Factory. It was being towed by one of the little steam-powered harbor tugs that had started appearing a few years back. The shape was familiar. Maggie hurried to the window, where she strained to see.

Soon she spotted his dark beard, could see him leaning forward to scan the shore for her, and now she knew — Ray had made it home one more time. He was bundled in a sou'wester bib and jacket, leather boots on his feet and wool mittens on his hands, his head kept dry by a wide-brimmed oilskin hat. Maggie flung open the door and rushed out onto the porch, where she waved and waved. Ray waved back with one hand, keeping the other steady on the wheel.

Much of the schooner's lower rigging was white where salt spray had frozen into a deceptively serene coating of ice. But the *Benjamin Parsons* was safe now in the relative calm of the harbor, and she was down on her lines — not full, as she'd run for home before they'd caught all she could hold. Still, she had enough codfish in her belly for this to be a fair payday for Ray and his crew, a hard gamble won this time.

After the *Parsons* turned into Harbor Cove to unload, Maggie secured the porch door and walked over to the mirror on the wall facing the harbor. Her hazel eyes captured the steely color of the sky, and when she caught sight of her own reflection she smiled impishly, as if she were tickled to meet once again an old co-conspirator. She smoothed her windblown red hair, now streaked with gray. She was barely five feet tall, but she sported a fine figure still, and her complexion was the same milky white it had been when she was a teenage lass new to Fannies two and a half decades earlier. Men still enjoyed looking her way.

By the time she had finished her coffee the snow had started, just a few flakes at first, but soon a blizzard so intense she could barely make out the water's edge. She couldn't see any boat traffic now, not that there was any to see. Even here, none were so foolish as to start a trip in weather like this, and now it was too late for anyone caught offshore to safely approach the coast. Her adrenaline spent, she sighed with relief and slumped in her chair. At least Ray was safe.

A few minutes later she got up to wash the breakfast dishes. A gust shook the back door; she shivered and bolted it shut. A drift already three feet deep was growing where the wind swirled around the back steps — this storm would be a bad one.

Maggie had spoken with Sylvie the day before, and now she remembered that Robby was at sea on the *Julia Gorton*. The world had seemed safe then in the cold sunshine; it had just been small talk. But now she thought of Sylvie sitting in her parlor, contemplating her own husband's unknown fate. Sylvie had overcome so much to build the family she never thought she would be able to have, but it was all at risk again, as it had been so many times before. If Robby were lost — Maggie shuddered at the thought.

Chapter 2

Anchored on Georges Bank — February 1885

From the wheel, Robby could barely see the bowsprit. Heavy snow mixed with frigid salt spray stung his eyes, melted on his forehead, and refroze into icicles that hung down from the soft red whiskers of his beard. Slush was piling up on deck, beginning to plug the scuppers, and ice was building rapidly on the scores of lines that supported the masts. Soon the crew would have to be called on deck to deal with it. "Gawd, I hate poundin' ice," he muttered to the wind.

Anchor watch was usually a one-man job, but this morning Robby was paired with Joey. The captain wanted to know the instant they sensed anything unusual, but there was little they could see through the blowing snow, and little they could hear over the roar of the storm. Robby was about to call for help with the icy rigging when Joey appeared out of the snow on the port side, picking his way carefully back toward the wheel. "Robby, we need to go forward and let the anchor line out! We're gettin' chafe!" Joey had to shout to be heard.

Like her sisters, the *Julia Gorton* was beamy and shallow, and she set a massive amount of canvas on two tall masts and an elegant bowsprit. These little ships were fast as lightning downwind, but in a blow they were unable to claw their way off a lee shore. When it got rough, as it had this day, they sailed on the edge of calamity, and all too often over that edge. Losses were high, but handsome profits compensated boat owners for putting their capital at risk, and there was an endless supply of men like Robby and Joey willing to take their chances. This perilous work paid far more than anything else they could do.

In a steep sea like the one she found herself in this morning, the *Gorton* pitched like a seesaw gone mad. It was enough to make most men sick, but Robby had been at this for over thirty years, and Joey had started in the Azores in a simple fishing smack at age eleven.

Joey gingerly retraced his steps to the bow with Robby in tow. Once they reached the windlass, Robby grabbed the anchor line just aft of where it was wrapped three turns around the drum, and Joey undid the knot from the bollard. When the schooner crested a wave and started back down, Robby shouted, "Now!" With the tension eased, they let out two feet of line and cinched it back up before the boat took the strain on the next wave face. Then, with the ease that comes from long practice, they shifted the chafe mat back under the line with a pry bar and a boat hook.

Just as they finished, a towering wave lifted the *Gorton* up and up, until her prow pointed into the sky and she could go no higher. Then the wave passed on and gravity took hold — she pitched down and fell headlong to the bottom of a deep trough where she buried her bow in the face of the next wave. Deep water swept over the foredeck, carrying Robby aft in a churning world of green liquid and white foam. He held his breath and reached instinctively for anything solid, anything to save him from being swept away, until the surging water slammed him chest-first into the foremast and then dropped him to the deck.

It took two wave cycles for Robby to get back on his feet, and when he looked aft Joey was nowhere to be seen. Before Robby had regained wind enough to yell, "Man overboard!" he saw Joey staggering forward out of the driving snow. The sea had carried him all the way to the aft rail, yet somehow he had stayed on board.

Joey struggled up the pitching, plunging deck, then slipped and fell face-first into the slush. Robby started to laugh, but just then the schooner was hit by a wave coming in on the starboard side, unlike the rest. The boat rolled. Robby fell and then slid on his back across the icy deck to join Joey in the semifrozen muck at the port scuppers.

Soaked to the bone, both had lost their oilskin hats. Robby's head was white with frost, and Joey's thick black hair had frozen into a wild forest of spikes and random curls. They sat up and looked into each other's eyes — and laughed, not the happy chortles they might emit in response to a bawdy joke, but the adrenaline-soaked guffaws of men who had escaped drowning in an icy sea, of men who had been hurled into the void together, but had been thrown back to live a while longer.

Chapter 3

Enniskerry, Ireland — June 1859

Maggie O'Grady's journey to America began on St. John's Eve — Bonfire Night, an ancient solstice celebration, a time to appeal to the Celtic gods for fertile fields and fertile women. She had made a new dress for the occasion, green with white lace trim lining the bottom of the skirt, short sleeves, and a low neckline — saucy, but respectable enough for her to pass as a proper lass of seventeen.

Jake Anderson, the oldest son of Paddy Anderson, the most prosperous tenant farmer on the Powerscourt estate, escorted her into town that night. The tenancies had always passed from father to oldest son, and Mervyn Edward, Viscount Powerscourt, had declared his intent to continue the tradition, so Jake would have his father's land one day.

"What a night this is — just smell the air!" Maggie exclaimed on the walk to town. "Jake, do you know o' California?"

Maggie, daughter of one of Enniskerry's few college graduates — the estate's veterinarian — was a voracious reader. She had just finished Richard Henry Dana's *Two Years Before the Mast*. "The Spaniards built their California missions hundreds of years ago, but most o' the land is still as wild as can be, a thousand miles o' coastline and just a few wee villages. They have horses, they do, and cows too, just like we've got here. You'd feel at home, surely you would. Ships sail from Boston around Cape Horn to trade for hides. Some o' the crewmen are Kanakas, mysterious men from the Sandwich Islands, men with strange customs and stranger tattoos. What an adventure it would be to make a life in California, wouldn't it now?" she said hopefully.

"Well, I don't know about California, do I?" Jake responded. "I don't know much about any place other than right here. But I know this place, and make no mistake. Our peaty sod — what a fragrance it has in the first heat o' spring — no richer soil anywhere on God's green earth. And, for sure, there's no prettier sight than an October sunset o'er the Wicklow Highlands. . . . Me da says we're part o' this land, just like the bones o' the ancient ones, we are. No matter how many cows they have in California, it'd never be home, now."

Maggie sighed, and they walked in silence to the clock tower in the town square. The celebration began with a potluck supper; when the sun set, a bonfire was lit and the dancing began. Everyone was there; it would have been bad luck to stay away. Maggie and Jake danced the first dance, and then the next, and the next after that. She soon lost herself in the spins and the whirls, in the crackling intensity of the bonfire, and in the surging energy of the crowd.

As darkness blackened the hills, Jake invited her to jump through the edge of the fire. His proposal was not without meaning — it was said that young couples who danced in the fire were destined to marry, although that was more ancient lore than binding promise. Flushed with excitement, she said yes, and through the edge of the fire they leapt, danced a few steps, and leapt back. The crowd drank to their health and cheered them on. They jumped through again and again, the fire their prop and the crowd their drug. This year, Bonfire Night belonged to them.

Finally the musicians rested, and it was time for pudding. Maggie joined her mother to serve it to the crowd, and Jake joined the men to share a jug of *poitin*, distilled locally for the occasion. It was the rough-and-ready liquor for those who didn't worry too much about the revenue agents. After pudding was served, Maggie and her mother had time to talk. "Well, Margaret, you were making a spectacle of yourself out there, back and forth over that fire like that, you sure were. 'Tis said to bring a young couple good luck."

"And many babies too!" teased her younger brother, Michael, passing by with a stack of dirty dessert bowls.

"Oh, shush now, the two of you. We were having an entirely lovely time, paying our respects to St. John. That's all — nothing more."

"Maggie, that young man has every reason to expect more from you. Your da and I jumped the flames in our time, you know. Before we knew it the wee ones started coming, and a great life it's been too. I rejoice for you. That Jake will be a fine provider, he surely will. And your brother's right. No mistake, you'll make handsome wee ones."

"Oh, Ma, I'm not to breeding. I may never be. I have great things within me, and they're not all babes. I want to go places. I want to write. Anna Jameson's a writer, grew up not far from here."

"Don't be silly, child; she's barren and withered. But you'll be blessed with children, for sure. Your da and I want wee ones around the fire when we're old and worn. It's what God made you for, Maggie; it's what He made us all for, surely 'tis."

Maggie wandered away from the fire to look for Jake. She did not need to look far; he was down by the old mill, drinking with a dozen other men. The miller's cousin, who lived alone up in the Highlands, owned the still. Before Maggie laid eyes on them, she heard the old drinking song they belted out with enthusiasm:

Now learned men who use the pen
Have wrote the praises high;
Of the sweet poitin from Ireland green,
Distilled with wheat and rye.
Forget your pills, it will cure all ills
Of the Pagan, Christian, or Jew,
Take off your coat and grease your throat
With the rare old mountain dew.

They broke into raucous laughter, and Maggie could hear them cheer each other on as they passed the jug around. She retraced her steps to the bonfire. It was nearly midnight, and while the celebration was likely to go on until dawn, she had had enough, so she started home. The gibbous moon was low in the sky, and the shadows faded to black as she left the bonfire behind her. When she was halfway home, Jake caught up with her. He was out of breath.

"Maggie . . . where you off to? The night's young . . . there's lots o' dancing still to do!"

She crossed her arms and looked hard at him. "Do you mean dancing or drinking, Jacob Anderson?"

"Maggie . . . 'tis the shortest night o' the year . . . but surely 'tis long enough for both. I wouldn't be a right man if I didn't share a jug with the lads, now would I?"

"Well, short it may be, but 'tis long enough for me to want a few winks." Maggie unfolded her arms and frowned theatrically. "You can walk me the rest o' the way home, though, if it would please you."

Jake smiled, and Maggie tried unsuccessfully to hide the smile that came naturally in return. They started down the road, together now, walking slowly. After Jake found his wind, he proved unusually talkative. "We jumped the fire tonight. You know what they say about that: we're destined to be together now, me and you, my beautiful Margaret O'Grady!"

She blushed; he'd never called her beautiful before. "Well, Jake, I don't believe things are destined to happen. For sure, it's people who make things happen."

Jake slipped his arm around Maggie's waist and pulled her close. She did not resist. He kissed her; their tongues touched.

She broke away and cocked her head. "Jake, you surprise me," she said softly.

"Yes, but it's a good surprise, isn't it, now? That's a kiss for a grown woman; you're not a little girl anymore. I've something else for you." Jake straightened up and looked over Maggie's right shoulder, as if reading from a big poster board behind her. He cleared his throat and recited:

Nothing in the world is single;
All things by a law divine
In one spirit meet and mingle.
Why not I with thine?

14

"Oh, Jake!"

"'Tis Shelley. You probably knew that, the way you've always got your nose in a book." Now she stepped forward and kissed him.

Jake took her hand. "When I was little, I'd go out to me da's field on nights like this and just lie down and stare at the sky. Come on, Smitty's field's right over here." She followed him over the low split-rail fence, and soon they were walking in damp, knee-high grass. Well away from the road, Jake stopped, tamped down a patch, and lay down his jacket. "Here, sit on me coat, now." She did, and he sat beside her. "I brought this for us, you and me." He pulled a small flask out of his trouser pocket, removed the cork, and handed it to her. "Ever tried poitin? It'll make you see the stars in a way you never seen 'em before."

"Jake, that's not for a lady. Does your ma drink poitin?" Maggie asked, feigning offense.

"No, but then I didn't figure you to be like Ma, for sure. I heard all the ladies in America drink spirits right along with their men. I thought you might be entirely like them." Jake smiled broadly and held the flask out for her.

She nodded reluctantly, then took the flask and held it under her nose. It smelled of old hay in the dead of winter. She put it to her lips and swallowed way too much. It burned the back of her throat, and she coughed. Jake laughed. "I did the same first time I took

15

a swig, so I did. If you keep at it, you'll find it's right as rain — warms the insides of you, now." He took a gulp, more than Maggie would have thought anyone could stand, having just tasted how strong it was.

Jake corked the bottle and lay down on his back. "Look at the stars. That's the Big Dipper. Follow those two in the cup, and they take you right to Polaris, the North Star. Polaris will always lead you home, so it will."

She lay down beside him. Her da had taught her about the stars, and looking at them now put her at ease. "Yes, and over there, that bright star is really the planet Jupiter. Four little moons are running around it. Galileo was the first to ever see them." She closed her eyes and exhaled deeply. *What a marvelous evening*, she thought. Jake nudged her hand with the flask. She took it, and this time she sipped.

Jake rolled onto his side, facing her. "It'll be a grand day when you're me wife."

She rolled to face him. "Oh, Jake, I'm not ready for marriage. I may never be. I want to travel; I want to see America. You've got your farm, and that's your life. I don't see that it's meant to be."

"'Tis meant to be, Maggie, 'tis entirely meant to be. We've been raised for it our whole lives, you and me. And tonight we danced in the fire. 'Tis our fate to be together." He drew her closer and looked into her eyes.

Alcohol and unfamiliar hormones coursed through her; she ran her fingers through his hair and then down over his broad shoulders. They kissed again. With lips pressed hard against her, he rolled them both until he was on top of her, then pulled her hard against him. She leaned her head back far enough so she could speak. "Jake, mind yourself, now," she said quietly, but he ignored her.

He arched his back, pushing his pelvis hard against her, then straightened up to ease the pressure, then arched again. Her mind started to clear, and louder than before she said, "Jake, you must stop now! That's enough. . . . Jake . . ."

He did not stop.

"Maggie, this is what jumping through the flames is about. This is what all God's creatures are meant to do. We're the stallion and the filly, spindly legs grown firm and strong, full in the flesh and ready for each other." He pulled up the bottom of her skirt, grabbed her drawers, and yanked straight down, ripping a seam as he went. He rolled her bare bottom onto his jacket.

Scared now, she screamed: "No, Jake, no!"

"'Tis meant to be!" he cried in a hoarse voice.

She pounded his back, but he did not yield. When he loosened his grip to free a hand, she grabbed his hair and jerked his head back. In pain he rolled away from her. She jumped to her feet and started to run, but had gone only a few steps when he caught her by the shoulder, ripping her dress and exposing her right breast.

Now he threw her down onto the wet grass and planted one foot on each side of her. Standing over her, he slid his arms out of his suspenders and, one by one, undid the buttons, letting his trousers drop away. She looked up at him. He was engorged, ready to take her.

But she would not be taken. She grabbed him tightly with both hands and yanked herself upright into a sitting position. Then, holding him against her, she threw herself back down toward the dewy field, twisting and rolling as she went, using her body as a lever, as if trying to rip a sapling and all its roots clean out of the ground.

In surprise and agony, he screamed and collapsed. She landed face-first in the thick grass, then jumped up and ran, and she didn't stop until she was all the way home. But she needn't have run so hard and so long, for he did not follow. He lay curled up, whimpering, for a long time before starting his slow walk home, one jarring step after another, on that rutty country road.

Maggie ran up the steps of her childhood porch and collapsed on the bench where she had so often sat and read with her da. Her mother had arrived back from the bonfire minutes before, and hearing the commotion, she stepped out to investigate. "Oh m'God, Maggie, what the devil's happened to you? Your dress is all ripped, and you're busting out of it. What happened, me child?"

Maggie tried to answer, and at first nothing came. Kathleen O'Grady sat down next to her daughter, took her head into her arms, and let her weep. "'Tis all right, Maggie, 'tis going to be all right. God's in his heaven, the sun'll rise in the morn, and we're here for you. Your family's here for you, now."

They sat, clutching each other, while the candle in the kitchen burned itself out and the moon set, leaving only the gentle light of the star-rich solstice night. Finally her explanation came: she'd egged him on some, the dress was too revealing, she had wanted to be kissed, she never should have danced in the fire, and he was drinking — could any man be trusted when he was drinking? But surely it wasn't right of him to grab her and throw her to the ground after she'd told him no. She did not tell her mother exactly how she had managed to get away. But no, she said in answer to gentle questioning, he'd not bedded her; she'd fled before he'd gotten all he wanted.

"Well, that's a blessing then," Kathleen said softly, cradling her daughter's head in her arms.

By now the bushes and the trees were black patches against a sky dimly illuminated by a smidgen of light. It was just enough to reveal Maggie's brother Seth coming through the gate, returning home late from the night's celebration. "Ma, Maggie, you didn't need to wait up for me. I'm not a child anymore," Seth said as he climbed the steps to the porch.

When he got closer, he could make out Maggie's ripped dress, her bruised arm, her eyes red from tears, and the grass stain on her cheek. "What's happened to you?" he asked.

There was no sense in trying to lie about it. "It was Jake. He tried to take advantage o' me — but I'm all right, no harm now."

"God damn him, drunk for sure, damn him. Did he hit you?" Seth asked, his concern turning to anger.

"No — well — no — for sure — no. He ripped me dress — he tried to — he ripped me drawers — he wanted — but he didn't — I got away — I might have hurt him." The tears started to flow again, and she couldn't talk.

"By God, I'll see that he never hurts you again!" He turned and started back down the steps.

Kathleen jumped to her feet. "Seth O'Grady, you get back here right now. We don't need that kind o' trouble. Don't be a bloody fool. I can see that Jake isn't the only one who's been drinking this night, and the drink don't make you any smarter than it makes him."

Seth turned back toward the porch. "That may be, Ma, but she's me sister, and a man — a man can't let this happen to his sis now, can he?" His mother did not respond. "I'm not afraid o' Jake Anderson!" he exclaimed.

With just the right soothing tone, Kathleen said, "I know you'll protect your sister, but she's home now. Protect her here tonight. Go to bed, Seth. We all need sleep. We'll all have clearer heads in the morning."

Seth's posture softened. "All right, Ma, let's go to bed."

After four fitful hours of sleep, Maggie woke and found her way to the kitchen. She fried herself two eggs, lightly cooked three strips of bacon, and sat down at the rough-hewn kitchen table to eat. Her mother was already up, hanging the laundry out to dry. She walked into the kitchen and sat beside her daughter.

"Feeling better this morning, are we, my dear?"

"Tired, Ma, tired and hungry." Maggie dabbed at the eggs with her fork.

"Let's see that bruise." Her mother rolled up the sleeve of Maggie's cotton shift. "'Tis a wee bit black-and-blue, but it will be right as rain in a few days. Is that the only place you're hurting, me child?"

"Aye. Thanks be I got away before he did more damage."

"Well, no permanent harm, then. . . . No reason we can't patch this up with Jake, is there now?"

"Patch this up?" Maggie asked in confusion.

"Your da and I will call on the Andersons. Jake's basically a good lad. Too much in his cups last night, for sure. But he'll be sorry for what he's done. Paddy and Maureen will see he apologizes. The Andersons are decent folk, so they are."

"He tried to violate me."

"Now, Maggie dear, you said yourself that you led the boy on. And all that dancing in the fire — he just assumed you'd be his wife. Now, he was supposed to wait 'til his wedding night, for sure, but this is hardly the first time poitin's caused a lad to jump the gun."

"But Ma . . ."

Kathleen O'Grady leaned over and grabbed her daughter's shoulders. "You're not a little girl anymore; you're a woman now, and you must start thinking like a woman. We need a man to put a roof over our heads and food in the mouths of our wee ones. Look around — see what you've got to choose from. Jake's a good worker, and the Andersons have a fine farm that'll be his one day. As for the rest of the lads your age, well, it's like a summer without rain. It's parched, barren ground out there, and you're not the only potato in the pot, now. If we don't fix this up quick, Jake will find another young lass, and you'll be out in the cold. You can't let a few minutes of unpleasantness destroy your whole life. Think about it, now."

Kathleen went back outside to finish hanging the laundry. Maggie stared blankly out the window. The thought of kissing Jake, so tantalizing only twelve hours earlier, now nauseated her. Submitting to him was more than she could contemplate. She returned to her room and lay back on the bed, but she couldn't sleep. There on the small table was Anna Jameson's thin volume, *Winter Studies and Summer Rambles in*

Canada. She'd read it many times, and it was already showing wear along the binding.

Maybe there was another man out there for her, and maybe there wasn't. But being alone was better than being with Jacob Anderson, and if it were her fate to be barren and unmarried, well, so be it; she would dedicate herself to becoming a writer like Jameson. She walked with determination into the kitchen, where her mother was cleaning up.

"Ma, I can't do it. If it's Jake or no one, then a spinster I'll be. I'll find a way to feed meself. I cannot be with Jake, not ever, not after what he did last night."

Her mother looked away and said nothing.

Five nights later, Jake finally felt well enough to venture out, and down to the Bull's Head Tavern he went. Seth, who was working in the kitchen, saw him straightaway, but just gave him an icy stare and went back to frying bangers and mashing potatoes. Jake noticed the look, but he ordered his pint, turned his back to the kitchen, and sat down with his friends to unwind after a long and painful week.

It was two hours and many pints later that the trouble started. One of Jake's friends asked when he and Maggie would wed, an innocent enough question since everyone in the village had seen them jump though the fire together. Jake responded in an altogether too loud voice that he'd never marry that tart Maggie O'Grady, no matter how much fun she was in the wee hours.

No one remembered what Seth said, but what he did was a tale long told. Jake was the bigger man, but perhaps he was still hobbled by his delicate injury, or maybe Seth had gained extra strength from his righteous rage. No matter, Jake soon found himself flat on his back, with Seth pounding fist after fist into his head. By the time Seth was manhandled out the door, Jake had a broken jaw, a broken nose, two black eyes, and a pretty good concussion. Seth had hit him so hard that he broke two of his own fingers and bloodied all of his knuckles. It wasn't much of a fight, but for years it was known down at the Bull's Head as the Great Beatin'.

The next morning, the Wicklow County constable arrived on the O'Grady porch and rapped three times on the old oak door. Kathleen answered. "Katie, I've come to investigate a fight last night. It's Seth I need talking to."

"Come on in, Danny. Why is it you're here, now? Do you get involved these days every time two boys get into a scuffle? You were pretty quick to bloody your own knuckles when you were a lad. I remember that, I surely do."

"It's more serious than that, Katie. I need to see Seth. Fetch him, if you please."

"Seth," she called out. "Come on down here. Constable Sullivan wants a word." Soon Seth appeared in the kitchen. His right hand was heavily bandaged, and two of his fingers were in splints. Seth and the constable sat across from each other, elbows at rest on the worn pine table.

"Seth, I've just come from the Andersons' farm. The doctor was there, and he said Jake was in a bad way, although he doesn't think any lasting harm's been done. He'll be out shoveling manure again in a week or two, he surely will, but you wouldn't guess that from the way he was moaning every time he moved this morning."

Kathleen put a fresh loaf of bread and a crock of butter on the table. "Have a slice o' this soda bread still warm from the oven, Danny. I'll pour you a glass o' milk."

The constable helped himself to a slice of bread and buttered it liberally before continuing. "Jake told me you jumped him. Said you threw the first punch, and the second punch, and pretty much every punch after that. I've got two witnesses who say the same thing. What do you say for yourself?"

Seth tried to cut a slice of bread, but his bandages and splints got in the way. His father had just fixed him up that morning, and he had not yet learned how to manage. "Constable Sullivan, he called Maggie a tart. He all but said he'd had his way with her. I couldn't just stand there and let him slander me sis like that, now could I?" Seth threw down the knife in frustration. "I've known Jake me whole life, and I'm glad he's going to be all right. But I'm not sorry I knocked him about. He had it coming, and I'd do the same next time." He straightened up and said with conviction, "If defending your sis is a crime now in Wicklow County, then I guess you'll have to take me in, so you will."

"Seth, let me give you a little lesson in the law. Beating a man who isn't threatening you is a felony. You didn't just wrestle Jake to the ground and give him a little love tap. You could have killed the man. If you had, you'd be in jail for manslaughter now.

"As it is, Jake wants to bring charges, and if I can't talk him out of it, I'll have to lock you up and you'll stand trial. And as God's me judge, you've not got much of a chance if it comes to that. You'll be spending the next couple o' years breaking up rocks on the new turnpike to Knocksink."

Kathleen jumped in. "Danny, you know Seth's a good boy. You can't be serious, now."

"Katie, I'm going to let everyone cool off for a day or two. But Seth, if I can't get Jake to back down, I must do me duty. Good day, now."

Kathleen cut her son a slice of bread and buttered it for him. "Ma, Jake's stubborn as a mule," Seth said. "He's not to backing down." His mother nodded sadly.

Patrick O'Grady soon returned from his early-morning trip into the village. As he walked into the kitchen, he placed an envelope on the table in front of Seth. "That's your last pay from the Bull's Head. Charley says he doesn't have many rules, but he can't have his cook attacking his customers. ''Tis bad for business,' he says. Son, you're out o' work, although Charley says if you want to take up prizefighting he'll back you, he surely will. He says you beat the daylights out o' Jake.''

"Da, Constable Sullivan was just here. Not only am I out o' work, I might be off to jail too."

By nightfall Seth knew what he had to do. He'd been saving up money for the last three years, hoping one day to open his own tavern. Unlike Maggie, he had no love for the New World, but now it looked like the place for him.

Maggie wanted to get right on the boat with him, but her family would have none of that. Kathleen needed her at home now more than ever, and Seth didn't want the added pressure of looking after his little sis while making his way.

That night Patrick and Seth borrowed two horses from a neighbor and rode under cover of darkness into Dublin. The *Dublin Packet* left the next morning for New York. Patrick last laid eyes on Seth standing alone at the aft rail, his bandaged hand waving goodbye as the *Packet* cleared Ringsend and put out to sea.

Maggie was sullen after Seth left. She declined to attend the summer fair in late July, and she stayed away from the dance that followed, and the dances after that. She slept late, yet she was always tired. She withdrew from the life of the village as completely as if she had been the one who'd gone to America.

Toward the end of August, Patrick asked her to help with his visits to the farms. He had slipped into a ditch when trying to get hold of a young calf and had badly sprained his ankle. He needed help until he healed, he told her, although that was stretching the truth — he knew he had to get her back out into the world.

One day they went to Mike Smith's farm. She walked right past the field where Jake had attacked her in June. Mike Jr. was Jake's age, and he knew Jake well. While their fathers tended a lame cow, Maggie and Mike talked in the barn. He filled her in on who was going with whom and other local gossip.

Then the tenor of the conversation changed. Mike put down the scythe he had been sharpening and put his hands on Maggie's shoulders. "Maggie, you're the prettiest lass in all o' Wicklow County," he said.

Confused, Maggie pushed him away gently. "Thank you," she replied apprehensively. Then he leaned forward and kissed her. She slapped him and backed away. "For the love o' God! Stop that!"

Mike was as startled as she. "I thought you might fancy a little fun," he said.

"Why would you think such a thing?!" she exclaimed. "There's never been that kind o' feeling between us, and you're practically engaged to Mary Sweeney. How could you, now?"

"You seemed to be liking me and, well, I hear tell you enjoy the company of a man now and again. I thought this might be me time, so I did."

"Enjoy the company of a man! What kind o' girl do you think I am?"

"Well — Jake told us all what happened on Bonfire Night. He said you were — well — experienced and that you, ah, really fancy that sort of thing." Maggie's jaw dropped. "I'm twenty-one now, and I've never — well — I thought you might enjoy — well — that we'd both enjoy — well — you know. Nothing serious, now, just a lark."

"That Jake is nothing but a liar! He beat me. He wanted to have his way with me that night, right here in your field. I was lucky to get away," Maggie pleaded, hoping he would understand.

"'Tis for sure not the way Jake tells it."

"Oh m'God, does everyone think I'm that kind o' girl? They can't think that, they just can't!"

"I was there for the Great Beatin'. If we hadn't hauled Seth off Jake that night, he might have killed the poor man. None of us thought it was right for Jake to talk about, well, his frolic with you when your brother was in earshot. In a way, Jake deserved what he got. But the Beatin' was a big story, and it got even bigger when Seth ran off to America. I guess everyone was to thinking Jake was telling the truth after Seth skedaddled the way he did."

The next day Maggie sought out Molly Tierney, who had been her friend since grade school. Molly didn't want to talk, but Maggie was persistent. She had to know what her other friends were saying. "All right," Molly said finally. "You've been the talk o' the village this summer, you sure have. They say you've a couple o' boyfriends in Bray and you've been whooping it up there every weekend. That's why you're never around.

"Night o' the bonfire, you made Jake get you some poitin. Then you took him out in a field and showed him a fine old time. He broke it off with you when he sobered up the next day. Rumor is you gave him the French disease, and being a good man who'd made a mistake, he told you he'd not see you again."

"What a big lie! He attacked me that night, and I've been staying home ever since to keep away from him. Oh m'God! How will I ever straighten this out?"

"Whatever the truth is, I don't think any o' the respectable boys would be seen in public with you — the randy ones, aye, that's a different story, for sure. As for the girls, they're not much better, I have to tell you. Even I was reluctant to let you come through me own door today, so I was."

Strangely, Maggie felt a new clarity, and with clarity she found strength. What a liar Jake was — the French disease! Clearly she could no longer live in Enniskerry. She was not going to waste her life trying to convince her neighbors she was worthy of their respect.

That evening Maggie sat her parents down at the kitchen table and told them she was going to America. Her ma cried and pleaded with her to stay, but her da just shook his head in resignation. He hated to see her go, hated it with all his heart, but at least she had the fire in her belly again.

Two weeks later, Maggie boarded the *Packet* for the trip to New York. She shared cramped, windowless quarters with seven other women, two of whom became seasick with the first ocean swell. Going topside to take the air, Maggie saw a dramatic display of vibrant color dancing across the northern sky. Once before she'd seen the pale white edges of an aurora borealis as it strained to reach Ireland, but this display lit up the sky with transcendent brilliance. Maggie sat up the whole night, watching the colorful bands of light dance across the heavens. By dawn she was spent, but infused again with hope and wonder. She was off on a grand adventure and determined to make the most of it.

Chapter 4

Gloucester — August 1859

While Maggie sat on the deck of the *Packet,* transfixed by the aurora's glow, a small supper was winding down in Gloucester. Sixteen-year-old Ray Stevens had finished the last day of his summer job at the Cape Ann Savings Bank, and he was celebrating with his mother, Elizabeth; her best friend, Emily Wonson; and Emily's daughter, Jane. They had nearly finished dessert when Elizabeth prodded her son. "Raymond, you've been sitting across from Jane the whole supper without remarking on her new dress. Isn't it pretty?"

Jane's dress was pale blue and went all the way to the floor, supported by a series of ever-larger hoops. There was no possibility of seeing her feet, and the high neckline and long sleeves kept the rest of her safely covered as well. To Ray it looked like the same conservative dress Jane had worn with a bonnet every Sunday to church, but he was a bright boy and knew that a compliment was required. "Yes, it's a fine dress. It flatters you, Jane."

"Thank you," Jane said proudly. "I've spent the better part of a month making it. These hoops are all the rage."

"Jane's an excellent seamstress," Emily said. "A dress this fine would cost a pretty penny from a Boston dressmaker and would never fit this well. She's making me one for the September social at the Universalist."

"Raymond, you should use some of your summer earnings to buy some new going-to-church clothes," Elizabeth suggested.

"If you buy the fabric, I'll make a suit for you," Jane offered.

"That's generous of you, but I've got barely enough to buy that Henry Fitz telescope I've been eyeing."

"Telescopes are all well and good," Elizabeth said, "but you'll need a new suit for the savings bank next summer. I don't know how much I can keep letting your old one out."

"I don't want to go back there, Mother. All that sitting around, all that chitchat, it's not for me. I'm going to sea next summer."

"Raymond, we've talked this over many times. Your father and I want a career ashore for you. Look at what he's going through now. Out of work a whole year, and all those trips to Boston to plead for a job from some dandy who couldn't even row a boat across the harbor."

Ray stared down at his plate, empty but for streaks of blueberry and flakes of piecrust.

"And when he was working, he was gone for two years at a time, with me back here not knowing if he was alive or dead. And now he's out of work. It's not the life for you. It's not the life for anyone who has any sense at all. You'll understand when you're older, so that's enough of that."

After an uncomfortable silence, Emily caught Elizabeth's eye, and she nodded almost imperceptibly. "Raymond, Em and I are going to clean up. Would you be so kind as to walk Jane home?"

"Of course, Mother," Ray replied. He shifted his gaze to Jane. "It would be my pleasure." Ray had walked Jane home after many such meals, but he had yet to initiate the offer.

As soon as they stepped outside, it was evident that something unusual was afoot. It should have been fully dark, but Middle Street was as bright as day. A dozen people were milling about, looking up into a northern sky that was painted with brilliant purples, reds, and greens, vast ribbons of flowing color so bright a pamphlet could be read in their glow.

"Ray, what is it? What is it?" Jane asked with increasing agitation.

"I think it's an aurora borealis," Ray said with wonder. "I've read about them, but I thought you had to be in the Arctic to see one. Look how beautiful it is!"

"We should go back inside. Something bad's happening."

Ray had known Jane his whole life, and he had seen this sort of behavior many times before. Rowboats, horses, black cats, dark nights, that first kiss way back when — anything new — she was spooked by it all.

He tried to comfort her. "Nonsense, Jane. It's perfectly safe."

But he was no more successful than he'd been all the other times. "If you say so," she said. "Please take me home."

They set off for the Wonson home, just a few blocks away, with Jane holding up the front of her hoop skirt to avoid tripping over it. She hurried inside as soon as they arrived, too distracted to even thank Ray for escorting her home.

Ray walked down to the Vincent Cove dock, where he could look out over the water and all the way down to the northern horizon. He gazed skyward while the bands of color jumped across the heavens, and dreamt of sailing to some exotic port under those heavenly lights. It was after midnight before he returned home to find his worried mother waiting up, wondering what had become of him.

Chapter 5

Gloucester — September 1859

Ray's father, Captain Augustus Stevens, had
sailed seven times around the Horn. He had purchased
tea in China and silks in India, swum with schools of
colorful reef fish in the clear waters of Raiatea, and sat
with Polynesian mystics while they prayed to their gods
and barbecued their enemies. He had never lost a ship,
and he had lost fewer crewmen than most.

While none of his voyages had been wildly
profitable, he had made steady money for Jordon &
Graham, the last of the Gloucester-based Far East
shipping companies. But Boston, with better river
access and now better rail access too, had come to
dominate the New England merchant trade. Finally,
Jordon & Graham sold out to the N.S. Hudson
Company of Boston.

Gus tried to get on with the new owners, but the
Hudsons didn't want him. Not aggressive enough, they
said — he'd heave to in a gale rather than sail on to be

first to port. Getting the cargo home a few days earlier was real money to a shipping company.

Gus knew that, but he had grown up with the men who worked for him, and he respected them too much to be reckless with their lives. Dick Graham and Bill Jordon had accepted his judgment on such matters, but now they were out of business, and who could say whether they might still be at it if Gus had pushed harder all those years. Without profits there was no business, and without business there were no jobs.

Gus had sent letters of inquiry to other shipping companies, but got no offers. After a year on the dock, his money was running out. His oldest son and namesake, Augie, was at college, and Ray would start college in a few years. Perhaps most notably, Gus had recently bought the house his grandfather had built in 1782. It was an elegant three-story on Middle Street near the center of Gloucester, with a granite slab foundation, yellow clapboard siding, and a cedar-shake mansard roof. It had been expensive, but Gus had a keen sense of family history and could not pass up a house he had admired since boyhood.

So he was becoming desperate. Yet he hesitated to seek a job in the fishing industry, the source of most Gloucester-based jobs now that the merchant ships had gone. He was a master mariner, licensed by the Coast Guard to sail across any ocean. The grand, square-rigged ships he had commanded were ten times the tonnage of the largest fishing schooner. Running a schooner would be a humiliating step down.

But that wasn't all. While Gloucester was the nation's most productive fishing port, the community leaders were not fishermen. When fishermen got ahead, they became fish brokers, boat owners, and the owners of the businesses that supplied the fishing industry. They were men like John Pitt, who had risen from humble beginnings to build a fish-packing business that marketed Gloucester's fish to the world.

Fishermen just weren't Gus' kind. It wasn't so much where they came from — though many were immigrants, the Novis and the Newfies, and lately the Irish and even the Portagees and the Sicilians. It was their behavior. The waterfront was home to six saloons and as many brothels, and the fishermen kept them in business. The debauchery repulsed Gus. This was his hometown, where his kids played in the street and his Elizabeth took her evening strolls.

For Gus, to become a fisherman would be to descend the social ladder, and he was loath to lower himself. But by the spring of 1859 he was out of ideas. John Pitt owed him a favor — he'd given Pitt's son a mate's job a few years back — so it was to Pitt that he went. Pitt was having boats built to feed his growing fish-packing business. His sixth schooner was in frame up at Joseph Story's shipyard in Essex, and she would need a skipper.

Pitt had gone to grammar school with Gus, and ever since Jordon & Graham had sold out, he had been expecting Gus to come to him looking for work. Pitt knew Gus could handle the schooner just fine. It was his reputation for caution that concerned Pitt. In the old days, when all the catch was preserved with salt, speed had not been critical. But now much of the fleet carried ice. Fish that was iced down on the grounds and brought quickly home could be shipped by rail and sold fresh to restaurants and fish markets from Boston to New York. That was where the big money was these days. Pitt wanted the fish delivered fast — caution be damned.

So Pitt would have rebuffed his old schoolmate, but for one factor: in his great rush to expand, he had gotten overextended. In a spring storm, one of his five schooners had sunk with all hands on Georges Bank. He had insurance, of course, but he would need that money to replace the sunken schooner. His revenues were down by twenty percent, and he had a cash flow problem. The best solution was to take on a partner in the new schooner.

Gus met Pitt in his office behind the drying racks on Smith Cove in East Gloucester, about a twenty-minute walk from Middle Street. It was a bright, brisk spring morning when he set out, his vest and jacket buttoned up, but warm enough for him to have shed the jacket by the time Smith Cove was in sight. Gus found Pitt on the dock outside his office. "I'm here because I need work," he said. "The merchant trade is all done in this town. I hear you've got a new schooner in frame up, and she'll need a skipper. I'd like the job."

"Why start somethin' new at this point?" Pitt said. "You earned your time on the beach. Why don't ya take it easy?"

"I could tell you I miss the briny smell and the bite of the wind, but that would be bull. I need the money."

"Well, I'll be just as straight with you. You're a fine skipper, but handlin' these little speedsters is a young man's game. It takes boldness, and I . . . I ain't sure ya got it in ya."

"For Chrissake, I've sailed around the world in real ships. I can handle a dinky little schooner."

Pitt looked into Gus' eyes. He knew Gus had been to every shipping company over the last year. He could see the desperation behind the arrogance. "Well, you're an ol' friend, and you been good to my boy. I'm willin' to put ya in charge a' my new boat, but I need a partner, not an employee. You're the skipper — if ya buy half the boat. I'll buy the fish, and I'll get ya a good crew and some first-rate fishin' charts — the rest'll be up to you. Whaddaya say?"

Gus was stunned. "I don't have the money for that. Jesus!" He put his chin in his hand and stared at the worn planks of Pitt's dock. Pitt let him stew. Finally Gus broke the silence: "How much are we talking about?"

"Story gave me a firm price a' thirty-eight hundred. It'll take five hundred to outfit her, but I'll front that against the first year's profits. You'll need to come up with nineteen hundred."

"Let me think about it," Gus said.

Gus wandered toward home, lost in thought. Maybe this was a blessing in disguise. Respectable men owned fishing boats; men like Pitt were the leaders in this town. Being an owner would take some of the sting out of his disgrace. But getting the money would mean going into debt. He'd never been in debt before, and he'd always ridiculed those who were. "Only a fool would be beholden to some banker," he'd lectured Ray at supper just a few nights back. But by the time he reached Middle Street, he was resigned to mortgaging his new home.

Never a lollygagger, Gus walked straight to the Cape Ann Savings Bank and applied for a loan. The banker knew his house, of course; it was only two blocks from the savings bank. And the name Stevens meant something in Gloucester. When the banker heard the loan was to buy into a schooner with John Pitt, that sealed the deal. "Still need to do some paperwork and run it past the trustees," the banker told him, "but we'll approve the loan."

By the end of the day, Gus was back at Pitt's. "You've got a deal" were the first words out of his mouth.

"Good" was all Pitt said. They shook hands, and that was agreement enough for them both.

"Does she have a name yet?" Gus asked.

"Nope."

"Then I'd like to call her *Raiatea Sunrise*."

"Done," Pitt said, without voicing a bit of curiosity.

The next day Gus rode a horse out to Story's shipyard in Essex to inspect his new investment. He began just after dawn, and it was nearly ten in the morning when he came around the last corner and found himself looking down the Essex causeway. By then he was sore, and the stink of horse sweat permeated his whole being. "I'd go senseless if I had to sit atop you every day," he grumbled.

Off to his right was the salt marsh, a flat expanse of eelgrass through which the Essex River meandered to Ipswich Bay. When he was a boy, Gus' mother had taken him each summer to a cabin near Wingaersheek Beach. From there he had often taken a sailing skiff around to the Little River in a salt marsh like this. He'd beach her in the white sand and dig for clams with his bare hands. Many thought clams good only for bait, but he loved steamers dipped in melted butter or fried and topped with his mother's sauce of mayonnaise, chopped sour pickle, and onion.

Joseph Story was alone in the small shack he used for an office when Gus rode up. Story's face was rough and heavily lined, his dress simple, his manner plain, and his hands huge. Gus could feel the hard calluses when they shook. "I'm Augustus Stevens, John Pitt's new partner in the schooner you're building. I'm here to take a look."

Story pulled a half model from the shelf behind his desk. "The *Lookout* was the first Georgesman schooner we made off this model. Built her two years ago, built two more since. Yours will be the fourth."

Gus took the model and turned it slowly around in his hands, feeling the smooth curves and the silky slipperiness of its spar varnish finish. These boats would never be as seaworthy as the ships he was used to commanding, despite their speed — or perhaps because of it. Yet he did not have it in him to scorn the shapely little schooner that Story was building. "Has the *Lookout* or any of her sisters been caught in a real blow yet?" he asked mildly, as if only in idle curiosity.

"The *Lookout* was on Georges durin' a whole gale last March, and she came back when four others didn't. Don't really know 'bout the sister ships; this is their first season. But she'll suit your purpose, Cap'n. She's not just some summer mackerel catcher. She's designed for the weather."

Gus looked out toward the Essex River. "Is that her?"

"Yup."

Her main framing was done, and about half of her hull was planked. She was sixty-three feet long on deck, beam of nineteen feet, and she would draw seven

43

feet eight inches. She looked to Gus like a toy — a beautiful toy, a fast and nimble toy, but a toy nevertheless. Four men were fastening planks to her frames. They clamped a plank in place, then used a hand auger to drill holes for the treenails that would hold her together. Story introduced Gus to the planking crew, each of whom gave him a polite nod and continued working. "These men are quick. In a month's time we'll have her in the river and on the way to Gloucester for fittin' out."

Gus walked slowly around the hull, then climbed up inside to get a better look at her. Her frames were straight-grained oak, her planking was quarter-sawn yellow pine, and her scantlings were prudently sized without being overdone. No seam was so large that tar and oakum could work free, and the fastenings were strong and properly installed.

"Nice work, Mr. Story. It's obvious you know your business."

"Thank'ee, Cap'n," Story said, with the flat affect of a man who did not need to be told that he knew his business. "What name shall I paint on her?"

"*Raiatea Sunrise*, if you please."

"Is that a place, Raiatea?"

"It's an island in the South Pacific, northwest of Tahiti."

"You're a lucky man, Cap'n, to have seen such places. I've not been farther south than Boston, and

44

there only once. Never goin' back to that Satan's den, I'll tell ya."

Gus left for home with melancholy memories of Raiatea in his head. But soon he was thinking of his new command. She was small and pretty, and he could see she would be handy. He was already feeling affection for her despite the obvious shortcomings of her design. Before, he might have called them her fatal flaws, but not now. She was shallow and excessively beamy, but she had a gentle sheer and an alluring angle to her cutwater; and she would be tall when her topmasts were in her. Why was he seduced by her? Were good looks that important?

Six weeks later, Gus went aboard the *Raiatea Sunrise* in the early-morning twilight. A single lantern hanging from the end of the wharf reflected across the still surface of Smith Cove. The tide was out, so he had a long climb down slime-covered ladder rungs to the deck. As he stepped aboard, the gunnels creaked — the familiar sound of wood moving against wood, relieving stress — and she heeled ever so slightly.

Gus leaned against the rail and looked out at the cove, where four decades earlier he had been a fisherman of sorts, catching minnows in a small trap his father had given him. Back then the old Chebacco boats moored here had seemed huge. For the first time since being stranded ashore, Gus was at peace. He was home again.

From below he heard the hard, hacking cough of someone who had smoked for decades. It was his first mate, Asa Burnham. Fishing schooners did not usually have a first mate; generally there was a skipper, a cook, and the rest of the crew. Asa had accumulated the skills to be a skipper long ago, but he had never held a command. He loved booze and loose women too much for that.

At the start of each fishing trip, Asa's skipper would round him up at his favorite flophouse, usually broke and often drunk. Asa was never fit for the shore duty demanded of skippers, but at sea, where he was sober and chaste, he was the finest kind.

Pitt and Gus had put Asa aboard the previous evening. They had found him at Fannies, at the corner of Duncan and Locust Streets. He hadn't resisted. On the contrary, he'd claimed, in a voice loud enough to be heard halfway across the harbor, that Sarah Jones was his one true love, and he was going to sea to earn money to buy her a little cottage on Rocky Neck. As the men were pulling away with Asa singing in the back of the wagon, three ladies appeared in a second-floor bay window of the brothel and shouted their boisterous goodbyes. Asa was excited to see them, and if one of them was his Sarah, he showed no preference.

As soon as Fannies was out of sight Asa fell sound asleep, and when they arrived dockside he had to be lifted out of the wagon and carried down to his bunk. Gus had doubted he would still be there in the morning, but Pitt had assured him that Asa would be quite responsible once he was back on board.

An orange glow now filled the eastern sky, and Sirius was the only star still visible. Gus could see the faces of the lumpers, who were assembling to unload salt cod from a schooner that had spent three months fishing on the Grand Banks. He tried to imagine three months on the banks in such a tiny boat. After spending a lifetime keeping his ships moving in deep water, Gus was uneasy at the prospect of sitting still, anchored, waiting for the inevitable bad weather to arrive.

But he looked forward to getting out of the house. Being home this past year had strained his relationship with Elizabeth. She had always been glad to see him when he arrived home from his long trips at sea, or so it had seemed. These days, though, it seemed she enjoyed Emily's company more than she did his own. Although nothing had been said, it was clear he had overstayed his welcome this time.

The oaky smoke of a galley fire drifted up from the foc's'le. Gus slipped down the companionway to find Asa standing by the stove, eyes red and hair disheveled but, considering his state the night before, doing remarkably well. "Mornin', Skipper. If we get some wind, this will be a mighty nice day for a pleasure sail. Ready for mug up? The coffee's 'bout done, and I found us some bread and jam."

"That would really hit the spot. Thank you."
Gus had left home early, so Elizabeth had not been up
to cook for him.

"Don't thank me; I'm just takin' care a' myself.
Lucy's long on feedin' the soul, but pickled eggs and
fried smelt from the bar's the only grub I been gettin'. It
don't fill your belly after a while."

"Lucy? Who's Sarah, then?"

"Why, Skipper, Sarah's Lucy's cousin, but
they're close as sisters. Sometimes they, uh, work as a
team. So you know Sarah, do ya?"

Gus didn't know Sarah, and he didn't want to
know about their teamwork. But he soon forgot about
them as ham and eggs came off the stove to accompany
the third biscuit he was wolfing down. He ate a hearty
meal and enjoyed it. Like most fishermen, Asa had
served as a cook a time or two, and he knew his way
around a galley. Fried ham and scrambled eggs were
not gourmet fare, but Gus was surprised by how good
they tasted this morning. It was the first of many
pleasant surprises Asa had in store for him.

By midmorning, Gus, his crew, and Pitt, along
with various family members and friends, were on the
deck of that modest schooner for her inaugural cruise
around the harbor. Gus gave the order to raise the
mains'l. The five men on the halyard and the four on
the topping lift made short work of it. As soon as the
forty-foot boom lifted out of its gallows, the smaller
fores'l was on its way. The lighter sail seemed to fly up

the mast, and the stays'l went up quicker still. Gus rigged a spring line from the port quarter forward and ordered all other lines cast off as three men on the foredeck backed the stays'l.

The wind nudged the schooner's bow into Smith Cove, the spring line was released, and when the sheets were trimmed, the *Sunrise* gathered way under her own power for the first time. She cleared the Rocky Neck Railways shipyard on a beam reach, and then she was hard on the wind and headed out of the inner harbor. "Not too shabby," Gus said with a satisfied nod. Three short tacks later, they entered the outer harbor; over to starboard tack, and they cleared Ten Pound Island.

With more sea room, Gus had the crew hoist the flying jib, followed by the two tops'ls and finally the fisherman's stays'l. Even in this light breeze, the schooner heeled noticeably under the full press of all that canvas. Her gurgling bow wake was audible, and she pitched gently to the long swell that refracted around Eastern Point into the outer harbor.

Pitt stepped over to the wheel. "How's she feel, Cap'n?"

"She's a handy little boat. Turns on a dime compared to what I'm used to."

"She'll show ya a good turn a' speed. Drive her hard and she'll make us money, and them too," Pitt said with a sweep of his arm toward the crew, leaning against the windward rail, clustered together with clay pipes lit. "Don't gentle her. If ya break a spar or two, we'll replace 'em."

Chapter 6

Boston — February 1860

Maggie had moved in with Seth to share one corner of an abandoned sail maker's loft on a South Boston pier. Their room, if it could be called that, was partitioned off from the rest of the loft by bedsheets strung from old lines left behind by the sail maker. They had space for a bunk bed and the two trunks holding their belongings, and that was all. They cooked on a two-burner alcohol stove they shared with the eleven other Irish immigrants. The commode was perched over a hole cut directly through the pier.

Seth had planned to get Maggie a chambermaid's job at the hotel where he was a cook's assistant, but the day after she arrived in Boston, an Irish dishwasher was caught with the wallet of a New York banker, and after that the hotel refused to hire any more Irish. "You're all thieves and drunks!" the banker had yelled.

Seth discouraged Maggie when she suggested going around to Boston's many taverns and saloons. He wasn't keen on his kid sister working in a place like that, and her trying would just be a waste of time anyway. The tavern owners believed the surest road to ruin was to let anyone Irish loose behind the bar. So she was left with looking for a maid's job. She applied for every one she could, and finally she read an ad saying that a man named Hudson was seeking a maid at his townhouse on Beacon Hill. She gussied up, as she had done a dozen times before, and walked the two miles from South Boston.

William Hudson was twenty-six years old, with brown eyes, thin lips, and a chiseled jaw. He kept his hair neat and closely cropped; he had ramrod-straight posture, slight musculature, and little fat, along with the pallid complexion of a man who rarely faced the sun or a fair breeze. He wore spare but elegant suits, custom-tailored on Essex Street by the same firm that had cut cloth for his father and grandfather before him.

William was the only child of the sixth generation of Boston's most successful merchant family. He had grown up with nannies and maids and cooks and butlers — but not with other children. He spoke only when spoken to, and he was invariably polite to his elders. To the many visitors at his father's several homes he was the perfect child, well scrubbed and neatly dressed, never disturbing the serene seriousness of the household. He was up early every morning, reasonably attentive to his studies, and on time to bed every night. He learned to control his emotions, to shake hands but refrain from hugs and backslaps, to smile and frown but not laugh or cry. He strived to fit his father's mold — competent and reserved, a serious person of high character and impeccable morals.

His father, Nathaniel Hudson, was driven to excellence in his work and to prominence in civic activities. As an elder of Old South Church, he was leading the fight for the abolition of slavery. He was also a crusader against strong drink and the evil of promiscuity, and he often used, or tried to use, his considerable influence to pressure tavern and brothel owners to close up shop. He was the prime sponsor of a program to offer Boston prostitutes a one-way ticket around the Horn in lieu of prosecution for public indecency, theft, or the many other crimes that often brought them into conflict with the law. He was thus indirectly responsible for staffing many of the classiest bawdy houses in San Francisco's Tenderloin District, and for that alone, many there toasted his good health.

William attended church every Sunday, and every Sunday afternoon the family gathered around their polished mahogany table for a dinner of roast beef or mutton, often with their minister or other leading citizens in attendance. At that table, where he usually was the only child, William absorbed the proper habits of a Boston Brahmin.

After William graduated from Harvard College with a gentleman's grades, his father set him up in business. Nathaniel owned a fleet of merchant vessels, recently expanded by the addition of Jordon & Graham's ships. He had formed an insurance company as well, initially to protect his own holdings, but the company had grown and prospered. He put young William in charge of it. It was, he thought, a reasonable way for the boy to break into business. William proved suited to his new job, and the insurance company prospered under his steady, if unimaginative, leadership.

With his career in hand, it was time for William to marry and assume his predestined place in the social order. He had known Victoria Lowell since he was four years old. Her father had roomed with his at Exeter, and the two families owned adjacent summer cottages on Lake Winnipesaukee. It had always been assumed that they would eventually marry.

But William had dawdled, and finally Victoria announced that she had waited long enough. "William," she said with an icy chill, "I have just celebrated my twenty-second birthday. Caroline threw me a delightful ladies' luncheon. All my friends were there, and every one of them was married — every one except me." She paused and lifted her chin toward the ceiling. "Avery Barnes will escort me to Sissy's New Year's Eve party this year. You shall have to find someone else to go with. I shall not wait on you any longer."

She stared defiantly at William as he pondered her words. The thought of Victoria marrying someone else concerned him deeply. He would never find another woman as suitable, and he certainly did not want to have to get to know someone new at this stage of his life. And his father expected him to marry her. He shuddered at the thought of explaining this turn of events to the imposing Nathaniel Hudson.

He thought in silence while Victoria waited for his response. Finally, he finished his contemplation and made a momentous decision. "Victoria, I have delayed far too long. Will you marry me?"

There was no pretense of romance in his proposal, but that did not bother Victoria. "Oh, William, of course I will marry you" was her straightforward reply. She offered her cheek so he could kiss it, which he did with polite formality.

The grand wedding to merge two of Boston's great families was set for the following December, in accordance with Victoria's preference for a winter wedding. In January, to allow time to prepare a proper home for his new bride, William moved out of his father's house and into a four-story brick townhouse on Beacon Hill overlooking Boston Common, just a few hundred yards from the Massachusetts State House. White columns guarded its entrance, and the bay windows on the second story were decorated with rugged but elegant wrought iron filigree. The sidewalk out front was paved with brick and illuminated by gas lamps that matched the windows.

William hired Harvey Percival, his uncle's coachman, to be his butler; his father's pastry chef to cook his meals; and Harvey's cousin, Seward Buckley, to be his coachman. All were long known to him, and each was happy to move up. Now he needed a maid, so he asked his new butler to put out the word. An ad was placed, and Harvey was surprised when a dozen women arrived at the doorstep to see him. Only three had experience. Harvey favored one of these, a woman from Arlington who'd worked for a professor, but she reminded William of his austere Aunt Edna. He had never been able to relax when Edna was around.

William had Harvey summon the other candidates and line them up, so he could see them all at once and with his own eyes. With nose slightly elevated, he asked the group why they thought they were suitable to work for him. Silence followed. It was unusual for the master of a household to ask such a question, or even to speak to a maid at all. Then a short young redhead stepped forward and said in an Irish accent that she had been making beds and cleaning clothes for her brothers since she was a wee tyke, and she was sure as sure could be that she could do the same for him.

She was wearing a dress of indifferent origin — not a maid's dress but a peasant's dress, perhaps. *Why had she not worn a maid's dress?* William asked himself. This dress covered her breasts without flattening them, and it showed the slight roundness of her belly that should have been smoothed out by a corset. The dress did not hide the soft, fleshy curves of the young woman's hips either — she was reasonably slender, but not too much so.

William had had carnal feelings before, of course, but he had always quickly suppressed them. Indulging such urges did not fit the Hudson image of British reserve and phlegm. But for the first time, perhaps because he sensed a new freedom in his new home, he let his baser emotions influence him. He hired her on the spot, then thought to ask her name.

"Maggie," she said.

Maggie moved into a tiny room on the fourth floor of the townhouse. Her first days on Beacon Hill were hard. Harvey was not pleased with his new master's choice; he resented having to train a new maid who knew nothing of a maid's work. But Maggie was bright and energetic. She quickly learned her cleaning, waxing, and polishing chores, kept her uniform and cap pressed and spotless, and before long was more help than hindrance.

The hardest part of the job for Maggie was dealing with the household's guests. She had not been raised around aristocrats, and subservience did not come naturally to her. Two weeks after she was hired, William held his first Sunday dinner party, hosting Victoria and their parents to show off his new home.

As Maggie cleared the soup bowls, William's mother expounded to Victoria about her Irish gardener. "Dear, when you get your summer cottage, you need to pay careful attention to the help. I let Nathaniel do all the outdoor hiring, and he put a ne'er-do-well named Mickey O'Brien on the payroll to trim the hedges and edge the lawn. I declare, every day after dinner he was so drunk he was a danger to himself. And every year, he and the missus had a new baby. Why, by the time your children are grown, our country will be overrun with red-haired drunks named O'Brien and McGinn."

Maggie was unable to hold back. "Why, Mrs. Hudson, sure an' you're being unfair! We're a hardworking people who may be down on our luck, but as good and upstanding folk as there are anywhere."

Harvey rushed Maggie out of the dining room, and she spent the rest of the meal in the kitchen doing dishes. The poached cod was delayed until Seward, still in his touring clothes, could be summoned from the stables to help Harvey pass the plates. William was saved from complete humiliation only by family tradition, which absolutely forbade the type of emotional explosion that otherwise would have burst from his mother.

As it was, William had to withstand his guests' cold appraisal of his household staff — and of his judgment in hiring one of "those people" to work inside his home, a decision the ladies agreed was even worse than Nathaniel's to hire O'Brien.

But William was strangely sanguine about the whole affair. Maggie had taken on his mother, something he had not done in all of his twenty-six years, and for reasons he would have found hard to explain, he had enjoyed it.

Chapter 7

At Sea — February 1860

When the light breeze died, all movement
perished with it, leaving the full moon reflecting across
the polished sea as if it were a gas-lit causeway. Gus
leaned against the starboard rail. His cheeks and nose
were cold, but the rest of him was warm underneath
layers of wool. He shook some tobacco into the bowl of
his clay pipe, tamped it just so, and lit it with a wooden
match.

This was Gus' third trip out to Georges Bank,
but the other two had been in early fall, when good
weather was the norm. The weather was good now too,
but winter was when the storm winds blew, and when
they blew hard, conditions were hellish. Georges was
shallow, just a few fathoms in places, so storm-driven
waves turned into steep and sharply crested mountains
of water that could rip a vessel from its moorings and
hurl it against another, or carry it into the shallows to be
crushed by more waves. Over the years, thousands of

fishermen had died in the hundreds of schooners that left Gloucester to fish on Georges and never returned.

Nevertheless, the fleet came to Georges because currents from the Gulf of Maine mixed there with warm water from the Gulf Stream, which in turn nurtured the creatures feasted upon by the cod and haddock that swam here in the millions. All told, Georges was one of the richest fishing grounds on the planet.

The fishing started in the pre-dawn twilight. Each member of the crew rigged his gear, save Gus and the cook, Doc — so called because he was responsible for first aid as well as for meal preparation. Each fisherman attached a lead ball to a tarred line. Below the ball, multiple lines and hooks were tied to a trapeze arrangement. The hooks were baited with herring, and the whole contraption was lowered until the lead ball hit bottom, then raised slightly so the hooks trailed out with the current.

The gear was left down until several fish had taken the bait, then brought in hand over hand. As each fish cleared the surface, it was gaffed in the gills and flung onto the deck. Usually they were big codfish, five to ten pounds, sometimes heavier. The fisherman clubbed his catch, extracted the hook, and cut out the tongue — a man's share depended on the number of tongues in his tally. He rebaited his gear, set it out again, and tied the line to the rail. Then he headed, gutted, and split each fish and lowered its butterflied carcass into the fish hold to be stored between layers of

61

ice or salt, depending on how long they planned to be at sea.

The fishing was good this morning, as it usually was in February. Doc, the cook, fried up beefsteaks, eggs, and potatoes, and brewed gallons of steaming coffee. After two hours of fishing, the men went below and wolfed down their breakfast. Half an hour later, they were back on deck. They continued fishing, with one more short meal break, until it was too dark to see. After supper they mended their gear, smoked their pipes, and told lies.

On the third day of fishing, Gus was sitting in his small cabin when there was a rap on the door. Asa stepped in. "Gotta minute, Skip?"

"Of course, Asa. What's up?"

Asa was still in his fishing gear, coated with salt crystals, fish scales, and the remnants of viscera. He had taken off his gloves; his right hand was calloused between the thumb and first finger from handling his fishing line. "I don't know how to say this sweetly, Skip, so I just gotta blurt it out. There's some things the crew doesn't like much — there's been talk."

"Talk about what, Asa?"

"It's that you ain't helpin' out with the fishin'. Most skippers go down into the hold when they got nothin' else to do and shovel ice on a layer of fish. Or when the fishin's real good, they'll help with the headin' and the splittin'. It keeps the guys at the rail bringin' 'em in. But, ya know, you're mostly just watchin' us work."

Gus respected Asa, but this was too much. "Jesus H. Christ, Asa, I'm the captain of this boat, not its slimer. Don't they know what it means to be captain?"

"Skip, it don't mean the same as you're used to it meanin'. On a schooner, the skipper's only the skipper if the men agree he should be."

"I don't command by agreement. The law covers this. I'm the captain, and anyone who says otherwise is talking mutiny."

"Skip, I'm just tellin' ya, this ain't some grand ocean-crossin' bark; it's a little Gloucester fishin' schooner. You lose the respect a' these men and they won't work for ya, and when we hit the dock you'll see nothin' but their backsides. I seen it happen. If ya can't man the boat, you're not skipper no more, and it don't matter what the law says."

"All right, have you had your say?" Gus asked, more resigned than angry.

"Yup, I'm off to get my grub."

Gus slumped in his chair after Asa left. Such a conversation would have been unthinkable on any ship he had commanded in the merchant marine. It was more proof of how far he had fallen.

The next day he swallowed his pride. Much of the time, he had captain's work to do. He had to point the schooner off the direction of the current so the fishing lines didn't tangle. He would put the rudder to one side or the other, where it worked in conjunction with the riding sail they flew at anchor in lieu of their big main. He could lash down the rudder and sail once they were set, but as soon as either wind or tide changed, he needed to adjust one or both. And he needed to inspect the anchor line for chafe periodically, and take soundings to make sure they weren't dragging anchor.

But when he wasn't needed for any of these things, Gus helped out on deck. He jumped into the hold to spread ice, helped head and split the catch, and even took a few turns at the rail, line in hand. At the end of the day, he was covered with the unholy goo of a working fisherman. A newcomer would never have guessed he was the captain just by looking at him.

After a few days of this, Gus earned a grudging respect. The crew still did not accept him as one of their own, but their complaining ceased, and they went back to bitching about the cooking, the unfaithfulness of certain ladies ashore, and the sad disappearance of the really big halibut — all the usual topics of fishermen's conversation.

At dawn on their eighth day, Gus noticed a few high, horsetail cirrus clouds moving in from the southwest. The barometer had begun to fall at midnight, though not precipitously yet, and the wind had shifted during the night. The changes weren't much, but they were enough to put the old sailor in him on high alert.

After breakfast, he asked Asa to come down to his cabin. "The glass started to drop last night, and the wind's shifted to the southeast. What do you think?" he asked.

"Skip, I think this great weather's comin' to an end."

"Me too. A nor'easter could be coming our way. I'm thinking of weighing anchor and heading for home."

"Skip, the men won't like that. The fishin's been great, but we're not even half full. Some a' the men are dreamin' 'bout a big wad a' cash. They won't like bein' cut short."

"And what about you, Asa? How do you feel about it?"

"I'm with the men, Skip; this is some a' the best fishin' we've seen. I got my ladies on Duncan Street, and they'll keep me real happy if I come in with fifty bucks."

This was about what Gus expected to hear. "All right, Asa. We'll keep fishing for now, but I'm going to take another look when the sun goes down."

Ten hours later, as dusk was settling, Gus looked hopefully around at the rest of the fleet, but no other boats were preparing to weigh anchor. The barometer had kept dropping all day, and the wind had backed around farther to the east. The swell had increased, but the crests were still far apart, so the *Sunrise* rode gently over them. All looked serene enough, but Gus knew better. His decision would have been easier if other boats were doing the same thing, but this was his command, and he had made up his mind.

"Men," he said after they had stored away the fishing gear, "we're heading for home. Let's shorten up on the anchor line and then get the mains'l up."

At first there was no movement, just grumbling. Finally, Sooky Wilkins, a weather-beaten old-timer, spoke up. "Skipper, none a' them other boats are movin' yet. Why do ya wanna run for it?"

Gus had his story ready. "Sooky, I have a serious feeling that we're about to get bad weather. If I'm right, we'll be the first in, and we'll be the only one in for a couple of days. I know we're not full, but we'll get a good enough price to make up for it. So that's why we're going in."

Robby Sprague, a young man already in his eighth winter-fishing season, spoke up next. "Skip, no one else is leavin'. They'll all think we got no guts."

"Robby, this isn't about proving who the bravest man is. You don't fish Georges in February unless you've got guts. This is about making money. We'll unload, we'll get a good price, and after the storm blows through, we'll be back on Georges making more. Now let's get going. If we wait too long, we'll have a hell of a time."

No one moved for what seemed to Gus an eternity. Finally Asa said, "All right, men, if we get crackin', it's supper in bed tomorrow at Fannies." Thus inspired, the men raised the working sails and retrieved the anchor. They had left Gloucester in winter trim and without topmasts, so they were unable to set the tops'ls or the fisherman's stays'l. When suppertime came they went below, leaving Gus alone at the wheel. It had taken less than fifteen minutes to get the boat under way, once he had talked the crew into obeying his commands.

Gus had the good sense not to say directly what he felt: that it would be dangerous to stay out on Georges in the coming storm. The crew would never have agreed to be the first boat to run from danger. Had he been that honest, he could have been faced with mutiny. He knew the risk he was taking. If this storm wasn't a bad one, or if they didn't get a better price by coming in early, he would be tagged as being too cautious or, worse, being a coward. Either way, his fishing career would be over before it had truly begun.

By the end of the graveyard watch, the wind had built to twenty knots and had backed farther to the northeast. The clouds had moved in at midnight. It was inky black; all Gus could see from the helm was the compass, dimly lit by a small kerosene lantern, and the occasional wave-top illuminated by the dull red and green of the schooner's running lights.

Gus had been hoping to wait until first light to reduce sail, but the wind was continuing to build, and the leeward rail was in the water much of the time. He called for all hands to reef. It took only five minutes for the crew to wake, get into their winter gear, and feel the way to their stations. He ordered them to take the jib down, put two reefs in the big main, and put one each in the fores'l and stays'l. They efficiently manhandled the sails in the pitch black, but it still took half an hour to get the reefs tucked in. The watch was changed, and everyone not on duty retired to their bunks.

Gus went below as well. He pulled out his chart and plotted their course since leaving Georges. They were about halfway home, but the glass had been dropping rapidly during the last six hours, and the wind had come up more quickly than he had anticipated. Still, they were close enough to make it in before the weather got really bad.

Gus ate a hunk of cheddar cheese and a thick slice of dark bread that Doc had baked when they were still anchored on the fishing grounds. He washed both down with a few gulps of water. He would have liked coffee, but the ship was pitching and rolling too much for a galley fire to be safely lit.

He lay back in his bunk. The heel of the ship pressed him tightly against the hull. He closed his eyes for a short rest and immediately fell asleep, secure in the knowledge that he had done everything he could.

He was awakened by Asa. "Skip, it's gettin' kinda blowy up here. I think we need to reef."

Gus emerged on deck to a familiar cacophony. The wind came through the rigging with a roar that drowned out all but the most determined conversation, but even it was muted by the voice of the sea. The waves were now twelve feet high, the crests closely spaced. The bow pitched over one wave only to slam immediately into the next, with a crash that reverberated through the timbers of the little ship. Spray flew off the bow, hurled to leeward by winds that were now gale force.

Asa was right about the sail she was carrying. The wind was laying her hard over. Gus lowered the fores'l entirely and tucked the second reef in the stays'l. This was the easiest way to reduce sail and still keep her moving forward. The wind was now almost out of the north, and they were close-hauled on starboard tack aimed straight for Eastern Point, just thirty miles ahead.

"Asa, what's the bilge look like?" Gus asked as soon as sail had been reduced.

"'Bout an hour ago she was pretty wet in the well. I started a few a' the boys on the pumps, and we're keepin' up with it nicely."

Gus was not surprised. No ship could sail in weather like this without opening up some. "You're a good man," he said.

At noon they sighted Eastern Point three miles to the northwest. Big flakes of wet snow had started to fall, leaving just enough visibility to make out the lighthouse. They continued west almost to the shore, then tacked around to the northeast to enter the harbor.

Just as they settled on their new heading, the jib came loose from where it had been furled on the bowsprit. Left like that, it would flog itself to shreds. Sooky went forward to tie it back down, but when he stepped onto the boltrope, a gust laid the schooner hard over. He lost his footing and dropped into the sea.

"Hard alee!" screamed Gus as five voices shouted, "Man overboard!" The *Sunrise* shot into the wind, and in seconds she was hove to on starboard tack just twenty yards to windward of where Sooky was thrashing in the frigid sea.

"Launch a boat!" Gus yelled, but Asa and three of the fishermen were already unlashing a dory, getting it ready to go over the side. Off to leeward, Sooky was going under, arms flailing.

"The bastard never learned to swim," Gus said, swearing under his breath. Many fishermen never did; they would say they preferred a quick death from drowning to a lingering one from freezing. The dory would reach Sooky in minutes, but it was clear that would be too late to save him. Gus threw off his heavy oilskin jacket and boots, and with no time to get rid of the rest, he dove in.

The ocean was frigid. Gus gasped on surfacing. In the rough seas he couldn't see Sooky most of the time, but the fisherman's yellow oilskin hat kept popping up when a wave crested under him, and that was enough to point the way. He tried an overhand stroke, but his overalls filled with seawater and it was

70

too hard to breathe, so he used a breaststroke and then a sidestroke. By the time he reached Sooky, the older man had stopped struggling. Gus grabbed him, turned him face up, and waited for the dory.

Now it was Gus who struggled to breathe. He dropped his head underwater in the crests and breathed when he popped up in the troughs. He lost the feeling in his feet first, and then his arms began to go numb. He could hear the dory and Asa's firm commands, hurried but not panicked. He started to drift off but was jarred awake when he inhaled seawater. He gagged and couldn't get the water out of his lungs before going down again. Then there were arms around him — then someone was thumping on his chest. He vomited into the bottom of the dory, and then he passed out.

When he awoke he was still in the dory, but now it was lashed down on the schooner's deck. The seats had been removed. He was lying on his back, and Doc was pouring hot water in on top of him. *How did they get the fire going?* Gus wondered.

He closed his eyes and dreamt of the palm trees in the sand atop the coral reefs that guarded the lagoon between the South Pacific islands of Tahaa and Raiatea. He heard the gentle breeze ruffle through those big tropical fronds. He felt the press of soft thighs, glorious dampness and warmth, the luscious fragrance of her plumeria lei.

Out of this sweet haze, Gus slowly awoke to the winter storm still in full fury all around him. Robby and

Doc were hovering over him. He had not come aboard the dory alone, Robby told him. He had been clutching Sooky tight to his chest, as if he meant to carry him all the way to Fiddler's Green, the heavenly afterlife for longtime sailors. But Sooky was dead — he'd drowned before Gus had gotten to him.

Asa had put the schooner onto port tack as soon as Gus was safely aboard. They were now enough under the lee of Cape Ann that the waves were far smaller than those rapidly building offshore. Once they were in the harbor, the sea moderated further, and in the smooth water the *Sunrise* made nine knots close-hauled under its small sail plan. Asa sailed her into the inner harbor, where the wind had just enough easting to allow him to come all the way up harbor and anchor to windward of Pitt's dock.

Asa launched a dory and ran warps to the dock. As they slowly paid out her anchor line, a crew from Pitt's reeled them in. Once they were secure, the unloading began. Gus was put into dry clothes, wrapped in blankets, and carried ashore into Pitt's office, where they set him down next to the Franklin stove. Robby stayed with him and fed the stove until its innards glowed red.

The storm continued to build that afternoon and evening. On Georges the wind peaked at sixty-five knots, with the waves twenty feet high. One boat anchored in only four fathoms hit the sandy bottom in a trough and broke her back. A helpless sister ship watched as she sank in less than three minutes.

The anchor lines of four other ships chafed through at the height of the storm. Two of the four, the lucky ones, shot through the rest of the fleet, avoiding collision by fortunate backing and veering of the gusty winds. They eventually got enough sail up to heave to in deeper water, and each survived to fish another day. The third schooner barreled into an anchored boat that hadn't cut its line in time. Both boats sank — the Essex shipbuilders had made them to withstand the elements, not the extreme trauma of a storm-driven collision. The fourth schooner blew downwind onto the Georges Shoal, where violent breaking surf crushed her planking and splintered her frames. Four schooners lost in a bad but not exceptional winter storm, twenty-eight men dead, twenty widows, and fifty-two fatherless children.

So Gus Stevens was not a hero that day, not outside his own crew anyway. Pitt raised an eyebrow on learning he had brought home only forty-four thousand pounds of cod in a boat that could hold ninety thousand. One of Henry Wonson's boats would limp home four days later with ninety-four thousand pounds. But Henry's boat came in with the rest of the fleet, so the price she received was lower than the price paid to the *Raiatea Sunrise*.

"It worked out for ya this time," Pitt told Gus. "But we don't wanna get in the habit a' comin' in less than full; that won't do."

"Our boat might have been lost if I'd stayed on Georges," Gus responded with an indignation he couldn't suppress.

"This is a risky business. That's why we buy insurance. Henry lost two boats in the storm, but Hudson'll pay off, and Henry's already commissioned the replacements."

"What about the men who died, and the widows, and the kids whose fathers are never coming home?"

"There are bound to be losses. But we're all better off in the end if we push hard." He gestured toward a pier where another of his schooners was unloading. "In what other line a' work can those kinda men make the money they make?"

Not needing an answer to his rhetorical question, Pitt ended the conversation. Gus watched as he climbed into his carriage, which drove off through the hard-packed snow toward his Eastern Point mansion. From there, Pitt would be able to watch the ice-covered survivors beat back upwind with holds full of codfish.

"Aye," Gus said to himself as he turned to walk home, "it's a risky business, but not for you, you bastard."

Chapter 8

Boston — April 1860

On the first Sunday in April, Maggie followed
what had become her regular Sunday routine since
moving out of the loft to work for William Hudson. She
attended services at St. Joseph's Church in the North
End, then paid a visit to Seth in South Boston. He took
her to an Irish-owned pub in the neighborhood — the
first of its kind in the city. They ate potato pancakes and
drank beer, sitting on a rough wooden bench, and
looked out across the street at stables owned by the post
office.

Seth asked how she liked being a maid. Maggie
had to speak loudly to be heard over the buzz of
constant conversation. "'Tis fine enough for now, I
suppose. But I sure don't fancy cleaning goblets and
spittoons me whole life. Master William's right enough.
He's well read, and smart, and he's such a wealthy
fella. You should see the clothes he wears — fine wool
suits, and they fit him to a T."

"Don't let anyone tell ya there isn't plenty o' gold in Boston, little Margaret O," Seth said. "The way some of them throw money around at the Ritz would make yer noggin spin."

"Master William comes from quite a family. His da's a right high muck-a-muck. But the master seems fair enough to the regular folk — he's always treated me right. His ma's another story, now. Queen Victoria wouldn't be good enough for her. . . . Are you missing home, Seth?"

"Aye, to be sure, I miss the family and the blokes down at the Bull's Head, but there's no sense complaining about spilt milk. . . . I met a lass a couple weeks back. She's Italian, and her da's a baker. She helps with the deliveries to the hotel. I'd like you to meet her — she might be the one."

"I could give Ma a report," Maggie said with a twinkle in her eye. Then she sighed. "I'm aching lonely. I'm stuck in that brick palace six days a week. I work, I go to church, and I work. I don't know a soul in Boston except you, and I don't see how I'm to find time to meet anyone."

"Ah, you'll bump into somebody. That's how it works. Just when you're least expecting him, there he'll be. But don't worry about that. Here you are in America, Maggie! 'Tis where you always wanted to be. Maybe you should start writing that book, just like what's her name — that one Ma said was barren."

"Jameson. Anna Jameson. But she had things to write about, didn't she, now? She traveled to the wilds and knew the savages. I'm sweeping floors and starching shirts. I've got nothing worth saying, now do I?"

William gave the servants April 19 off. The anniversary of the battles of Lexington and Concord was quickly becoming a sacred holiday in Boston. Maggie put on her best dress and bonnet, the ones she usually wore to church, and joined the early-morning festivities on the Common. A large crowd cheered as hundreds of blue-coated men in white breeches and tricornered hats marched with powder horns and muskets, stopping periodically to fire volleys in the air. A white-wigged man in colonial dress rode a big stallion from Faneuil Hall to the State House, calling out, "The British are coming, the British are coming!" Beer and hard cider flowed from kegs lining Beacon and Boylston Streets, and vendors with carts sold small flags, fried dough, and pickled eggs.

In contrast to all the gaiety, a line of six black men in rags and leg shackles stood silently on the edge of the Common, right in front of the State House. By their side were four white women in black dresses and veils, holding placards saying, "All Men Are Created Equal" and "Free the Slaves."

Maggie bought some of the fried dough and a glass of cider. By midafternoon, though, she'd had enough and returned to the townhouse. It seemed deserted, the other servants enjoying their day off.

Still in her going-to-church frock, she cautiously opened the door to the library, which she was normally allowed in only once a week to dust. Inside, richly stained cherry bookcases filled with leather-bound volumes lined the walls. A fireplace with an imposing mahogany mantel stood opposite bay windows. A quarter cord of split ash was stacked ready for burning on one side, with brightly polished brass fire tools in a wrought iron stand on the other. An oriental carpet with a complex floral design set against a deep blue background covered the middle of the hardwood floor. Oil paintings of serious men and bold ships in vigorous seas hung on every wall.

Perusing the shelves, Maggie discovered a copy of *A Short History of the Battle of Breed's Hill,* an old volume that seemed to have been passed down through the generations: the inscription inside declared it the property of a James Hudson, though she did not know who that was. She had been studying the Revolutionary War for her American citizenship test and had heard of this battle, which had become known as the Battle of Bunker Hill. She knew it had been fought in 1775, not too far away. She sat down on the leather couch and took off her shoes, then carefully swung her legs up onto the couch and sank into its cushions.

Being on this forbidden ground was a gamble; Maggie knew that well enough. She was to venture outside the servants' quarters only to clean and dust and wax, never to read, and certainly never to lounge on the master's fine furniture. But this was no ordinary day, the master had said so himself, and, no one was due home until suppertime.

With her head resting on an arm of the couch, Maggie read with increasing fascination about the occupation of Boston and the events leading to the fight for possession of Charlestown Heights. Scores of soldiers assembled behind breastworks hastily thrown up near the top of Breed's Hill as the officers distributed gunpowder and lead shot. A colonel named James Hudson — the name in the book's inscription — rallied his men. "It's time to end the siege of Boston!" he cried. "If we hold this hill, we can drive the redcoats out! End the tyranny!"

Maggie read on. But warm sunlight flooded through the bay windows, and she was full of dough and cider. Before long she was asleep, the book lying open on her chest.

When she opened her eyes he was standing in the doorway, quietly watching her: William Hudson, descendant of the hero of Breed's Hill, not in the blue uniform and tricornered hat of his great-grandfather, but no less magnificent in an elegantly tailored three-piece suit, every hair in place, his cravat tied just so. She looked through the fog of history and into his eyes. She could easily have been frightened, but she knew he liked her — she could see it in his eyes, in the tilt of his head and the turn of his lips. She jumped to her feet, hurriedly straightening her dress and smoothing her hair underneath her day cap.

"Are you reading about Breed's Hill, Maggie?" William asked.

"Aye, what a time it mu . . . mu . . . must have been," Maggie stuttered, having realized that her shoes were off to one side and her feet were bare. "Your great-grandda was quite a man, now," she said, curling her toes as if to make them disappear.

"That he was. Those were great times, and great times make great men."

"You must be proud, sir."

William walked to the mantel and gazed for a moment at the portrait of his great-grandfather, rendered some eighty years before by John Singleton Copley. "We are a great family," he said matter-of-factly. He turned to face her. "Are you interested in American history?"

"Aye, to be sure I am. I want to be a citizen one day. I've already started the studying." She blushed as he stared at her.

"We made history here," he said earnestly. He pointed at a painting of a full-rigged ship under sail on a rough sea. "My grandfather commanded this frigate in the War of 1812, and my father — well, he will defeat slavery yet. He *is* the Republican Party in Massachusetts. We will beat them, those Southern *gentlemen*. You can take that to the bank." He turned to face her. "You are in a good place to learn American history; there is no better place anywhere in the world."

"I'm grateful to be here, sir. I've loved America since I first read about it as a wee tyke."

William walked over to the couch. "Please, sit back down." She did, cautiously, and he sat across from her. "This is the land of opportunity; if you are industrious, you can improve yourself. You can achieve great things here despite your modest upbringing."

As he was talking, she leaned forward, bringing them closer together: "Yes," she said, now intently focused on his eyes, "that's why I'm here."

He looked into her eyes, then abruptly stood up again. "I would be most pleased for you to borrow any of the books in my library," he said with an expansive sweep of his arm. "I studied history at Harvard. There is no finer college in America. You may ask me any questions you have." He clasped his hands behind his back and tilted back his head and shoulders, as if he were Napoleon sending the Polish legions into battle.

Maggie was flattered; she had never heard him volunteer to help anyone before.

"Of course, it is best that we do not discuss this when others are within earshot. We would not want the servants to think you are getting special favors. But I do wish to help you improve yourself. My own ancestors were immigrants once, and we owe it to the nation to pass on our wisdom."

"Sir, you're very generous, now," Maggie said. "I'll take good care of your books. I do love to read, and I so want to learn more about America. Thank you, sir!"

Over the next month, Maggie finished her study of the Battle of Breed's Hill and moved on to other Revolutionary War topics. She wrote down questions from time to time. About once a week she would find herself alone with William — once when she was sweeping a hallway floor, once when they inadvertently met on the Common, and once in William's study when he was paying bills and she was tidying up. Each time he was eager to answer her questions; sometimes he would throw in an anecdote about a relative who had been present when history was made.

Maggie's new obsession with history led her to curtail her Sunday visits with Seth. Now, if the weather was nice, she would go to a historic site. She visited the Old North Church and imagined the lanterns hanging there as Paul Revere might have seen them. She walked to Breed's Hill and thought of the valiant James Hudson rallying his inexperienced farmer-militiamen to stand their ground against King George's army of professional soldiers. Later, she would tell William about her visits. He always listened with rapt attention, even if her tales were of places he had visited himself many times.

One Sunday in early June, Maggie rode the horse-drawn omnibus all the way out to Concord to stand on the small wooden bridge where the minutemen had forced the redcoats to begin their long and bloody retreat to Boston. From the bridge she watched a boy drift slowly downriver in an old skiff, jigging for alewives. The fields on both sides of the river were crisscrossed with low walls made of loosely piled stones; the grazing dairy cows reminded her of her home in Enniskerry. A bronze statue of a minuteman stood defiantly on one approach to the bridge, the first verse of a poem inscribed at his feet:

> By the rude bridge that arched the flood,
> Their flag to April's breeze unfurled,
> Here once the embattled farmers stood,
> And fired the shot heard round the world.

The author was Concord native Ralph Waldo Emerson. At a small bookstore, Maggie found several pamphlets containing various essays and poems he had written. The proprietor advised her to start with the essay called "Nature"; it was Emerson's first important work, he said. She purchased it and began reading on the way home.

June 17, 1860, was the eighty-fifth anniversary of the Battle of Bunker Hill. A special celebration took place at the Bunker Hill Monument that day, and William's father, Nathaniel, was one of the speakers. William attended, of course. After returning home, he discreetly asked Maggie to see him that evening in his study, a modest room adjoining his bedroom, so he could tell her of the day's festivities. She tidied up as quickly as she could and hurried upstairs, knocking softly on the door of his study and slipping in without being seen.

William was at his mahogany desk, writing a note in his journal, a nightly practice he had recently begun. He stood when she entered. "Maggie, here, sit down," he said, pointing to the edge of the small couch next to his desk.

He began recounting the day's events with an enthusiasm she had never seen in him before. "I wish you could have been there to hear the speeches. Colonel Lee from the army spoke about the tactics and strategy employed that day. The mayor gave the usual sort of political speech, and then it was my father's turn. A hush came over the packed crowd — the ladies and gentlemen and the common folk too. Everyone knew it was a Hudson who had led the militia into battle. I could almost smell the gun smoke, the sweat, and the blood. Maggie, one day I will speak at this event. I never gave it much thought before, but now I cannot wait for that day. I want to take my place in history."

"Sir, I wish I had been there to see it. 'Tis many times I've imagined that battle. I can picture Colonel Hudson with his musket, leading his men against the British, I surely can."

William sat next to Maggie on the couch. He paused, emotion muting his voice, then said huskily, "I felt that I too could be a great man."

Maggie leaned toward him and said with conviction, "Oh, sir, you are a great man!"

Impulsively, William leaned forward and kissed her. Then, just as suddenly, he jerked back. His face turned red.

"Maggie, I'm sorry, I . . . I . . . I have never done anything like that before. It is so improper. Forgive me."

Confused, she said nothing. During these last two months William had become her professor. He knew everything there was to know about American history, or so it seemed, and she was consumed with learning all she could from him. But there was more. She had begun to fantasize about what it would be like to be the mistress of this house, even though she knew that was impossible. Remaining composed, she spoke. "No bother, sir. I'm not offended, not at all. Still . . . I wouldn't want it to be said that I can be so easily kissed."

"Of course not. You have my word: I will keep silent."

She suppressed a smile as she imagined what William's mother might say if she knew her only son had kissed a maid, and an Irish one at that. She knew she did not have to worry about this man telling anyone what had happened. "I know you're a gentleman, sir," she said with kindness and respect.

"Maggie, thank you for being so understanding. And in the future, when we are alone . . . ah, I mean, if we should again find ourselves alone, please call me William."

She nodded, then stood and walked with dignity toward the door. With one hand on the brass doorknob, she turned to face him. "Good night, now . . . William." They both smiled.

Maggie slept fitfully that night. She rolled and rolled in her narrow bed, bunching the flannel sheets underneath her. Three times she got up and remade the bed. She wanted no repeat of the events of the previous summer, but William had been quick to see how she could be hurt, and quick to promise that he would keep the kiss a secret.

And William Hudson was no Jacob Anderson. William came from the greatest family in the most marvelous country on earth. He was no crude farmer prone to drink and lacking all manners. He had misbehaved, but every man was sometimes governed by impulse. His breeding and good manners had shown through in the end. Surely now, it was the Christian thing to forgive a man who apologized so sincerely. And it was only a kiss, after all. She had nothing to worry about.

After supper the next night, William lingered in his study with the door open a crack. But when Maggie's duties were done, she retired to her room and read alone in her bed. And so it was the next night, and the night after that. On Sunday, Maggie returned to her old routine; she went to church in the morning and then to South Boston to visit Seth. That evening, before turning in, Maggie went to see Gail, the scullery maid, in her room.

"Do you have a minute?" she asked after Gail opened the door.

"Surely," Gail replied. "Come on in and sit. Are you in any trouble?"

"Have you ever been in love, Gail?" Maggie asked.

"It's like ya read my mind. I been broodin' on that. Yes, once, ten years ago. He was handsome. He came from a modest but proud family, and he was so smart. He was goin' to college. When he first kissed me — oh my, I knew then that the love was real. The next year was the most marvelous a' my life."

"What happened?"

"I was a fool. He asked me to marry him, but his parents didn't approve, threatened to disown him. My family's poor, ya see, and my pa drinks too much. I couldn't go through with it, couldn't separate him from his family."

"Where is he now?"

"Married to another," Gail sighed. "He's got two young 'uns — they might a' been mine. But he wrote me just last week, Maggie. He's not happy; he wants to see me. I wrote him back just this mornin' and told him no. What else could I say? I'm not one to take a father from his children. But if I could peel back the years and hear him ask me to marry him again, oh . . . I would say yes in a jiffy. I wasted my chance, Maggie."

Gail looked down and shook her head. "Oh dear . . . what was it you wanted to talk 'bout?"

"Oh, I'm missing me family, Gail, that's all. Thank you for telling me your story. There'll be another man come along for you, surely there will."

"Anythin' can happen, I suppose."

The next night William was sitting in his study, reading his father's latest letter to the Massachusetts Abolitionist Society. It was a warm evening, and he had taken off his jacket and cravat and rolled up the sleeves of his starched white shirt. His bare arms were pale, his hands scrubbed, and his fingernails neatly trimmed. The door was open a crack, as it always was in the evening now.

Maggie knocked gently on the doorframe. "Maggie, come in," he said with a big smile. "Come in, please be seated." He stood and closed the door behind her, then reseated himself behind his desk.

"Thank you — William." She was still in her maid's uniform, but she had taken off her white day cap and removed the pins from her hair, letting it fall down onto her shoulders. "If you don't mind, I have a question about slavery."

"Of course. What do you want to know?"

"Well, the Declaration of Independence says all men are created equal, but Americans have slaves. How can that be?"

"Here in America, at least in *this* part of America, we believe what the Declaration says." William crossed his arms and leaned back in his chair, as a professor might. "But we never would have convinced the Southern states to join the Union if we had not let them keep their slaves. It was a bad compromise, but the reckoning is nigh."

"What about me kin? Do you think the Irish are equal too?"

"Yes, I do. The Irish are just as good a people as any other. I am sad to say I do not think my own mother agrees with me on this, but times do change. She will come around one day."

Maggie smiled. "I'm not sure *that's* ever to be — William."

He chuckled. "Yes, she may be beyond all hope."

They smiled at each other, and then Maggie said she must be going.

"I've missed having you come around with your questions," he blurted as she reached the door. "I . . . ah . . . I enjoy discussing history."

"I thought it best I stay away," she said, turning to face him.

He stood and took a step toward her. "It was because I behaved badly."

"'Tis not that . . . I like you . . . too much, perhaps . . ."

"But staying away from someone you like is not a sensible thing to do . . . is it?" He was not more than a foot away from her now.

"No, maybe not." She was looking up into his eyes.

"I like you too," William said, inching closer. He put his hands on her shoulders and brought her to him. They kissed.

"I really must go now," she said softly.

"Yes, of course," he replied. "Perhaps you will have another question tomorrow night?" Now halfway out the door, she turned and nodded. He kept watching her until she disappeared down the hallway.

Every evening for the next two weeks, Maggie came to William with a question. They discussed history, their families, and life in general. Every evening ended with a polite kiss. Then, at dinner on a Saturday, William asked the cook to prepare a cold meal for him the next day. After church he would be up in his study tending to some unfinished insurance business, he said, and he would like a bite to eat.

After a hurried visit to church the next morning, Maggie returned to the townhouse; the other servants had gone to Dorchester for a picnic. William was working at his desk when Maggie knocked gently on his open door in the early afternoon. She had put on the same dress she had worn when he hired her. He was still in the fine suit he had worn to church that morning. Cold chicken, bread, and an apple sat uneaten on the side table by the desk. She set down the book on the War of 1812 that she had brought with her and began the discussion. "I don't understand why the British burned the White House."

"I think they just wanted to show they could do it, that they were much stronger than we were."

"Wasn't Dolley Madison a hero in that war?"

"She certainly was. She was a smart, inquisitive woman, and a beautiful one too . . . much like you."

She blushed. "You flatter me, now, William. . . . You're the handsomest man I've ever laid me eyes on."

They embraced and kissed. Cautiously at first, he ran his fingers through her long red hair; she stroked the nape of his neck. Her lips covered his.

They parted. "Oh, William, I think of you every minute."

Eyes closed, lips joined again. More excited than she'd ever been, she forgot about the impossibility of being with William. One of them went through the door to the bedroom; the other followed.

They lay down on the bed. He brushed his fingers across her breast and over her warm belly. Her breathing quickened. He reached beneath her dress and gently pulled and twisted, without effect.

"Wait, William, wait." His name had become so easy for her to say.

He let go. She lifted herself and slipped off her drawers. He stroked the inside of her thigh, barely touching the damp apex. She trembled. He undid the buttons of his trousers, and she put her hand on him. It felt so different than when she had grabbed Jake in self-defense. He pushed and pulled in her grasp, sliding in the loose hold she had of him.

He rolled on top of her, and she opened to him. "Be careful, now," she said. "I've not had a man before." He pulled back instinctively, then came powerfully forward and was through. She cried out in surprise and in pain.

He pulled partway out and thrust back in, then withdrew quickly, but not quickly enough. He was done, and he held her tightly. She burned, but kept her arms around him. They lay still until their breathing slowed.

He got up and pulled himself together. He nodded, buttoned his trousers, and stepped out of the room.

Maggie hurt. She stood and looked at herself in his mirror. Her dress was bloodstained, as were the bedsheets. She stripped the bed and went to her room to clean and change. Next, she soaked her dress and the sheets in cold water. Thank God the other servants were away. She focused on cleaning and was pleased to see the stains come out. She went back to William's bedroom with new sheets and made his bed. He had not returned.

Back in her room, she was honest with herself. She could not blame William. She could have stopped him at any point. No, it was even worse than that. She had brought it on. She loved learning from him, but she hadn't wanted to discuss the War of 1812 that day; she had wanted him. She had opened her mouth to his, she had touched him, and she had wanted him to touch her. But she did love him — oh, how she loved him — and he loved her back. Wasn't Gail right? Wasn't that what really mattered?

She knew one thing she could do. She could confess her sin. She did not know anyone well in the North Boston parish yet, and that made it easier. So it was off to St. Joe's. It helped that the priest was an older man. Maggie reasoned that he had heard it all before and wouldn't be as shocked as some youngster right out of seminary might be.

"My child, did the man force himself on you?" the priest asked after Maggie had gotten it out.

"Father, he was entirely willing, to be sure, and he did start it. But no, I let him in. 'Tis truth to say I encouraged him."

"It's a grave sin, my child, one that can ruin a promising young life. Is the man going to do the right thing and marry you?"

"Father, I don't know." A wave of emotion surged over Maggie. A linen hankie was pushed under the confessional screen. She picked it up and dabbed at her tears. "He is a powerful man, Father. But he does love me, I think, and surely I love him."

"Then all is not lost, child. Counsel him to do the right thing. You two can come here together and talk. Is he of the Faith?"

"I'm afraid not, Father."

"We can deal with that as well when you bring him in. I want you to say a hundred rosaries, and all the while think of the enormity of your sin. By the grace of Almighty God, you are forgiven. Praise be to the Father, the Son, and the Holy Ghost. Now go forth free of sin, my daughter."

"Thank you, Father." Maggie pulled out her rosary and started her penance on the walk home.

William had walked straight out his door, down to the Charles River, and all the way to Brighton and back. On the walk he became more and more agitated. He was deathly afraid that his father would find out what he had done. One day Nathaniel Hudson had caught one of his gardeners out behind the pines at Winnipesaukee with the Lowells' scullery maid. In a tirade of self-righteousness, he told them they would both rot in hell and only marriage could save them.

They were so cowed that they agreed, perhaps forgetting that a reverend was visiting that weekend. An hour later they were married. William witnessed the brief ceremony, and even through his usual fog of indifference, he felt the gardener's misery. The scullery maid seemed pleased until the ceremony ended with their being handed two weeks' pay, given a carriage ride to the local inn, and told never to come back.

William was sure he would suffer the gardener's fate if his father were to discover his indiscretion.

He continued to ruminate on the way to the Lowells' house that evening for dinner. He could see now that Maggie had enticed him. The way she had kissed and handled him had thrilled him. He had thought she was an innocent girl, but now he wondered. Could it be she was experienced? The Irish were known for their promiscuity. That he, a man of high morals, had so completely lost control was certainly evidence that he had been led on.

No, he was sure of it now, she was no novice. But still, he should have resisted her temptations. She was so beautiful, though; perhaps she was too much for any man to resist. But he would never give in to temptation again. He would give Maggie her walking papers the next day, and that would put an end to it. This was a good lesson for him; now that he knew the power of evil firsthand, he could resist the next time. He was a Hudson, after all.

By the time he crossed the Lowells' threshold, William had achieved a measure of peace. But later that night, while Victoria was discussing the food to be served at their wedding reception, his mind wandered back to his bedroom. He had never before seen skin as pure as on those thighs, always hidden from the sun, and there was that damp triangle of wispy red hair. As he slid in he had reached around and grabbed the soft round fullness of her bottom. He let out an audible sigh of remembrance.

She was so young, he reasoned. Discharging her would be too harsh; he would not want to ruin her for just one mistake. A stern talking-to would be just the thing. It would be better to educate her than ruin her, as his father had ruined that gardener. Tempering justice with mercy was the Christian way. She would understand the paramount need for secrecy. She was basically a good girl who had made a mistake. She would not want this to get out any more than he would.

Slowly, he became aware that all conversation had stopped and the Lowells were looking intently at him, waiting for him to say something. Mr. Lowell saved him. "Come, my boy, surely you have an opinion on the ratatouille niçoise question."

"Yes sir, absolutely, we must have ratatouille. It would not be a proper reception without it."

With a nod, Victoria turned to a discussion of the soups to be served.

Chapter 9

At Sea — June 1860

The tired crew of the *Raiatea Sunrise* had been on Georges Bank for almost three weeks, and the fish hold was nearly full; one more day and they could head for home. The married men looked forward to spending the Fourth of July with their wives and children; most of the rest anticipated a raucous celebration fueled with fat shares from the sale of a boatload of codfish. A greenhorn was also on board, a first-timer fishing for a half share. Gus had reluctantly agreed to take his son Ray fishing for the summer.

Ray was old to be starting out — most of the crew had first gone to sea at twelve or thirteen. To them, he seemed slow and inept for so nearly a full-grown man. He was not a novice in the ways of the sea, though; Gloucester boys rarely were.

When Ray was eight, Gus had given him and his brother a dory to muck about in. They tied it up with the other small boats on the backside of a wharf in

Vincent Cove, and from there they rowed out to Ten Pound Island to explore its seagull rookery, to Niles Beach to swim, and through Blynman Canal and into the Annisquam River to dig for clams. They mounted a small mast and sailed whenever the wind was favorable. The dory wouldn't go upwind — it had no keel — but it was a tolerable downwind sailer. They fished too, for mackerel, cod, and pollock, and even for small halibut now and then. They put out traps and brought home lobster as well, although Ray never developed a taste for the crustacean, so little admired that it was often on the menu at the Essex County Jail.

So Ray was a sailor of sorts, but a schooner was serious business, and he had much to learn.

By breakfast time the deck was getting warm enough to develop that distinctive odor that everyone in a fishing town knows all too well. When the crew went below to eat, Ray grabbed a mop and swabbed the fish scales and other remainders over the side, where several dozen gulls noisily fought for every scrap. He got to breakfast late, but Doc took care of him. Soon he was digging into a heaping plate of eggs and sausage with a fresh-baked biscuit to sop up the juices, and coffee to wash it all down.

Asa and Robby had finished eating, but they lingered to play out an ancient fisherman's ritual with Ray. "What are ya gonna do with your share when ya get paid off?" Asa asked as he sat down next to the boy on the bench, close enough to rub shoulders with him.

"Save it for college, I guess," Ray replied, leaning away.

"That don't sound like no fun. I'll introduce ya to some *fine* ladies down at Fannies — deposit your pay there, and I guarantee you'll be satisfied with the return."

"Listen to him, Ray," Robby said, feigning solemnity. "Asa's an expert on the ins and outs down at Fannies, ain't ya, Asa?"

"Now, don't be crude," Asa said, shaking his finger across the table with mock disdain. "Those are ladies you're talkin' about. And young Ray here's a gentleman." He turned back toward Ray and asked in a serious tone, "Have you bedded your first lady yet?"

Robby broke out into a broad grin, and Ray couldn't hide his embarrassment. He thought about lying, but it was too late, and he'd never been any good at it anyway. "No, Asa, not yet," he said glumly.

"Consider it part a' your education." Asa put his arm around Ray's shoulder. "And it's a far sight more important than college, I'd say. I know just the gal for ya." He leaned in, his face inches from Ray's. "Lucy's a natural-born teacher. Why, she's instructed a Harvard professor or two in her time. Even I still learn a new trick from her now and again, and like Robby here says, I'm considered to be somewhat of an expert in this area of study."

"Sometimes Lucy team-teaches with Sarah," Robby chimed in. "There's lessons to be learned from those two. You stick with Asa when we go ashore; he'll see that you're educated in the fine art a' pleasurin' the ladies." With a hearty laugh, Asa slapped Ray on the back, and he and Robby went topside. Ray was grateful that it was time to get back to work.

They quit fishing at midafternoon and set sail. Asa took Ray aloft and showed him how to unfurl the maintops'l. He talked Ray through the setting of the foretops'l and the fisherman's stays'l while they watched others do that work. After all the sails were set Asa climbed down, but Ray stayed up in the rigging as the schooner began her reach to Gloucester. The *Sunrise* sped along in the light air. A gentle swell rocked the little ship, and the motion was exaggerated sixty feet above deck. The maintops'l filled as the boat rolled to windward and slacked as she rolled back to leeward, the topmast groaning rhythmically as it shifted to the changing load.

Exhausted from weeks of hard but happy work and soothed by the regular motion, the friendly sounds, and the late-afternoon sunshine, Ray dozed off. A few minutes later, he awoke with a start — he was slipping off his perch! Frantically he grabbed a line, and after his heart stopped racing, he slid down a backstay.

Gus was on deck, holding an odd-looking instrument. "Ray, if you're going to be a real sailor, you must learn to use a sextant." He had instructed dozens of young men in the art of celestial navigation, but this would be a first; he had never been home long enough to teach his sons much of anything. "This half-silvered mirror lets you see both the horizon and the sun at the same time, so you can measure the sun's angle of elevation. Once you learn to use a sextant, you can find your position anywhere on the face of the earth."

Ray held the sextant awkwardly. At first he couldn't see anything, but after a few minutes he managed to get the horizon and the sun in the same frame. "Tomorrow, meet me here half an hour before noon, and I'll show you how to take sun sights. Some of the youngsters think you can't navigate without a fancy chronometer. But if you keep a good plot of your course and speed, and pay attention to what the sea and its creatures are telling you, a sun sight's all you'll ever need."

Ray took the sextant back to his bunk that night. There wasn't enough light for him to see it, but he ran his hands over it until he could tell all its parts by feel.

At midnight, he was called for night watch. He pulled on his overalls, a warm jacket, and a wool watch cap; even in summer, Massachusetts Bay was cold at night. The moon was nearly full, and its light cast solid shadows across the deck. Sailing on a dark night could be trying, but this night was nearly as bright as day. The wind remained light, and it was steady; the little ship heeled over gently, making an easy six knots over a gentle swell that had been kicked up long ago by a far-off storm.

Ray was teamed with Robby. Half the time Ray would steer, and half the time Robby would. They were to hold a course according to the big binnacle compass right in front of the wheel, but Ray had trouble interpreting it. His dory didn't have a compass, and he'd never sailed at night before.

"No, turn the other way," Robby said five minutes after Ray took the wheel. "You need to imagine the boat turnin' round the compass card. That card may look like it's dancin', but it ain't; it's the boat that's doin' the movin'." This was not obvious to Ray, and he kept turning the wrong way. He was glad when it was time to be relieved. Robby made it look easy.

"Do you know how to use a sextant?" Ray asked once Robby had settled in behind the wheel.

"Nope. Been goin' to sea my whole life, but no one ever bothered to teach me that. I suppose it don't matter. We're always close in, ya know. Still, I sometimes dream a' sailin' across the ocean. The Flemish Cap's halfway to Portugal. I been there plenty."

"My father's teaching me. If you like, once I learn it, I'll teach you."

"Nah, that takes a lotta figurin', and I don't have much schoolin'."

They stood quietly and listened to the rhythmic sounds of gaffs and booms working against wooden masts. After a few minutes, Ray spoke again. "Have you been in any big storms, Robby?"

"Sure, I been in some pretty good blows. I guess the worst was in April a' '52, when I was just startin' out. I was on the ol' *Ruthie J* when the *Wilson Graves* broke loose. It musta been blowin' sixty knots, and she was comin' right down on us. I was on deck when we cut the anchor line. Drifted off just in time to miss her, but then *we* were loose in the fleet. Went by two boats so fast I never did figure out who they were.

"Before we could get a ridin' sail up, we got rolled by a monster wave. Mainmast went down into the water. Three a' the crew got swept off; my big brother, Tommy, was one of 'em. Last I ever saw a' Tommy was the soles a' his boots as he went over the side. We finally rolled back up, but Tommy was gone.

"Papa said it was Tommy's job to keep me outta trouble. I was just thirteen, ya see. I wish I coulda taken care a' him instead. I couldn't help him, though; I was too busy holdin' on for dear life. Once we got a little sail up, we were able to ride it out. Took two full days before we could get under way, and by then we'd blown all the way down to the Jersey shore. Ya know, now I think of it, a sextant woulda come in handy then. It took us a while to figure out where we were. When we finally got back to Gloucester, we found out two schooners had gone down in that storm. One of 'em was the *Judith Simpson*. My papa was her skipper, and my other brother, Horace, was on board."

Looking out to the horizon, Robby continued in a far-off voice: "My pa and my two brothers, gone in one day." He looked back at Ray. "Yup, the storm a' '52, that was the worst I seen."

Ray looked up at the stars. "Were you scared?" he asked.

"Scared — when she was lyin' down with her masts in the water, I thought we were goners. I didn't wanna die. I started cryin' and begged for another chance. We ain't churchgoers, but . . . well, when we finally came up, I said thank'ee. I guess I was talkin' to God. I remember looking up anyway. But I don't know whether God had anything to do with that boat rollin' back up. Most likely it was them Essex shipbuilders I shoulda been thankin'. But was I scared? Yup, I was real, deep-down scared."

"How come you went back out fishing?"

"It's what I know. It's *all* I know. And with all the men in my family dead, somebody had to support Ma and my sister. They didn't want me to go back out at first, but we had no choice. They saw it soon enough.

"I live a pretty good life when I'm back on shore, ya know. I give Ma half my pay, but I always got money for rum, and I got enough extra to keep the ladies interested. By the time it runs out, I'm back out to sea, and that ain't bad either. There's plenty of good grub, the men are first rate, and the work's honest. I'm lucky to been born a fisherman. . . . We all gotta die, Ray. I'd sooner die a quick death in this cold water than a slow death in some bed full a' my own pus. I'm gonna keep comin' out here 'til I can't do it no more, or 'til some storm sweeps me off the deck. That's what my papa did. It was good enough for him, and it's good enough for me."

It was time for Ray to take over steering again. "My father wants me to go to college, wants me to become a banker or something like that. I don't know, though."

Ray was already a point off course.

"No, Ray, turn to starboard. If ya can hear the jib luffin', you're way too near the wind. You need to develop a feel for these things, feel when she heels and when she lays back, listen to the sounds she makes. A good touch will keep ya outta trouble when you're confused by the compass."

Ray got back on course.

"There's somethin' to be said for goin' home to a nice warm bed and a good woman every night," Robby offered. "And there's a lot to be said for bein' rich. It's not the life I was born to. But if your papa can make it happen, maybe you should take him up on it. He's a good man, and he wants the best for ya. I followed my papa to sea . . . God bless his soul. . . . I'm proud to be followin' in his footsteps . . . he was a first-rate skipper. . . ."

Ray stared at the compass, pretending he didn't notice the tears in Robby's eyes.

"But that don't mean goin' to sea is right for you. Goddamn it, Ray, now you're too low; see how the whole boat's lost its liveliness? You need to come back

105

into the wind this time. The course is north-northwest, and we're on a beam reach — pay attention."

"Sorry. There, north-northwest."

"That's right. You can feel the boat sing when the course is right. She just won't go unless the wind and the sails are lined up. You'll get it. None of us learned this overnight."

The next morning Ray was on deck with the sextant. As Gus watched, he looked through the eyepiece, moved the arm back and forth a few times to locate the sun on the horizon, then settled on a spot: "Sixty-two degrees, but I don't know how to read the fractions."

"This wheel here has what's called a Vernier scale on it. Where the two lines meet measures the fractions. So this here is sixty-three degrees fourteen minutes. Keep measuring every few minutes; the highest measurement is the one you want."

And so Ray made his first sun sight. When he had his number, he and his father went down to the master's cabin. Gus took out the nautical almanac, and after a calculation that didn't look all that hard, he found their latitude to be forty-two degrees twelve minutes north, five miles south of the latitude determined by their dead-reckoning plot of course and speed. "Ray, that's a damn respectable result: good enough to find a South Pacific island, and certainly good enough to find Gloucester Harbor.

"I'm going to give you a book your grandfather gave me." Gus pulled a heavy volume off his small bookshelf. "By Nathaniel Bowditch. *The American Practical Navigator*. It's the bible for real sailors. If you want to be a professional . . . I mean . . . a competent mariner, study it. I'll help you." Ray opened the book and saw his grandfather's writing: "To Gus: Learn well what is written here. It will take you around the world and bring you safely home. Love, Father."

Late that afternoon they rounded Eastern Point, and before dark they were snugged up to Pitt's dock; by midnight, they were done unloading. With the office closed, the crew had to wait until after breakfast to get paid.

Ray slept in and was glad to find Asa gone when he picked up his pay. He did not want to be kidded about Fannies, and there was no possibility of his going there. Pitt's bookkeeper carefully counted out his half share: thirty-two dollars for three weeks, more than he had made for the whole summer at the savings bank. Not a bad way to make a living, he thought, and this is only a half share. He walked back to Middle Street with a smile on his face and a bounce in his step.

Chapter 10

Boston — September 1860

In the early-morning twilight, Maggie could see the leaves of the big chestnut through the open window — just outlines of the leaves, really, but there was enough light to see that insects had gnawed on most of them. Maggie had watched through this window as the leaves aged from the supple bright greens of early summer to the brittle hues of fall. Soon the tree would be bare, its branches exposed to the harsh winds of the New England winter.

An hour ago, Maggie had pulled William's finely woven English wool blanket over her bare arm and tucked it under her chin. She was on her right side, bent into an S-shape, and he was a longer S-shape looped around her backside. His left arm was under hers, his palm loosely holding her bare right breast, his midriff pressed against her naked cheeks. A light sweat coated the back of her thighs where his legs met hers.

They had so easily slipped back together. After that first time, he had pulled her aside and told her they had to stop. She agreed without reservation. No matter how much in love they were, they had committed a horrible sin. She considered finding work elsewhere, but after he assured her that he too knew they had made a grievous mistake, she decided to stay. She had a fine job that had been hard to find. Why make life difficult by moving on?

Just three days after they had resolved to stay away from each other, she was walking slowly by his study after supper when he spied her through the open door and called her in. He was working on an article about one of the sea battles of the War of 1812. Could he read a bit to her? Of course he could; she still loved history. It was as if they suffered from mutual amnesia, as if they had forgotten the convictions expressed just days earlier.

William began reading, and she walked around behind him and gave him a friendly shoulder rub. He casually reached up with his free hand and put it atop hers. Then he stopped reading and closed his eyes as she rubbed his shoulders with both of her hands. He stood up and turned to face her. They embraced. He loved her, he said. She loved him back, she said. Then he led her to his bed.

Aside from a painful four days when he went to stay at Lake Winnipesaukee with his family and Victoria, they had shared his bed every night these past three months. He read poetry; she listened adoringly. Their lovemaking lasted for hours. Sometimes he would wake at three in the morning and they would begin again; often they would greet the dawn with passion. He went to sleep holding her in his arms; she awoke with her arms around him. He told her she was the most beautiful woman who had ever lived. She cherished him and said so. They slept little, but they were never tired.

She felt the guilt most in the pre-dawn hours, when fear reigned. It consumed her then. What they were doing was wrong; it violated every Catholic principle. But they were in love, she reasoned when fully awake and courage returned. Wouldn't love cure all?

The date for William's marriage to Victoria was approaching, but she knew he could not go through with it now. He'd call it off soon, and then they could wed. He would do the right thing. He was the most wonderful man from the most wonderful family in the most wonderful country in the world. Their love was just more proof that anything could happen in America.

But there was a problem.

It was now fully light, and Maggie had to hasten. She hopped out of his bed and into her maid's uniform and cap, then directly to Harvey's roll call. She was a little late, as she had been more often than was proper, but no one seemed to notice. She went about her morning chores. Near noontime she found herself alone with Gail.

"Gail, I'd like to talk to you about something. 'Tis a . . . well . . . in Ireland we'd call it a ladies' matter."

Gail leaned close to Maggie and whispered: "Oh, Maggie, my dear, Master William's not put ya in a family way, has he?"

Maggie was so surprised that she said nothing.

"You may think you've been careful, but your comin's and goin's have been noticed. Harvey's checked your room a few times. You're never there anymore, not even at three in the mornin'. Don't worry, I won't tell. I don't think the others will either. We're all worried, though, what with Master William's weddin' comin' up. Now tell me he hasn't put ya in a family way. Please, dear Jesus, say he hasn't?"

"Oh m'God, Gail, I'm scared. I've missed me second straight month, and some mornings I can't keep me breakfast down."

"Maggie, have you and the master been takin' precautions?"

"Well . . . most of the time he pulls out before he . . . you know . . . before he's all done."

"You haven't been usin' a skin?"

"I don't know what that is, Gail. I don't think we have those in Ireland."

"It's a little cover that goes around . . . around him, ya know, his man part, to keep his juices out a'

111

you. My sister, Mabel, started usin' them after her fourth boy was born."

"No, we haven't used anything like that."

"Well, I'm a spinster lady. What do I know? But I'd say you're in a family way."

Maggie started to cry. "Oh, what's to do?"

"Talk to him. Maybe he'll do the right thing by ya."

"He is a very good man. But, oh, this is so hard. I'll talk to him, though, and I'll do it tonight. Please keep this quiet."

"I'll do what I can. God bless ya."

William was sitting in an armchair, reading and smoking a cigar, when Maggie slipped into his bedroom that evening. He was already wearing his white silk robe, the one with the Hudson family crest embroidered on the breast, and he had on matching rabbit-fur slippers. He greeted Maggie with a hug and a kiss. "I have been waiting for you, my little redheaded beauty. Let us go to bed straightaway."

She pushed him away and sat on the edge of the bed. "William," she started, but her voice cracked and she could not continue.

He sat down beside her and put an arm around her. With head cocked slightly, he asked lovingly, "What is it, my dear?" Tears were running down her cheeks as she looked into his eyes, just inches away from hers.

She blurted it out at last. "I think I'm going to have a baby." She buried her face in his chest, dampening the filigreed "H" on the white silk robe.

The news took a minute to sink in, but then blind fear took hold of William. He looked at his luxurious surroundings — the four-poster bed, the lath and plaster walls of this fine room.

If his father turned against him, and by God he surely would when he found out, William knew he would lose his position at the insurance company — and then all of this. He held the title to this expensive townhouse, but without income he would lose it to the bankers in a few months. He would become a pauper.

He knew no one in the family would stand up to Nathaniel Hudson, patriarch of the dynasty, the original Brahmin. His mother certainly would not save him — not after hearing he had taken up with an Irish maid.

He released his grip on Maggie. "What are we to do, William?" she asked meekly.

He looked at her and started to open his mouth, but no words came. Maggie saw his fear, but she was too caught up in her own grief to comfort him. Her eyes red and her strength spent, she slipped between the silk bedsheets, clutched a pillow, and curled up into a tight ball.

William stood up slowly. His right leg began to shake when he put weight on it. He turned gray, his stomach churned and acid burned his throat, and then his whole body began to sweat. He lunged for the chamber pot, where he vomited, and vomited again, and then heaved a third time, but nothing more came up. He knelt there, hands around the cold porcelain, until his joints ached and the pain forced him away.

When she woke hours later, Maggie found him sitting at his desk in his study, eyes bloodshot, hair matted. Streaks of vomit had dried on his silk robe. He was staring straight ahead. "My love, you're a sight," Maggie said kindly. "Give me that robe. Let me clean you up."

He stared blankly. "It is over. My life is over…. Go now."

"But William, we must decide what to do. I need you. I'm in trouble."

He replied, no longer tender: "I need to be alone. Leave me." And then, in the tone a master uses with a servant: "I will call for you when I want you back."

Maggie stepped out, and he closed the door firmly behind her.

The next morning William summoned Ted Stark, an investigator he had hired two years before, after an old Gloucester pinky had suspiciously sunk in fine weather with no loss of life. Stark was a hard-bitten former Essex County sheriff's deputy who knew where all the bodies were buried on the North Shore. Eventually he had persuaded the crew member who had opened the pinky's sea cocks to confess, saving William from paying on a fraudulent insurance claim.

Maybe Stark would know how to deal with this disaster and keep it quiet.

Stark was more than happy to help. Getting Maggie out of the way was no problem. He knew a woman in Gloucester. For a price, she would take on William's little problem. Keeping Maggie quiet was the trick. Given William's circumstances, extortion was a real danger — he knew Maggie's kind. But there was usually a way, he assured William. He'd check around and see what he could find out.

Four days later Stark was back in William's office. "Good news, sir. I have friends in the Irish community. Your Maggie's brother is wanted for felony assault back in Ireland. He entered this country under false pretenses, and we can have him sent back whenever we want."

"I do not follow you. How does that help take care of Maggie?"

"Sir, reports are she is close to her brother. She will be, shall we say, more amenable to doin' the right thing if she understands what could happen to him."

William was still confused. "I see, Stark, but I do not think that kind of threat is necessary. She will be embarrassed by this whole thing and want to keep it quiet as much as I do."

Stark shook his head and frowned in disbelief. "Sir, with all due respect, I know more 'bout this kind of woman than you do. Without a lever like this, she'd be back to ya for more and more money. Her silence would become so dear that even you couldn't afford it. Believe me, sir. I seen it happen.

"You should also know that your little lady left Ireland under a bit of a cloud herself. Some say she gave a poor farmer the French disease. But no need to run to a doctor all worried 'bout your own johnson. If you're not infected by now, sir, and *believe me,* you would know if ya were, you'll be all right."

"But no matter what happened back in Ireland, the point is that her troubles are good news for us. She won't want those rumors spread here. They make her seem more the tart that she surely is, and she won't want her brother shipped home in chains to rot in some primitive Irish jail. I can use this information to protect ya, sir."

William paced, hands locked behind his back. "I see, Stark. I have so little experience with this sort of thing. I'm lucky to be healthy, it seems. Quite good news about her brother, indeed. Now tell me, what do we do next?"

"Leave all the arrangements to me, sir. It won't be cheap — you'll hafta pay for her care for a few years. If she gets desperate, we can't control her no matter what we got over her. But for a price, my friend will take her in and eventually put her to work. Pretty young ladies with your Maggie's talents are always in demand with the lower classes. She'll be able to pay her way after the baby's born. You have her meet me tomorrow in the Public Garden, down by that fancy new pond they just put in, and I'll take it from there."

"Thank you, Stark. I knew you were the right man to call about this. My future depends on keeping this quiet. I see you understand. Let me know how much it will cost, and I will take care of it."

"I'll furnish ya with a statement after I make all the arrangements. Don't worry, sir; she's given us all the tools we need."

The cobblestones on Beacon Street were damp and slippery, and the air was thick with the sweet fragrance of rain on cut grass. Few were in the Public Garden on this dreary morning, so Maggie had no trouble spotting Stark. He wore a rumpled overcoat and a bowler hat; his shoes were badly scuffed. His eyes were dark and set close together, and he had a boxer's nose and a two-day-old stubble. Next to Stark was a large, thick-boned man with matted black hair, bloodshot eyes, and a scar on his right cheek. He was missing one of his lower front teeth, and he smelled as if he hadn't bathed in weeks.

Stark recognized Maggie at once. "Miss Maggie O'Grady, is it?" he said. He kept his hands at his side; he was not given to shaking hands, especially with women.

"Yes," she said cautiously, "and you must be Mr. Stark."

"I am, and this is Timkins." Timkins cleared his throat of a large phlegm blockage and spat it out. A viscous string hung from his lip until he wiped it onto the palm of his hand and then onto the front of his trousers. "We're here to take ya to your new home."

Staring at Timkins, Maggie cocked her head and furrowed her brow. "I know nothing of a new home." Turning to Stark, she continued with more confidence. "And I must say, I'm not ready to go anywhere today."

"Miss O'Grady, you'll do what I tell ya to do. Your brother, Seth O'Grady, is wanted for assault back in Ireland. He lied when he entered this country, and I can have him deported for incarceration in Ireland anytime I choose. If I have him picked up, he'll serve three years in the Wicklow County Gaol. I hear it is an unusually dirty place filled with thugs, lepers, and sheep lovers. But perhaps you already know this."

Maggie stood silently.

"If he goes there, his blood will be on your hands. The poor mick beat up Jake Anderson," Stark continued. "I'm sure ya know the name. Tryin' to protect your tarnished reputation, he was. You're a saucy one, that's for sure, and it's plain you're trouble when it comes to men. You fled your homeland because a' man trouble, and what did it get ya? Pregnant with a bastard child, and I don't hear ya sayin' some man forced himself on ya.

"You claim the father is William Hudson. Between you and me, I don't know what the truth is, and I don't care. But Miss, I can tell ya that Hudson will deny fatherin' your child. He's respected; people will listen to him. And once I'm done tellin' what I know to the authorities, there'll be no one, and I mean no one, who will even give ya the time of day."

Maggie started to respond, but Stark kept right on talking.

"Now, you can go your own way and accuse Hudson of adulterous acts, but it won't do ya any good. And if ya do that, you and that babe a' yours will starve. As a' right now, you've no home in the Hudson household. No more pay for ya. And you'll not find work anywhere else, not with that bastard inside ya, and not without a reference. Harvey knows which side a' his bread the butter's on. He won't speak on your behalf. So if ya don't care 'bout whether you and your babe have food to eat, and if ya don't care 'bout whether your brother spends the next three years a' his life locked up with the buggers and lepers of Wicklow County, then you just leave here and go your own way. You're a free woman. America's a free country."

Maggie's shoulders slumped. Stark could see that his speech was having the desired effect.

"But if ya come with me and keep your mouth shut, you and your babe will be housed and fed, and your brother can keep workin' at the Ritz, and maybe one day he'll own his own tavern. So what's it to be, little lady? I don't have all day. I got a train to catch."

Maggie spoke softly, as if only to herself. "Mr. Stark, you don't know my William. 'Tis his babe that's

119

in me belly. He will not let this happen. For sure, he won't."

"Oh, is that so? Who told ya to come here, Miss?" Stark did not wait for an answer. "William Hudson sent ya here. He hired me, and he hired Timkins." As he said this, Timkins took two steps forward, stopping directly in front of Maggie's right shoulder, close enough that she could smell the blood sausage he had eaten for breakfast. "These ain't my words I'm sayin'; they're Hudson's. If ya don't do what *I* tell ya to do, you and your baby will be alone in the world. You got another to think 'bout now. You're gonna be a mother. You got responsibilities; don't forget that, little lady. If you make the wrong decision, you'll be murderin' your child, and you alone will be to blame."

"William . . . ," she said weakly, her eyes not focused on anything real. She lifted her head to look at Stark. "All right, I will . . . I don't . . ."

Stark did not need the words Maggie couldn't get out; he knew the battle was won. "Come this way, Maggie," he said, no longer the bully, more the friendly uncle. "I have a carriage to take us to the Boston and Maine terminal. We're goin' to Gloucester. It's a fine place; I'm sure you'll like it." His patron would be pleased, and he would be able to name his fee. He was in a generous mood.

"Gloucester — is that near Salem?" she asked.

120

"Yes, we go right by Salem on the way there. Salem's where they hung those witches long ago."

"Yes, 'tis where the House o' the Seven Gables is," she said.

"That's right, you can go look at that famous house one day."

"I'd like that," Maggie said, as if in a dream. She climbed into the carriage. Stark and Timkins sat close on either side of her. With a touch of the whip, they were off to the train station.

Chapter 11

At Sea — June 1861

Ray and his brother, Augie, started the summer of 1861 together on the *Raiatea Sunrise.* The previous summer Ray had made many times what Augie had earned filing papers in the city clerk's office, and this summer Augie wanted in on the big money. But he soon discovered that fishing wasn't for him: he hated the long hours, the tight quarters, and the unpleasant odors, and unlike Ray, he had no interest in learning to be a professional sailor. During their second trip to Georges, Augie told Ray he would stick it out for the rest of the summer, but he was looking forward to returning to Bowdoin College and having the career ashore that their father wanted for both of them.

Ray had different plans. He and Augie were sitting together on the bowsprit of the *Sunrise,* enjoying the ride back to Gloucester, when he revealed them. "Augie, I'm not going to college. Robby can get me a job on the *Benjamin Parsons*. I'm going to be a fisherman."

Augie wasn't surprised. "You do have the knack for it. The men respect you; that's easy to see. Father's going to explode, though."

Ray nodded.

The clang of the ship's bell announced dinner, and they crawled back over the bowsprit to safety. When they reached the foredeck, Augie extended his hand. Ray took it, and then Augie pulled him close and wrapped his arms around him. "Take care, little brother, especially once winter sets in. I don't want to lose you."

They had never embraced before. "Don't worry about me," Ray said. "Everything will turn out all right."

To his relief, Augie let go. "It always has for you. See that you keep it that way."

They were home by noon the next day. Ray waited three more days, until the morning the *Parsons* was to depart. He packed his sea kit, then walked back to the *Sunrise* and told his father straight and simple: he was a man now, and he was going fishing. College could wait, maybe forever.

Gus didn't explode the way his sons had thought he would. "You're a man; you get to make your own decisions," he said in that authoritative tone Ray had heard him use on so many occasions. "The truth is," he said, his tone softening, "I'm damn proud of you. You're a natural-born sailor, just like your grandfather.

Teaching you things I learned from him has been one of the great pleasures of my life." Gus bit his lip and looked down at the ground, but he was unable to hide his emotion.

After a moment of silence, father and son shook hands. Ray thought of following Augie's lead and hugging his father, but a lifetime of tradition stopped him. "Thank you, Father," he said.

"But son, your mother will disapprove of your decision. She sees you as a banker or a lawyer. She'll not be happy."

Ray looked at his father and nodded.

"You've learned a lot, but you still have a lot to learn. Remember that. And never forget: one hand for the ship and one for you, always one hand for you. Always take care of yourself."

Six weeks later, Ray and Robby were on the Grand Banks, a thousand miles east-northeast of Gloucester, not far south of Newfoundland, in a twenty-foot dory. Schooners carried dories to the Grand Banks, where the men fished by setting long lines of baited hooks, called trawls, from the dories and retrieving them after an interval that allowed many fish to bite. It was an efficient way to fish, but it couldn't be used on Georges Bank because the currents were too strong there.

This evening, Ray and Robby were rowing back to the *Parsons* in a dory overloaded with cod freshly pulled off the hundreds of hooks that their trawls had strewn across more than a mile of ocean bottom. When the swell lifted them up, they could see the *Parsons* in the twilight of a late-summer night, kerosene lamps already lit. Down in the dark troughs, Ray and Robby were hemmed in by walls of deep blue water. Their dory was so heavy that it felt as if they were rowing in a viscous porridge of corn meal. It was slow going.

They were the last of the eight dories to come in. As soon as their dory was stacked on deck with the others, the *Parsons* hauled her anchor. While their crewmates made sail, Ray and Robby headed, gutted, and split the cod they had just caught, placed the carcasses in the fish hold, and shoveled on salt from bins that were now nearly empty. When they reached Gloucester, the fish would be placed on drying racks in the sun until it had the leathery consistency of fully cured salt cod. It could then be stored for years.

The weather had been good except for one powerful late-summer gale that had forced them to heave to for forty-eight hours, while their ship was tossed about like a toy in a bathtub with a rambunctious toddler. The rain had been so warm and intense that it seemed like a tropical waterfall. Their captain, Paul Tobey, said they had passed through the dying remnant of a hurricane that had ridden the Gulf Stream all the way from the Caribbean to the cold waters of the Labrador Current.

Six days after leaving the fishing grounds, the *Parsons* sailed into Gloucester and tied up to the unloading dock. Ray and Robby were working together in the fish hold, putting the salt cod into baskets to be lifted ashore by a hand-powered crane, when one of the crew yelled down that Tobey wanted to see Ray in the captain's cabin. Ray climbed out of the fish hold and descended from the bright sunlight into the darkness. When his eyes adjusted, he saw his father standing next to the navigation table. Gus' shoulders were hunched over, but he straightened up to look at Ray.

"Ray . . . Augie's dead."

"That can't . . ."

"Son, we ran into a hurricane. We saved the ship, but Augie was swept overboard. Tobey says you're relieved from unloading duties. Come home to your mother. The storm that hit us headed east, and she was scared that it might've killed you next."

Toward the end of the day, Ray walked back to the Harbor Cove dock, where the *Parsons* had just finished unloading. He found Robby, and the two of them went to get paid. Robby had heard the news; by then, everyone had. As his crewmates emerged from the fish company office, they all came over to Ray. Most just nodded and then looked respectfully at the ground; a few gave Ray a pat on the shoulder. Robby said he was awful sorry. Augie was a good man, he said, the finest kind.

Ray had to know what had happened. He asked Robby to find Asa Burnham, and Robby said Asa always went to Fannies between trips. It didn't take long for the two of them to walk the few blocks there.

Fannies had once been a grand three-story home. Now the white paint on the clapboards was worn through in places, the black shutters were missing a slat here and there, and the roof sagged. The wooden steps leading up to the entrance were hollowed out from the footsteps of thousands of men home from the sea, looking for comfort ashore.

Ray followed Robby through the bright red door into a dimly lit bar, where the air was heavy with tobacco smoke. They stepped on wide pine floorboards that creaked and groaned against old oak joists. The hum of quiet conversation was occasionally broken by a boisterous laugh. A middle-aged woman greeted Robby with a grin and a big slap on the backside. "I'm glad to see ya, Robby. I hear the ol' *Parsons* had a hell of a trip." She looked at Ray. "Who's the young fella?"

Robby gave the woman a big kiss square on the lips: "Fannie, this here's Ray Stevens. He's becomin' a right fine fisherman. But today he's here because he just found out he lost his brother on the *Raiatea Sunrise.* He'd like to talk to Asa 'bout it. Is he around?"

The woman turned to Ray. "Sorry 'bout your brother, young man. It was a devil of a storm, I hear. It's lucky any of 'em made it back. Asa's here, sure enough. Normally he wouldn't accept visitors, busy as he is, but I'm sure he'll make an exception for ya."

Fannie turned around and shouted. "Maggie, come in here!"

Out from a room behind the bar came a short redhead wearing a green dress with a low-cut, tight-fitting bodice, her white petticoat visible below the ankle-high hemline. She cocked her head, subconsciously letting Fannie know she was ready to listen. Her bright eyes stood out in the smoky room like the Twin Lights of Straitsmouth Island. "Maggie," Fannie said, "go up to Sarah's room and see if Asa's decent. Tell him Ray Stevens is here. He wants to talk 'bout his brother. What was your brother's name, Ray?"

"Augie."

"Augie's the name. Now run along." Maggie bounded up the stairs two at a time. Ray watched her go, and he kept looking at the stairs after she had disappeared. "Now you two, have a drink while you're waitin' — on the house," Fannie said loud enough to bring Ray back to the present. "Skip," she yelled to the old one-legged man behind the bar, "fix these two up, whatever they want."

Robby walked over to the bar, but Ray stood still. "Come on, Ray," Robby said. "You might as well have your first drink. If I know Sarah, she'll clean Asa up before she sends him down. It'll be a few minutes. Come on, it won't kill ya. Two rums, Skip," Robby said, turning to the bartender.

So Ray had his first drink. The old man behind the bar smiled when Ray gagged on the first swallow.

"That'll put hair on your chest, youngster," he said to Ray. Skip had captained a pinky back in the '20s and '30s; his fishing days had ended when his leg got caught in a loop of mooring line. The descending anchor had pulled the line so hard it crushed the veins in his shin; gangrene had set in, and Skip's lower leg had to be amputated. The doctor gave him half a bottle of whiskey, Skip would tell anyone who asked, and stuck a piece of thick line in his mouth so he wouldn't bite his own tongue off. He remembered it hurting "somethin' awful."

Ray looked around as he sipped his drink. A large mirror hung behind the bar above shelves lined with bottles of rum and whiskey. A dozen stools were at the bar, half of them occupied, and three of the half dozen tables were full. All the customers were fishermen. Several looked as if they had come right off their boat, clothes still covered with dried-up gunk, hats encrusted with salt. After a few minutes, Fannie signaled one of the men who had been sitting at the bar. He downed the remains of his drink and went upstairs.

Robby went over to Fannie and whispered in her ear. Then he handed her something and came back to sit next to Ray. "What did you say to Fannie?" Ray asked.

"I feel real sorry 'bout Augie. But life does go on. I asked Fannie if Miss Sylvie might be available once we completed our business with Asa. I spend time with Sylvie when we're in town; she's a remarkably flexible lady. Fannie said she's busy right now, but I'm next in line."

Ray didn't know what to say, so he just nodded and silently sipped his drink. He was feeling the effect of the rum by the time Asa came down the stairs and sat on the stool next to him. His hair was combed, but he hadn't shaved, and his breath smelled of stale tobacco. Skip automatically poured him a drink, and seconds for Robby and Ray.

"Ray," Asa began sleepily, then downed his shot of rum in one throw. "I'm awful sorry 'bout Augie. There was nothin' anyone could do." The rum seemed to perk him up.

"What happened, Asa?" Ray asked. "My father hasn't told me how it happened."

Skip poured Asa another rum. "It was the worst summer storm I seen in all my years," Asa said. "We were anchored on Georges, and the bottom dropped outta the glass. Your papa ordered us to stop fishin' and we set sail, but the storm came on too fast. We went from a nice breeze to a full-blown williwaw in less than half a day, not enough time for us to get home. The air was warm, almost hot. And my gawd, how it blew. The seas built to thirty feet in no time, and some of 'em started to break. The sound was fearsome. We hove to with nothin' but a triple-reefed fores'l, but the wind was still holdin' us over, puttin' the rail under."

Asa paused and downed his rum. Skip poured him another. "Four of us, including Augie, were on deck when the fo'stay let go. It parted down low, right where it connects to the bowsprit. The only thing holdin' up the top of the fo'mast was the jib halyard that's lashed down with the furled jib to the bowsprit, and those lashings weren't gonna hold for long with the mast tugging at 'em.

"Augie and Stan Smith went out onto the bowsprit to splice a piece of heavy line into the fo'stay. Your brother wasn't the handiest man on board, but he was a gamer. I think Gus wanted to stop him, but how could he send another man where he wouldn't send his own son? Augie and Stan crawled out there, and they had to hang on pretty tight; even hove to, the bowsprit was going under every third wave or so." Asa tipped his head back and drained his glass. Skip filled it again.

"Just as they got all the way out at the end, all that yanking on the halyard broke the lashin', and the jib flew free and filled out to leeward. It shoulda blown to bits right away, but it didn't. The cloth held, and the *Sunrise* just lay right over on her side. It woulda sunk us for sure if it had gone on, but then there was a loud crack.

"That sail just ripped the bowsprit clean off the boat, and then the fo'mast exploded 'bout ten feet off the deck. Now she was free of all that sail, and she just popped back upright. But most a' the fo'mast, along with the fores'l, was hangin' from the boat like a sea anchor, still tied to her with all those lines. I got a gang workin' to cut the riggin' away." Asa took a sip from his glass.

"Gus . . . well . . . he ran forward. The bowsprit was all splintered, Ray. Small pieces of it were hangin' from some a' the lines, but nothin' anyone could stand on. Augie and Stan were somewhere in that water, but we couldn't move the boat with all that riggin' holdin' it down. And we couldn't see fifty feet anyway — it was rainin' that hard. We finally got the mast cut away, but then all we could do was jury-rig a ridin' sail. We never saw Augie again, or Stan either." Asa downed the last of his fourth rum.

Ray put his hand on Asa's shoulder and nodded his thanks, then turned and left.

From the sidewalk he looked toward the harbor and thought of a day long ago when Augie was tying their dory to the Vincent Cove dock. Still down on one knee, he had looked up at Ray, his face bright in the orange glow of the setting sun. "Great row," he said. Ray could see the freckles on his cheeks and the gap in his upper front teeth just as clearly as if he were kneeling before him still. "Great row, Augie," Ray now whispered back into the empty wind.

He walked the few blocks to Vincent Cove and found what he was looking for. Next to the small boat dock, wedged in among the prams and other small boats, was their old and battered dory — little used, neglected now, and half full of rainwater. It was there that Ray sat down, head in his hands, to weep for his brother.

Chapter 12

Gloucester — August 1861

Sarah plopped herself down in the second-floor sitting room next to a bay window that looked out over the Harbor Cove dock. She carefully tamped tobacco into a clay pipe, struck a wooden match, and lit the bowl, the tobacco glowing cherry red as she inhaled. Just as the captains' wives took to their cupolas to watch for their men returning from the sea, the ladies of Fannies came to this window when a boat carrying one of their regulars was due to arrive, or when a boat feared lost was miraculously reported to be sailing into the harbor.

Today Sarah had come here for a break while Asa slept in her room, one of seven bedrooms on the second floor. She wore a translucent crème-colored robe and soft leather moccasins. Her light brown hair fell down in waves below her shoulders. Her makeup, though applied with a heavy hand, was not thick enough to conceal an old scar under her chin.

With arms full of clean bedsheets, Maggie poked her head through the door. Sarah blew a perfectly round ring of white smoke that rolled over itself, encircling Maggie's head. "Oh, I do love a pipe. Learn to blow smoke rings, little one; it's good practice for so many things."

Maggie coughed on the harsh smoke.

"Asa's taking a shine to ya. He brought your name up three times today, once in the throes of passion. When he wakes up, why don't ya go in there and relieve me? Don't let his drinkin' bother ya. Asa's the finest kind, never beat up on any woman that I know of. He's generous, and he won't make ya do anything odd. Just let him love ya is all ya have to do with Asa." Sarah tapped the pipe twice on a side table. "You do have to clean him up, though. I'm surprised ivy doesn't grow up that slender stalk a' his when he's out to sea. But he'd be a real good one for ya to start on. I washed him just this morning — he's good to go right now."

Maggie coughed and waved the smoke away with her right hand, as if trying to swat a fly. "'Tis a kind offer you're making, Sarah. I'm honored that you'd give up your favorite to get me started, surely I am. But I've only been with one man, and that didn't work out. I'm keeping me drawers up tight for now." Maggie coughed again, and her eyes watered.

"My dear, I don't know who the bastard is that got ya that babe and then abandoned ya here. A special corner a' hell is reserved for men like that. My papa's there right now. He ran off on Ma when I was a year old, but he hung around town — I seen him every once in a while.

"A few years back he comes waltzin' in here. He walks right on into my room and starts to haul his thing out. I says to him, 'Ya don't know who I am, do ya?' 'You're a whore, ain't ya?' he says. 'I'm your daughter, ya bastard,' I tell him. Ya know what he says then? 'No daughter a' mine's gonna work in a place like this.' So proud, he was, all the while standin' there with junior still stickin' outta his trousers. What nerve!

"This ain't the easiest work. For all his kindness, Asa can take forever if he's been drinkin', and that's near all the time. And it ain't the safest work." Sarah pointed to her scar. "But it's easier than a lotta jobs, and it's a hell of a lot safer than what Asa and those other poor bastards do for a livin'. The pay's pretty good, and you have time to yourself. It's not so bad; don't turn your nose up at it."

"I meant no offense."

"None taken." Sarah inhaled again, and Maggie took a step back.

"Sarah, do you know who that man was who came in today, the one Asa went down to talk to?"

"Asa said it was Ray Stevens. His older brother was a greenhorn who died on Asa's last trip. His father's the captain of Asa's boat. He's an ol' Yankee

136

— family's been in Gloucester since Moses came down from the mountain, but Asa says he's all right."

"He sure an' looked out of place here; you can just tell when a fella's uncomfortable. He was looking me over, though."

"And it sounds like you were ganderin' at him too. Be wary a' men, little one. Few are as good as Asa. And you got a tough way to go. You need a lover and a father. But you got one thing going for ya — you're very pretty. Asa and young Ray ain't the only ones around here been looking your way. If ya decide to uncross those pretty legs a' yours, you'll be a busy lady." Her pipe had gone out, and she stood up and tapped the ashes into the spittoon beside the chair. "Asa'll be awake soon, so it's back to the salt mines for me. Don't worry 'bout the sheets. We been pretty tidy, so nothin' needs to be changed tonight."

Maggie had more beds to make that night, and in between she had an infant to nurse. She'd had a rough delivery. Doc Gray was finally called after she had struggled for thirty-six hours. He managed to save her and the baby, but he said she would not be able to have another. The news pleased Fannie.

Maggie lived in a tiny room in the cellar that Fannie reserved for women who had gotten pregnant on the job; Mabel and Winnie had been living there before Maggie moved in. Both had since delivered. Mabel and her daughter moved away, and Winnie gave her child up for adoption and went back to work upstairs. So now

137

Maggie and Seamus, named after her favorite grandfather, were alone in the cellar. Some of the ladies would check on Seamus between dates — Winnie especially liked to do that — but Maggie was never too far away.

Later that night, after she had tucked Seamus in, Maggie went to Winnie's room to change the bedsheets. Heavy lace-edged curtains covered her partially open window, but some light from a streetlamp seeped through, mingling with the yellowish glow from the kerosene lamps inside, turned down low. A glass bottle topped with a pump, a silver-backed hand mirror, and a pot of lipstick sat on a lace doily atop Winnie's varnished pine dressing table. The wide pine floorboards were painted light green and partially covered by a multicolored braided rug. Maggie pulled the light quilt off the bed and began to remove the sheets. They had been well used.

Winnie was slumped in a plush red upholstered chair by the window, sipping whiskey. She wore only her drawers. Her breasts were engorged, still full with the milk meant for her recently born child. Her jet-black hair was pinned in a chignon that had come partially dislodged, and one long fall trailed down the right side of her face. Her lipstick was smeared, and there was a bit of it on the tip of her nose. "Maggie, I'm beat. Nine boats in today, and they been in and outta here all night. Eleven of 'em so far, and I got another waitin' down in the bar. I'm sore as hell; that last one was big as a fence post. I . . ."

Winnie was interrupted by a scream from next door and then a loud bang, as if something were being thrown across the room, then more screaming. They ran next door, where a naked man had Lucy by the throat and was banging her head against the wall. Winnie jumped him from behind. He let Lucy go and landed a punch that knocked Winnie unconscious. When he turned to grab Lucy again, Maggie picked up a brass candlestick that had been knocked to the floor and swung it as hard as she could. She caught him just behind the right ear and down he went, out cold. Then Fannie burst in, gasping for breath, followed immediately by Asa, his trousers only partway on.

The police arrived before the man regained consciousness. He was a Swede off the *Halibut Point,* a boat that had caused trouble before. After he had been hauled away, Lucy slumped in a chair and explained what had happened. "Everything seemed to be goin' just fine. This big fella was poundin' away, and I was movin' and makin' all the right noises, like I was enjoyin' myself, and then he just stops.

"'This ain't workin',' he says, and he pulls out and stands up. 'We gotta do it the other way.' Then he grabs me real rough-like and rolls me over. Well, he's meanin' to stick his thing up my arse, and I don't do that. So I tell him no, I'm a girl, and he's gotta do me like a girl. He yells at me, says he's paid good money

139

and he'll do me his way. I say, 'We're done,' and I get up, but he grabs me real rough-like. I punch him in the nose, and then the bastard starts beatin' on me. I start screamin' and, well, ya know the rest."

"The same thing happened the last time we had trouble. I don't need that kinda aggravation," Fannie said. "I'm bannin' the whole *Halibut Point* crew. From now on they can drink in the bar if they want, but they ain't gettin' upstairs. Skip will know who they are."

Fannie turned to Maggie. "Winnie and Lucy are both outta commission. I got a coupla more downstairs. Whaddaya say you take one of 'em and I'll do the other, the new and the old? I think one's drunk enough to have an ol' hag like me."

"No, Miss Fannie, I've told you before, no."

"You're gonna have to earn your keep."

"Ease up there, Fannie," Asa said. "I don't need Sarah anymore tonight. I'll lend her to the cause." He bowed and gave a theatrical wave of his arm.

"All right, Asa, that will do for now," Fannie said. "But young lady, we'll be havin' this talk again."

The next morning Maggie was in the kitchen making breakfast when Lucy came down to the cellar. Both of her eyes were black, she had a big bruise on the right side of her jaw, her lips were swollen, and her neck was red where the Swede had grabbed her. Maggie poured her a cup of coffee. "I didn't thank ya last night. You saved my life. That bastard was tryin' to choke me to death."

140

"Fannie and Asa were right behind me. For sure, they would have taken care of him if I didn't," Maggie replied.

"That may be, but it was you that got him. This ain't an easy life; you're right to be cautious 'bout gettin' started. I been beat up a dozen times now, and Cousin Sarah almost had her throat cut once. It's hell if ya fall in with the wrong man."

"I thought Sarah was your sis."

"We're that close, but in truth she's my cousin, daughter of my ma's older sister. Sarah's father ran out on 'em, and my aunt just couldn't take raisin' a little girl alone."

"How did you get started in the business, Lucy?"

"Sarah and me, we grew up in one a' them abandoned shacks in Dogtown. Papa died at sea when I was just startin' school, and Ma became a drunk. I was fifteen when she passed out one night and burned our place right down. Knocked over a candle, we think. Sarah and me climbed out a window, but Ma didn't make it.

"Sarah was put in an orphanage, and I was out on the street. A nice ol' man from Annisquam took me in. At least, I thought he was nice. When he found out 'bout Sarah, he went and got her too. 'Better to have the sisters together,' he told the orphanage. Even then, everyone thought we were sisters.

141

"And it was better — for him — and I guess for us too. We learned to be a sister act with him. One of us would kiss his mouth, and the other would kiss his . . . his . . . well, ya know what. Then we'd take turns bendin' over. Not like last night — he always put it in the right place.

"We stayed with him two years, and then one day he brought us down to Fannies. He sold us to Fannie. Never learned how much he got. We been here ever since. We can leave if we want, but it's what we know. And mostly it's good. Doin' the sister act with Asa's kinda fun for us. It's like ol' times, ya know. We're lucky we're still so close; some families drift apart. And Asa's a good man. He loves us and he pays well.

"So that's *my* story. Who's the bastard who got you a baby and dumped ya here?"

"I just can't say. I was told he's paying Fannie for me to be here, and that Seamus and I would be out on the street if I ever said who he was. I can't take that chance."

"You're a good mother, Maggie. I wish I'd had a mother like you."

By now the rest of the house was gathering for breakfast. Lydia, a slender woman with beautifully clear blue eyes and long dark hair, not much older than Maggie, sat next to Sylvie at the long pine table. Winnie plopped down at the other end of the table, peeled back her chemise, and strapped on a gadget Asa

142

had made to pump milk out of her breasts. She had a regular customer who paid triple just so he could put his lips on her and get some milk out, so she was keeping it coming for as long as possible. Maggie let Winnie nurse Seamus when she could, but he had had his fill this morning.

Fannie took her spot at the head of the table. She had been up to the police station and learned that the Swede had been released already. "I asked the sergeant why they let that bastard go after he almost killed one a' my girls, and ya know what that lazy arse said? 'He's a good family man, Fannie,' that's what he said. 'All he needed was soberin' up.' So now he's gone home to the little woman on Rocky Neck."

"If I was her I'd watch my backside," Lydia quipped.

"Poor woman," Lucy said. "I wouldn't wanna be in her shoes. Nothin' worse than throwing your lot in with one man and findin' out he's no fuckin' good. At least when we get a bad 'un, it's over inside an hour."

"Hell, sometimes it's over in less than a minute," Sylvie said, to laughter.

"Give me a minuteman every time!" cried Winnie. "I'm a patriot!"

"All right, enough of that now," Fannie said. "This is a discussion I need to have with Maggie, but you might as well all be in on it. Maggie, Lucy can't work 'til those bruises heal, so that makes it decision time. You can step up and take one a' those beds upstairs, or you and Seamus can pack your bags. What's it gonna be?"

"Wait a minute, Fannie." Lucy stood up. "That young lady saved my life last night. She needs this place, and I don't think ya should force her into whorin' just to stay here. She changes sheets, she cooks better than anyone we've had since ya promoted Lydia, and she listens to all our bellyachin'. You been decent to me these last ten years — this place feels like home to me, more than any other place I been, anyway. But I swear, if ya put Maggie and that little boy out on the street, I'm goin' with 'em."

Lucy stared down at Fannie. Then came the grating sound of wooden chairs being pushed back across a wooden floor, and Sarah stood up as well. "I go where my Lucy goes."

Winnie stood up next. "Hardest thing I ever did was put my baby girl up for adoption. I'm not staying here if ya put that baby out on the street." Maureen, a buxom young woman from County Cork in the old country, stood with Winnie.

Sylvie looked down the table at Lydia, who nodded. Both stood up.

Everyone now stared at Fannie, the only one still sitting down. "But girls," she said, "we can't have freeloaders here. We'll go broke."

"Maggie works hard doing the laundry," Winnie said. "And there's plenty else she can do. She's good with figures. She could help ya with the books and see that the bills get paid."

"She could help Skip in the bar too," Lucy chimed in. "He's gettin' on; nowadays he has a tough time stayin' awake 'til closin' time. Whaddaya say, Fannie? Give her time. She may change her mind yet 'bout workin' upstairs."

"Yup," Sarah said, "try to entice her with a little honey. Get that Ray Stevens fella in here. I'll bet she'd soil the sheets for him."

Maggie's cheeks turned pink.

"All right, all right," Fannie said, with a wry smile. "Our candlestick-bashing heroine can stay on, *with* added duties. Maggie, we run this house like a Georges Bank schooner. All the money gets pooled. Food and booze comes off the top, and then I get half a' what's left for ownin' the place. The girls split the other half. You seen how we work it. Every time a girl entertains a customer, I put a chit in her lockbox. At the end a' the month I count the chits, and each girl gets a share based on how many men she's done. I'll give ya three chits each day for doin' your three jobs — maid, bookkeepin', and relief bartendin' — just like you'd done three men that day, and then you'll get your share, just like everyone else. You'll find soon enough that it's a lot easier to do the men than what you'll be doin'. Anyway, welcome to the crew."

After breakfast Fannie went upstairs to her small office on the first floor. She'd been watching

Maggie for a year and was sure she could handle her new responsibilities. She was far better educated than any of the others — indeed, better than Fannie herself. She considered whether it was a mistake to share too much of the business with Maggie, but quickly dismissed that concern. Stark had filled her in on Maggie's brother. She could always use that if she had any trouble.

Fannie pulled the leather-bound accounting ledgers off the shelf and placed them before her on the small oak desk. She'd been running this place for twenty-four years now. She leaned her chair back and gazed out the window. The barber across the street was out in his white apron, sweeping off the sidewalk.

This morning she had hoped to pressure Maggie into working upstairs. She was beautiful and young, her skin soft and her figure perfect; she would draw the men like flies to the gurry pile — for a while. Nevertheless, Fannie was pleased with the way events had played out. She was tired of doing the bookkeeping, and she was looking forward to spending more time out, away from this house.

She looked out again. That barber got away from his work every night; she never got away from hers, but that would change with Maggie doing some of the work Fannie had always done. And now she could put off replacing Skip. The girls were right — he was getting too old to work all night, but he'd been her very first customer all those years ago, and she was not looking forward to letting him go; the old one-legged man had nowhere to turn.

Best of all, the girls were so pleased to have faced her down that they hadn't stopped to realize that Maggie's pay would come out of their shares. Fannie would get help, and the girls would pay for it. That alone was enough to put a big smile on Fannie's face.

She'd just been bluffing anyway. She was getting fifty dollars a month from that fat cat Hudson for keeping Maggie. She had to kick fifteen back to Stark, but thirty-five a month far exceeded the cost of keeping Maggie and her baby in the cellar, and now she could keep on collecting that money for a good long time.

There was no reason to let Hudson know Maggie was paying her way, and Fannie was sure Stark would not upset this apple cart. She'd worked out arrangements with him before, and she knew he wouldn't let a misplaced sense of loyalty jeopardize his commission. She opened the right-hand drawer of her desk and took a big swig from the half-empty bottle of rum she kept there. It was thick and sweet, and it warmed her gullet on the way down.

Chapter 13

Boston — December 1861

William had changed into his crimson robe. It was a gift from Victoria on this, their first wedding anniversary; she had bought it the previous summer during her three-month stay in Paris. He was not able to join her, of course, not with a business that needed to be run. She said the robe was in Harvard's colors, but he thought it a little off.

His journal lay open before him. He had taken up writing during that summer with Maggie, but had given up on it after sending her away. He'd had so much energy back then, but now he was always tired. Running the business had become routine; there was little excitement or challenge there anymore. And his home life was not much of a life at all.

The war interested him. He had read every account he could find of the Battle of Bull Run, fought the previous summer. He knew what had gone wrong — McDowell had failed to follow up on his original advantage. William would write about the battle, and everyone would recognize that he had the key to victory. He fancied that President Lincoln would appreciate his insight and appoint him general. After his first few battlefield victories, who knew how far he would rise? But first he had to write his article, and the words were not forthcoming.

He yawned and looked toward his bed. The silk bedsheets were turned down, waiting for him. He wondered whether Victoria had turned in yet, but he would not knock on her door to find out. Twice, early on, he had been invited in there. The first time was quite awkward. She told him she was submitting out of a sense of duty. She had scrubbed her face clean of all makeup and kept her nightgown on, lifting the bottom up just enough to allow him to get the job done. Her nightcap was tied tightly under her chin, and she kept her arms by her sides, grimacing the whole time. It was painful for her, a fact she made no effort to hide.

For the next three months she was in recovery, and only when it was clear she was not pregnant did she allow him to try once more. If anything, the second go-round was worse than the first. It took him a long time, and toward the end she complained loudly, urged him to hurry up, and let him know how unpleasant it was for her. He finally announced a false completion and withdrew.

They both knew an heir was expected, but submitting to that process a third time was too much for either of them to contemplate, so now her door stayed closed at night. In March she would sail for Italy to spend the summer with her mother at their favorite villa outside Naples. He would not be sorry to see her go.

William slid under the bedclothes. He recalled Maggie's triangle of wispy red hair and soft, milky-white skin, and tried to emulate her perfect touch. He settled quickly into sleep once he was done. Ninety minutes later he awoke, the remnants of a dream still in his head. There was Maggie, as he had never seen her, her soft white belly full with his child, her breasts enlarged, ready to feed their rich milk to his heir. He tossed and turned for half the night before sleep came to him again.

Chapter 14

Brunswick — February 1862

Ray sat next to the window in rhetoric class and watched as blowing snow drifted over the pathway to Massachusetts Hall. Professor Chamberlain was droning on, and Ray was finding it difficult to hold onto the thread of the lecture. This storm was fast becoming a blizzard in Brunswick, Maine; it would be much worse out on Georges. The *Raiatea Sunrise* might have up-anchored by now, run for the safety of Gloucester Harbor if she had gotten going soon enough, hove to and rode it out if she hadn't. At anchor the shallow water would be rough and the crew would have an uncomfortable night, enduring steep seas while watching anxiously for something to go wrong. It would be dangerous, but they would be living fully; no one would be bored.

Ray looked away from the window at his professor. Chamberlain was not an old man, and he looked vigorous enough. But he must be a meek character, going through life never experiencing the excitement of a storm or the challenge of conquering the elements. How could he truly be a man if he never risked it all? Only the fearful would choose a career as a college professor. Ray shook his head in pity as he watched him walk back and forth in front of the class. That poor man must be afraid of his own shadow.

Ray drifted off again. He regretted not fighting back harder last fall, but really, what could he have done? Augie was dead.

His parents had sat at the dining table with him, across from Augie's empty chair, its eternal silence dominating their conversation. Gus repeated what he had said a month before: Ray was a grown man, and this was his life and his decision. But then his mother spoke: she wouldn't be able to go on living if Ray went to sea and never came back. She looked at Augie's empty chair, and tears formed in her eyes. His father was staring forlornly at the empty chair too.

Ray made the best deal he could. He would go to Bowdoin for a year and see what it was like. If it didn't suit him after a year, he'd go back to fishing.

Gus had seen Ray off on the train the next day. Two sea bags in hand, Ray was about to board when Gus put his hand on his shoulder. "Ray . . . Ray, I . . . I should have stopped Augie from . . . I could have saved him."

Ray looked away from his father's swollen eyes, then looked back. "You couldn't have stopped him, Pa.

Augie was a man; he had to walk out onto that bowsprit." Now Ray's own tears began to flow. He dropped his bags, and father and son embraced. When they let go, each nodded uncomfortably. Ray picked up his bags and boarded the train without looking back.

The shuffling of chairs woke Ray from his daydream; rhetoric class was over. He buttoned his coat tightly. With hands stuffed deep in his pockets, he crossed the quadrangle to his small room in Appleton Hall. It was getting dark, and the gas lamps cast a yellowish glow on the unshoveled pathways. By the time he got to the dorm, he was out of breath and his socks were soaked. He removed his hat and boots and rubbed life back into his frigid toes.

Later that evening, after a hearty meal of overdone meat and baked beans in the dining hall, he climbed into bed and pulled up his heavy quilt. The dorm was indifferently heated, and it felt good to be covered up. In the feeble light of a single candle, he began to read the next day's English assignment, "The Wreck of the Hesperus," written by Bowdoin's own Henry Wadsworth Longfellow:

It was the schooner Hesperus,
That sailed the wintry sea;
And the skipper had taken his little daughter,
To bear him company....

The storm tossed about an old beech that rose up outside Ray's second-story window. Drafts blew the calico curtains away from the sash, and a gust shook the window against its frame. Ray pulled the quilt up high under his chin and read on:

Colder and louder blew the wind,
A gale from the Northeast.
The snow fell hissing in the brine,
And the billows frothed like yeast....

Ray could feel the sea as the schooner pitched up over breaking crests and dropped into deep troughs. She rolled hard to leeward and a dory broke free, smashed through the gunnels, and disappeared. Now another ship raced out of the blackness to windward, out of control, the faces of its crew frozen in fear. The violence of the collision threw him to the deck as spars came raining down to the sound of timbers splintering and lines snapping. Men armed with hatchets began to cut away at the tangled rigging, slipping in the ice as the boat rolled in beam seas.

He peered down into the bilges to see the black North Atlantic racing in though broken planking. The starboard side was stove in, and she was flooding fast. She wallowed. Men put aside their hatchets to hang on and to pray. Water washed over the leeward rail and up the deck. Half-frozen men lost their grips and slipped into the sea.

154

A wave washed clean over the deck, sweeping Ray against the shattered stub of the mainmast; an inert mass left by the receding water bumped against his shins. It was a man in oilskins. He struggled with the unresponsive body and finally turned it over. The unshaven face was lost in the darkness, and then in a burst of lightning he could see: it was Gus, his father, staring up toward the heavens, his lifeless eyes and mouth wide open.

Ray jerked awake in a cold sweat. The candle had burned out and his quilt lay on the floor, where he had thrown it when thrashing about. He curled into a ball and covered himself, then shivered for a long time.

The next morning he went straight to the dean's office. A family emergency had arisen and he had to go home, he said.

He took the train south. It was slow going in the aftermath of the epic storm.

In Gloucester, the townspeople were frantic. Seventy boats had been out on Georges when the storm started; only a handful had straggled in by the time Ray arrived. He took his telescope and rode out to Eastern Point to watch as, one by one, they limped back to port. They were crippled and hurt: gaffs missing, masts gone, deckhouses and dories carried away.

Day after day he made the trip out to Eastern Point, hoping to sight the *Sunrise*. Each day, as darkness settled in, he made the trip back home: sorrowful, anxious, exhausted from fretting.

After a week the arrivals dwindled to a trickle, and then they stopped.

There are stories enough of men who return home months, even years, after being given up for dead. But by the second week of March, Ray and his mother had given up hope — Ray, because he had felt his father die that night as he lay in his bed in Brunswick; his mother, because she was of this place and had seen friends, neighbors, and family disappear at sea her whole life. The *Sunrise* was gone, as were fourteen other Gloucester boats sunk that stormy night. One hundred twenty men were dead. New widows filled the waterfront homes and tenements, and schoolrooms full of children were now without fathers.

March 14 was the worst day down at Fannies. That was the day the *Cape Ann Advertiser* gave up praying for a miracle and published the names of the men who had died in the storm. Asa Burnham was among the dead, and Sarah was inconsolable. She couldn't work. He had not been her only customer, of course, but he had been her anchor, and now she was adrift. He had cherished Sarah; he was the only man who ever had.

Up the hill on Middle Street, Ray was now the man of the family. His mother needed Gus' share of the insurance money to pay the mortgage, so Ray went to John Pitt to get it.

It started well. "Ray, I been meanin' to come see ya and your ma," Pitt said. "I'm sorry 'bout what happened. Your papa was a good man."

"Thank you, Mr. Pitt. He sure was," Ray said. Knowing no other way, he got right to the point. "I've come to collect Mother's share of the insurance. Also, I'd like to talk about going to work for you. I think you'll find I'm a hardworking hand."

"That's what I heard. Asa, God rest his soul, said you'd be a good skipper one day. His word on such matters means much to me. I'll find ya work on one a' my boats. Now, as to your papa's share a' the insurance, we ain't done with the figurin' yet, but don't get your hopes up. Your papa had a half interest in the boat, all right, but when the *Sunrise* sank, all the gear was lost, and I owned the gear, so it's gotta come outta your papa's share. That's what happens when a captain loses a boat; he pays for the loss. And then there's the fish. The *Sunrise* had been out for two weeks when the storm hit; she musta been pretty full, and that fish belonged to our partnership, so that comes off your papa's share too.

"Your ma ain't gonna have much comin'. It might turn out she owes me money." Pitt put his hand on Ray's shoulder, then spoke with as much dramatic conviction as he could muster. "But Ray, I've known your ma forty years . . . I wouldn't dream a' demandin' she write me a check, given what's happened."

157

This didn't sound right to Ray, but then again, he didn't have much experience with such things. "You're saying Mother owes you money?" He sounded more confused than defiant.

"That was the deal your papa and I made," Pitt said.

"Can I see this *deal*?" Ray asked, his voice rising. "Do you have something I can take back and show to Mother, something to explain to her why she gets *nothing*?"

"Calm down, young man," Pitt responded. "You don't understand the way business works between honorable men. Ain't nothin' written. A handshake's enough for men like your papa and me."

His father was honorable; of course a handshake would have been good enough for him, as he always kept his word. Yet this couldn't be right. Still, what could he say? Pitt just stood there as Ray's indignation turned back into confusion and then embarrassment. "Well, ah, thank you for your time, Mr. Pitt" was all he could think to say.

"You're welcome, Ray," Pitt said with a little too much enthusiasm. He swung open the door. "Say hello to your ma for me. And come see me when you're ready to go fishin'. I'll fix ya up."

The only man still alive whom Ray knew he could talk to about Pitt's refusal to pay was Robby. Ray found him at home with his mother and sister, told him the story, and asked for his thoughts.

"That don't sound right to me. A' course, I don't know the ways a' business. But it seems like Pitt's trying to put the blame on Gus for losin' the *Sunrise*, when you and I know he did everythin' a man could to save that boat. It was the storm that sunk her, not anythin' he did. But Pitt's got all the cards here. Maybe it's best to just get back to fishin'."

Ray shrugged. Maybe that was all he could do. He thanked Robby and headed for home, trying to think of a way to explain this to his mother.

Robby headed to Fannies, and Maggie greeted him at the door. "It's good to see you again. Sylvie's been pining away; shall I let her know you're here?"

"Miss Maggie, I'd like to have a drink or two with Skip first. But once I'm warmed up, Miss Sylvie's the one I wanna see."

"Excellent. I'll tell her to get ready. Skip, give Robby one on the house."

Over the past eight months, Maggie had moved from bookkeeper to assistant madam. As soon as Maggie took over the books, Fannie had started spending more time with her lawyer friend, Rufus Harrison, and by the end of January she'd moved in with him.

At first she came back every evening to usher the customers upstairs and make sure everything ran smoothly, just as she'd always done. But then she missed a night when Rufus took her out to a fancy supper at a private club, and then another night when he took her to a show in Boston, and then another when they went to hear an opera singer perform in Salem. Each time she found that the house ran just fine without her. So she spent more and more evenings with Rufus, and less and less time at the brothel. Gradually, without any distinct handing over of the reins, Maggie took over day-to-day operations.

As Maggie assumed more responsibility, Fannie agreed to hire a new girl to do the maid's job. They put out the word, and soon half a dozen applicants had visited Duncan Street. Fannie decided to hire Anne; she was the least experienced, but young, eager, and quite pretty. Maggie was shocked by Fannie's reasoning.

"The maid job's a trainin' ground," Fannie said. "Sooner or later there'll be a vacancy on the second floor. A girl gets too old to attract the customers, or she gets a bad case a' the clap, or she gets beat up and becomes too skittish for the work. Whatever the reason, you need to let her go, and then the maid's the one to fill the job. You, my dear, are the only exception to that rule in twenty years. So you pick a nice, pretty one who'll attract the men. That's the most important qualification for the maid job — get one they'll drool over. You gotta think ahead in this business. And this Anne — she's perfect. I get a little hot myself lookin' at her."

Maggie held her tongue. Running Fannies wasn't a job she was going to do for long. But it was a job; she had a place for her son, and it beat working on her back upstairs. It would do until she could find something better, so she did not want to antagonize Fannie by speaking her mind.

But turning an innocent fifteen-year-old girl to prostitution was not something Maggie would ever tolerate. It was fine for Fannie to hire Anne as the maid, but they were going to have it out if Fannie ever tried to force Anne to sell her body to the fishermen.

Robby took a barstool and ordered a rum. "Skip, did ya ever hear of a skipper being charged for the gear and the catch lost when his ship sinks in a storm?"

Skip put a heavy shot glass full of dark brown rum on the bar in front of Robby. "After a boat's lost, the skipper's down with the rest a' the crew paying compliments to Davy Jones. Don't know any owner who would go down there to try and collect for lost gear."

"Well, let me tell ya what I heard from Ray Stevens. He was the young fella in here with me last summer to talk to Asa after his brother died." Skip remembered, and so did Maggie, who had just returned from Sylvie's room and now stood by the end of the bar, eavesdropping.

"I know 'bout the *Sunrise* bein' lost," Skip said. "It's a damn shame. We all miss Asa; he was a favorite a' the ladies."

"I miss him too. Asa taught me how to fish and, well, lotsa other things. It's the *Sunrise* I wanna tell you 'bout." He filled Skip in on the story. "So Ray's ma is gonna lose her home if she can't get the insurance money. But Pitt says she won't get anything because all the money's owed to him for the gear and the fish that sank with the *Sunrise*. Whaddaya think 'bout that?"

"I been around the docks for fifty years, and it don't sound right to me at all. The devil made that storm blow. You can't blame the skipper for that. The poor widow shouldn't lose her home right after she's lost her man."

Maggie broke in. "What did Ray say he was going to do about it, now?"

"He doesn't know what to do 'bout it. Don't know if there's anythin' he can do. Pitt owns a bunch a' boats and that big fish-packin' company in East Gloucester. What's a kid like Ray gonna do?"

"For sure, he could hire a lawyer," Maggie suggested.

"Lawyers work for the ones who have the money," Skip said. "There ain't many with as much money as that Pitt. That poor kid's not gonna find a lawyer who'll help him out."

"I talked to a lawyer once," Robby said. "My leg got broke when a line let go and I fell fifteen feet to the deck. This lawyer asked me if the boat was unseaworthy. 'Well, no,' I says, 'the boat was sound enough, just some damn greenhorn didn't know how to tie a bowline.' 'Well,' the lawyer says, 'I can't help ya then.' It doesn't matter that some damn fool's careless and I'm outta work for three months. Lawyers are no use to the workin' man." Robby downed the rest of his drink and popped the glass on the bar. "Well, I can't have Sylvie waitin' all night for her one true love."

The next morning after breakfast, Maggie stepped into Winnie's room. She was using the breast pump Asa had made for her; she had to use it all the time now that Seamus was weaned. "Winnie, how long will you be keeping up your pumping?"

"I'm gettin' mighty tired of it. But it pays well."

"Isn't that thirsty calf of yours named John Pitt?"

"Yup, he's the one."

"Let me tell you a little story, now."

Chapter 15

Gloucester — March 1862

The next day was damp and cold, the kind of day that could start a man shivering no matter how bundled up he was. A few flakes had started to fall, and it was obvious that another storm was building. Those whose loved ones had returned to sea began to worry all over again.

Five blocks up the hill from Fannies, Elizabeth Stevens sat alone. Ray had left that morning for Brunswick to withdraw from Bowdoin. He had told her not to worry. He could make enough as a fisherman to support her and himself. She had to accept his decision; what else could she do? There was no way she could earn a living. So Ray was off to Brunswick to gather his things and beg for a tuition refund. And when he came back, she would have to live with the fear she knew would consume her every time he put out to sea.

The front door opened, and Emily Wonson let herself in and joined Elizabeth in her sitting room.

Emily had been at Middle Street especially often over the last few weeks. Elizabeth had held up well enough until Ray brought the news about the insurance, but then melancholy had taken hold of her. This morning her eyes were bloodshot, her face was drawn, and her wrinkles were deeper than ever. She looked as if she'd aged a decade overnight.

"I just don't understand that John Pitt," Emily said. "Remember when we were in Central Grammar, and the Miller brothers were beating up Stinky Pederson all the time? One day Pitt got right in the middle of it and stood up for Stinky. Got his nose bloodied, too, but after that the beatings stopped. And Pitt didn't even know Stinky that well. It was one of the kindest things I ever saw a boy do. Whatever happened to that John Pitt? How did he come to be the type of man to steal your insurance money?"

"He changed when his father died at sea, remember?" Elizabeth said. "It was the same year he stood up for Stinky. Before long his ma lost that little shack of theirs. Then John had to go to sea. He couldn't have been more than twelve. It changed him."

Elizabeth put her face in her hands. "What am I going to do? I pay twenty dollars a month on the mortgage, and if I don't keep up the payments, the savings bank will take my house. I have taxes due next month too. The bills don't stop just because Gus is gone. Isn't there some way I can make John Pitt pay what he owes me?"

Emily took Elizabeth into her arms.

"Did you talk to Enoch's brother, Henry?"

"Yes, I spoke with him this morning, but he just said it was between Pitt and Gus. Whatever they agreed to goes. But Henry's bound to see Pitt's side of it, being a boat owner and all. I want to hear what my Enoch thinks." Emily rocked Elizabeth back and forth and kissed her forehead.

"If I lose my house, what will happen to me? I can't go to the workhouse," Elizabeth sobbed. "I'll kill myself first."

"Don't worry," Emily said in a calm, loving tone. "Ray will take care of you, and if he can't, I will. You'll never go to that nasty place."

"Oh, Em, I don't want Raymond to go out in those boats again."

"Now, Libby, we've been around long enough to know that going to sea is what our men do. Ray's always been a lucky boy. He'll be all right. It's up to us to put on a brave face."

"I'm so tired. I didn't sleep a wink last night."

Emily took Elizabeth's hand. "Come on, then. I'll put you to bed. You'll feel better after you've slept."

Back down at Fannies, Seamus, now almost a year old, was eating his morning meal in the cellar with Sylvie, who had volunteered to look after him, and Robby, who had stayed the night and was lending a hand. Sylvie had prepared mashed cod, left over from

166

the previous day, squash, and pureed blueberry scooped out of last night's pie. Seamus liked the cod best; he could throw it the farthest. He and his high chair, the breakfast table, and much of the floor were splattered in varying shades of white, blue, and orange.

Robby had been the youngest in his family. He had no experience with infants, but Seamus fascinated him. After a bit of observation, Robby grabbed a spoon and pretended to be a seagull, swooping in to deposit a piece of fish in Seamus' mouth.

At first the boy wouldn't open up. Lots of people had helped feed him, but they'd all been female. He leaned back unsteadily in his high chair as Robby's pretend-gull approached, then turned his head away as the spoon got close.

But Robby was patient, and he had a talent for making odd and interesting sounds. Finally Seamus reached up with squash-stained hands to grab Robby's bushy red beard. Sensing what Seamus was aiming for, Robby moved in close. The boy grabbed hold and yanked, bringing forth a startled "ouch" from Robby. Seamus let go and looked for a second as if he would cry but, noticing the big smile crossing Robby's face, he squealed with delight instead.

Robby leaned back and Seamus again grabbed his beard, this time without tugging. With a broad smile, he let out another gleeful squeal. Letting go, he accepted the spoonful of squash and blueberries Robby reoffered. From then on, they were friends.

Sylvie had been working at Fannies for a dozen years now, and in all that time she had never had a real relationship with a man. Like Seamus, she lived in a world of females. Robby was her steadiest customer, but she had never considered him to be anything other than a good customer. Seeing him react as he did to Seamus was a slice of male humanity she hadn't known existed. This pleased her, but it also reminded her of everything she had missed, of how unlikely it was that she would ever have a normal relationship with a man or have a child of her own. Sylvie was in her late twenties, old to be marrying, even if she weren't a professional woman.

Soon Seamus had his fill, and Sylvie cleaned him up. Robby said his goodbyes, washed the squash out of his beard, and returned to his mother's house. What he remembered most the next day was not his night with Sylvie, although it had been most satisfying, but his morning with Seamus. Robby had never given a thought to settling down and having a family, and he didn't give it serious thought now. But he did think he would enjoy spending more time with Seamus.

Chapter 16

Gloucester — March 1862

A week later, right after dark, John Pitt came up Fannies' back stairs and slipped into Winnie's room, just as he'd done many times before. He'd been there for a few minutes when her door opened and two men walked in, followed unobtrusively by Maggie. One of the men sat in the plush red chair, pulling it next to Winnie's bed, while the other stood next to the chair, hands at his side, towering over the bed. Pitt yanked the bedsheet over his naked body.

"Who the hell are you? Get outta here!" Pitt yelled, then grabbed the edge of the sheet to wipe the milk off his chin. Winnie lay naked and uncovered, her right breast dripping onto the mattress.

"My name's Stark," the seated man said, "and this here's Timkins." A drip of saliva from the corner of Timkins' mouth dribbled down his chin. "We're here to collect the insurance payment for Elizabeth Stevens. I understand thirty-eight hundred dollars was deposited into your account this morning. Mrs. Stevens' half is nineteen hundred. We prefer cash."

"Are you crazy? I ain't gonna give you that kinda money."

"Suit yourself, Mr. Pitt. When Mrs. Stevens' claim comes to trial, Miss Winifred Parker, this young lady here from whom ya been takin' much nourishment, will testify that between gulps ya been braggin' 'bout outmaneuverin' young Stevens — 'the gullible young fool' is what ya called him. I'm quite sure a jury a' your peers will do the right thing. What a spectacle that trial will be; it will give the Cape Ann Morals Society plenty to talk 'bout, no doubt. I understand Susan Mason's the president a' the society this year. She's your mother-in-law, ain't she?"

Pitt looked accusingly at Winnie. "Whaddaya doin'?" he demanded.

"I'm gettin' outta the dairy business. And stop being so high and mighty. All this man wants is for ya to pay a widow what ya owe her. If ya don't, I'll testify, just like Mr. Stark says. And I won't hold nothin' back. Now here," she said, leaning over, "you still got some milk on ya." She wiped a spot off his chin with her thumb.

Pitt turned to Stark. "I ain't got that kinda cash on me."

"We're willing to accept your check. Just remember, the lawsuit will follow right quick if ya don't honor it."

Furious, Pitt pulled back the covers and got out of bed. He was short, with little chest hair and a belly that drooped over his waist. His privates were now at rest, shriveled into three small yellowish orbs. His thinning brown hair was combed over from left to right in an ineffective attempt to cover a bald patch.

He walked around Timkins, giving him as wide a berth as he could in the small room, to the chair where his trousers hung. Resigned, he pulled a blank check out of one of the pockets and turned toward the dressing table. His buttocks were small and wrinkled, like partially deflated balloons, and he had an isolated patch of hair on the right side of his back.

Pitt moved a doily off the top of the dressing table and made out the check to Elizabeth Stevens for nineteen hundred dollars. After Pitt finished, Timkins reached for the check with a large, calloused hand. His sleeves were stained and covered with random strands of animal fur; his fingernails were jagged and dirty.

Pitt pulled back, as if he were afraid Timkins would rip off his arm. He shoved the check at him and leaned back until he was pressed against the dressing table. With check in hand, Timkins stepped away and watched in silence as Pitt hurriedly threw on his clothes, picked up his hat, and left.

The next morning, right after breakfast, Robby led a bewildered Ray Stevens into the bar at Fannies. Standing there was the beautiful redhead he'd met the year before, and behind her were six ladies still in their morning robes. Everyone was smiling as the redhead spoke.

"Mr. Stevens, me name is Maggie O'Grady, and these are the ladies of Fannies: Winnie, Lydia, Sylvie, Maureen, Lucy, and Sarah. We all loved Asa Burnham — especially Sarah." Sarah smiled and surprised everyone by blushing. "We know Asa loved and respected your father, and we wanted to do something in Asa's memory, so we've gotten you this." Maggie handed Ray the check.

"Is it real?" Ray said in astonishment. "How did you get him to write this?"

"It's real enough, but it's best we don't talk about how we got it. It belongs to your mother, for sure, that's all that's important. But one more thing: don't think that John Pitt's your friend. You should go fishing with someone else."

Not knowing what to say, Ray thanked them, put the check safely in his pocket, and left. Maggie opened up the bar, and everyone toasted Asa. Stark and Timkins had cost them twenty-five dollars, but they all agreed it was the best twenty-five dollars they had ever spent. Asa's memory having been suitably honored, Sarah went back to work that night.

Chapter 17

Gloucester — May 1863

Another year went by, and on a fine day in May there was a knock on Maggie's office door. It was Rufus Harrison. "Top o' the morning to you, Rufus," Maggie said. "No need for you to have come over, now. I was about to walk the accounting up to your office."

Rufus carried a cane, and today he leaned heavily upon it. He spoke with a soft voice; he was the kind of lawyer who worked behind a desk, so courtroom bombast was not his style. He always wore a three-piece suit and tie. On this day his face was pale, his voice even softer than usual. "I'm not here for the accounting. . . . Fannie's gone, she's . . . she's dead."

"Oh m'God! What happened?"

Rufus slumped in the chair in front of Maggie's desk. "Last night I came home from the office around five o'clock, as usual. I was taking my hat and coat off in the parlor and I called to her . . . but there was no answer. . . . She was in the sitting room, on the floor next to the divan . . . went down enjoying life, just the way she would have wanted."

Rufus stared at the floor, as if he were looking down on Fannie once more. "There was a burn hole in the carpet by her right hand where her pipe landed. She was clutching her favorite shot glass in the other hand — that heavy one with the anchor engraved on it. I got Doc Gray over; he just lives down the street. It was a stroke. He thought all the smoking and the rum did her in. 'Women weren't meant for that kind of thing,' he said. He probably thought all the men she'd pleased had something to do with it too, but he was too polite to say that.

"She could be a hard woman, but she was soft with me. Took good care of me since you've been running things here. I never married, you see. At least I had a taste of it. . . . We didn't go out together much — the way people talk, you know. But we had our moments."

"Fannie was good to me too," Maggie said, "putting me in charge here and all. I haven't gotten out much either, but I've been able to take care o' me son. I'm grateful for that."

Rufus straightened up in the chair and put his hands on the desk, palms clasped together. "I wanted to come and give you this news personally. I didn't want you to worry. Fannie left me this house and this business. I know because I drafted the will. Did it properly, of course, with all the legal formalities."

174

"Rufus, I'll run this place faithfully for you, just like I did for Fannie. If you'll keep me on, I'll take care of everything."

"Maggie, my dear departed mother would spin in her grave if I ran a house of ill repute. . . . I'll sell you this building. It's worth at least fifteen thousand dollars. We'll put a mortgage on it for that amount, and you can have twenty years to pay it off. I know how much you've been sending Fannie every month; you'll have no problem with the payments. This business, I give to you. I can't keep it, and I certainly couldn't put it on the market. You can have it, with my thanks for making it possible for Fannie to live her last days with me."

"I don't know what to say. You are a very generous man."

"You could say a prayer for Fannie. She'll need our prayers."

"I'm worried that I may not be on the Lord's good side, but I will, Rufus."

Rufus departed. Maggie was proud of the good job she was doing, but running a brothel was shameful. She was doing it only because she had a son to support and no good alternative. Owning the place, though, would change things. Until now she could say truthfully she was a victim of bad treatment. But if she bought the business . . . what then? Before she could finish the thought, Skip opened the door to her office, tears in his eyes. The word was out; she'd have to address her moral dilemma later.

Three days later, Maggie, Rufus, Skip, and the ladies of Fannies gathered at the Harrison family plot at the Mount Pleasant Cemetery. Rain had been falling before they got there, and the pile of recently dug earth that would cover Fannie for eternity was dappled and wet. Rufus read a few passages from the Bible, and they all sang "Amazing Grace."

Then Fannie was lowered into her grave. Skip limped forward and threw a white rose in after her, then walked over to Rufus. "She was my favorite when I was younger, and when I was an old and broken man, she saved my life. I'm damn sorry she's gone." Rufus nodded and patted Skip on the shoulder. Skip acknowledged the gesture with a nod of his own.

Early the next morning Maggie climbed the stairs from her tiny cellar bedroom to the third floor, where she opened the door to Fannie's room. They had kept it ready for her even though she hadn't slept there in months. The largest and finest bedroom in the house, it had a bay window that looked out toward the water, just like the sitting room the ladies frequented directly below, and a small anteroom that would be perfect for Seamus.

This morning the bedroom was bathed in the orange light of dawn, reflected and intensified by the still water of the inner harbor. Maggie opened the window to the early-morning chill and heard the caws of the gulls begging for handouts from the men now stirring on the Harbor Cove dock.

The bed was big and soft. The sheets were Chinese silk. Maggie ran her hand across them and felt the once-familiar sheen of luxury. She had not thought of William much these past three years; there was no sense in dwelling on a past she could not change. But the touch of silk brought back the ecstasy of those nights from the recesses of her mind. The few months before William betrayed her trust had been the happiest of her life. She lay on the bed and looked up at the ceiling. She was so alone.

When she had first arrived in Gloucester, she had written Seth and her parents. She had a chance to go west, she told them; a Salem sea captain would take her around the Horn to San Francisco, where she could have her grand adventure. Stark had mailed the letters from Salem so Seth wouldn't think to look for her in Gloucester if he got suspicious. She had not written again. They probably thought she was dead, but she dared not write even now. Seth would find her, and then he'd find Seamus. He could count — he would wind up in an Irish jail, or even worse if he got to William. Better that her family thought her buried at sea in some shipwreck at the end of the world than for Seth to come to more grief because of her.

When she stood, her solitary shadow was projected on the wall in warm sunlight, a symbol for how she now felt: cut off from her past, isolated, alone.

But on that still morning she accepted what life had given her. She would not sleep another night in that damp cellar. She would become a madam. This was her business now. Giving up all hope of contacting her parents and her brothers again was the heavy price she would pay for her summer with William, but she refused to wistfully pray for the undoing of what could not be undone.

Chapter 18

At Sea — June 1863

The *Benjamin Parsons* was on the way home after two months on the Grand Banks, sliding through thick fog at four knots in a light southerly. From the helm Ray could see hints of blue sky above, but otherwise everything was a uniform gray. The silence was broken only by the groaning of the main boom against the mast and by the gurgling of the smooth sea being pushed aside by the schooner's spoon bow. Fog-born dew coated every surface.

Captain Paul Tobey was an old-timer. He had grown up on the Annisquam River, two houses down from Ray's mother, and he'd sailed with Gus in the merchant trade. A year ago, Tobey had picked up Ray's training where Gus had left off. Ray studied hard. He learned the esoteric mathematics of spherical trigonometry and mastered celestial navigation. Ray was always asking Tobey or other experienced crewmen how to do this or how that worked.

And he was not just a bookworm. He enjoyed skylarking in the rigging and long days in the dory. He learned to splice line and mend sails, and he excelled at boat carpentry. He liked the men he fished with, and they liked him back. Tobey had never known anyone more at home on a ship than Ray.

The *Parsons* sailed out of the fogbank, and several boats came into view two miles ahead. Ray called for Tobey, who emerged on deck munching on a biscuit.

"What do we have, Ray?"

"Three ships ahead, Skipper, all hove to, a bark of some sort and two fishing schooners. Seems odd they'd just be sitting still in this easy weather."

Tobey put his head down the companionway and shouted, "Doc, grab the glass and bring it up here." Soon the cook appeared with the telescope, and Tobey studied the boats ahead. "I don't like the looks of it, Ray. Bear off to the north." He put his head down again. "Everyone who's awake down there, on deck to trim the sails!"

Four men came topside and began letting the sails out.

"Skip, the bark's getting under way!" Ray yelled over the racket created by the crew working the sails. They all looked back to see the bark unfurling its sail. Then a puff of smoke emerged from her bow. Several seconds later a waterspout appeared a hundred yards in front of the *Parsons*; then they heard the boom of a cannon.

"Jesus Christ!" exclaimed Robby. "What the hell's goin' on?"

"Men, I think we've stumbled onto a Rebel Raider," Tobey said evenly.

"Skip, that fogbank's still right there behind us," Ray said, no hint of panic in his voice.

"So it is," Tobey said. He called for all hands on deck — an unnecessary command, as the rest of the men were pouring out of the companionway in various states of undress.

"Prepare to jibe." The men scrambled to their positions.

"Jibe ho!" The little ship's stern came through the wind, and the spars came across the deck. The bark fired again, and with a whistle and a thud a neat hole appeared in the mains'l.

"That's no warnin' shot," someone said in a shrill voice.

"They mean to sink us!" hollered Angus Cahill. "We can't fight 'em! They got a cannon!"

"We'll lose our fish if we heave to, Angus, and I'll lose this boat. We'll be back in the fog in a jiffy," Tobey said with calm determination.

"She's gainin' on us," Robby said. There was no denying it: the bark had set every stitch of sail, and in these conditions she was clearly the faster boat. Another puff of smoke was followed by a crash as a cannonball smashed through the gunnels. Angus was down, blood flowing out of his right arm.

"Jake, Doc, get Angus below and take care of that arm. Everyone except Ray get below forward; you'll be safe there," Tobey ordered. Angus was helped below, but no one else moved. "Get below! What's the matter with you?!" Tobey yelled.

"We ain't no cowards, Skip. We're not leavin' this fight to you and Ray," someone said. Another puff of smoke was followed by a crash above their heads as the main crosstrees exploded, raining spruce splinters down on the deck. The topmast leaned perilously to leeward.

Robby and three other men raced up the shrouds to haul down the tops'l, then rigged lines around the topmast to keep it from falling. Then came another crash, this one on the transom beneath where Ray was steering. Planking and framing were smashed, and water was coming in. Tobey sent two men to work the pumps, and two more to go below to slow the leak.

Then it was gray all around. They were back in the fogbank.

"Two points to starboard, Ray," Tobey calmly commanded. A bright orange flash lit the fog astern, and immediately they heard the boom of the cannon. They had entered the fogbank barely two hundred yards ahead of the bark. But this time the cannonball did not strike home. The bark had not seen the *Parsons* turn. A minute later they heard the bark fire again, but now it was well off to port, and farther away. Then there was only the rhythmic sound of the pump, the groan where the throat of the main boom rubbed against the mast, and the gurgling of the sea as the spoon bow pushed aside the cold water of the Atlantic.

The *Parsons* rounded Eastern Point two days later. They had gone south in the fog almost to Long Island before turning back to the north. The town was abuzz. The bark was the *Tocony,* and she had captured and burned four Gloucestermen. The men of the *Parsons* were heroes. Wherever they went, they were stopped to tell their yarn: cannonballs, blood, and the smell of gunpowder.

Gloucester had sent its share of young men to fight in the Great War, but very few had yet returned home to tell their stories, and those few told unromantic tales of muddy encampments, dysentery, and malaria. This was different. While they were still unloading, Maggie sent word that each member of the crew was entitled to free drinks and a romp with the lady of his choice. That night Maureen earned bragging rights by serving under three of the *Parsons'* heroes, more than any of the others.

Ray was tempted. Was Maggie among the ladies from whom he could choose? After they finished unloading, he stayed with the boat and helped Tobey move it across the harbor to the Railways for repairs. When the boat was secure, he walked back downtown, right up to the corner of Duncan and Locust. He stood

183

in front of that red door, staring at the doorknob. But he lost his nerve and turned away to walk home.

That night Ray had supper with his mother, Emily, and Jane. Emily's husband, Enoch, was out on the Grand Banks and not expected back for at least another week. Emily was agitated. "Ray, do you think that Reb boat is still out there?"

"I don't know. The bark headed off to the north after it burned those schooners. We know that from the crews she put ashore."

"I'm worried about Enoch."

"I hear the navy's sent gunboats from Boston to look for the Rebs. Now that our navy knows about them, they won't be able to get away with much. I'm sure Captain Wonson will be all right."

Elizabeth was concerned too. "Raymond, I'm worried about you out there in a defenseless fishing schooner. Wouldn't you be safer if you joined the navy?"

"Both the Bishop boys joined last week. That makes a dozen from our class, Ray," Jane said.

"I can help the war effort more by doing what I'm doing. Most of the salt cod these days is going to feed our troops. The Rebs seem to think our fish is important. Otherwise they wouldn't be up here trying to stop us."

The room went uncomfortably quiet, and then Jane changed the subject. "Will I see you at church tomorrow, Ray? There's a picnic afterward."

"You should go," his mother urged. "You miss so many services when you're out to sea. The Lord will do a better job of protecting you if he sees your face once in a while."

"All right. Will you be there, Jane?"

"Yes, I will. I'll make a basket for you, if you have time to stay for the picnic."

"Thank you. That's nice of you."

The two mothers nodded approvingly.

The next morning Ray and his mother walked the few short blocks to the church together. Built in 1806, it was one of the grandest buildings in Gloucester. Its tall yellow spire was visible all the way from the tip of Eastern Point, and he always felt a twinge of pride when he saw it on entering the harbor. This was the first Universalist congregation in America; the tax collector had seized its first building when the parishioners, Ray's ancestors among them, refused to pay the levy to support the state-sponsored Congregational Church.

Ray walked through the massive oak doors and scanned the pews. He did not see Emily or Jane, so he escorted his mother to the front.

Then he saw her. She was on the right side toward the back, wearing a conservative full-length white cotton dress with short sleeves and a high neckline. Her dark red hair was pinned in a chignon and partially covered by a stylish wide-brimmed hat. Next to her was a diminutive child in short pants, a suit

185

jacket and bow tie, white socks, and polished brown shoes.

Ray seated his mother in the second row of benches and walked back to her row, where he stood until she noticed him. "Miss O'Grady, I'm happy to see you. I never properly thanked you," Ray said, trying hard not to stare.

"Mr. Stevens, no thanks are necessary. May I introduce you to me son? Seamus, this is Mr. Stevens. Say hello, now."

Seamus looked silently at Ray.

"Seamus, it is my pleasure to make your acquaintance," Ray said as he extended his hand.

"Seamus dear, take Mr. Stevens' hand."

Seamus moved his hand, and Ray reached out and grabbed it. "Hello, Seamus."

"For sure, he's a shy lad; he's not yet had his third birthday."

"I wouldn't have said a word myself when I was his age. Will you be staying for the picnic afterward?"

"No, I don't think we shall. This is only our second time here, and I don't know quite what to expect — given what I do for a living."

"This is the Universalist Church. We believe everyone is entitled to salvation." Then, with a slight compression of his shoulders, he added, "At least, I think that's what we believe."

"'Tis what I've heard. I'm Catholic, or I was Catholic. I don't really know if I still am or not. Last month Seamus and I went to St. Mary's, but one of . . . one of our customers recognized me. The next Sunday the monsignor met us at the church door. He said we should leave and not come back. I said, 'Father, I want to get me son baptized, introduce him to the Church and, when he is old enough, enroll him in the catechism.' The monsignor said that was not possible. I hope it's different here." She frowned.

"I'm sure it is. I'm not much of a regular, but my great-grandfather was a founder of this church. I want you both to feel welcome."

"Thank you, Mr. Stevens. How very kind of you, now."

Emily and Jane came down the aisle. "Good morning, Ray," Jane said.

"Good morning, Jane, Em. May I introduce Maggie O'Grady, and this is Seamus. Miss O'Grady, this is Emily and Jane Wonson."

"Top o' the morn to you, ladies."

"Good morning, Mrs. O'Grady," Emily responded.

"What an adorable little boy!" Jane said. "How do you do, Seamus? My name is Jane."

Seamus looked up at Jane and leaned away, toward Maggie.

"Say hello, now, Seamus," Maggie said as she leaned down to his eye level. Turning back to Jane, she said apologetically, "He's shy, for sure."

"He is a handsome boy, Mrs. O'Grady. Ray, we should find our seats. The service is about to start."

"Of course, Jane, this way," he said with a backward glance at Maggie. "Mother is down in front."

The next morning, Maggie was sitting in her office after breakfast when Stark walked in. He was wearing the same rumpled overcoat and bowler hat he'd had on each time she had seen him. Both were damp; it had showered intermittently since midnight.

"Mr. Stark, what a surprise seeing you here. Please, take off your coat and pull up a chair. Would you like some coffee?"

"Thank you, Mag — Miss O'Grady. I would take a cup. It's cool for summertime." He sat down without taking off his coat.

"Anne!" Maggie shouted down the hall, then turned back to her visitor. "You can call me Maggie; most everyone does. And what might your first name be?"

"It's Ted, Maggie."

A young woman holding a broom poked her head in the door.

"Anne, please bring Mr. Stark a cup of coffee, and I'll have another too."

"Yes, Maggie," Anne said. "How do you take it, Mr. Stark?"

"Regular, Miss," Stark replied.

Anne nodded and disappeared down the hall.

"So, Ted, what brings you across me doorstep this damp morn?"

"It's the matter of a commission. Fannie was collectin' fifty dollars a month from an account in Boston. I brought the business to her, and our arrangement was she would forward fifteen dollars a' that to me. It's a finder's fee a' sorts. Did she mention it?"

Anne delivered two cups of coffee, cream and sugar already added. Maggie took a sip.

"I know about the fifty-dollar payment. When I took over the books, Fannie told me to send that to her straightaway. When I reviewed last year's books, I did notice a monthly payment of fifteen dollars to you, and it was called a commission. She must have been paying you out of her personal account after I took over."

"That's right. I assume the checks are still comin'?"

"Yes, they are. They're drawn on the account of a Boston firm called the Beacon Hill Housing Company. The signature on the checks is familiar to me — H. Percival — me old boss Harvey, if I'm not mistaken. It's for keeping me and Seamus in the cellar, isn't it?"

"I won't deny it. Fannie promised me fifteen a month for bringin' ya here instead a' somewhere else. The circumstances have changed, but it's only fair that Mr. Percival keep writin' these checks, wouldn't you agree?"

"Yes, Ted, I do think this is the least the poor boy's father could do for him. It's bold of you to come here for your cut, though. For a time I thought you were the devil himself, carting me off to hell."

Stark sat still while Maggie eyed him.

"But I have forgiven you for that, Ted," she eventually said. "Life is what you make of it and, for sure, I'm not going to wallow in regret. I never could have called you when I needed help dealing with that milk-lover if I hadn't let me anger go. And a bonny job you did of it too." She smiled. "Pitt thought that brute Timkins was going to toss his wrinkled little behind right out that second-floor window."

Stark relaxed. "Between you and me, Maggie, I bring Timkins along just for show. He looks the beast, but he's a gentle soul. Lives down the causeway in a cellar with three cats. Treats them cats better than most treat their own kin."

Maggie mulled over Stark's request, staring out the window until she came to a decision. "Ted, I'll honor your commission for as long as William keeps paying. But I would like something in return. I've cut off all communication with me family. I want to know that me brother Seth is all right. Can you find out about him?"

"I make it my business to keep up on people who might . . . well, ah . . . be important to my work. He's still at the Ritz, and he's head breakfast chef now.

190

Due to be married in August, to an Italian girl, I understand."

"Oh, I wish I could go to the wedding. But I won't do anything that puts Seth in harm's way. But Ted, you and that man who hired you should know that if something happens to Seth I'll raise hell, and I won't be so easy to deal with the next time."

"I don't doubt it. I've no interest in crossin' you, and as for . . . for, well . . . as for the *other* person you were referrin' to, I'm sure he won't do anythin' a' that sort unless I tell him it's a good idea."

Maggie wrote out a check. "This should cover the past. I'll send you your cut in the future each month after I receive the check from Harvey. We're odd ducks to be in business together on this, you and me," she said as she extended her hand.

"That we are, Maggie, that we are." Stark hesitated, then shook her hand.

A moment after he left, Maureen stepped into Maggie's office. "I got a letter this morn from Cork," she said. "My schoolyard sweetie is coming to America to pour beer at his uncle's tavern in New York. He wants to marry me!"

"Oh, Mo! Will you take him up on it?"

"Fast as I can!" Maureen said.

"That's wonderful. But we'll miss you."

"I hate to leave you in the lurch, but I'd like to meet him when his boat arrives. I don't want the lad

191

coming up here, for sure. I haven't told him the entire truth about what I've been doing."

Maggie nodded. "I've been wondering meself what I'd tell me family."

"He knows I'm pretty good with a needle and thread. He thinks I've been making fancy dresses for the fine ladies of Boston."

"Well, there's no reason for him to know anything different. Let me see here — with last night's receipts, your share for June comes to eighty-one dollars. Let's make it ninety dollars even. Consider the difference to be a little wedding gift from me."

"Thank you, Maggie. You're damn decent. Truth is, I didn't think you were cut out for this job, but you're doing all right. If you would accept a little unsolicited advice, though, I think you need to be tougher on the girls. Some have been grumbling that Sylvie's not pulling her weight, you know."

"Is that so? Has she been slacking off?"

"Lately when she's begged off work, she's not really been sick. I think she's losing the stomach for it."

"What should I do?"

"Well, one day you're going to have to put her out on the street. Might as well do it sooner rather than later; that's what Fannie always did. Said it was business, not personal, now."

"I can't put her out with no place to go."

"You'll need to throw some girls out eventually. No one wants an old whore."

"Sylvie stuck by me when I needed her. But enough o' this, we have celebrating to do! Have you told the others the news?"

"Just Winnie, so far." Maureen frowned. "She didn't take it so well. . . . I don't think she fancies the idea o' husbands."

"Well, let's get everyone else together. We'll drink to your good health and to a happy marriage!"

An impromptu party followed, and everyone except Winnie joined in the fun. The next morning Maureen was on her way to New York. After the celebration Maggie talked candidly to Lucy, who confirmed Maureen's impressions of Sylvie. Maggie decided to keep a more careful eye on her. In the meantime, she had Maureen's bed to fill. She sought Lucy's advice on that too.

"We've always been paid pretty well, and we've got a great location. For many it'd be a step up to work here. I don't think you'll find it hard to fill a bed."

"When they start coming in, how do I know whether they'll be any good?"

"It does take a while to figure that out. Fannie would start new ones on a trial basis and see how they did. She'd usually encourage one or two regulars to give the new girl a try and report back. It's too bad Asa's gone. He was good at evaluatin' new talent — though he was an easy grader, bless his heart. But usually the maid wants to move up, and Anne's mentioned to me a coupla times that she needs the money."

"Fannie told me the same thing. Anne's had a birthday since we hired her, but she's still only sixteen."

"Most of us started younger than that, and it's good for the house — the men really like young 'uns. If ya decide to go that way, Sarah and I'll be happy to show her the ropes."

"I don't know. . . ."

"Don't get preachy. I think ya should give Anne a chance."

Lucy went back upstairs, and Maggie walked Seamus, who had been playing in the sitting room, down to the cellar. Anne had prepared a stew and baked fresh corn bread. Maggie watched her as she served and cleaned up. She was at the other end of childhood from Seamus, yet Maggie hadn't been much older when she first shared a bed with William.

She had her talk with Anne that evening. Anne stood in front of Maggie's desk with head slightly cocked, one hand loosely draped over her breast, as if about to caress it. She was wearing a simple blue cotton frock tied with a sash around her narrow waist, the soft curves of her nymph-like body plainly apparent. Her mouth was of average size, but her lips were full and open just a crack, as if she were ever so eager to be kissed. Her complexion was light, her eyes deep brown, her auburn hair falling halfway down her back in rich, lazy curls. She appeared curious and innocent, and she exuded a sensuality that was impossible to ignore.

Maggie stared at her. Finally she cleared her throat and forced herself to speak "Anne, with Mo leaving, we have a vacancy upstairs. I heard you might be interested."

"Oh yes, Miss Maggie. I have my family to support. I would love a room of my own."

"Do you have any . . . well, any experience? I mean, have you ever been with a man before?" Maggie asked.

"I sure have," Anne said proudly. "My mother was widowed a coupla years back. It was that big storm in March a' '61. Papa went down with the *Nathan Douglas*. Since then it's just me and Ma and my little sis. But a coupla months before I came here, Ma took in a boarder, a fella off the *Islander*." Without thinking, Anne slowly started rubbing her breast.

"The first time Ma was grocery shoppin'." Anne exhaled and smiled as she remembered. "I coulda resisted more. . . . Truth is, I *was* a little curious, and he'd been very kind to me. He told me I was pretty and he'd never fancied anyone like he fancied me. One thing led to the next and . . . well . . . after that, we found some time every day, and I got pretty good at bringin' him around." Anne smiled and nodded her head, obviously savoring the memory.

Then her smile turned to a frown. "One day Ma walked in on us, and that was the end of that." Anne wiped her hands together and shook her head for emphasis. "That fella was out on the street, and Ma gave me a whippin'. I deserved it, I guess. A coupla weeks later I heard ya had an opening for a maid. It sounded interesting, and a . . . a bit naughty. I'm givin' almost all my money to Ma; she's got nothin' but a few pennies from the fishermen's fund and a bit from bringin' in laundry. If I could move upstairs, I could make enough to have a little left for me, enough to buy a new dress or maybe a pretty bonnet."

Maggie took a deep breath and forced herself to concentrate. "Anne, a lot of folks look down on what we do here. I was thrown out o' me church because I run this place. It's a big decision you're making."

"I guess," Anne said cavalierly, "but it worked out for Mo. I don't see what else I can do. Ma and Vicky, that's my little sister, they look to me to pay the rent. I may only be sixteen, but I got responsibilities. With Papa dead, it's up to me . . . and I *do* like fishermen."

"Not every man we see here is a gentle soul. We do our best to protect each other, but the men get rough once in a while."

"I know, Miss Maggie, but I'll take my chances."

Maggie swung her chair around and stared into the distance; then, her mind made up, she turned back to Anne. "All right, you can have Mo's room for now. But we both need to see how it goes. I'm considering you a greenhorn; you'll get a half share until you prove yourself. Lucy and Sarah will train you. I want you to talk to them and follow their lead. And I want you to check in with me every morning for a while. Is that acceptable to you?"

"Yes, Miss Maggie. Thank'ee. You won't be disappointed."

"I'm sure I won't."

Anne stepped out of the office and ran upstairs to her new room.

Maggie shuddered at the thought of her mother ever finding out about this. But Anne did seem uniquely suited to the profession. She would draw the customers in; there was no doubt about that. Besides, Fannies needed a new girl, and if it weren't Anne, it would just be another young one. Maybe this was meant to be. Maybe it was all right.

Chapter 19

Gloucester — July 1863

Ray got to church early the next Sunday and was there to greet Maggie when she arrived. "Seamus, so glad to see you," Ray said, extending his hand to the boy. Seamus stopped short but then, without prompting from Maggie, reached out. Ray grabbed his tiny hand and shook it vigorously. Seamus looked up at Ray with a puckering frown. As soon as Ray let go, he retracted his arm and backed up against his mother.

"Mr. Stevens, it is a pleasure to see you this fine morn," Maggie said cheerfully, in spite of the gray gloominess of the day.

"Miss O'Grady, the pleasure's mine. May I escort you and Seamus to a seat?"

"Thank you."

"Come with me, young man," Ray said, and he led the way down the aisle.

"Not too close to the front, if you please. I don't want to attract too much attention."

"Well, how about here then?" Ray said, leading Seamus to a bench about halfway down.

"Thank you. This will be just fine." Maggie sat down next to a tall man in a brown suit.

"Sergeant Smith, this is Maggie O'Grady, and this is Seamus," Ray said.

"Good morning to you both," Sergeant Smith said. "And good morning to you too, Ray. So nice to see you in church." Turning back toward Maggie, he said, softly enough so Ray could not hear, "You are the matron at Fannies, aren't you?"

"Yes, sir, that I am. And this is me son, Seamus. I don't recall seeing you before. How is it we are acquainted?"

"I'm the night sergeant at the police department. We keep track of the houses."

"I see. Well, it is a pleasure to make your acquaintance."

"Likewise, I'm sure. But I must say, I'm surprised to see you here."

Ray, who had turned away to look for his mother, came back to the conversation. "Seamus will be entering our Sunday school soon, Sergeant. The sooner the better, wouldn't you say?"

"We'll see about that, Ray."

"Here come Mother and the Wonsons. I'll take my leave now, Miss O'Grady, Sergeant."

The sergeant turned to Maggie after Ray had left. "Miss O'Grady, I have a matter of some importance that I would like to discuss with you. Would you have a minute outside after the service is over?"

Maggie said yes, and after that she couldn't concentrate — all through the hymns and the prayers and the sermon, she worried about what the sergeant wanted to discuss. Finally the service ended, and

Maggie walked out hand in hand with Seamus. When they reached the door, Seamus caught sight of a squirrel on the church lawn and, letting go of Maggie's hand, took off in pursuit. Soon the sergeant caught up with Maggie.

"Miss O'Grady, my men put in long, stressful days serving the public. A little relaxation is very welcome and conducive to good police work. Recently, some of the houses in town have been providing special support to the police department, as a public service, you see."

"Sergeant Smith, I can assure you that Fannies is very public spirited."

The sergeant cleared his throat. "Yes, I'm sure. But you may not realize the limitations of municipal employment; my officers are not well paid."

Maggie looked at him quizzically. "Are you suggesting that I give discounts to your officers?"

"It's no charge at Betty's up on Prospect Street. I can assure you my men are grateful for the service, and they do not abuse the privilege."

"I'm sure they don't, Sergeant. Let me ask you, did Fannie have a policy similar to Betty's?"

"She had a special arrangement with Chief James. But the old chief had a few too many special arrangements, and now he's doing three to five in Charlestown. He'll be out on parole next year, if he's lucky. . . . Best all around for money not to change hands."

Seamus was now sitting in the wet grass, flinging acorns up a tree in the direction of the squirrel. Maggie watched him until she had made up her mind. "Sergeant, we pay our taxes, just like other property owners. We should be treated as they are, no better and no worse."

Sergeant Smith's back stiffened, and he threw his head back. "Of course, Miss O'Grady, you should expect no less." He turned away abruptly and marched back up the church steps. Maggie shivered and pulled her coat tightly around her.

Ray had hurried out of his pew at the end of the service, but he was too late to reach Maggie before she was engaged in conversation with the sergeant. Jane caught up to him at the church door. "Ray, who are you looking for?"

"Oh, no one in particular." The crowd was now dispersing in front of the church. "It's getting colder, don't you think?"

"It's Miss O'Grady you're looking for, isn't it?" she demanded.

Elizabeth and Emily now joined them. "Raymond, do you know who that young woman talking to Sergeant Smith is?" Elizabeth spoke in the firm tone she reserved for the times when he had misbehaved.

"Yes, she's a young mother who wants to enroll her son in our church," Ray said defensively.

"Raymond, she runs a bawdy house on Duncan Street. The deacons are meeting tonight to ban her from the church. It's been noticed that you've been talking to her. My own son talking to a harlot — this is not easy for me."

"Nor me," Jane said petulantly, arms akimbo. "I thought you and I had an understanding, but now I just don't know what to think."

"You're being unfair to Miss O'Grady," Ray said, his resolve building. "She was the one who got your insurance check, Mother. She got the check in honor of Asa Burnham, Father's first mate. Asa did frequent her house, but he was as decent a man as I've ever known, and he had earned Father's respect."

"You knew all along she was a harlot," Jane said incredulously. "How could you introduce my mother to a woman like that? In church, no less. It's shocking!"

"I'm sorry you feel that way, but this woman has been very good to my family, and I'm not going to apologize for being polite to her."

"Oh!" Jane exclaimed. She spun around and started down the church steps so abruptly that her bonnet flew off. Ray reached down to pick it up, but she beat him to it and snatched it away. Hair askew, she scurried off.

After an uncomfortable silence, Emily said it was time to go, and she and Elizabeth walked away together, leaving Ray standing by himself atop the church steps.

They don't know Maggie, Ray thought. She's a good woman, well brought up; all you had to do was look at her and her well-dressed little boy to see that. After all she'd done for his family — why, Mother would be out on the street but for her! Jane had acted so high and mighty, as if she were soiled by Maggie's mere presence; she was prissy, always needing protection from the real world. Ray stood atop the steps and then started for home in a huff, but before he'd gone a dozen strides he stopped, turned around, and bounded back up the steps two at a time; then he stood paralyzed, all the while rubbing his fingers together in a frenzy of static activity.

Ray might have stewed for a good long time, but his childhood friend, Spashy McCloud, noticed him. The McClouds were an old-time Gloucester family, like the Stevens. Spashy had gone straight from high school to a sales position at McCloud Cordage, the family business that supplied rigging to most of Gloucester's fishing fleet.

"Hello, Ray, how are you?"

"Oh, I'm all right, Spashy."

"You don't look all right. Looks like you got the shakes."

"Aw, crud. I suppose I'm all worked up."

"What's the matter, have a fight with Jane?"

"She's offended that I introduced her to somebody."

"That cute little redhead?"

"You know Miss O'Grady?"

"Jeez, everyone's talking about her. You do know she's a hooker, don't you?"

"I think she runs the place, actually."

"Well, how do you expect Jane to feel? Hooker or madam, it's not exactly one of your God-fearing professions, now is it?"

"She's awful nice, Spashy." Ray was calming down.

"Damn pretty too. That's plain enough. You'd expect Jane to be jealous if you're paying attention to her."

"Yes, I probably should have seen that coming." Talking to his old friend was a tonic. "Say, I heard the deacons are going to be talking about Miss O'Grady. You know anything about that?"

"Yeah, I hear they're going to ban her from the church."

"I'm thinking I might go and speak up for her."

"Good luck with that. The elders are never going to let a hooker sit in this church with their wives and children. It's just too much. Me, I think she brightens the place up, but if I had kids I'd probably see it the same way the elders do."

"But don't we Universalists believe in grace, or something like that?"

"I think you're sweet on her. I see why Jane's so upset with you."

Ray smiled. "Good talking to you, Spashy. I'm going to see if Mother will still feed me." The two friends parted company.

The next morning, the deacons met in an anteroom off to the side of the altar. When Ray knocked on the door, seven men were already seated around an oval oak table — Reverend Smithson at one end, John Pitt at the other. The latter was a surprise; Pitt was not one of the deacons. They had obviously been deep in discussion before Ray arrived.

The reverend spoke first: "Ray, welcome. I'm always heartened to see a young man interested in church business. How is your mother?"

"She's fine, Reverend, thank you."

William Sewall, one of the deacons, spoke next. "Like the reverend says, Ray, we appreciate your interest. But this is a deacons' meeting and you're not a deacon. Why are you here?"

"Mr. Sewall, I understand that you're considering banning Miss O'Grady and her son from our church. She has been a friend to my family, and I want to speak on her behalf. It's true I'm not a deacon, but John Pitt's not one either, yet I see he's part of this meeting."

"I'm here, Stevens, because I care 'bout this church. I've given it considerable support over the years — more years than you've been alive, in fact,"

Pitt snapped. "You got no right to tell me I shouldn't be sittin' at this table."

"If I may ask, Ray," Sergeant Smith said, "how is it that this . . . this . . . woman . . . is a friend of your family? I must say I cannot see your dear mother inviting her over for tea."

Ray ignored the smirks this last comment elicited from Pitt and a few others. "Sergeant, after my father died, my mother was entitled to a substantial insurance payment." Ray turned and looked down the table at Pitt before continuing. "Miss O'Grady was instrumental in helping her get what she was owed." Ray's eyes did not leave Pitt's, and Pitt sat still as a stone. Ray turned back to address the sergeant. "Without her help, my mother would have lost her home."

An awkward silence followed. Ray began to rub the bottom of his coat between his thumb and forefinger. Most of the others looked down, avoiding eye contact with both Ray and Pitt. Reverend Smithson broke the tension. "I am satisfied that we should hear what Ray has to say. After all, he comes from one of the founding families of this church. Are we in agreement, then?"

Everyone except Pitt nodded. "Very well," Smithson continued. "Ray, we have been told Miss O'Grady runs a house for harlots on Duncan Street. Do you know whether that is true?"

"I understand that is true, yes. But she's a kind soul who has generously helped my family. And while none of us can approve of what she does for a living, is not every soul entitled to redemption?" Ray thought the answer to his rhetorical question was yes, but now he wished he'd paid more attention all those Sunday mornings.

"Every soul is entitled to redemption, but not every soul is equal in the eyes of the Lord," Reverend Smithson said. "There is a difference between a saint and a harlot, and we cannot have the latter mingling with the good God-fearing members of our congregation."

"But isn't she more likely to find the path to redemption if she is allowed to come to church? How else is she to hear the wisdom of the Lord's word?" Ray did his best to mimic what he had heard in church, but he was out of his depth.

"This is ridiculous," Pitt said. "We ain't gonna have no whores minglin' with the upstandin' ladies a' the parish. What of our children? Are we to let her in here to recruit our young girls as prostitutes and our young boys as their customers? Maybe ya got no scruples, Stevens, but it ain't all right with the rest of us."

"I have to agree with John," Sergeant Smith said. Ray could see the others nodding. "And she doesn't really care for us anyway. She's a Papist. She's only here because she's been thrown out of her own church."

"Ray, if she had given up her sinful ways and was truly repentant, it would be different," Reverend Smithson said. "Our Lord counsels forgiveness; everyone from the purest saint to the vilest harlot is entitled to salvation. But while Jesus forgave the adulteress, he said to her, 'Sin no more.' Miss O'Grady is not changing her ways and seeking forgiveness for past sins. She is plying her trade right now — she is still sinning, and brazenly so. We cannot have her among us every Sunday while she practices prostitution."

Seeing the main case lost, Ray tried to salvage a partial victory. "Well, what about her boy? The child is not guilty of any sin."

"That is a good point," the reverend said. "When he is old enough to come to church on his own, he will be welcome." The reverend could see Pitt about to object, but he pushed ahead, looking straight down the table at him. "The Lord does not punish the child for the sins of the mother; we *all* agree with that, I am sure." Without waiting for any response, the reverend continued, "Ray, thank you for coming and expressing your views today. I can see you have a kind heart, and I hope to see you in church more often. Go with God."

Ray was angry and frustrated. This was the second time Pitt had gotten the best of him, and while he did not know the details, he knew the man was a hypocrite. Ray stomped off down Church Street and kept going, passing his mother's house. He wanted to cool off, so he walked down to the dock, where it was quiet. He sat down on an overturned dory to think over what had just happened.

An hour later, he opened the door at Middle Street to find his mother and Emily Wonson chatting about a half-knitted sweater laid out on a table in the sitting room. "Well, Raymond, how did it go?" his mother asked.

"About as you expected, Mother." Ray fidgeted; he couldn't keep his fingers still. "Pitt was there," he said with disgust, "and they've banned Miss O'Grady and her little boy from our church. I've been proud to belong to the Universalist, but now . . . It's just mean-spirited for them to turn their backs on that nice woman and her child."

Elizabeth put down the ball of yarn she'd been holding. She rarely saw her son so upset.

"Ray, most people are afraid of anyone who's different," Emily offered. "Miss O'Grady is very different from the good folks at the Universalist. I don't approve of what she's doing, but I think everyone is entitled to love and kindness, and that goes double for people who have different ways. If it makes you feel any better, I would have voted to allow her to attend our church."

"Thank you," Ray said. He poured himself a cup of tea.

"Em and I have been talking," Elizabeth said, "and I've realized I overreacted. The world would be a better place if everyone were more accepting." Ray took his mother's hand and nodded. "But son, please be careful. I will love you and support you no matter what. But if you keep seeing this woman, there will be many who will shun you."

"I know, Mother, I know."

"Now, let's have some dinner. We have a lovely scrod, and I made rhubarb pie." Elizabeth opened the oven door, and the familiar smell of a warm pie cheered Ray, as did his mother's unexpected sympathy.

After dinner Ray walked down to Fannies. He swung open the red door to find Lucy joking with Skip at the bar. "Look who we have here," Lucy said, laughing. "Maggie will be pleased to see ya." Lucy yelled out, "Maggie, you have a visitor!"

"Care for a drink, youngster?" Skip asked.

"No thanks, not today. I've come by to give Maggie a message." Ray could think of nothing else to say, so he stood there in silence.

"Well, Mr. Stevens, what a pleasant surprise." Maggie smiled as she rounded the corner. "Can I treat you to a drink?"

"No, thank you, Miss O'Grady. Is there someplace private where we could talk?"

"Of course," she said as her smile disappeared. She led Ray to her office and closed the door.

"Miss O'Grady . . ."

"Please call me Maggie."

"Maggie, I went to a meeting of the church deacons this morning. I spoke on your behalf, but it wasn't enough, I'm afraid. They voted to bar you from the church. I wanted to let you know now so you wouldn't get this news on the church steps. I am so sorry; this is just not right. I wish it were different."

"So your church isn't much different from mine after all, is it? And me son," she asked, "did they bar him too, now?"

"They said he would be welcome . . . when he was . . . when he was old enough to come by himself. I'm so sorry."

"That's something, I guess. Mr. Stevens . . ."

"Ray. Please call me Ray."

"Ray, thank you for speaking on me behalf, and thank you for coming here to give me the bad news in person. You're a gentleman."

"It's the least I could do." Ray looked down, summoning his courage.

"There is something I want to ask you. Do you ever have the time to go out? Perhaps . . . perhaps I could take you out sometime."

"Are you sure you'd want to be seen with me? You've just gotten a taste of what the good citizens of Gloucester think o' me."

"The deacons may control who gets into that church, but they don't control who I spend my time with. That bastard John Pitt is the one I would be ashamed to be seen with. How about tomorrow night?"

Maggie smiled. "I accept."

"Excellent. Shall I come by at seven? There's a new tavern in the West End that serves a good brisket, I've heard."

"I'll be ready at seven. Thank you for your kindness."

After Ray left, Maggie walked back into the bar and sat down on a barstool. "Skip, I need a drink, a stiff drink. Rum."

Skip poured Maggie a double shot. "You look like ya have the weight a' the world on your shoulders, little one. What is it?"

Maggie took a big swallow and coughed. "How am I ever going to get Seamus to know God? I've been thrown out of the Catholic Church, and now I've been thrown out of the Universalist Church too. I'm raising me son in a whorehouse, and I'm being shunned by all the decent folk. Worst thing is, I'm feeling I deserve it. I'm ruining me boy, surely I am."

"Don't go talkin' like that," Skip said, shaking his head with conviction. "Don't do that to yourself. God can see past the labels people give us: drunk, whore, bastard. God can see right through these walls and right down into your heart. 'Blessed are the pure in heart, for they shall see God' — that's what Jesus said. Just teach that son a' yours to love people and to be kind. He'll know God, Maggie."

Anne's training was the subject at the breakfast table the next morning. She wasn't allowed customers on her own yet. Whenever Sarah or Lucy had someone suitable, they would ask if he'd be willing to help train the new girl. Robby had come by the previous night to see Sylvie, but she wasn't up to working. He'd chosen Lucy instead, and she'd asked him if he'd help out with Anne's training.

"How'd it go, Lucy?" Winnie asked.

Lucy swallowed a bite of egg and wiped the yolk off her lips. "Oh, that Robby was willin', he sure was! I called Anne in, and Sarah came along too, to help with the trainin'. 'Three, I get three!' Robby says. His eyes were bulgin', like a boy in a candy store.

"We concentrated on the basics. I put my mouth around Robby and got started and, well, it was great having Sarah there, because she could tell Anne just why I was doin' what I was doin', where the most sensitive spots are and the best ways to get at 'em. Without her, I'd have had to stop to explain; my mouth can't do two things at once.

"So after a while I let him go and say, 'All right, Anne, now you give it a try.' She was too dainty at first, not near enough pressure. Ya know, we all been there. Well, Robby was calmin' down, and Sarah, she's pretty impatient. She hopped up on the bed and said, 'Let me show ya the way I do it,' and she had Robby groanin' again in no time. Then she hands him back to Anne.

"That Anne's a quick learner. Pretty soon Robby was all herky-jerky, gaspin' and such. He's one of the louder ones, and then he really lets go — havin' three of us charged him up pretty good. Anne didn't feel it comin', but she came up smilin', just like a pro. Sarah and me gave her a big hand."

Everyone laughed. "So, Anne, how'd ya feel 'bout your professional debut?" Winnie asked.

"Well, his thing was a lot bigger than I expected. The only one I knew before was 'bout this big," she said, holding up a breakfast sausage on the end of her fork.

Sarah slapped Lucy on the back. "Oh, Robby is one of the bigger ones."

Sylvie looked as if she were about to say something, but thought the better of it.

"He was salty too," Anne said. "But it felt good to get the job done. I'm lookin' forward to branchin' out."

"You will," Sarah said. "Last night we stuck with oral trainin'. Best to get the basics down solid. We had three more sessions after Robby."

"And three more satisfied customers too, I might add," Lucy said.

"Old Able Tarr was the hardest," Anne said. "I thought he was gonna take all night. My jaw was achin'."

"Able's gettin' too old for this," Winnie said.

"Hey!" Skip protested. "He was in my little sister's class in grade school. He's just a kid!"

"No offense intended, Skip. We all know you never have that problem; you're twice the man Able is," Winnie said.

"More than twice, I'd say. I seen full-grown hosses smaller than you, Skip," Sarah said with a respectful nod. "A' course, even you can't hold a candle to the Johnson twins. Remember them, Lucy? Mark and Luke?"

"Biggest I ever seen, those boys," Lucy agreed. "Remember when we did them as a foursome? That was somethin'. It was a sad day when their boat went down."

"After the *Dauntless* was lost, the flag was at half-staff at every house in town," Sarah said.

"Hell, they're all at half-staff compared to the Johnson twins," Lucy said.

"So, Lucy, are you and that sister a' yours takin' on new students?" Lydia winked. "I hear our matron's goin' on a date tonight. Maybe she'd like a lesson before she brings him home."

"A date! Maggie, tell us 'bout your boyfriend. How does he stack up against the Johnson twins?" Sarah asked with a mischievous smile.

"Ladies, I'm just going to a tavern with Ray Stevens, nothing more, now," Maggie said, obviously embarrassed.

"It's a first date, Maggie. We know what happens on first dates. Tell her, Anne. You just had four first dates last night — tell her what happens," Sarah said.

"All right, that's enough. I have to get to work." Maggie beat a hasty retreat to her office upstairs.

Ray arrived at Fannies that night in his Sunday best, clutching a bouquet of sweet peas. Conversation stopped and every head turned to watch him walk across the room to the bar. Skip slowly shook his head.

"Skip, would you let Maggie know I'm here, please?" Ray asked, trying his best to ignore the bartender's reaction.

Still shaking his head, Skip hobbled to the stairs and hailed Maggie.

A tall, husky fisherman, a real bear of a man, got up from one of the tables and walked over to Ray. He looked him over from top to bottom, then spoke. "You look a little like Ray Stevens."

"You know who I am, Shorty," Ray said.

"But the Ray Stevens I know is pretty smart. You don't look smart at all."

"I don't know what the hell you're talking about."

"Christ, Ray, you're in a whorehouse. You don't need flowers and a tie; all you need's a couple of silver dollars."

There were guffaws from other fishermen in the bar, but before Ray could react, Maggie came down the stairs. "Oh, you are so sweet to bring flowers," she said, then put them to her nose and inhaled. "And they smell wonderful. You're such a gentleman. We're going to put them in water and leave them right here at the corner of the bar, where Shorty and the other men can enjoy them." She turned and gave Shorty a wink. "Please take care of that, Skip," Maggie said, handing over the flowers. "Now, shall we go?"

Maggie offered Ray her arm. He hesitated but then took it, and they headed for the door. He held the door open for her and she stepped out. Before he followed her, he turned back and exhorted, "Enjoy the flowers, Shorty!"

"You handled Shorty just right," Ray said as they started uphill toward the tavern. "I was thinking about taking a swing at him before you came downstairs."

"You sound just like me brother Seth. He was mighty quick to use his fists, he sure was. It never did him any good, though."

"Truth of the matter is, it's never done me any good either. But it's the only thing that makes sense sometimes."

"You found a better way to handle it this time. Maybe Shorty's back there sniffing those sweet peas right now."

Ray chuckled, and Maggie laughed.

"I never got on well with Shorty. He was nearly that big in the sixth grade. He pushed all of us around, and he beat the hell out of me once. I felt like I was back in grade school for a minute there."

They had a pleasant evening. Maggie was delighted to discover that Ray's favorite book was *Two Years Before the Mast,* and he was pleased to find that she knew so much American history. They both were excited to hear of the other's interest in astronomy. Ray promised to set up his telescope some clear night so Maggie could see the moons of Jupiter. When they finished their meal, Ray walked Maggie back to Fannies. She resolved an awkward moment outside the door by offering her hand. They agreed to get together again when he returned from his next fishing trip.

When he was next home, Ray took Maggie to see the stars. He set up his telescope on the backshore, where there were no nearby houses or streetlamps. With the sound of the surf in the background, Maggie finally saw the moons of Jupiter as Galileo had first seen them. Then Ray turned his telescope toward Mars, the red planet. Finally, he led Maggie on a tour of Betelgeuse, Rigel, and the other navigation stars. The night ended with another handshake outside Fannies' red door. A few days later, Ray returned to the Grand Banks on the *Parsons.*

Chapter 20

Gloucester — October 1863

Before long it was October, when fall storms sporadically shatter the peaceful warmth of Indian summer. Ray was overdue, and Maggie was beginning to worry about him. One night at twilight she sat, as she now frequently did, in front of the big bay window in her bedroom and scanned the docks, hoping to spot the *Parsons* back from her long trip. But with no sign of the schooner, she went downstairs to work.

Anne was already busy with her third customer of the night when two fishermen off the *Martha Bay* walked into the bar. They were big men, nearly six feet tall; both had dark hair and broad shoulders. They had obviously come straight from the boat, sporting flannel shirts and dungarees stiff with dried scales, greasy and matted shoulder-length hair, and the odor of decaying fish and dried sweat. Maggie greeted them as she greeted everyone: "Welcome to Fannies, gentlemen. Will you have a drink?"

"Nope," one of them said. "We're here for the young one." His face was flushed, and he slurred his words. "What room's she in?"

"That would be Anne. She's seeing a gentleman right now, and then this fellow here," Maggie pointed to an older man sitting at the end of the bar, "is next in line. You could wait, or I could get you started right now with Lucy and Sarah. They are two o' me best ladies."

"We want the young one," the other man said. He turned to the man waiting at the bar. "Give ya five bucks for your spot in line." This generous offer was accepted, and then one man said to the other, "Ed, since we gotta wait on the fella upstairs, let's have a drink."

"Fine idea, Sam," Ed said. They ordered two double shots of whiskey.

Ten minutes later, Anne's customer came unsteadily downstairs and plopped down on a barstool. Maggie hailed the *Martha Bay* men: "Whichever one wants to go first, it's the third door to the left at the top of the stairs. It'll be two dollars."

Ed pulled four silver dollars out of his pocket and handed them to Maggie. "Here you go, Miss. We'll go together."

"I'm sorry, boys, we've got a rule here — one at a time," Maggie said firmly.

"We do everything together," Ed insisted.

They started to walk around Maggie, but she stepped in front of them and said firmly, "No! That's not the way we do it here." One of the men pushed Maggie hard. She fell over backward, hitting her head on the base of the bar.

"We paid our money and we're gonna have our fun. Stay outta the way, Missy, or you're gonna get hurt," Ed said. They stepped over Maggie and went upstairs.

Maggie staggered to her feet, while Lucy ran to get the police. Skip grabbed the billy club he kept behind the bar and mounted the stairs one at a time, pulling his wooden leg up behind him. Maggie shook off her dizziness and followed. Before they reached the second floor, they heard Anne scream.

Now Maggie ran ahead of Skip, but the *Martha Bay* men had jammed the door to Anne's room shut. Skip finally arrived, and it took the two of them pushing and shoving to force open the door. Anne was facedown on her bed. The man named Sam was pressing her shoulders into the mattress, while the one named Ed, trousers at his ankles, was violently thrusting into her from behind.

"Stop!" Maggie yelled. "Stop!"

Ed pulled out and stepped toward Maggie, but he tripped on his trousers and fell to the floor. Sam let go of Anne and rushed Maggie. Skip stepped in front of her and swung the billy club, hitting the outstretched arm that Sam had raised to deflect the blow. Sam swung wildly at Skip and missed, almost falling over, and Skip landed a solid blow on Sam's shoulder blade.

But when Skip reared back to swing again, he slipped on his peg leg and lost his balance. Sam grabbed Skip's good leg, knocking him over, then grabbed the club and beat Skip with it. Maggie screamed and jumped on Sam's back, but by now Ed had his trousers all the way off and was back on his feet. He grabbed Maggie by the hair and threw her to the floor. Then he wrapped his arms around Sam.

"Sam," Ed said, gasping for breath, "leave the ol' man alone. Let's finish up with this pretty little redhead." Skip lay unconscious on a throw rug now stained with blood.

Sam dropped the billy club. "She's a feisty one."

They picked Maggie up off the floor and threw her on the bed next to Anne, who lay there groaning. Maggie struggled, and one of them stunned her with a fist to her jaw. They turned her on her stomach, and Sam held her down while Ed lifted her dress and ripped off her drawers.

Maggie gasped in pain as Ed forced his way into her. He pulled partway out and, grabbing her hips, slammed back in with powerful thrusts that became faster until, with a yell, he was done and out of breath. Then the men switched positions, and Sam took his turn.

In a few minutes it was all over. The brothers unhurriedly dressed and went down to the bar. They took a bottle of whiskey, left two dollars as payment, and walked out into the brisk fall air, passing the bottle back and forth as they walked up the street.

The women rushed into Anne's room, and Doc Gray was summoned. After a gentle examination, he said Maggie and Anne would be all right, but Skip was still unconscious, and it was serious. They put him to bed and applied cold compresses to his forehead. Maggie's jaw ached, and her privates were sore and bleeding. After the doctor left, she cleaned herself up and gingerly walked down to the bar, where Lucy poured her a rum. The bar was empty.

"The pain passes," Lucy said. "You'll be all right if ya don't brood on it."

"I've just been raped. Those animals held me down and raped me." Tears started down her contorted face.

Lucy pulled her chair up close. "Men are kegs a' gunpowder; ya gotta be so careful around 'em, and even then they still explode sometimes. You'll be all right. We been raped since the beginnin' a' time. We survive — we have to."

Maggie stopped crying. "What happened to the police?"

"The night sergeant, that pig Smith, was just sittin' at the reception desk. I told him two thugs had broken in and were up to no good. He said all his officers were busy, but *he* sure didn't look busy. There'd been a disturbance up at Betty's, he said. He'd send someone down here when he had a man free. I said it would be too late then, but he said it was the best he could do. He said somethin' 'bout explainin' all this to ya at church. Don't know what he meant by that."

The door to the bar opened, and in walked Sergeant Smith. "Good evening, ladies. What seems to be the problem here?" Lucy walked across the room, where she noisily spit into a brass pot.

"The problem is that two men burst in here, raped me, brutalized one o' me ladies, and beat me bartender senseless. He's lying unconscious upstairs right now, and Doc Gray says he may not make it. So *that's* the problem, *Sergeant*."

"Well, that sounds pretty serious. Who are these men you say did these things?"

"Someone said they're off the *Martha Bay*. They called each other Sam and Ed. They were real big. Could be brothers. In their twenties, I'd say."

"Did they just bust in here without paying?"

"No, they paid. But then they forced themselves on Anne, the two of them together, and they beat Skip with a club. . . ." Maggie's voice cracked. "Then they raped me."

"In a place like this, it's reasonable for them to expect services once they've paid."

"Sergeant, they could have killed us; Skip may die yet. For sure, we would have been all right if you'd sent someone right away."

"Like I told you that day in church, Miss O'Grady, we're stretched pretty thin at the police department. We can't be two places at once." Lucy coughed loudly and spit again.

"Lucy says your officers were up at Betty's."

"That's right. This sort of thing hasn't happened up *there* in years."

"I see." Maggie paused and looked toward the empty bar, then continued with resolve: "Well, Sergeant, Fannies doesn't play second fiddle to anyone when it comes to our love for the police force." Lucy looked over at Maggie with an expression of astonishment. "We'll match whatever Betty's doing."

"Miss O'Grady, the hardworking men of the force will be grateful. And may I say, I am deeply sorry this has happened to you tonight. I'll do everything in my power to see that these men pay for their crimes."

"Thank you, Sergeant. I understand."

"I see that you do, Miss. I'll take my leave now. I'll have something for you tomorrow."

After he left, Maggie turned to Lucy in resignation. "Like you said, Lucy, we do what we have to do."

"Aye, Maggie. That sergeant's gonna do it to us one way or the other. We might as well get somethin' outta it. Still, I don't like the stink of it."

The next day Maggie walked to the station. Her privates burned with every step, her jaw was bruised and achy, and there was a lump on the back of her head the size of a chestnut. She had no trouble identifying Ed and Sam. They were the Swinson brothers, and their story was that they had paid, and that Maggie and Skip were between them and what was rightfully theirs.

The prosecutor charged them with assault, then upgraded the charge to manslaughter after Skip died two days later. He did not charge them with rape. "You'll never get a jury to convict these two lads on rape charges," he told Sergeant Smith. "They're basically good boys who'd had too much to drink. They even paid for the bottle they took when they left; that shows they didn't mean any harm.

"Still, we can't have strong young men beating on a poor old cripple; that's not right. I think they'll do jail time," he concluded with a satisfied nod of his head.

Four days later, Maggie, the ladies of Fannies, and a couple of old-timers gathered at the Mount Pleasant Cemetery to bury Skip. He had no living relatives that anyone knew about, so Maggie purchased a burial plot and held a private graveside service. She read a few passages from the Bible, and the ladies sang "Amazing Grace." Then old Able Tarr stepped forward. His long, untrimmed gray beard matched the stringy gray hair hanging down from under the black bowler he always wore. For the service he had put on a clean flannel shirt, clean dungarees, and a black scarf that he secured neatly around his neck with a polished bronze ring in the old style. Over coarse wool socks he wore a battered pair of paint-stained boots, the only footwear he owned. Before he spoke, he removed his hat, revealing a pink, bald crown.

"I've known Skip since I was six years old, when I started grade school with his little sister, Beatrice," Able said, hanging his head respectfully. "When Skip was eleven he went to sea on the *Stalwart,* one of 'em ol' Chebacco boats, same kind our ancestors sailed back in the days when they burned them witches in Salem. The *Stalwart* was so old she had taken fire from that British sloop that raided Gloucester right after all the shootin' started at Lexington and Concord. Skip showed me where the musket ball was still buried in her rail. Whenever the weather got snarly, her captain would pat that spot for luck.

"In the '20s the pinkys came into fashion, and Skip sailed on some real highliners. He was young and strong back then; we all were." Able nodded. "I sailed with him on the *William A. Helsell* and then on the *Richard S. White,* grand names for what folks would see as modest boats these days.

"But I'll take the ol' *Helsell* in a big nor'easter over one of 'em speedsters the youngsters fish in these days. They don't make 'em like that anymore. Ain't gonna be many a' today's crowd that get to wait out eternity under the shade of a nice maple like Skip here. There's a price to be paid — it's a watery grave in the prime a' life for most o' them poor souls fishin' today.

"I guess I knew Skip 'bout as well as anyone still livin' on this earth. Believe me when I tell ya, he died proud. Ya see, Fannie saved Skip's life when she took him in. Maybe you can be a pirate with a peg leg, but fishin's too hard for that. Skip took charity for a while, but then he was out on the street.

"One day Fannie found him half dead. She cleaned him up and gave him the bartender's job — she saved him. He found religion after that. He loved Fannie, and he loved all a' you, too. And I'm not talkin' 'bout just when he had a few extra silver dollars to spend." That elicited a few giggles from the mourners, and like any good speaker, Able waited for quiet before continuing. "We all gotta die. Skip died defendin' ya, the people he loved the most — it's a good way to go.

"Well, I'm goin' on and on . . . but you've come to expect me to take forever." Able looked up at Anne with a crooked smile; she couldn't suppress a giggle. "I don't think we should be sad today. Skip lived a full life and died well. He believed in heaven, and if there's such a place, surely Skip's there now. Many deserve it a lot less. So that's what I gotta say."

Able turned to face Skip's casket. "Goodbye, ol' friend. I'll miss ya." Notwithstanding his admonition, a tear rolled down his cheek and caught in the gray hairs of his beard. He put his bowler back on and limped slowly away. The mourners watched his rhythmic motion in silence until he disappeared behind a tall elm.

A few days later, a slab of polished granite was in place over Skip's grave. The inscription was chosen by Maggie:

Ezra (Skip) Adams
Born around 1800
Died defending women in distress
October 1863
Blessed are the pure in heart:
for they shall see God

A week later, Maggie had her talk with Sylvie. "Maggie, I've lost my nerve," she confessed. "It started way before the Swinson brothers busted in here. One day Keith Justice came to visit me. He's been a regular a' mine for years, and he's nice enough, but this time he undresses and there's this green pus all over his johnson. The thought a' that disgustin' thing stickin' into me made me sick. I handled it. I cleaned him up and put a skin on him. He didn't mind. But all the while he's doin' me I couldn't help but think a' that pus.

"And now it's like that with all of 'em. I have to hold my supper down every time I got one a' their things in me. I know I'm lettin' everyone down. I been sick, like I said, but the sickness is in my head. Been scared too, scared 'bout this talk we're havin' now. I don't have a place to go. I don't got no one but the other ladies." Sylvie winced like a dog that was about to be hit.

"Sylvie," Maggie said as a mother might to a frightened child, "now that Skip's gone, we need a bartender." Maggie took hold of both of Sylvie's hands. "Do you think you could get enthusiastic about serving drinks? I'd want you to be friendly with the customers, make them feel real welcome like Skip always did, for sure. But you wouldn't have to take them upstairs."

Sylvie burst into tears. "I'll be the best bartender you ever seen. Thank'ee, Maggie, thank'ee!"

That evening Sergeant Smith came back. He wanted to talk privately, so they stepped into Maggie's office. "I thought you'd like to know," he said as soon as they were seated, "the Swinson brothers have been formally charged with manslaughter."

"Thank you for coming to tell me that, Sergeant. I hope they are put away for a long time."

"That'll be up to the judge and the jury. We've done what we can do. I regret that the prosecutor didn't pursue rape charges. I hope you're recovering from your injuries."

"Thank you, Sergeant. Me wounds are healing."

"When will you be well enough to handle new customers?"

"Sergeant, I don't provide services meself. I'm in charge here. Me job is to see that things run smoothly."

"As a sergeant, I have similar responsibilities. Could you make an exception and see me personally?"

"No, Sergeant. I appreciate your interest, but no. But I can recommend one o' me ladies I'm sure you'll like. I think you'll have the time of your life with Sarah."

"Very well. I'm pressed for time today; I have to be at the station in half an hour."

"Please wait here, Sergeant; I'll ask if Sarah can see you straightaway." Maggie soon came back and escorted the sergeant to Sarah's room. He conducted his business quickly, and Sarah showed him the back stairs, where he could exit discreetly.

Maggie slept fitfully that night. In her dreams she lay on her back in a field, and the dark outline of Sergeant Smith stood over her. His trousers were down at his ankles and, though he was in shadow, she could see he was erect. She reached up and grabbed him as she'd grabbed Jake years earlier, but he was covered with pus. She let go in disgust.

She drifted away, but then she was on a bed, being held facedown, and she could feel the pounding from behind. She strained to turn around to see her attacker, but her head was pressed tightly against the sheets. She struggled and struggled, but couldn't get loose.

Finally that nightmare ended, and she drifted away again. Then, as she lay on her side, she felt a body pressed against her back and an erection against her bare bottom. An arm was draped around her, and a hand was on her breast. She rolled over, and it was Ray. She awoke with a start and was surprised to find herself alone.

The next morning Maggie had bags under her eyes, but she had to get to work. With Sylvie in the bar, they were shorthanded. Anne had bounced back quickly, but she was overworked and could not be expected to keep up her current pace. Sergeant Smith, knowing Maggie was looking for help, brought by a young woman named Faith. She'd been married less than a year to a fisherman who'd been lost on the Grand Banks in April. After a few weeks alone in the tenement with little to eat, she had started walking the street. This went on until her landlord found out and called the police to shoo her out. That's when she'd become known to the sergeant.

Faith had taken up residence in an abandoned schooner that had sunk into the mud next to a Rocky Neck pier. The schooner's stern had settled to the bottom, but its midsection was hung up on a submerged boulder, leaving her bow pointed toward the sky and her fo'c'sle bunks out of water.

To get to the fo'c'sle, Faith would shimmy down a creosoted dock and then descend into the hull on slimy stairs that were partly underwater at high tide. Once below, she would climb up the steeply sloped deck to reach the bunks on the high side of the hull. She shared the fo'c'sle with a family of water rats that came out of hiding every night to forage for food.

When she was brought to Maggie, Faith stank of decay. Her arms, hands, and feet were black with creosote, and her torn clothes were stained with green slime and black oil. They looked like the rags a teamster might have used to clean up with after lubricating his wagon. Maggie had never seen a human being who looked as bad as Faith did that day. But rather than throw her back on the street, Maggie gave her a bath, a bed to sleep in, and a clean dress to wear.

The next morning, after a hearty breakfast, Faith admitted to Maggie that she had resigned herself to dying on that derelict schooner. She pulled up her dress, revealing where rats had taken nips out of her ankles while she slept. Her legs were bony, her cheeks hollow and gaunt. But now, clean and well fed, Faith said she felt better than she had in months — as if she might live after all. If Maggie would give her a chance, she would work hard and earn her keep.

Over the next few weeks, Faith slowly became once again the attractive woman she had been. She lacked Anne's simmering sensuality, but she was tall, dark, a little mysterious and still quite young — nineteen, she said.

Maggie now knew the truth of what Fannie had once told her — the younger ones got the men in the door. She gave a fleeting thought to what her mother might say about such reasoning, then let it go. Faith was desperate; she needed this chance.

Lucy and Sarah taught Faith the techniques of her new profession, and all the ladies helped with makeup and clothes. Before long, Faith was Fannies' most popular lady — after Anne.

Chapter 21

At Sea — November 1863

Out on the Grand Banks, Ray and Robby had just started to haul their trawls when a wet, gray wall rolled in from the east. They put their gear back over the side and pulled for the *Benjamin Parsons*. Guided at the end by the bell the cook had started ringing, they found their way, as did the other dories, all except the one manned by Jeff and Willy Burgess.

The crew fired the boat's rifle every thirty minutes and kept ringing the bell every ten, sounds that became so regular they stopped hearing them. After four days, they gave up. The Burgess boys were nineteen and seventeen, so no widows or children were left behind this time, just a mother who had also lost her husband to the sea a few years earlier.

The *Parsons* weighed anchor and sailed toward where Ray and Robby had left their trawls. They were lucky to find one of the buoys despite the fog. Once the catch was on board, they set sail for Gloucester with everyone in a somber mood. The weather cleared just north of Provincetown, and from there it was an easy day-sail home.

Ray thought about Maggie every day he was gone, but he knew that being with her made little sense. His mother disapproved, and most of his childhood friends would too. But sensible misgivings could not overcome strong desire. The day after the *Parsons* pulled into port, Ray called on Maggie. "It's good to see you. This was a long, sad trip," Ray said once they were seated at a table in Fannies' bar.

"I heard about the Burgess brothers. I'm sorry."

"You feel so helpless. You know they're not far away; if it would just clear up, you could find them. But if you up-anchor and go hunting for them, all is lost. You have to stay put and hope they find their way back."

"Were you close to them?"

"They've never had dinner at my house; I've never been over to theirs. But this trip lasted three months, with seventeen of us bunking in a space no bigger than your office. I know who Jeff's first sweetheart was and why they broke up, and I know the way Willy liked his beans. I packed their duffels, and I knew each piece of clothing I put in those bags. I guess we were close, close in the way shipmates get close, anyway."

Ray handed Maggie a package. "I brought this for you. I know you like history." Maggie peeled the wrapping back to find John James Babson's newly published *History of the Town of Gloucester*. She looked down at the volume and frowned. "Did I do the wrong thing?" Ray asked.

"Oh, no, not at all. I was just reminded of someone from long ago, someone who is . . . well, someone who is surely dead. 'Twas me Uncle Clyde, the first one to tell me of America. He gave me a book once. Thank you — I can't wait to read it. For sure, you're a darling to be thinking o' me."

Ray nodded. "There's a talk at Town Hall tomorrow by one of the officers who was at the Battle of Gettysburg. Would you like to go?"

"Ray, I don't think so, not with the way people talk." But on seeing his crestfallen expression, she changed her mind. "Oh, why not? Yes . . . yes, I would love to go."

The next night they walked the half mile to Town Hall, a two-story building in Gloucester's West End, built in the 1840s in the Greek Revival style with white Ionic columns. This night it was packed with citizens eager to hear the details of the Union's greatest victory. Captain Truscott of the 10th Massachusetts laid out how the battle had developed.

There were a lot of heroes at Gettysburg, Truscott said, but none greater than Joshua Chamberlain, colonel of the 20th Maine. On the second day of the battle, the Confederates attacked the left flank of the Union Army. If they turned the flank, the battle, and perhaps the whole Army of the Potomac, would have been lost. The 20th Maine was on a hill called Little Round Top, and the fighting was fierce. Wave after wave of Rebs charged, only to be beaten back. Finally the 20th ran out of ammunition. Rather than retreat and give up the flank, they fixed bayonets and charged down the hill, yelling and whooping the whole way. The Rebs never figured out that the Mainers had no more bullets — they turned tail and ran.

"I'll be damned," Ray whispered. "Chamberlain was my rhetoric professor at Bowdoin." On the walk home, Maggie asked Ray to tell her more about Chamberlain. "He was a slender man, fit it seemed, and he had an enormous moustache; he looked like one of those Scottie dogs if you left the big moustache and shaved everything else off. But I don't really know him at all, even though I listened to him talk for half a year. I thought he was a weak, mousy sort of man. Obviously, appearances can be deceiving."

When they reached Fannies' red door, Maggie gathered her courage and invited Ray in. They sat down at one of the tables, and Sylvie came over. She was wearing a sleek black dress with a plunging neckline that exposed a bit of a lacy brassiere. The dress swung as she walked, exposing the bottom of her petticoat. A towel was draped over her bare forearm, and she wore the easy smile of someone who enjoyed her work. "Well now," Sylvie asked, "what can I get the young couple to drink?"

"I'm ashamed to admit this," Ray said, "but I don't know. What would you suggest?"

This innocent question put Maggie at ease. "I can't say I'm an expert, but I do like rum with a little water and lime juice."

"All right, that's what I'll have."

"Make it two, Sylvie."

Sylvie walked back to the bar. Ray asked about Skip.

"Skip's dead, Ray. He was beat up last month by a couple of thugs who busted in here. They're to be tried for manslaughter next week."

"Jesus, that's horrible! What a fine old man; why would anyone harm him?"

Maggie bit her lower lip and tasted the iron in her blood. "I suppose you should know." She described the night. "So one of them was coming at me, and Skip stepped in and tried to stop them, but they were young and strong and fortified with liquor. They got Skip down and beat him senseless. . . . After they beat Skip, they attacked me." Tears came to her eyes, but she continued. "They raped me, Ray, both of them." Her voice cracked and her jaw clenched as she tried to hold in her emotions.

Ray looked at her silently, then said softly, "I don't know what to say. What an awful thing."

"You've been nice to me. I know you were grateful for me help with the insurance. But that

238

account is paid in full. If you don't want to see me anymore, I'll understand."

Ray didn't delay. "But I do want to see you." He leaned across the table. "I thought about you the whole time I was out at sea. My mother thinks I'm crazy." He stopped talking as Sylvie delivered their drinks. He took a sip and smiled. "The last time I had a drink here I thought I was going to choke, but this is pretty good."

"The lime juice cuts the harshness of the rum. That's why I like it this way."

"There is another thing on my mind, and maybe it's best if I just say it. Drinking isn't the only thing I'm inexperienced at. I've never . . . well, never been upstairs, here or anywhere else, if you understand what I'm driving at."

"Yes, Ray," Maggie smiled. "I think I take your meaning."

"With you being such an expert in this area . . ."

"Wait just a minute, Ray Stevens." This was too much like the kind of talk that had driven her out of Ireland. "I can understand why you're saying what you're saying. But you need to know that I run this place. I don't work upstairs. I've never worked upstairs, here or anywhere else," Maggie said emphatically.

"I'm sorry, I just assumed that . . ."

"Oh, Ray . . . I didn't mean to be so harsh. It's the same assumption pretty much everyone makes, I suppose. Oh m'God, people have been making that assumption about me since I was seventeen, and I don't know how to shake it." Now her voice softened. "Most people just go by how things look, as you did with that professor of yours. And you need to know this too: the ladies who work upstairs are good people. They're all doing the best they can, and they deserve respect. Most of all, they deserve it from me. I shouldn't take offense because you thought I was one o' them."

"Hey, Ray," came a booming voice from across the bar. It was Robby, who'd just come downstairs. He sat down at their table. "Miss Maggie, you were completely right. That Winnie's a fine lady." Robby turned to Ray to explain. "Miss Sylvie retired, so Maggie set me up with Miss Winnie."

"Can I get you something, Robby?" Sylvie had walked over from the bar.

Robby stood and put his arms around her. "You're not jealous, are ya, sweetheart? You're still the best."

"I'm not jealous — it's all business anyway," Sylvie said, but her voice dropped, and she looked away. "I'll buy you a drink for old times' sake," she said, perking up again. "What'll it be?"

"A whiskey," Robby said cautiously, trying to make out her mood. Then he brightened and turned to Ray. "So are ya headed upstairs? Winnie's free right now, and I'm sure you'd like her." Robby winked at Sylvie, who now grinned.

Ray blushed. "No, I'm visiting Maggie. We just got back from a lecture," he said with obvious discomfort.

"A lecture? Christ, Ray. All the great things you can do with a lady, and you take her to hear someone talk? Is he boring you, Maggie?" Robby asked with feigned concern.

"Not at all, Robby; I loved the lecture. I'm glad you enjoyed your time with Winnie." Then, with an impish smile of her own, she said, "But I'm not sure Winnie is the right one for Ray."

Robby laughed loudly. "Maybe not, but she's sure a good one. That Winnie knows how to keep a man right on the edge 'til he can't stand it no . . ." He stopped abruptly and looked for Sylvie, but she was back at the bar and seemed not to have overheard him. He downed the rest of his whiskey in one gulp. "Well, I'm going home to Mother. I'll be back tomorrow night, Miss Maggie. Save a spot for me."

"See you tomorrow, Robby."

"Robby seems to have made the transition from Sylvie to Winnie without too much heartache," Ray said playfully, then added, with a smile, "And you're right, Winnie's *not* the one for me."

"Good," Maggie said, smiling broadly.

Ray looked down at his glass, and after a moment he picked up his lime and squeezed it. This was unfamiliar territory, and he did not want to say the wrong thing, but he was curious. "How do the ladies get started in this business, Maggie?"

"I don't know how it works in other places, but in Gloucester most of them find their way here because their father or their husband gets killed at sea. They start out selling themselves to get food or rent money, like Faith, or to support a mother and a sister, like Anne. It's nearly impossible for a woman to find a good-paying job. But most of the ones who stick with it, the ones who are good at it, they come to accept the life and make the most of it. It's not all bad. We're like a family — an odd sort of family, but like one in many ways."

Now Ray got to the question he truly cared about. "If it's not too much to ask, how did you wind up here?"

Maggie cautiously told Ray her story. "I was sent here by Seamus' father. I was a maid in his house and, well, as we would say in me church, I sinned — we both sinned. For one whole summer we were together. We thought we were careful about, well, about things. But by the end o' the summer, Seamus was on the way.

"This man . . . well . . . he was engaged to someone else. I had dreams that he would change his mind and marry me, but I was young and naive. We read books together. We talked about history. I learned so much from him. His family was rich and well known; he was an impressive man. I thought I loved him, and I thought he loved me.

"But I was wrong. As soon as I was in a family way, he shipped me here to get rid o' me. His reputation was more important to him than I was. He was afraid to own up to what he'd done, to what we'd done. Fear's an awful thing; we do so much out o' fear."

"Why did you put up with him shipping you here?" Ray asked. "Why did you go along with it?"

"I have a brother in Boston. This man, Seamus' father that is, threatened to have him sent back to Ireland. Seth, that's me brother, he's wanted for assault back there, you see. . . . Oh, Ray . . ." Maggie took a sip of her drink. "Seth beat up a man, a farmer who tried to take advantage o' me. This farmer told everyone back home that I was easy, a tart. Honestly, Ray, what that farmer said was a lie, a disgusting, unfair lie. . . . Being me big brother, Seth beat up the farmer. He beat him up so badly that he had to flee Ireland. I followed soon after."

Ray sat still, thinking things over. After a silence that seemed to last forever, Maggie stood up. "I see you don't accept any o' this. I don't blame you for thinking poorly o' me, but maybe it would be best for you to go now."

Ray squeezed his now-mangled lime one last time and put it back in his glass. "I have so little experience with things like this. I've been thinking about you every day for months, and that isn't going to stop because of some farmer in Ireland or some rich bastard from Boston. The only thing I'm really sure about is that I want to keep seeing you."

Maggie slowly sat down.

"Do you think Sylvie would get us another drink? This rum is pretty good." He picked the thoroughly squeezed lime out of his glass and smiled. "And I definitely need another piece of lime."

Maggie ordered another round. Ray took a swig before he continued. "My mother expects me to marry Jane Wonson. You met her at church. Jane's the only girl I've ever kissed; the first time was down in her cellar, when we were only ten years old. There were a few more kisses later, but she's always seemed like a cousin to me. I thought maybe that was the way marriage was supposed to be, more a convenience than anything else. There weren't any fireworks between Mother and Father, none that I could see anyway.

"But then I saw you that day Robby brought me here. You probably don't remember, but I can still see that green dress you were wearing, the smile on your face, and the way you ran up the stairs to get Asa." He paused and stuttered, but his courage held, and he continued with a lowered voice. "The way the lace from your petticoat showed above your ankles, and that . . . beautiful, soft, white skin of your neck and . . . and your . . . your chest." Ray took a big swig of his drink. "You got my heart beating faster in thirty seconds than

Jane's done in all the time I've known her. That's the God's honest truth, Maggie."

Maggie reached across the table and took Ray's hand. Her soft touch sent a shiver of excitement down Ray's spine.

"That feeling hasn't gone away; it's gotten stronger — so much stronger." Ray downed the last of his drink. "So I want to forget your past life, and if you want to forget it too, that's good enough for me. After all," he said, breaking out in a smile, "I belong to the church of universal salvation."

Maggie giggled, and she squeezed his hand. "Ray, you're a lovely soul, now. I've never met anyone like you. But you're wrong about one thing; I did notice you that first day you stopped by, and I've been unable to get you out o' me thoughts ever since."

Emboldened, Ray asked, "Are you free Sunday?"

"For sure, I am," she said with conviction.

"Good. Then let's be brave. Come to Sunday dinner at my house. We always have a big meal after church. It's time my mother got to know you."

"Oh . . . do you think that's wise, now? Your mother . . . she won't accept me; it will be so uncomfortable. I don't think so."

"Maggie, the only way she'll ever accept you is if she gets to know you. This may be hard, and it may take a while. . . . Down deep, where it really counts, she's got a good heart. Please come."

"Oh . . . all right, I'll come."

On Sunday, Ray called on Maggie and they walked to Middle Street together. They entered the parlor, where Persian rugs covered the wide pine floorboards and paintings of ships and men covered the yellow plaster walls. "Is this your da?" Maggie asked, pointing to one of the portraits.

"That's my great-great-grandfather, James Stevens. He was in the General Court during the Revolution. I've got ancestors that sided with the Tories too — don't have any of them hanging on the walls, of course. My father's portrait is over here." Ray pointed to an oil painting of a middle-aged man with a full dark beard, a round face, and hazel eyes. He bore a definite resemblance to Ray.

"He was handsome."

"I wouldn't know about that, but he was a first-rate sailor." He escorted her into the dining room, where silver flatware and china were set for four on a polished mahogany table. Candles in pewter holders were reflected in a large mirror, and two leaded-glass windows faced the harbor, which was visible over the roof of the Cape Ann Savings Bank building.

Elizabeth Stevens came through a swinging door wearing a dress Maggie had seen her wearing in church, but now a colorful cotton apron protected it. "Miss O'Grady, welcome. Would you have a glass of sherry? We'll be dining in fifteen minutes." Maggie curtsied and said she would be pleased to have sherry. Ray poured it into cut-crystal glasses.

Emily Wonson emerged from the kitchen, also in a going-to-church dress protected by an embroidered apron. After exchanging formal greetings and commenting on the unseasonably cold weather, Elizabeth and Emily returned to the kitchen to finish making the dinner.

Ray led Maggie back to the parlor and told her about the ships in each of the paintings. Maggie's favorite was a square-rigged ship under full sail in a strong breeze. White clouds raced across a blue sky, and a bright white wave piled up in front of the blunt bow. The ship was the *William Wallace*; Ray's father had commanded her in the China trade.

Elizabeth announced that dinner was ready, and they migrated to the dining room. A steaming pot roast on a turquoise porcelain platter sat in the middle of the table, with potatoes, carrots, and onions swimming in the thin brown juices that encircled the roast. "I love pot roast, Mrs. Stevens. It was a special treat in me house growing up, and it wasn't often we had a lovely piece o' meat like this one. Thank you for sharing it."

Elizabeth smiled and nodded as she passed the plates.

"Do you still have family in Ireland?" Emily asked.

"One brother, Michael, and me ma and da; they live in the village of Enniskerry, not far from Dublin.

Me da is the cow doctor." Maggie went on about her family, the Wicklow Mountains, and the fragrance of lilacs blooming in the late spring.

"How did you happen to come to America?" Emily inquired kindly.

"I've wanted to come here since I was a girl, Mrs. Wonson. I read about America a great deal. When I had an opportunity, I came. This is certainly a lovely house, Mrs. Stevens. Did you and Mr. Stevens design it yourselves?"

"Oh, no. It's been in Gus' family for nearly a hundred years. Gus was my husband, Ray's father. . . . He died at sea, and so did Ray's older brother."

"Yes, Ray told me. I understand they were fine men. I'm sorry for your loss."

"Thank you, Miss O'Grady. I have something else to thank you for too. I understand you persuaded John Pitt to pay me the insurance money he owed me. I don't know what I would have done without it; I would have lost this house for certain. Raymond didn't tell me how you managed to get it. Could you enlighten me?"

"Yes . . . I suppose." Maggie paused as she considered how much of the story to tell. "Please keep what I'm telling you under your hat, though. Mr. Pitt was a customer o' one o' the ladies down at Fannies. That's the — the house I'm running. When I heard that he was, well, I don't think it's too harsh to say he was stealing your money, well, I . . . let's just say I found him in a compromising position and was able to persuade him that justice demanded he pay you what was rightfully yours."

"That scoundrel!" Emily exclaimed. "Consorting with harl . . . oh, dear, I am so sorry. I meant no offense."

"No mind, Mrs. Wonson. Me own mother would say the same thing," Maggie said sadly.

"Is John, that's Mr. Pitt, is he still frequenting your house, Miss O'Grady?"

"No, ma'am. He's mad at us, surely he is. He's taken his business up to Betty's on Prospect Street, if I'm not mistaken."

"Betty Crabtree? You were right about her, Libby," Emily said.

"Maggie's a history buff," Ray broke in, trying to change the subject. "She knows more about the Revolutionary War than anyone I know."

"Is that so? How did you develop that interest, Miss O'Grady?"

"I've always loved to read, and I've always loved America. It was natural for me, I suppose. Me first employer in the States had a library o' history books he let me read. On me days off I'd visit some o' the places I read about: the Old North Church, Breed's Hill, Faneuil Hall, even the battlefields at Lexington and Concord. I haven't had much time to read lately, but Ray has given me Babson's new history o' Gloucester. I've just started it."

"That John Babson's always been a bookworm, a real shy one. Remember, Em? Nobody could ever get him to dance."

"Yes, but then Mary latched on to him, and before you knew it, they had five children. John didn't have any time for writing while poor Mary was around."

Ray snorted.

"Mary always liked the quiet type, God rest her soul," Elizabeth said. "Remember how she swooned over Mark Johnson — you know, one of the Johnson twins? I never heard that boy say a word. He let his brother, Luke, do all the talking. She couldn't get enough of Mark, though; I never understood the attraction."

Maggie smiled.

As Elizabeth rose from the table to clear the dishes, she asked her son when he was going fishing again.

"We'll do short trips in Ipswich Bay until February, and then the skipper wants to give Georges a try. He's been dory fishing ever since he built the *Parsons.* He thinks he's been missing out on the big money by staying away from Georges."

"Raymond, can't you do something else? Your father and your brother died on Georges Bank. It is so dangerous. As it is, I can't sleep nights when you're away."

250

"I'll be careful, Mother. Nothing to worry about. Captain Wonson's fishing Georges right now, isn't he?"

"Yes, Ray. But your mother's right. It is dangerous. My Enoch is a lucky man. You have to be lucky to fish all the years he has. Two of his three brothers were lost at sea. The odds don't favor lasting as long as my Enoch has. He'd tell you the same himself if he were here."

"I don't suppose what you do is all that safe either, Miss O'Grady," Elizabeth said. "Don't you, ah . . . you ladies come to grief from time to time?"

"Sometimes, Mrs. Stevens. It's usually caused by drinking. Some men get violent when they've had too much."

Nodding in agreement, Elizabeth said, "Alcohol is at the root of so many of our problems. I'd give up my sherry if it meant we could ban the sales of all spirits."

"Oh, Libby," Emily said, "I like my sherry, and I know you do too. Maybe we could pass a law that prohibited men from drinking. They're the ones causing the trouble."

"We'll have to get the vote before we can make that happen. What do you think of giving women the vote, Miss O'Grady?"

"I don't see why not. I can tell you that some of the men I know shouldn't be trusted with anything as important as the vote. I don't mean you, Ray, of course. But as a rule, women are usually more thoughtful than men. We'd have a better government if women were the ones doing the voting."

Emily nodded approvingly.

"Raymond, how do you feel about giving women the vote?" Elizabeth asked.

"It's a very new idea."

"It's not that new. Don't you have an opinion?"

"I don't know that we're ready for that sort of thing. Most women are ruled by their emotions; it's better to have voting decisions made thoughtfully, by men who know how to run a business and who understand money and finance."

"What poppycock!" Emily exclaimed.

"Miss O'Grady, you see what we are up against. My own son is a fine man in so many ways, but he is as backward as any when it comes to women's rights."

"It's been me experience that many men aren't ruled by their brains, but rather by a body part more centrally located. . . ." Maggie was stopped by a gasp from Elizabeth. "Oh dear, I've said too much. I'm so very sorry."

Emily threw back her head and laughed. "That's all right, Miss O'Grady. While I'm sure my experience is a good deal more limited than yours, I tend to agree with your conclusion."

After an uncomfortable silence, Emily stood up and announced that it was time for dessert. "Elizabeth makes great cobbler," she said, glancing over her shoulder at Maggie and winking.

Once the blackberry cobbler was served, Ray poured more sherry. Elizabeth took a sip and asked, "Miss O'Grady, do you plan on raising that boy of yours in — what is it you call it — in Fannies?"

Emily gave her friend a disapproving look, but said nothing.

"Mrs. Stevens, Fannies is me home. I've nowhere else to raise him."

"Yes, so it is, but certainly it is no place for a child."

"The ladies help a lot. They're very sweet to Seamus."

"My. But how will he turn out, how will he turn out?" Elizabeth said, half to herself.

"Now, Libby, the Lord works in mysterious ways."

"This cannot be the Lord's plan, Em. Where is the boy's father, Miss O'Grady? Why are you raising him alone?"

"He is in Boston, ma'am. He's the one who sent Seamus and me to Fannies. We never married." After a period of silence, Maggie continued. "Perhaps I should go now. I think I may have overstayed me welcome."

"Libby, you're being rude to our guest."

"No, Mrs. Wonson. No one has been rude. I worry about Seamus too. Every day o' me life I worry. I do think I should go now." Maggie got up from the table, her cobbler untouched.

Ray walked Maggie home in silence. As they approached Fannies, Ray said with more cheer than he felt, "That wasn't so bad."

"Oh, Ray, for sure, it wasn't good. Em is more understanding than most will be. But they were both uncomfortable having me over. I don't think your ma is ever going to accept me."

"Just give her time. She'll come around." Ray paused. "I promised to get back and help clean up, so I'll leave you now." He stepped forward and kissed her on the cheek. She didn't offer anything more.

"Thanks for trying. When do you leave for the fishing grounds?"

"Tomorrow, but we're staying close to home. We should be back in three or four days, sooner if the weather turns bad. May I call on you when I'm back?"

"As you wish," she said without enthusiasm.

Maggie went straight to her room to find Seamus sitting on the floor wearing a white shirt, a plaid bow tie, and his Sunday-best wool trousers held up with red suspenders. Lucy was on the floor stacking wooden blocks with him, and Sarah was sitting up on the bed, knitting. They both wore full-length black gowns. "Ma, look, look," Seamus said as soon as he spotted her.

"What a beautiful house, Seamus. Did you make it all on your own?"

"Me and Aunt Lucy. Not a house, a church."

"And a lovely church it is. Don't you three look fancy!"

"It's Sunday, so we thought we'd get dressed up," Sarah said. "Seamus was just finishin' our church when ya got here. How did it go?"

Maggie sighed. "About as I should have expected. Not at all well, to tell the truth. How do I get his ma to accept me? How do I do that, now?"

"It's hard for us," Lucy said. "Remember Aunt Bertie's funeral, Sarah? Bertie was our closest relative after Ma and Pa died. She passed away right before ya came here. We went to her wake. Uncle Joe, that's Bertie's husband, was polite enough. He even gave us a drink and thanked us for comin'."

"But then there was Louisa, Bertie's oldest daughter," Sarah said. "Lucy had bumped into the most darlin' little boy at the table with all the food. He was 'bout as old as your Seamus and all dressed up for the funeral, just like Seamus is now. But he'd stuck his hand right into a pot a' jam and was smearin' it all over his face. He was tryin' to lick it off his fingers and makin' even more of a mess. So Lucy gets out her hankie, kneels down, and starts cleanin' him up, and that's when Louisa comes around the corner. The little boy was her son, it turns out. We didn't know. We hadn't seen Cousin Louisa for years. What a scene she made."

"She starts screamin', right there in front a' everyone," Lucy said. "'Get away from my boy, you harlot, you whore! Take your filthy hands off him!' I was just tryin' to clean him up, tryin' to help. . . ."

"Everyone stopped what they were doin' and looked at Lucy," Sarah said. "She was still kneelin' in front a' that boy, her white hankie all covered in purple jam. He looked so startled with his mother goin' on like that, but then he yelled, 'Whore!' and slapped Lucy, leavin' a smear a' jelly on her cheek, and ran cryin' to his mother."

Now Lucy leaned her head against Sarah's shoulder. Seamus cocked his head, then leaned into Lucy and put his little arms around her as far as they would go. Maggie sat on the floor with them and did her best to embrace them all.

Chapter 22

At Sea — January 1864

For the next two months the *Benjamin Parsons* made short trips, rarely going more than thirty miles from home, never staying at sea more than five days at a time. The last of these trips was different from the others. Paul Tobey remained ashore — it was Ray's first command.

On the third day out, high thin clouds moved in from the southwest. Noticing the change in weather, Ray left Ipswich Bay and sailed south to anchor on Stellwagen Bank, just fifteen miles southeast of the mouth of Gloucester Harbor. The next morning the crew resumed fishing under an overcast sky. The wind came up before noon and kept building throughout the day, but knowing he was so close to home, Ray delayed leaving the fishing grounds. By the time he finally ordered a halt to the fishing and got under way, it was late afternoon and a strong breeze was blowing.

Ray set all the sail he could. He wanted to make the harbor before it got completely dark. Soon the wind was blowing twenty-five knots. Ray called for all hands, but before the crew could get to their stations, one of the weather stays parted with a snap loud enough to be heard over the commotion of the developing storm. A tremendous cracking followed as the mainmast fractured just above deck, sending it over the side. The leverage exerted by the wreckage spun the boat, first dead downwind and then through an uncontrolled jibe that sent the fores'l and stays'l flying across the boat. The fores'l boom broke in the middle and the gaff broke at the jaws, sending these spars tumbling overboard and ripping the sail into pieces as they went. The *Parsons* then came to a stop broadside to the wind, held in that vulnerable position by broken spars, ripped sails, and a rat's nest of tangled lines.

Ray and his crew sprang into action. They rushed to cut away the rigging before the shattered mainmast, now surging back and forth in the growing sea, could smash a hole in the hull. In minutes they were sweating despite the winter gale now roaring around them.

The sun had set while they were dealing with the damage. The Eastern Point Light was visible behind them to the northwest, but the *Parsons* was drifting down on Halfway Rock, hidden in the blackness to leeward. To go upwind they had to set a sail aft of the foremast, and every moment they delayed took them farther from the safety of Gloucester Harbor.

"Pat," Ray said to McCurdy, who was back on the helm, "come right, toward land as far as she'll go. Everyone else, let's jury-rig the tops'l on the foremast." The deck exploded into activity as the sail was hauled up from below and laced onto the remaining mast. Ray hoped that the tops'l, their newest sail, would hold up in the growing breeze. If it didn't, he had a backup plan. He told Robby to get the stays'l ready to go up the foremast if the tops'l tore away.

The tops'l was raised and the *Parsons* heeled hard over, but the rail stayed clear of the water. "This will work," Ray said, more to himself than to anyone else.

Then the snow started. At first just a few flakes came down, but before long the Eastern Point Light disappeared in heavy snow. Thirty minutes later the wind increased again, and in a gust the tops'l exploded. The *Parsons* was momentarily without sail, but now Ray's foresight paid off. The crew raised the pre-rigged stays'l. It wasn't pretty and the *Parsons'* speed dropped to three knots, but she balanced well and was going in the right direction.

Ray had to guess how much leeway the *Parsons* was making. With the unusual sail-plan it had to be significant, but with no visual references, he had little to go by. If he didn't correct enough, the *Parsons* would come to grief on Norman's Woe reef; if he corrected too much, he would wreck her on the windward shore of Eastern Point. He brought up a mental picture of the harbor entrance and ordered Pat to turn her one point to starboard. Spray flying over the starboard rail was now freezing on the lower rigging, so he started some men breaking it up with clubs.

An hour and a half later the wind was stronger than ever, but the sea wasn't so steep. They must be under the lee of Cape Ann, but none of the familiar landmarks could be seen. Ray started the lead, and twenty fathoms became eighteen, fifteen, ten, and then, alarmingly, six. But then they had eight fathoms and nine and eight again. Ray guessed they had skirted Dog Bar and the harbor entrance was off to starboard. If he was right, he had to turn; otherwise, the broken hull of the *Parsons* would lie forever alongside Longfellow's fabled wreck of the *Hesperus.*

Ray tacked and sailed as far as he dared before dropping the anchor in seven fathoms. An anchor watch was posted, and Ray and the rest of the men went below. Now that they were in a sheltered spot, the cook stoked the fire, and with the hatches battened down, the boat warmed up. Hot coffee was followed by eggs, potatoes, and ham, and soon everyone relaxed. So far the men had been quiet, focused solely on the job at hand. Now Pat broke the silence. "Ray, that was some first-class sailin' getting us to this anchorage."

Another shipmate agreed. "Having the stays'l all ready to go when the tops'l blew away was real smart." There was a general murmur of agreement among the crew. Everyone stood up and shook Ray's hand when he headed back to the small captain's cabin.

The wind blew and the snow continued all night and all the next morning. Ray was up on deck every two hours with the change of the watch, but there was no need. It was obvious from the lack of any significant sea that they were in a safe place, although he could not say exactly where that place was. The snow abated at noon, and finally they could see the shore. They were in Gloucester's outer harbor, in an area known as the Pancake Ground, half a mile south of Niles Beach — just where Ray had hoped they were when he dropped the anchor.

The wind shifted to the south, allowing them to raise the stays'l and sail into the inner harbor and right up to the Harbor Cove dock. They attracted quite a crowd, coming in without their mainmast or their foremast spars. Paul Tobey was there to take their lines. and as soon as the *Parsons* was secure, he joined Ray in the captain's cabin. "What the hell happened?" he asked.

"Well, Skipper . . ."

"Don't call me skipper. This trip isn't over until the *Parsons* is unloaded and the men are paid off. You're the skipper here, and this is your cabin. I'm just the owner. Now tell me what the hell happened, Skipper."

Ray explained to Tobey how it was that his schooner came in missing its mainmast and most of its rig.

"Jesus Christ, Ray."

"Well, I sure am sorry to have lost most of the rig like I did. But shrouds do sometimes break. . . . I did get her home. The crew thinks I did all right."

"I can imagine what you're glossing over. You've learned a lot, Ray. . . . But I can't say I think much of the judgment you showed out there. You knew there was bad weather coming, but you pushed it for a few more codfish. And then you piled on too much sail in a rush to get in before dark. Those men out there who are unloading this boat right now — you almost killed them all yesterday."

Ray looked down at the floor.

"Let me tell you about a man I knew once. He was the new captain of a small bark, only a couple years older than you. It was his first command, and he was running a shipment of salt cod down to Charleston. He was supposed to go down and back in two weeks, but the trip took him almost four.

"When we got back, the owner demanded to know why the hell he took so long. The captain said he had to wait out bad weather down in the Carolinas before starting back. The owner swore up and down at him — on deck, in front of everyone. He said if he were ever late again, it better be because the mast broke; otherwise, he'd be fired. The captain just stood and

262

took it. Then he looked the owner in the eye and said as long as he was captain, he would decide when the weather was good enough to sail, and he wouldn't ever let anyone else make that decision for him. The owner fired him on the spot.

"Ray, when you take one of these boats to sea, you've got the lives of the crew in your hands. Think of them first — always. It's not easy sometimes. Your own men may disagree with you. They may even say you're a coward if you leave the fishing grounds when everyone else stays. You may lose your job, like that new captain did. But if you put the men first, you can always hold your head high.

"You got away with it this time. Part of the reason is because you're a damn fine sailor. But don't ever put yourself in that position again."

"Maybe I'm not cut out to be a skipper," Ray said.

"Nobody said that; just learn from this."

"What happened to that captain?"

"His whole crew walked off that boat with him. I know. I was his first mate. We all got on with another owner, and that captain became one of Gloucester's finest. Don't you recognize who I'm talking about? That captain was Augustus Stevens, and you can be damn proud he was your father. Now, you get this boat unloaded and I'll find someone to fix the rig. If we move quickly, you may get in another run to Ipswich

Bay before we take her to Georges." Tobey went ashore, leaving the young skipper alone in his cabin.

He wasn't alone for long. "Skip, you got a visitor!" Robby yelled down from the deck. Maggie hurried down the steep companionway ladder, almost falling before she reached the bottom. "Ray," she said, nearly out of breath, "thank God you're all right!" She threw her arms around him. Ray gingerly wrapped his arms around her shoulders.

"Winnie said the *Parsons* was in, but when I looked out the window I didn't recognize her." Maggie loosened her grip. Her eyes were damp, her cheeks smudged and her hair disheveled underneath her winter bonnet. She was wearing slippers that were soaked from running through the heavy snow. She was the most beautiful thing he'd ever seen. He kissed her.

When their lips parted, Maggie pressed her head against Ray's chest. "I've been pretending your visits these past few months were just pleasant diversions. . . . I've been telling meself you should go ahead and marry Jane like you're supposed to. I couldn't see how this would ever work. But all last night I was worried sick about you. I had a premonition that you were gone. Then I saw this boat all beat up, and I couldn't wait another minute. I don't know what I would have done if . . ."

"Maggie, I . . . I . . . I love you." Ray stumbled over words that he had never heard his parents say to each other.

264

"Oh, Ray, I so love you." They embraced again.

After they finally let go of each other, Maggie said she had to return to Fannies. Ray insisted that she borrow his fishing boots, even though they were several sizes too big, and promised to come by as soon as he could.

Unloading didn't take long. Buckets were lowered, and the men filled them with fish that had been split and stored between layers of chipped ice. The buckets were weighed on the dock and sold right there to the fish packer for three cents a pound. The packer trimmed the fish and put it in wooden boxes that were shipped south by rail. By the time they were done unloading, Tobey was back. He had arranged for the Railways to take the *Parsons* that afternoon so they could get started replacing the rig right away. With the help of a harbor sloop, she made her way over to Rocky Neck.

It was dark by the time Ray hitched a ride back. Two feet of snow had fallen, and some drifts were eight feet high. Paths had been shoveled, so Ray was able to make his way up Duncan Street without much effort. It was cold, and the packed snow crunched underfoot. The bright light reflected by the snow under the streetlamps contrasted with the impenetrable darkness of the shadows. Ray opened the red door and saw half the *Parsons* crew in the bar. "Have a seat," Sylvie said. "I'll let Maggie know you're here."

Ray sat down at a table with Robby and Pat. "Gentlemen, it's been a long day. Let me buy you a drink."

"That it has, Skip," Pat said. "For a while there, I didn't think I'd ever step ashore again."

"I knew we'd be fine the whole time," Robby said. "Hell, we coulda swum home from Stellwagen if we had to."

"Jesus, Robby," Pat said. "You woulda frozen to death inside a' ten minutes, if ya didn't drown first."

"So, Ray," Robby asked, "was Tobey sore 'bout us trashin' his rig?"

"He was damn decent about it. Didn't think I was too smart, though. Said I should have come in sooner."

"I remember arguin' with Gus once when he took us in instead a' waitin' for a winter storm to whack us," Robby said. "Everyone else on Georges stayed put. I wanted to hide my head in shame — I knew they'd all think we were yellow. But four boats sank in that storm and we got home safe, all of us except ol' Sooky Wilkins. He fell into the drink and drowned, and it didn't take even ten minutes. Your papa was right to be cautious, Ray."

"He's been right a lot of times, it seems."

"Hey, here comes your lady," Robby said.

Maggie wore a simple green cotton frock that set off her red hair. She looked about sixteen years old. Her makeup was back in place, and her hair was down

266

to her shoulders in a lazy curl. Ray reached over and took her hand as if it were the most natural thing in the world. He led her to an empty table in the corner.

"Robby," Pat said as they went out of earshot, "it looks like our young captain is sweet on the little redhead. She's a cut above the usual for this sorta place."

"She runs the place, Pat. I don't know why Ray doesn't just take her upstairs and get on with it. Speakin' a' which, I gotta date with Winnie. Hey, Sylvie," Robby yelled across the bar, "is Winnie free?"

"Yup. Just go on up."

Ray and Maggie sat down, and Sylvie brought them each a rum with lime juice.

"I made a bit of a spectacle o' meself today, for sure," Maggie said. "Your boots are at the front door. Thanks for the loan."

"I was damn glad to see you." Ray took a deep breath. "Maggie, I've been worrying too much about what others think. I almost lost the *Parsons* because I was worried that my crew would think I was too cautious. And I've been foolish to be concerned about those who'll disapprove of my being with you. But I've learned my lesson." Ray pushed back his chair and got down on one knee. He took Maggie's hand in his and looked into her eyes, but he was blind to the panic that was taking hold there. "I love you," he said with quiet sincerity. "I promise I'll be a good husband and a good father to Seamus. Will you marry me?"

All conversation in the bar stopped. Sylvie strained forward to listen. Maggie looked down into Ray's innocent hazel eyes. "My darling Ray," she choked. "It just won't work. Your mother . . . your friends . . . we could never . . . I can't . . . I can't . . ." She jumped up, knocking her chair over, and hurried away, leaving behind only the swish of her skirt and the fading staccato of her shoes as she rapidly ascended the stairs.

The air was still. Then, with frowns and sympathetic nods, everyone turned away; slowly, hushed conversation erased the silence and Ray got up off his knee. Sylvie walked over, kissed him gently on the forehead, and left another rum on the table before him. Ray sat back down in his chair, watery eyes unfocused on any worldly image. Then he downed the rum, retrieved his boots, and walked alone back up the snowy hill to Middle Street.

Chapter 23

Gloucester — February 1864

The last customer had left. Sylvie had gone to bed, and Maggie was on her fourth shot of rum when Winnie came down to the bar wearing a red robe. Her hair was down but carefully combed, and her makeup was perfect, as if it had just been applied. The scent of her most expensive perfume filled the room. She poured herself a whiskey.

"I thought I heard you down here, Maggie. Why haven't you turned in?"

"I can't shleep. Drinking eventually helps, for shure."

"I have trouble sleeping too." Winnie downed her whiskey.

"I'm scared o' him. Innocent he surely is, but the thought o' him undressing. . . . I went crazy when that boat came in . . . ran down and threw meself into his arms. For shure, he'd think I was willing. But when he . . . the dear soul was down on his knee . . . all I

269

could see was Jake Anderson . . . I could almost feel the grimy paws of the Shwinson brothers . . . and there was this lovely man. I didn't tell him no because o' his ma. I'm scared o' him, scared o' him just because he's a man."

"They're all capable a' great violence, every one of 'em. They keep it under control most a' the time, but when they let go, it could be the end a' ya. I been raped. I wouldn't have any a' the bastards. . . . Just be a matter a' time, and if you're married, you're stuck, even if the bastard beats ya every night."

"Ray's never lifted a finger. And I have to tell you, for shure, he excites me. But William excited me too. Even Jake got me heart racing before he forced himself on me. I can't shtay away from them. . . . I've been aching lonely."

"Ya don't have to be alone." Winnie looked into Maggie's bloodshot eyes. She took her cheeks in her hands and kissed her on the forehead, then gently on the mouth. "Ya don't have to be alone," she said softly. "Come up to my room with me."

"Oh, I don't know about that, now." Maggie almost fell over as she staggered back. "There washn't any o' *that* kind o' thing in Wicklow County."

"Poppycock! Women keep it hidden, in Wicklow County and everywhere else. Maybe it'll be different someday. Maybe after we get the vote, things will change." Maggie's support of the suffragists was well known at Fannies. "Ain't ya curious? Don't ya like adventure?"

"I . . . I don't know. I don't know anyone who's that way."

"Oh, my innocent babe." Winnie put her arm around Maggie's shoulders. "Whaddaya think Lucy and Sarah do together every night after hours? And I been drinkin' myself to sleep ever since Mo left to marry that damn boy a' hers. I wish she'd had the courage to stay with me. Real affection's hard to come by, and so's real satisfaction, especially after an endless parade of unwashed fishermen inside ya.

"It's a cold night, Maggie, and we're two lonely people tryin' to drink ourselves to sleep. Come on, my dear," Winnie said affectionately as she extended her hand. "Try it for tonight." Maggie put down her glass and let Winnie lead her upstairs, closing the door gently behind them. Winnie lit a single candle, and Maggie stared into the yellow flame as if in a trance. She felt Winnie's arms encircle her from behind and gently turn her around. Winnie had undone the sash that held her robe together, and now she pulled Maggie in against her bare breasts. She pressed her lips against Maggie's, and her tongue searched for an opening.

Maggie pushed her away. Winnie reached forward and grabbed her arms, digging in with long fingernails, but Maggie broke free. "No . . . no, for shure, not this." Maggie stumbled, banging her forehead against the door. She turned and almost fell over, then managed to open the door and flee.

Winnie sat on her neatly turned-down bed, poured a shot of whiskey from a bedside bottle, and stared at the open door. Eventually, the candle burned out.

Ninety minutes later Maggie awoke on her own bed, shivering and uncovered, ears ringing and mouth dry, enveloped in Winnie's scent. She drank a glass of water from the pitcher on her nightstand and climbed under the bedclothes, where she curled into a ball and fell into a restless sleep.

She dreamt she was in her old classroom, staring out through the wavy window glass at the gray mist pouring down the creek beds that cut through the Wicklow Mountains. The ridgeline held back the mist except where low spots allowed it to overflow like water cresting a weir. A harsh voice shattered the tranquility.

"Margaret O'Grady, are yah deef?" The nun's voice sounded as if it were in a tunnel. Her face was a flushed blur of splotchy color surrounded by a black-and-white habit.

"No, Sister." Her lips moved in her sleep as she mouthed the words.

"Hold out your hand."

Maggie stretched out her left arm, lifting the bedclothes. The ruler whipped down on her palm.

"Again," and down came the ruler once more, propelled by the full weight of the wiry spinster. Maggie jerked back, but she didn't wake.

"Now, I asked you a question." The voice was distant, disembodied. "What is six times seven?"

"Forty-two," Maggie grunted.

"Nine times eight?"

"Seventy-two."

"Twelve times twelve?"

"One hundred forty-four."

Without offering a word of praise, the nun turned to the plain-faced twelve-year-old who always sat next to Maggie: "Molly Tierney, what is four times five?"

Molly's forehead wrinkled in thought, as it always did whenever she was asked a question. Maggie wanted to reach out across the years and help once more. The nun put her hands behind her back and looked up as if seeking divine guidance, giving Maggie her chance.

"Twenty," Maggie silently mouthed, and a split second later Molly shouted in triumph, "Twenty!"

The nun was exultant; her prey was caught in the trap. With fire in her eyes, she grabbed the frightened girl by the shoulders and pulled her nose to nose. "Molly Tierney, tell me true or you will forever boil in hell — did Margaret O'Grady help you with that answer?"

Molly, her face contorted in pain, looked to Maggie. "Look at *me*," the nun commanded in a booming voice. With mouth wide open but vocal cords paralyzed by fear, the girl nodded, then began to cry.

The nun grabbed Maggie and dragged her to a windowless storeroom. She could feel the jagged fingernails still. Sister Mary Agnes opened the door and pointed, as she'd done many times before. Without looking back, Maggie stepped inside to sit on the short, hard oak stool that was waiting for her there. The door closed behind her, and blackness filled the tiny space.

Now Maggie awoke to the blackness again. Her forearms ached, and for a moment she thought she was in that storeroom, back in a time before she let fear run her life.

Chapter 24

Gloucester — May 1864

Outside the kitchen window, the tulips Elizabeth and Emily had planted in the fall were a brilliant yellow in the late-morning sunshine. Elizabeth poured tea. "Em, did Jane say anything about how the date went last night?" she asked.

Emily sipped her tea. "It didn't go well, not well at all. I think she's going to call it off."

"She should forgive him for seeing the O'Grady woman. It wasn't serious."

"Oh yes it was. Last night Jane asked him whether he still had feelings for the woman."

"I hope my boy had the good sense to say no."

"He's your husband's son, honest as the day is long, and like most men he has no sense at all. No, he told Jane he was in love with the O'Grady woman. And there's more: he actually proposed to her back in January!"

"Oh my! Well, I'm glad he came to his senses and refused to go through with it."

"He told Jane that *she* refused *him*. She wouldn't marry him because she knew you would disapprove."

"That tart! Who is she to refuse my son?"

"Libby, listen to yourself! For God's sake, you don't want Ray to marry that woman."

"Oh, Em, you're right, of course. But I don't like her hurting my boy. He should forget her and marry Jane. They're a good match — you and I could have grandchildren. You don't have to love your husband to have a successful marriage. We both know that as well as any."

"Yes, but we got lucky, didn't we?"

Elizabeth nodded, reaching out to take Emily's hand.

"It wouldn't be right for Jane and Ray to marry just for form," Emily said. "Ray's not going to be gone for years at a time like Gus was. If he really does love that woman, it won't turn out well. He'll resent Jane. She'll lash out in return. They'll make each other miserable. I don't want that for Jane, and you don't want it for Ray."

"What's wrong with him? He isn't supposed to fall in love with the madam of a whorehouse."

"A woman doesn't always love the one she's supposed to love," Emily said softly. "Why should it be different for a man?"

Down the street at Fannies, Maggie sat across the breakfast table from Sylvie, surrounded by piles of paper. She was training Sylvie in the administrative side of the business.

"I need your advice," Sylvie said. "Last night Robby was here celebratin'; they left first thing this mornin' for Georges Bank. I'm sure ya remember he used to be a regular a' mine. Last night he came down to the bar after spendin' his time with Winnie. I gave him a drink, even though he'd already had a few too many. He asked whether I ever thought a' gettin' married and havin' children. I told him that just didn't seem like it was in the cards, so I hadn't given it much thought. Then . . . then . . . he really surprised me. He asked if I'd consider settlin' down. . . ." She dabbed her eyes with her handkerchief and then blew her nose loudly. "I would consider it, I told him, but he'd have to court me, like a normal lady. He said all right, he'd take me out on a date as soon as he was back in port."

"That's wonderful, Sylvie. Robby's a decent man."

"I think so too. But then he asked if I'd mind if he kept seein' Winnie, 'purely on a professional basis,' he said. I sent him to Winnie in the first place, so it didn't seem right for me to be too upset . . . still . . . Well, I told him I didn't know 'bout that; I'd think 'bout it. Whaddaya think? Should I tell him it's all right for him to see Winnie while he's courtin' me?"

"You and Robby aren't exactly the typical young couple, for sure, but it doesn't sit well with me that he should be seeing Winnie while he's planning on marrying you. I think he should be a one-woman man, starting right now."

Sylvie nodded: "There's somethin' else. I got pregnant once; I was only seventeen. It was before ya came here. That fella Stark knew somebody in Manchester who could take care of it; Fannie even agreed to pay. He was a hoss doctor, and I don't think he'd washed all week. We got there after dark, and they took me into a shack that smelled a' manure. I was laid out on a grimy bed. Stark held me down, and the hoss doctor went into me with this iron scraper. It was cold, and then it burned, like nothin' I felt before or since. I musta passed out.

"Next thing I remember, we were on our way back to Gloucester. Stark told me everythin' had gone just fine, but it didn't feel fine to me. Every time that carriage hit a bump, it felt like that hoss doctor was jabbin' me all over again. I was still bleedin' the next day and runnin' a fever too.

"The day after that, Fannie called Doc Gray in, or so I was told. I don't remember seein' him 'til way later. Doc Gray saved me, but he said I'd never be able to have a baby….. I haven't told Robby any a' this. He should know — he wants babies — but if I lose him…."

"Well . . . a few months back I spurned Ray's offer o' marriage," Maggie said. "I thought I was doing the right thing. But now . . . every day when I wake up, I think I should have said yes. Me son would have a father, and I'd have someone to hold me when I have nightmares. Telling Robby the truth is the right thing, but if it means you'll be alone your whole life . . . I don't know that it's the best thing."

They were interrupted when Mildred stepped into the office. She was a cute fifteen-year-old brunette Maggie had hired as a maid to replace Anne when she moved upstairs. "Miss Maggie, there's two ladies here," Mildred announced. "Standin' at the front door. They won't come in, but they say they gotta see ya."

Elizabeth and Emily were wearing black-and-white print dresses — dots for Elizabeth, lines for Emily — and hats decorated with flowers. "What a surprise to see you, Mrs. Stevens, Mrs. Wonson," Maggie said as she gathered her wits. "Won't you come in and have a cup of tea?"

"No, thank you, Miss O'Grady," Emily said. "We think it is best we stay outside."

"Miss O'Grady, at the risk of being blunt, I would like to ask you a question," Elizabeth said. "Is it true that my son proposed marriage to you a few months back?"

This was not what Maggie had expected, but it was an easy question to answer. "Yes, he did, right inside this door, in front of about twenty people."

"And am I correctly informed that you refused him?"

"Yes, that's right."

"May I ask why?"

"Mrs. Stevens, maybe I'm a fool, but I thought many would disapprove of our marriage," Maggie said, then fell silent. "I was concerned it just wouldn't work out," she finally said.

"Do you love my son, Miss O'Grady?"

Maggie squeezed the doorknob. "Are you sure you ladies wouldn't like to come inside?"

"No, thank you. I know this is a personal question, and I know I have no right to ask it. But my son's happiness is important to me, so if you would tell me your true feelings, I would be grateful."

Maggie hesitated, then decided to answer honestly. "Yes, Mrs. Stevens, for sure I love your son. I love him more than I can say. Ever since I told him no . . . I . . . I've regretted it."

Elizabeth nodded, then looked at Emily. "Miss O'Grady, Libby and . . . that is, Mrs. Stevens and I would like to invite you and your son to Mrs. Stevens' house for dinner this Sunday. Would you come?"

Maggie wiped her eyes with her sleeve. "Ray will still be out at sea on Sunday, won't he?"

"Yes, I expect so. We were hoping we could all get to know each other better. Would you join us?"

Maggie thought it over while the ladies waited patiently. She was wary of spending an afternoon with Ray's mother, but finally said she would be honored.

Elizabeth and Emily said their goodbyes, and Maggie watched them from her doorway as they walked up Duncan Street, a pair of dominos in black and white. From a distance, they looked like twins.

Chapter 25

Gloucester — June 1864

After unloading the *Parsons*, Ray walked home, stopping first at the savings bank to deposit the bulk of his pay. Minutes later he opened the front door, threw his sea bag in the entryway, and yelled, "I'm home!" When there was no response, he went to the kitchen for a bite to eat.

As he was rummaging around in the pantry, he heard a high-pitched laugh on the second floor. Climbing the stairs, he caught a glimpse of a woman's foot disappearing behind the closing door of his bedroom. Cautiously, he climbed up the rest of the way and opened the door to come face to face with his mother, who put her finger to her lips and said, "Shhh." Then she closed the door, leaving Ray staring at a door panel. Next he heard the high-pitched laugh again, and out of his mother's bedroom charged Seamus O'Grady. The boy stopped short on seeing Ray.

For a moment they both stood still, and then Ray pointed silently at the bedroom door, nodded, and backed away. Seamus looked at Ray. He was confused at first, but then he broke into a big smile and charged over to yank open the door. Spotting Elizabeth, he screamed, "I got you!" She laughed, lifted him into her arms, and spun round and round. "You win again, Seamus! You're too good for me," she said, which started him squealing all over again.

For the next hour the three of them played hide-and-seek, and when they were all tuckered out, Elizabeth served cobbler and milk, then put Seamus on the couch in the sitting room and covered him with a down comforter. Once the boy was asleep, Ray asked his mother what was going on. "Well, it all started about three weeks ago, when Em and I invited Maggie and Seamus to dine with us. She's a smart woman, and an educated one too. And she's done a fine job with her Seamus; he's a lovely little boy.

"She's learned a lot about our faith since she moved to Gloucester. It's easy to see why universal salvation has an appeal to *her*, but I believe her interest is sincere. Em was especially impressed by how much she cares about the plight of women. You know how important women's rights are to Em, and it turns out they're important to Maggie too. It wouldn't hurt you to get interested in our right to vote, Raymond."

"I'm confused, Mother. Why is Seamus here? And where is Maggie?"

283

"Oh, Maggie went to Salem this morning. She's always wanted to see the House of the Seven Gables — the place Hawthorne wrote about. She went with Richard Wonson, Em's cousin. You remember Richard, the butcher; he's a widower now, left last year with two small children when the typhus took Eleanor. He had to go to Salem to meet with a wholesaler, and he offered to escort Maggie. Anyway, I said I'd look after Seamus so she could go. Isn't he a delight? I do love having a child in the house again!"

"I didn't think you liked Maggie."

"I can't condone prostitution. But Maggie's had a difficult time of it. Men have treated her very badly. And anyway, her beautiful little boy isn't to blame for what his mother does. Seamus is spending the night with us. Then Em and I are taking him to church in the morning. Maggie's spending the night with Em's cousin Charlotte in Salem. She's married to that doctor who's a second cousin of Hawthorne's. It's good for Maggie to get away; she needs a break from that horrid place on Duncan Street. We all need a respite now and again. Every woman does, Raymond."

"Has she known Richard for long?"

"I don't think so, dear. Em just introduced them last Sunday when we had them over for dinner. They seemed to hit it off, though. Oh, one other thing, you'll have to sleep in Augie's room tonight. I didn't know you were coming home today, so I made up your room for Seamus."

Ray did not sleep well that night.

After Emily arrived the next morning, the four of them walked to the Universalist with Ray and Seamus in the lead. As they rounded the corner to Church Street, Elizabeth asked Emily where Jane was this morning. Emily leaned over and answered softly, so Seamus couldn't hear: "She said she wouldn't come if we were bringing Seamus with us. She wasn't going to get the family 'in trouble with the Lord,' she said. I told her she could do whatever she wanted, but I was escorting this little boy to church this morning."

"I'm surprised at her, Em."

"I'm ashamed of her. If that John Pitt tries to stop us from bringing this boy to church, I'm going to spit in his eye."

"High time someone did, I'd say. You take one eye, I'll take the other."

By the time they reached the church, Emily and Elizabeth had caught up with Ray and Seamus. "We'll take it from here, Ray dear," Emily said as she took Seamus' left hand and Elizabeth took his right. Up the steps the three of them went, with Ray trailing behind.

Sergeant Smith and William Sewall were at the door greeting parishioners. "Welcome to church this fine morning, ladies. And who is this handsome lad?" Sewall asked.

"Good morning, Bill; good morning, Stewart." Elizabeth and Emily returned the greeting almost in unison. "This is Seamus O'Grady," Emily continued.

"Libby has been looking after him this weekend while his mother is out of town. He's here because he loves singing, don't you, Seamus?"

"I like music!" Seamus exclaimed.

Sewall and Smith looked at each other, and then Sewall shrugged and said, "Well then, welcome to church. May I escort you to your seats?"

"No thank you, Bill. We know how to find them," Elizabeth said, and the three of them marched on in.

Ray had observed this conversation from two steps back. Sewall greeted him pleasantly, but then he came face to face with Sergeant Smith, who stood with hands by his side, staring into Ray's eyes. Ray looked down to avoid the sergeant's gaze, but then something stirred within him and he broke into a half smile.

"Top o' the morn to ya, Sergeant," Ray said in the best imitation of an Irish brogue he could muster, and then he winked. He followed his family into church, whistling the melody of the sea shanty "What Do You Do with a Drunken Sailor?" With a grin still stretched across his face, Ray sat down next to his mother in their usual spot in the second row of pews.

The service ran its course. Ray stood up and sat down, and there were songs and a few sessions where everyone bowed their heads in prayer. Reverend Smithson's sermon was about someone named Saul who was traveling to Damascus for some reason or other. Ray tried to pay attention — the sermon often

286

came up in conversation over Sunday dinner — but his mind wandered. He'd been to Salem only a few times, and all he really remembered were the docks. Now he tried to visualize the House of the Seven Gables, but he couldn't get a picture of it in his head.

He could see Richard Wonson clearly enough, though. Richard was thirty-five if he was a day, much too old for Maggie. Surely she would see that. Everyone around Ray stood up and started to sing again. He stood too and looked intently over his mother's shoulder at the hymnal, as if he were reading the words. After a few more ups and downs, the service ended and they began strolling home.

"I'm glad that's over," Elizabeth said as soon as they were out of earshot.

"Surely that would have been more unpleasant if John Pitt had been in church today," Emily said.

"No doubt Pitt will be the biggest problem," Ray said, "but Sergeant Smith was not happy about the situation either. He'll talk to Pitt, and they'll make a stink. At the deacons' meeting, Reverend Smithson said Seamus was welcome when he was old enough to come alone. I think what he really meant was that he was welcome as long as Maggie didn't come with him."

"Perhaps we need to remind the good reverend of what he said before Pitt can get to him."

"Yes, Libby, and maybe we can get to the other deacons too, before they all get together and come up with some self-righteously stupid idea. If you can talk to Mr. Sewall, Mr. Tarr, and Mr. Babson, I can speak to the other three. Ray, perhaps you could talk to the reverend, since you were there when he said Seamus could come to church without Maggie."

"All right. I'll strike while the iron's hot." Ray started back to the church.

Reverend and Mrs. Smithson were still on the front steps, saying their goodbyes to the last parishioners. "Reverend, when you're done, might I have a word?" Ray asked.

"Certainly, Ray. Martha and I always have a cup of tea after the service. Would you like to join us?"

Soon Ray found himself in the parlor of the modest parish house, seated at a table in a simple wooden chair while Mrs. Smithson poured tea and served a plate of hard sugar cookies. The white plaster walls were bare, and two pewter candlesticks adorned the oak mantel above the fireplace. The reverend sat across from him. "I was delighted to see you in church today, Ray. How is the fishing?"

"Excellent. The cod are as big this year as I've ever seen them. Not many halibut on Georges, though. Some think we've caught all the big ones."

"With the number of boats increasing every year, I do worry that we'll catch every last fish in the ocean, and then what will we do?"

"It's a big ocean; we'll never clean them all out."

288

"I hope you're right. So what is it you wanted to see me about?"

"Reverend, you may have noticed that we had the young O'Grady boy, Seamus, with us this morning."

"I did notice him, indeed. He was right there with you in the second row. He has a strong voice."

"Yes, he seems to have taken to singing, although perhaps with more volume than art. I know the deacons are uncomfortable with his mother coming to church, but I recall you saying that Seamus was welcome as soon as he was old enough to come alone. He isn't exactly alone, but my mother and Emily Wonson have taken an interest in his religious education, and they would like to continue bringing him to church. They asked me to discuss the subject with you."

Mrs. Smithson sat down at the table and looked at her husband. It was obvious even to Ray that this was a subject they had discussed before. "Not everyone will approve," the reverend said, looking at his wife as she straightened in her chair, "but as I've said before, that boy cannot be blamed for the sins of his mother. I commend the efforts of your mother and Mrs. Wonson to give him a religious education. He is most welcome in our church."

Mrs. Smithson stood up and left the parlor without a word, and a moment later a door upstairs could be heard closing abruptly. "You should warn your mother what she is up against, though. Mrs. Smithson is a charitable soul, but she has a blind spot on this matter. Her reaction is likely to be repeated in many homes around the parish."

"Thank you. I think Mother knows that, but she believes bringing Seamus to church is the Christian thing to do. I'll take my leave now; I hope I haven't upset your Sunday dinner."

"Don't worry," the reverend said with a twinkle in his eye. "It is good for a man of God to fast now and again."

By the time Ray got back to Middle Street, everyone was sitting down to dinner, and Maggie was being shown to her seat by Richard Wonson. "Ray, how nice to see you," Richard said as he pushed in Maggie's chair. He extended his hand to Ray, who shook it without enthusiasm.

"Hello," Ray said. "Miss O'Grady, my compliments."

"Hello, Ray," Maggie said. "Certainly it could be Maggie now, couldn't it?"

"Yes, of course . . . Maggie," Ray said in a softer tone.

"Come now, dear, we're serving," Elizabeth said. "You can sit between Em and Seamus."

Ray sat down. "Richard," Elizabeth asked, "would you carve?"

"My pleasure," Richard said. He stood at one end of the polished mahogany table and sliced the brisket, his head bobbing happily back and forth.

"Richard knows everything there is to know about meats," Maggie said. "Last night he took Em's cousin Charlotte and me to a fine restaurant in Salem. You should have heard him tell that waiter just what cut of pork to bring us."

Richard smiled proudly.

"Well, I suppose a butcher should know his way around a pig," Ray said to no one in particular.

Elizabeth gave her son a disapproving look.

Emily changed the subject. "So how did you find Salem, Maggie? Was it your first time there?"

"Me first, yes, but it won't be me last. Mrs. Ingersoll was so nice. She gave me a tour o' the House o' the Seven Gables; it's been in her family for decades. Curious readers must be such a bother, but you'd never know it from how courteous she was. The odd thing is the house has only three gables. And I don't believe that business about it being haunted. Salem is proud of its ghosts and witches, but I think the stories are mostly made up to get the curious to visit. Richard was a darling; he escorted me all around town. And Ray, there was a merchant ship unloading at the dock. It made me think o' the great naval battles of the War of 1812."

She turned to Elizabeth. "I thought of your husband too, Mrs. Stevens. You must have been proud o' him handling such big ships."

"Indeed, I was very proud of Gus. He sailed those ships all around the world, to every continent. He was never comfortable with the little fishing boats that Ray likes so much." Elizabeth frowned on remembering the pain Gus felt when no one would hire him. "I don't like the fishing boats either; they're just too dangerous."

Ray let the conversation drift over him, hoping only that the dinner would come to a speedy conclusion and that Richard would go away soon. When Seamus made a fort out of his mashed potatoes, Ray helped him fill it with gravy and then, to the boy's delight, bombarded it with peas until Elizabeth put a stop to it.

When dinner was over, Richard walked Maggie and Seamus home. After they were gone, Ray took the last few editions of the *Cape Ann Advertiser* to the sitting room — his mother saved the newspapers for him when he was at sea — and sat down to catch up on the news. He wasn't normally a drinker, but as he sat there with his papers, he drank glass after glass of sherry. He shuffled the pages but couldn't concentrate on the news. Finally it was dark, and he told his mother he was going to the boat and she shouldn't wait up.

The buildings on each side of Duncan Street framed the Summer Triangle in the eastern sky. *Too late to take an evening star sight now,* Ray thought as he walked downhill. The sun had set long ago, and now Vega and Deneb reflected off the silent surface of the harbor in long streaks of white. Maybe the time wasn't

292

right for this, he said to himself. But no, he was twenty-two years old; this was overdue.

He opened the red door and walked in. A few men were sitting in the bar, all smoking their pipes; the blue haze hung in lazy clouds just above eye level. Sylvie was surprised to see Ray, but she said nothing. Maggie was at the corner of the bar, speaking with a customer. She saw him and looked up quizzically, not understanding at first. But there was no stopping him now; his courage was up. He walked over and slapped two silver dollars down on the bar. "I'll have your finest lady," he said to Maggie.

Maggie's face went blank. She looked at the coins, then looked back at him. "Me finest lady costs ten dollars," she said coldly.

Sylvie looked quizzically at Maggie — they'd always had just one price — but Maggie avoided eye contact. Ray fished into his pocket, and one after another, out came eight more coins. He looked up at Maggie and pointed at the ten silver dollars now sitting on the bar. She picked up the coins slowly and placed them in her apron. "Follow me," she said matter-of-factly.

Up the stairs they went: to the second-floor landing, then to the third. They came to a door; she opened it and directed him inside. In the middle of the room was a four-poster bed. From each post, translucent cloth hung like a loosely reefed tops'l. He ran his fingers across the silk bedsheets; he'd never felt anything so smooth, so luxurious. Out the bay window he could see the *Parsons* at her berth, Altair now just visible above her foremast. The door closed behind him with a gentle click. He turned, and she was standing there.

"*I* am me finest lady" was all Maggie said.

The next morning the orange light of dawn danced through the bay window, and the caws of the Harbor Cove seagulls echoed off the Rocky Neck shore. Maggie had just climbed back into bed after checking on Seamus, who was still asleep in the anteroom. She snuggled down under the bedclothes and stroked Ray's muscular back.

He rolled over to face her, his eyes two bright splashes of color between his deeply tanned forehead and his dark beard. "Good morning, Maggie," he said. "That was the best night of my life."

"Not Miss O'Grady *now*, is it?" she said playfully. She lay on her side in a diaphanous white robe. Her head was propped up on her arm, her elbow on the pillow, her hair in mild disarray.

"No, it's Maggie now, my beautiful Maggie."

He rolled toward her and took her into his arms. They kissed, but when his hand slid too far down her back, she pushed him away. "Do you have another ten dollars?" she asked coquettishly.

He frowned and pulled off the bedclothes as if to get up, but when he looked down at himself, in arousal now, the smile returned to his face. "I'll have to go to the bank," he said, "but I'm not dressed for that. Any possibility you could extend me credit?"

She giggled, then reached over and stroked the inside of his thigh. "There is another way," she said with a coy smile and a cocked head. "You had a fine proposal a while ago, but the time wasn't right. . . . You might have better luck now."

Ray's smile broadened to capture his whole face. "Maggie O'Grady, will you . . ."

"Now stop right there, Raymond Stevens. You can't propose to a lady while you're in bed."

Ray stood up and led Maggie over to the bay window. The sun was now up over Rocky Neck and she was in silhouette, every perfect curve visible through her robe. He stood before her naked, every inch of him brightly lit in the early-morning sunshine. He got down on one knee, took her hand, and looked up into her eyes. "Maggie O'Grady, will you be my wife?"

She got down on both her knees and kissed him, a long, slow, deep kiss. "Yes, Ray Stevens, yes, I will be your wife."

Two months later, in a gentle breeze and under a deep blue sky, Ray and Maggie were married on the deck of the *Benjamin Parsons*. Paul Tobey officiated. The *Parsons* was all dolled up, colorful flags and bunting fluttering in the wind. She was anchored off Niles Beach, not a hundred yards from where Ray dove after flounder and crab as a child.

Ray's crewmates and the ladies of Fannies lined the deck. Elizabeth and Emily were there in their Sunday best, and Seamus was a little gentleman in short pants, jacket, bow tie, and a derby. Jane did not attend, nor did any of the other parishioners from the Universalist except Spashy McCloud, who wore a colorful madras jacket, a festive red bow tie, and a felt flat top.

Robby was Ray's best man, and Sylvie was Maggie's bridesmaid. Maggie wore a golden lace gown and a broad-brimmed hat. Ray wore his brand-new Sunday suit for the first time. Robby had found a signaling cannon that was fired as they were pronounced man and wife. Sylvie caught the bouquet, and the next day she and Robby eloped. She had said no to his request that he see Winnie during their courtship, and Robby felt he had endured celibacy long enough.

Chapter 26

Gloucester — August 1865

Ray pulled his ancient dory up onto the pebbly sand of Niles Beach. Pavilion Beach was closer to home, but it was closer to the fishing docks too. Swimming at Pavilion when the wind was wrong could mean coming home with pogy oil in your hair and fish scales on your feet. Niles was not swish, not by any means; it was not one of those beaches of brilliant white soft sand that nurture grand hotels and exclusive beach clubs. It was small, rocky below the low-tide mark, and populated with seaweed, driftwood, and the occasional dead seagull.

Seamus took off his shoes, rolled up his trousers, and waded out into the chilly water, where he spotted a school of minnows that he chased in the shallows. Then a crab caught his interest, and he took off after it. Ray walked up the beach and sat on a weathered log to watch him play. A bush covered with the smooth orange fruits of wild rose brushed against the back of his shirt, and tiny gnats swarmed overhead. Out in the harbor a schooner rounded Eastern Point, headed for home.

One day long ago Augie had built a massive sand castle here, its walls reinforced with driftwood and pebbles. He had boasted that it would withstand the tides for a hundred years. Ray could see him still, hands on his hips, admiring his creation. The sand castle was long gone, of course, leaving no more of a trace than Augie himself had left. Ray brushed away the gnats and walked to the high-tide mark, where he looked down on the now flat sand that was once a great castle.

Before long, it was time to go. Seamus wanted to row, but the oars were too big for him, so Ray put him on his lap and they rowed together. When they reached Vincent Cove, Ray slid the dory in parallel to the small boat float, and Seamus scampered over the bow. He tied the painter to the foot rail with a clove hitch and two half hitches, as Ray had taught him to do.

In the cellar Mildred was cooking, and Lucy and Winnie were eating their eggs and bacon, when Ray and Seamus walked in through Fannies' back door with their *fruits de mer*. Ray had moved into Fannies on his wedding night, and now shared Maggie's spacious bedroom on the third floor. A small room that had been used for storage was fixed up for Seamus.

Seamus emptied his bag at one end of the breakfast table, and out came starfishes, mussels, and an energetic crab that scampered about and attacked one of Winnie's toes. "Get 'em outta here!" she shrieked as she leapt out of her chair.

"You're becomin' quite the fisherman, Seamus. One day soon you'll be tellin' your papa how to go 'bout his business," Lucy said.

"We got these at Niles Beach, Aunt Lucy — rowed there in our dory. The tide was real low; that's the best time."

Maggie came downstairs to the cellar after doing the books. She gave Ray a kiss on the forehead and admired the catch with motherly interest before sitting down across from him.

"My dear," he said, "I bumped into Paul Tobey at the dock this morning. He's finally made up his mind to commission a new schooner. I'll be skipper of the *Parsons* from now on."

"Oh, Ray!" Maggie reached across the table to hug him. "Did everyone hear? Ray's been promoted to captain!"

"That's not all," Ray said. "I've been to see Rufus Harrison."

"About what, m'love?"

"If you approve, I want to adopt Seamus. I thought Rufus would know how to do it. I want to be his father — officially."

"Oh m'love, of course I approve! What do we have to do?"

"Most of it's just paperwork, and he said he could prepare that, no problem. But the father will have to be notified. If he objects, it could be trouble."

"Oh m'God! Do we really have to stir that pot, now?"

"Rufus said if we didn't know who the father was, we could publish a notice in the paper that I planned to adopt 'Seamus O'Grady, father unknown.'"

"That makes me sound like a tart. I don't want to do that."

"No, I thought not. And the other problem is we *do* know who the father is, so it would be a lie. We'd risk losing Seamus."

"William won't want him, for sure, but he'll be none too happy if some court papers say he's the father. He might have Seth sent back to jail in Ireland. I can't risk that."

"Rufus says William can't hold that over your head anymore. Turns out one Seth O'Grady of Boston served this last year in the 11th Massachusetts. When he was mustered out, he became a citizen of the United States. He's safe now."

"You mean — I might be able to see him again?"

Ray reached into his pocket and pulled out two train tickets. "How about tomorrow?"

Seth was astonished to see Maggie on the doorstep of his father-in-law's North Boston bakery. He'd given her up for dead years ago. After recovering from the shock, he ushered Maggie and Ray upstairs to the living quarters he shared with his in-laws. He had a pronounced limp and needed a cane to get up the stairs. They were joined by his wife, Louisa, and their two boys, twins just learning to walk. Louisa's English was broken, but she could make herself understood well enough. After a bit of time, she took the boys to their room for a nap.

Then Maggie told Seth of her affair with William and explained why she had lied about going to San Francisco. She did not mention Fannies. She asked him to promise to stay away from William. The affair was long ago, and going after him now would be bad for everyone. But she needn't have worried.

"The war changed me," Seth said. "I was a cook in the army. It was hard work, but it kept me out o' harm's way, right up 'til we came to a tiny bend in the road called Cold Harbor. I'll never forget that day. Our captain came through the mess tent and said we were all needed on the line. One big push to end it all, he said, one big push and we'd break through to Richmond and the war would be o'er. I took off me apron and they handed me a rifle. I barely knew how to shoot it — a week's training with a gun is all we mess boys had. By afternoon, I was in a trench and the command came to fix our bayonets; this nice young fella next to me showed me how. Then the captain gave the order, and out o' the trenches we went.

"It was like every gun on the planet went off. The sound pounded your ears so hard you couldn't hear yourself think. I ran forward with me mates. Just held on to the gun, never did pull the trigger. We were out in the middle of a big field and the Rebs were behind these barricades firing away. Men started to fall. I tripped o'er one poor fella whose chest was blown open, but I got up and kept running. A cannonball hit in front o' me, and I was covered by dirt and stung by flying pebbles, but I kept running. There were big orange flashes, and the noise from the cannon was so loud you could feel it vibrate in your chest, but I kept running.

"And then . . . 'twas like a circus strongman took a fence post and swung it against me leg with all his might. I landed face-first in the mud, and when I tried to get up, I couldn't move. Then that nice fella who showed me how to put on the bayonet was kneeling o'er me. He asked if I was all right, and then his head just disappeared . . . what was left o' him fell right on me. . . . What a cannonball will do to a human being . . . the top part o' him was gone, and when the rest landed on me, his innards poured out. Me face was covered by his guts. It stung me eyes."

Seth spoke softly with a faraway look. "I was a cook, just a cook, mind you. I talked my way into being a cook. 'Twasn't hard, I had experience cooking, you see. I never thought I'd be there in the middle of it all.

"I lay there in that mud for two days. The day after the battle was hot as Hades. That miserable swampland — you wouldn't believe the flies that came round. The second night was worse. The wild dogs took to gnawing on the dead. I shooed 'em away from what was left o' me friend, but later I fell asleep, and he got eaten some. I woke up when the dogs took a nip o' me.

"I prayed, Maggie. I swore I'd never hurt another soul if God would just let me live. You don't have to worry about me fighting that rich bastard. He'll go to hell for what he did, for sure. That'll be his punishment. I'm just doing me best every day to lead a God-fearing life. That's the deal I made out on that horrible battlefield, and I'm keeping me part o' the bargain.

"Finally, two days after the shooting, they called a truce, and medics came and took me to the field hospital. They say it took so long because our generals didn't want to admit we'd been beat. I was lucky — they didn't have to cut me leg off as they did with so many of the lads. But the bone never did entirely heal, and part o' the bullet's still with me. I'll be using this cane here for the rest o' me days. At least I've days left; we had thousands o' dead, stacked like cordwood they were. I'm the only one from the mess tent who survived. And we didn't get a foot closer to Richmond, not a bleeding foot closer."

Ray and Maggie left Seth in the early afternoon. Once seated on the train, Maggie leaned against Ray and put her head on his chest. "I came pretty close to losing me brother and never even knew it. What a time he's had, poor fella."

"I'm lucky to have missed all that. Seeing those twins made me want to adopt Seamus all the more. What do you think? Is it too dangerous to try?"

"There is nothing I'd like more, m'love. We'll get Rufus started with the paperwork as soon as we get back home."

Two days later, the *Parsons* put out to sea with Ray in command — his first Georges Bank trip as skipper. Seamus wanted to go along; he liked to fish, he said. He threw a tantrum when Ray told him he had to stay behind to take care of his mother.

The next day Mildred escorted Ted Stark into Maggie's office. "Welcome," Maggie said. "Please have a seat. I asked you to come because I have a bit of a delicate situation. Ray would like to adopt me son, Seamus, and our lawyer tells us that the boy's natural father will have to be named. I thought you might be able to help us make things run smoothly."

"I see. Mr. Hudson will be pretty mad about this. Your brother's still in the States?"

"Aye, but he's a war hero. Rufus says William can't touch him."

"That may well be. But a man with his wealth and connections can cause you considerable trouble. His father died last year, so Mr. Hudson has his hands on the family fortune now."

"I didn't know that. Is there anything you can do that would make this easier for me?"

"There usually is. I'll poke around, but it won't be cheap. I want a hundred-dollar retainer. Sidin' with ya on this will cost me business."

Maggie pulled out her checkbook.

"Very good," Stark said as she handed him her signed check. "I'll report back by the end of next week, but I have one piece of advice right now. While this business is going on, you should move your family to respectable housing. You don't want to be explaining to a judge why you're raising your boy in a whorehouse."

"For sure, there are nicer ways to refer to Fannies, but I take your point. I look forward to hearing what you find out."

After showing Stark out, Maggie walked up to Elizabeth's house and knocked on the door.

"What an unexpected surprise, Maggie dear," Elizabeth said. "Please come in. Em and I were just having tea. Would you like a cup?"

"Thank you. I do love your Chinese tea."

"Gus used to bring it back for me by the case. It's hard to get now."

They sat down at the table in the sitting room, and Emily entered from the back hallway.

"Libby, I have a big favor to ask you. We've just started legal proceedings to have Ray adopt Seamus."

305

"I know, dear. I'm so excited about officially having a grandson!"

"He couldn't have a better grandmother. Here's me problem. Our advisors have suggested that it would look better to the judge if Seamus were not being raised at Fannies. So the big favor I'm asking is whether Ray and Seamus and I could live here with you until the adoption is approved."

Elizabeth glanced at Emily, and she spoke next. "How long do you think that would be?"

"It depends on whether the father raises a fuss, but I'm told that it normally takes three to six months. And . . . there's a bit more to the favor I'm asking. I'll still be running Fannies in the evenings, and Ray will be at sea much of the time, so I wondered if you'd mind babysitting Seamus in the evenings. He goes to bed early, so he wouldn't be much of a bother."

"So we'd — I'd be here alone with Seamus most evenings?" Elizabeth asked.

"Yes, but I could arrange for a babysitter if that's too much trouble."

Both Elizabeth and Emily looked relieved.

"No need," Elizabeth said. "It will be my pleasure to have you stay here for a while. Seamus can stay in Augie's room, and we'll put a double bed in Ray's room for the two of you."

They moved in that night.

Two weeks later, Rufus asked Maggie to come to his office on Front Street. "You're going to want to sit down for this," he said. "I'm so sorry, but Mr. Hudson wants the boy. Here, look at this." Rufus handed her a letter. "I got it in the morning mail." He pulled out the handkerchief he always had neatly folded in his jacket pocket and wiped his eyes and nose.

The letter was neatly written in a clear and elegant hand on heavy off-white paper. The law firm's name, Hughes and Black, and its Boston address were embossed in raised type. The letter read:

Dear Mr. Harrison:

We represent Mr. William Hudson and have your notice of action. Please consider this our appearance in this matter.

Mr. Hudson does not consent to Mr. Stevens' adoption of the child in question. The mother, a woman of low morals, seduced Mr. Hudson in a weak moment when he was not in complete control of his faculties. If this isolated weakness on his part resulted in a child, he will take responsibility and raise the child as a Hudson. The child shall be raised with the utmost propriety and Christian morality. He will matriculate at Brookline Country Day School, the Phillips Exeter Academy, and Harvard College. If your clients care about the welfare of the child, we are sure they will see that being raised a Hudson will be for the best.

Please forward a certified copy of the child's birth certificate so that we may begin our due diligence. Please also forward us a list of the names and addresses of all the men with whom the mother copulated in the six to twelve months before the child's birth, to the extent she is able to recall them all.

It will be to your clients' benefit to avoid airing all the sordid details of the mother's sinful past in open court. We propose a meeting at your earliest convenience to expedite resolving this matter privately to the child's benefit.

We request the favor of a prompt reply.

Very truly yours,
P. Rennyson Hughes

Maggie read the letter, but the first time through it was a blur. When she read it a second time, shock turned to anger. She jumped out of her seat. "That pompous, lying dog. I 'seduced him in a weak moment,' ha!" She stormed from one end of Rufus' small office to the other. "That 'moment' lasted for three months. I seduced *him*! I thought he was a gentleman. What tripe this letter is! No one will believe this, Rufus, no one."

She finished with her arms braced against Rufus' desk, the now crumpled letter in her right hand. Her face was flushed. "So what do we do next?" she asked forcefully, looking down at him.

Rufus tried his best to avoid acknowledging Maggie's outburst. "Well, he asks for the birth certificate. That's a reasonable request. I suppose we could get him that. About his request for the list of men . . ."

"Rufus, there is only one man on that list, and his name is William Hudson. But you'll need to write that name at least a hundred times because he was afflicted by this 'isolated weakness' o' his every day that summer. So you write this pompous blowhard of a lawyer and you tell him that, and you send him Seamus' birth certificate too. You can explain to him that William Hudson's son was born in the cellar o' the whorehouse where that self-anointed paragon o' Christian morality dumped the boy's mother.

"And you tell him we'll meet with him. We'll meet in Gloucester, and when he comes down here, he can also meet the son he hasn't cared a whit about 'til now. And finally, you can tell him it'll be a cold day in hell before he gets his hypocritical lily-white hands on me Seamus!"

Rufus looked plaintively up at Maggie and spoke haltingly: "I . . . ah . . . I don't know if I'm up to this. I don't handle conflict well, if the truth be known. Hughes and Black, they're out of my league."

Maggie took a deep breath and focused on Rufus. His shoulders drooped; he looked as if he wanted to slide right out of his leather chair and under his desk. She could see he was scared — scared of her after that outburst, and scared of going up against the fancy Boston lawyers and the rich William Hudson. Seeing him in such distress calmed her. "Don't worry," she said in a tone she might have used with Seamus. "This is going to be all right. Now, you write the letter back to Mr. P. Rennyson what's-his-name. Use your own words. It should sound like a lawyer and not like an enraged ma protecting her kit. If we have to go to court, I'll find someone else to do battle there."

Rufus dabbed his forehead with his handkerchief. This was the second time this morning she'd seen him use it. "I'll write the letter. Thank you for understanding. I've been avoiding confrontation my whole life. I'm too old to learn how to deal with it now."

Maggie walked up to Elizabeth's house through a fog that had crept in the night before and now chilled her to the bone. She'd made a mistake serving papers on William. Now that she'd calmed down, hollow fear had replaced her rage — she might lose her son. She had not seen this coming. Why did William want him now? What could have changed his mind?

When she arrived, she found Seamus in the sitting room playing with a cedar-plank boat Ray had made for him before going to sea this last time. Seamus announced that the boat had been attacked by pirates and he was fighting them off with cannons. "Boom, boom," he kept repeating as he maneuvered his boat around the rug.

"He's been fighting that battle ever since you left today," Elizabeth said. "The pirates may be winning."

"Are the pirates winning, dear?" Maggie asked.

"Walk the plank," Seamus said with a growl. "Arghh, walk the plank."

"I think you're right." Maggie slumped in her chair. "I'm afraid the pirates are winning their battle with me too. William wants custody. No, he *demands* custody; that's what his lawyer said. What have I done?"

Seamus dropped his boat on the floor and came to sit with his mother. "Don't worry, Ma. No more pirates — all gone. Don't cry."

That night, Maggie lay down on Ray's side of the double bed, the side she always slept on when he was at sea. Two hours later, she jerked awake. Seamus had been in her dreams, wearing a uniform of hat, short pants, blue blazer, and bow tie. He must have been going to the private school William's lawyer had mentioned.

That lawyer was right about one thing — with William, Seamus would get the best education money could buy, and when he was grown he would have a place in society. With her, he would be raised in a brothel, and what would become of him after that? She tossed and turned and stared at the ceiling until daylight slowly filled the room.

Chapter 27

Gloucester — September 1865

Maggie was chatting with Sylvie at the end of the bar when Josh Collins waddled down the stairs, holding up his trousers with one hand and carrying his plaid shirt with the other. He dropped the shirt on one of the tables and finished buttoning his trousers. "I want my two dollars back," he said as he was putting on his shirt.

"What's the matter, Josh? Didn't Anne take care of you?" Maggie asked.

"Anne ain't the problem. We'd just got started, and ol' Winnie burst in screamin'. She pulled Anne right off a' me, and then there was a big catfight. I got the hell outta there — that Winnie's nuts. Just give me my money back."

After Josh left, Maggie went upstairs. Anne was sitting at her dressing table, looking in the mirror, dabbing a cut above her right eye. Maggie asked what had happened.

"Winnie busted in here and attacked me just as I was gettin' it on with Josh. She shoved me off a' him and then started slappin' me around. I never seen Winnie crazy like that. She's strong for an ol' broad. Josh was no goddamn good. He just snuck outta here like a scared mouse."

"I offered Josh a free visit tomorrow," Maggie said. "I'd hate to lose him; he's been a steady customer for years."

"For Chrissake, you could worry a minute 'bout me sittin' here bleedin' before you start countin' your damn money!"

Maggie held her tongue and left without responding. The door to Winnie's room was closed. She knocked.

"Go away!" Winnie yelled.

"It's Maggie. We need to talk."

"Go away!" Winnie let out a loud hiccup. "I don't wanna talk now."

Maggie opened the door. Long ago, Fannie had removed the locks so she could more easily help a woman in trouble. Winnie was sitting in the plush red chair by the window, a shot glass in her hand, a half-empty bottle of whiskey on the small table nearby. Her face was flushed.

"What the hell is wrong with you?" Maggie demanded.

"That slut took Josh away from me. He's been mine for years — always kept him happy. That little whore." Winnie drained her glass in one gulp and poured herself another.

"Josh asked for her, Winnie. Lots o' men ask for Anne. You can't go beating her up for that."

"It ain't right."

"What's not right is you breaking in on Anne when she's with a customer. We may lose Josh's business because of what you did. And Josh will talk. Who knows how many more we might lose? I still don't know how bad Anne's hurt. For sure, it'll cost us plenty if you've put her out of service."

"Just send 'em to me. I'll take care of 'em."

"You're too drunk to take care of anyone."

Winnie threw her glass at Maggie, but it went high over her shoulder, splattering whiskey as it flew by. Maggie stepped forward and grabbed the bottle off the table. "You sober up. This will not happen again," she said in a steady, determined voice. She left with the whiskey bottle in hand.

The next day Maggie traveled to Salem to meet with David West, a former Essex County prosecuting attorney. "West's tough, and he knows his way around the courthouse," Stark had said when recommending him. West's secretary, an older woman with short gray hair tucked under a widow's cap and slightly stooped shoulders, greeted Maggie and directed her to a couch covered in cracked brown leather. A moment later, she escorted Maggie through an inner door to West's office.

West stood behind a desk covered with stacks of papers. The walls were bare, except for a bar certificate and a certified copy of a judgment, both framed and hanging on the wall behind his desk. He was forty-one years old, five foot seven, and clean-shaven. His hair was closely cropped, and he wore a brown suit with a white shirt.

Stark had already filled him in on Maggie's case, and she now handed him the crumpled letter from William's lawyer. He invited her to sit, and seated himself to read it. "Well, Mrs. Stevens, you have a difficult case," he said when he finished. "What do you want from me?"

"Truth be told, I'm sorry I've stirred up this hornet's nest, but for sure, there's no use crying about that now. I'd like the court to allow me husband to adopt me son. But . . . me main goal is to hold on to Seamus. If I could just drop this case and have William Hudson forget about me boy, I'd be pleased."

"I'm afraid it's too late for that. It's clear from this letter that Mr. Hudson wants the boy, and it seems he's willing to fight for him. I understand that you're running a brothel, is that right?"

"Yes."

"And until very recently, you've been raising the boy there?"

"Yes, but I don't know that William — that's Mr. Hudson — knows that."

"Stark told me Mr. Hudson's lawyer had a detective snooping around. I think we must assume that he knows the whole story by now."

"Oh m'God."

"Renny Hughes is a pompous man, but he's a first-class lawyer. He'll use your situation to his client's advantage, just as I would if I were in his shoes."

"Are you afraid to go up against him?" Maggie asked.

"Oh, no ma'am. There's nothing I like more than going up against a high-toned swell like Renny Hughes. . . . That's not quite right. It's not the going up against him I like; it's beating him that's satisfying. But winning your case is not going to be easy."

"Surely a court will be reluctant to separate a young boy from his mother."

"In a normal case, that's quite right, of course. But it's not normal for the mother to be running a bawdy house. The Puritans founded our Commonwealth, and while we may sometimes forget it in these looser times, that famously rigid morality is not far below the surface. The Hudsons are well known for their moral fiber. While it appears evident that this particular Hudson has strayed from the straight and narrow path, I'm concerned that a judge would still find him to be a far more righteous parent than — well — than a woman who sells sex for a living, if I may be so blunt."

317

Maggie stiffened. "Are you saying me cause is hopeless?"

"Not hopeless, no. I tell the most desperate of my clients to never lose hope, at least not until the last appeal is pursued and the hangman is tightening the noose, and even then there may still be a pardon. You never know what might turn up. No, I'm just telling you to be realistic. If we go to court, I'm afraid you'll be in grave danger of losing custody of your son. I don't say this to alarm you. It's my duty to give you the facts as I see them, and I'd be doing you a disservice if I sugarcoated it. But I sense you already know this. Stark says you're no fool, and despite his faults, he's a good judge of character."

"I appreciate your candid advice. So what can we do?"

"My advice is to settle with him. Let me negotiate an arrangement where you share custody."

"Oh, no, Mr. West! I can't bear the thought of sending Seamus off to that man. I don't trust him at all. William would lie to me son and then ply him with all the riches at his disposal. He would turn Seamus against me, for sure. No, no, I am not willing to share custody."

"Well, then we fight. Mr. Hudson won't want a public trial. He'll want to keep this quiet. Let's take him up on his offer to meet, and we'll do our damnedest to convince him to give up. We'll see just how much he wants the boy. But I must say, he's acting like a man who's willing to be embarrassed if that's what it takes.

Now, let me warn you: if he won't give up, I may talk to you again about some sort of joint custody arrangement. It would be better than nothing."

"I just wonder why — after ignoring Seamus for years, why is he doing this?"

"I understand that his marriage has been childless. He may want an heir and see this as the only way to get one. He probably considers it his duty to carry on the grand Hudson dynasty."

"Do you speak from experience, Mr. West? Do you have an heir?"

"No, ma'am. There is no West dynasty. My father was a locksmith, God rest his soul, and his father was a farmer. I have no heir, nor even a wife. I do have family, though; that's my mother you met on the way in. She's been my secretary since Father died. She took care of me when I was a lad; I'm taking care of her now that she's alone."

"You must be close."

"Yes, we are; I'm an only child, just like your Seamus. Mother would understand why it's so important to you to fight for your son."

"Yes, I daresay she would. . . . All right, please set up the meeting. I'd like to meet them in Gloucester, though."

"Yes, better to be on our own turf. I'll see to it."

That night most of the fishing fleet was at sea, so it was quieter than usual at Fannies. Lucy and Anne were busy upstairs, and another customer was waiting for Anne. Even though it was still early, Maggie was sipping her second rum. Her depressed mood was obvious to Sylvie, who, like any good bartender, asked Maggie if she wanted to talk.

"Sylvie, me new lawyer as much as told me I'll lose Seamus if we take this case to court. And now that I got it started, I can't stop it if William keeps pushing. I've mucked everything up." Maggie finished her rum and put the glass in front of Sylvie, who poured her another.

"I can't let him take away me boy. Seamus is the one part o' me life I could show me ma and da and be proud of. The rest o' this . . ." Maggie looked slowly around the room. "I should never have gotten in so deep here. One thing led to another. I might just take Seamus and run. . . . But I don't think Ireland would be safe. . . . And anywhere in America, they'd track me down. . . . Maybe Australia — do you know anything about Australia, Sylvie?"

"No, I don't. Where do you think Ray fits into this?"

"I don't know. . . . They must have fishing boats in Australia."

"His roots here are deep."

"For shure," Maggie said sadly, the rum having its desired effect. "I don't want to choose between the two o' them."

She finished her drink and went to greet a new customer. He also wanted Anne, but she managed to steer him to Faith. She took his two dollars, and he walked upstairs.

"I'm going to raise the rates on Anne," Maggie said, settling back in at the bar. "They all want her, for shure. We might as well make hay while the shun shines, and maybe the other ladies will pick up some extra work. . . . Australia, that's the place. I could get a fresh shtart — make me living as a writer. . . ."

Two more men walked in, and Maggie gave them a hearty greeting. They both wanted Anne, but when they heard she cost four dollars, they chose Lydia and Sarah instead. Both were available right away, and at two dollars each, they seemed a bargain.

Chapter 28

Gloucester — October 1865

The meeting with William and his lawyer took place three weeks later at Elizabeth's house. West showed them into the dining room, where Ray and Maggie were already seated. Renny Hughes wore a three-piece suit of the finest English wool. His shirt was starched white, and his leather shoes were brightly shined. His hair was neatly combed, his skin was pale, and his lips were thin. He carried a black leather briefcase with brightly polished gold clasps.

William was neatly dressed in a tailored dark gray suit. His hairline had receded some and he had put on a few pounds, but otherwise he had changed little in the five years since Maggie had seen him. Introductions were made, and everyone sat down at the table. Maggie spoke first. "William, would you like to meet Seamus?"

"Yes, he would, Miss O'Grady," Hughes answered for William. "And please refer to my client as Mr. Hudson."

"It's *Mrs*. Stevens," Maggie said sharply. "I referred to your client as William because he asked me to refer to him as such when we last discussed the subject. He'll be Mr. Hudson to me today, and if we do our business well, I shall never need to address him again."

"Arhumpf," grumbled Hughes. He was not used to being lectured by anyone, certainly not by a woman, and especially not by Maggie's kind of woman.

Maggie went to the stairs and called to Elizabeth, who brought Seamus down to the dining room. "Mr. Hughes and Mr. Hudson, this is Mrs. Augustus Stevens, me mother-in-law. Seamus, this is Mr. Hughes and Mr. Hudson. Say hello, now."

"Hello," Seamus said obediently.

William was stunned. He was reminded of the portrait of himself as a child that hung in his mother's sitting room. It could have been Seamus' portrait, the likeness was that close. "How are you this morning, young man?" William asked. Seamus stared quietly at him without answering, so he tried again. "What do you want to do when you grow up?"

"Be a fisherman — like Papa," Seamus said.

William winced as if he had been pricked with a pin. Maggie smiled, and so did Ray. William stared silently at Seamus, as if looking back in time.

"Is there anything else you would like to say, *Mr*. Hudson?" Maggie finally asked.

"No," William said in a soft, sad voice.

Maggie cocked her head. "All right," she said, telling Seamus he could go back upstairs and finish the jigsaw puzzle he was working on. He looked confused, but Elizabeth took him by the hand and led him away.

William whispered something to Hughes. "My client is satisfied that the boy is his son," Hughes said. "I have prepared papers to take full custody immediately. The sooner the boy starts learning to be a Hudson, the better. We shall permit Miss — Mrs. Stevens — to visit the boy one day a month, in Boston. We will make arrangements for a suitable place to meet; the boy's nanny will be present for the entirety of her visit." He took a stack of papers out of his briefcase and placed them on the table.

"Of course, Mr. Hudson will compensate you for your expenses over these past five years," he continued, looking across the table at Maggie. He pulled two stacks of twenty-dollar gold coins from his jacket pocket and carefully placed them on the table directly in front of her. "Mr. Hudson will pay one thousand dollars, which I am sure we can all agree is more than generous." Maggie pushed her chair back from the table as if the gold coins were infected with a pox.

Hughes turned to West and pushed the legal papers across the table to him. West did not look down, but instead kept his eyes locked on Hughes. Hughes noticed West's stare and paused, giving West his opening: "Mrs. Stevens brought this action because her

324

husband wishes to adopt Seamus, and we are here today to settle any issues that might slow that process down. Mr. Hudson abandoned his son five years ago when he learned that Mrs. Stevens was pregnant. Mrs. Stevens and Seamus have made their way in this world since then, and now Mrs. Stevens is married to an upstanding man, a fishing boat captain, and they are raising Seamus here in this fine home. No court is going to come upon these facts and separate mother and child."

"Really, Counsel, do you think I was born yesterday?" Hughes said. "Your client is running a brothel in this dirty little town. She is obviously a woman of low morals and . . ."

"Now wait just one minute," Ray said, rising out of his seat, fists clenched. "No one talks about my wife that way, especially not in my house."

"Ray, let me handle this. It's what you're paying me for," West said evenly. Ray paused and looked at Maggie, who nodded and silently pleaded with him to sit down. As he did, she grasped his hands in hers and they looked into each other's eyes. William's aura of stoicism cracked for an instant at their expression of affection, but he immediately regained his composure and resumed his trance-like gaze.

"William Hudson is known throughout the Commonwealth as a man of breeding and industry, a man of the highest moral fiber," Hughes continued. "His ancestors have been patriots since before the days of the Revolution, and his own father did as much as any man to free the slaves. No judge will favor a harlot over a man like Mr. Hudson."

Ray's arm muscles contracted, and the veins in his neck bulged. Maggie gripped his hand as much to hold him back as for her own comfort. "Your client would do well to accept Mr. Hudson's very generous offer. The money will not be offered again," he said, gesturing toward the stacks of gold coins.

"It's true Mr. Hudson is well known," West responded, "and there can be no doubt that some of his ancestors were patriots. But his ancestors won't be the ones taking the witness stand, he will, and he will have a lot of explaining to do: why as a grown man he seduced an eighteen-year-old immigrant who'd just moved to this country; why he bedded her every night for three months; and why he shipped her off to give birth in a house of ill repute once he had her full with his child."

"That, sir, is slander," boomed Hughes, bringing both of his hands down on the table. "She seduced Mr. Hudson one night after he had taken ardent spirits. When he came to his senses and realized he had hired a tart, he dismissed her the very next day. The butler of the household will back him up on this. If your client says otherwise, she is a liar."

Ray started to rise again, but Maggie said, "Please, Ray," and he sat back down.

"Well then, it will be an interesting trial. Mr. Hudson's scullery maid," West looked down at a notepad before him, "one Gail Richards, will testify that the affair went on for months until one day my client came in crying and confessed she was in a family way. Miss Richards advised my client to tell Mr. Hudson about it. She did so, and several days later, she was gone from the household."

"The word of a scullery maid and a prostitute — is that what you're basing your case on?" Hughes said with a rhetorical sneer.

"That's enough," Ray said, standing up, angry but in control. "If you insult my wife one more time, no matter my lawyer's wishes or hers, I will come across this table and break that arrogant, upturned nose of yours."

Hughes looked at West, who gave no indication that he would restrain Ray this time. Maggie held her breath, and William remained staring straight ahead, expressionless. West continued as if nothing out of the ordinary had happened.

"Miss Richards and Mrs. Stevens are not my only witnesses, no." He rose and walked calmly to the sitting room, while Ray slowly sat down. Hughes stole a worried glance in Ray's direction.

West opened the door of the sitting room and motioned to someone inside. Ted Stark emerged and followed him back to the table. Despite having been waiting for a considerable time, Stark was still wearing his rumpled overcoat and bowler hat. He remained standing at one end of the dining room table while West reassumed his seat.

"Mr. Hughes, this is Mr. Edward Stark. I know I don't have to introduce Mr. Stark to Mr. Hudson," West said, now addressing William directly. William gave no hint of acknowledging Stark's existence now, let alone any prior acquaintance. "Mr. Stark, please tell Mr. Hughes how you came to meet Mr. Hudson."

"Well," Stark began, "Mr. Hudson used my services to investigate a fraudulent insurance claim. That's how we first met. When he got a maid in a family way, he called me again. I was acquainted with a woman who ran a brothel in Gloucester — Fannie was her name. So I told Mr. Hudson we could ship his problem to the brothel and keep it quiet. He thought that was a grand idea. He was scared his father would find out about his indiscretions and disinherit him. The elder Hudson had a well-known prudish streak."

"Do not insult Nathaniel Hudson, a man I had the honor of representing for thirty years," Hughes said. "A finer man never walked the streets of Boston, rest his soul."

"If ya say so," Stark continued indifferently. "Anyway, this here Mr. Hudson wasn't as consumed with moral issues as his father. He sent Maggie to me, and I took care a' his problem."

"Did he pay you?" West asked.

"Oh yes, he paid well. Gave me two hundred fifty dollars for my trouble, and he's been payin' the brothel fifty dollars a month ever since."

"Ridiculous! Preposterous!" Hughes exclaimed.

West reached into his bag and pulled out a check. "Here's this month's fifty-dollar check. It is a corporate check, signed by an H. Percival, who happens to be Mr. Hudson's butler. One of your witnesses, I believe you said. I don't think it will be hard to prove that your client made the payments."

"Mr. West, I understand the game you're playing. You think Mr. Hudson will be too embarrassed to go through with this case — that you can scare him into giving up. Well, you cannot. He knows that if you both go before a judge, he will win. It might be embarrassing, but he has decided that having his son is more important than a few ugly newspaper headlines, or even the difficulty this may cause in his marriage.

"That means your client will be far better off taking the money and accepting my client's offer to let her see the child occasionally. If she goes to court, she will lose both, and she will never see her child again. None of this bluster of yours matters. Your client is still a . . ." He looked at Ray, who was glaring at him from across the table. "Well, she manages a brothel. My client is a Hudson, and that is all that will matter in a court of law."

West looked gravely at Maggie, then at his own hands folded together on the table. Finally, after a long silence, he looked up. "No, Mr. Hughes, it *all* matters. Your client is the one claiming moral superiority. He has put his morals at issue, and he comes up wanting, seriously wanting."

Turning to William now, West said, "You remember Evan Stipple, Mr. Hudson? He's the man you paid eight hundred dollars to take your place in battle. It was a poor bargain for him; he was cut in half by a Reb cannonball during the Battle of Cold Harbor."

"Mr. West," Hughes interrupted, "you know it is perfectly legal to pay for a draft replacement. Mr. Hudson is a very important man with a job that was critical to our war economy."

"Yes, no doubt, Mr. Hughes. But buying your way out of danger is not how the Hudsons built their reputation for patriotism, is it? What's-his-name Hudson didn't pay another man to defend Breed's Hill, after all."

"James Hudson," Maggie said. Hughes looked at her with annoyance, while William maintained his stoic expression.

"Please, Mr. West," Hughes said with obvious disgust, "whether Mr. Hudson went to war or sent another man to fight for him is completely irrelevant here. You do understand the concept of relevance, don't you? You must have had some sort of legal training."

"You miss the point, Mr. Hughes," West continued. "Evan Stipple had a younger sister named Prudence." At this William winced just for a moment, but Maggie, Ray, and West all noticed. "Miss Stipple lives on Mount Vernon Street, just a few blocks from Mr. Hudson's townhouse, and we understand that Mr. Hudson is paying the rent."

"What a nice gesture, in honor of her dead brother," Hughes said, affecting boredom.

"I'm going to be plain with you, Mr. Hughes," West said. "It is no secret that Mr. Hudson and his wife spend little time together. They are hardly under the same roof for a full month all year. She seems to fancy Paris and Naples, while Mr. Hudson tends to business in Boston — but it isn't *all* business, is it, sir?" West asked, looking toward William. Now looking back at Hughes, West said, "Under the circumstances, it is understandable that Mr. Hudson would feel the need for female companionship, and he finds it with Miss Stipple."

"West, if you breathe a word of this false accusation outside this room, I shall have your license to practice law, by God I shall," Hughes said, bringing both his hands down on the table again.

West picked up his battered briefcase. He methodically shuffled some papers and eventually fished out a photograph, which he set on the table in front of Hughes and William. It showed a man and a woman sitting up in bed together, drinking from wine goblets. Both were naked. The woman was young, with long curly hair that did not quite cover her bare breasts. Although the photo was dark and blurred where the

331

subjects had moved, there was no mistaking that the man was William Hudson.

"Nice-looking lady, Willy," Ray said, finally relaxing in his chair. "You should take this money and buy her some clothes." He leaned forward and pushed the gold coins toward William; as he did so, the stacks toppled over into a messy pile. "She'll catch her death dressed like that."

William's stoicism dissolved. He put his head in his hands, while Hughes tried to save the day: "This is the grossest invasion of privacy I have seen in my long years of practice!" But he couldn't find anything else to say.

"Interesting time to be a lawyer, isn't it, Mr. Hughes?" West said, leaning back in his chair. "Instead of just talking about an event, an actual photograph of it can come into evidence in a court of law." He leaned forward, picked up the photograph, and examined it closely. "It is so much more convincing than the bare testimony would be." He chuckled at his unintended wordplay. "Don't you agree?"

West placed the photograph back on the table, pulled a single sheet of paper out of his briefcase, and put it before Hughes, who looked at it silently.

West then turned to William and spoke to him directly. "The Stevens did not set out to embarrass you, Mr. Hudson. All they want is a quiet adoption. In this paper you acknowledge parentage, and you waive your rights so Mr. Stevens can adopt. You also agree to refrain from all communication with Seamus, absent Mrs. Stevens' express permission. If you sign today, we will quietly file the paperwork, and if all goes well, you will never hear from us again."

"I want the photograph and the plate it was made from," William said, lifting his face from his hands. His cheeks were red.

"Of course. The plate is here; you can have it right now."

"I'll sign," William said sadly.

"Mr. Hudson, please wait one moment before you sign that?" Hughes was asking rather than commanding. "Mr. West, do you have any other photographs in that briefcase of yours?"

"No, Mr. Hughes. This is the only one I have."

"And how about you?" Hughes asked, turning to Stark, who was still standing at the end of the dining room table. "Do you have any more photographs?"

"No, sir. I have no other photographs," Stark said.

In resignation, Hughes nodded at William, who took pen in hand and signed the paper. West pulled the glass negative out of his briefcase and handed it to Hughes, who put it and the photo into his own briefcase. He picked up the gold coins and, without uttering another word, he and William left.

After the door closed, Maggie slumped in her chair and sobbed with relief. Ray turned to West and vigorously shook his hand. "Thank you, Mr. West.

Thank you for preserving our family." Maggie leaned over and kissed the lawyer on the cheek.

"I just played a role," West said. "This worked only because Stark had the goods on Mr. Hudson. I almost felt sorry for him at the end. Stark, I'm not sure I want to know, but where did you get that photograph?"

"Mr. Hudson's not a hard man to follow. When I discovered his dalliances, I visited Miss Stipple. She was happy to talk. After her older brother was killed, she went to see Mr. Hudson. She was in some sorta financial trouble, and she thought he had a moral responsibility to help her. One thing led to another, and in a jiffy Miss Stipple had her little love nest on Mount Vernon Street.

"Then her younger brother found out about the arrangement, and he had a better idea. Seems he's a photographer. So he set up his camera in the armoire in her bedroom and bored an opening for the lens to look through. Then he sat in the armoire taking photographs while Mr. Hudson enjoyed his sister's company.

"When I told 'em the purpose a' my investigation, they were happy to sell me one a' the photographs. They wanted to sell me just the print, but I had a suspicion it would come in handy to own the glass too. They charged me a hundred dollars. I thought the price pretty steep, but I paid it. Maggie, it will be on my statement."

"Worth every penny, Ted, every penny."

"I don't understand," Ray said. "Do they have more of these photographs?"

"Oh yes, the brother sat in that armoire for three or four sessions. I had quite a selection to choose from. Most of 'em weren't as decent as the one we had here. I decided not to buy the most explicit ones; I thought they were just too much."

"Sounds to me like Mr. Hudson's lady troubles are far from over," West said.

"Yup. Prudence Stipple and her brother have visions a' great wealth. They see it as fair compensation for their brother's death. I felt compelled to point out to 'em that extortion is a crime; I mentioned this only after I had secured the photograph we needed, a' course."

"Well, I'm glad I didn't know the whole story," West said. "I don't think what *we* did sank to the level of extortion."

"*You're* the legal expert, Counselor," Stark said, with more than a hint of sarcasm.

In due course the adoption was approved, and Ray and Maggie moved back to Fannies, where Seamus once again had his aunties to play with every day.

Chapter 29

Gloucester — October 1869

Four years passed. Sylvie was off for the night, so Maggie was tending bar in her place when Angus Cahill, hair and clothes in disarray, hurried down the stairs out of breath.

"What happened, Angus?" Maggie asked.

Angus tucked his shirt in. "She damn near bit it off, that's what happened. Drunk ol' hag…. You need to do somethin' 'bout her. Someone's gonna get hurt."

"Can I fix you up with one of the other ladies?"

"Jesus, I'm hurtin' too much for that." He touched his crotch tenderly with his left hand. "Ouch…. Maybe after I heal up." Then, in a booming voice, "But I don't wanna see Winnie — not ever again — I'll tell ya that." He limped out the door.

Maggie went upstairs. The door to Winnie's room was half open, and she was sitting naked on her braided rug. Strands of long dark hair hung down in front of her face; tears had eroded channels in her thick makeup. She was clutching a whiskey bottle.

"That bastard," Winnie said, looking up at Maggie. "He called me a fat ol' whore." Winnie reached down and grabbed a roll of fat from her belly. "A fat ol' whore." She raised the bottle to her lips and took a swig. "Arsehole."

"Angus said you bit him."

Winnie looked up. "Aw, he's bein' a baby. A little nip, maybe. That's all." She took another swig and hiccuped.

"You've had enough of that. Give me the bottle."

"Go to hell." Winnie hiccuped again and took another swig.

Maggie clenched her teeth. But she left Winnie alone and went back to tending bar.

The next day was Saturday. Before breakfast, Seamus was pounding a punching bag made of canvas filled with rice while Ray gave him pointers on boxing. The boy had been getting beaten up at school, so some basic self-defense training seemed in order.

Winnie had just arrived at the breakfast table. Her hair was matted and tangled, her makeup still a mess from the night before, her eyes bloodshot. She put her head in her hands, but as she leaned forward her robe came open, exposing her right side from thigh to breast. She didn't seem to notice.

Ray looked the other way, but Seamus walked over and put a hand on her shoulder. "Aunt Winnie," he said softly, "your bubbies are hanging out." While Winnie slowly tied her robe back up, Seamus poured her a mug of coffee, adding two spoons of honey. Winnie nodded and took a sip. Mildred finished cooking breakfast, and Ray and Seamus sat down to eat.

"Now, Seamus," Ray said, "fighting is a last resort; your mother would not be happy if you started picking fights. Settle your differences with your head whenever you can."

"Yes, Papa. But the other boys don't want to talk much."

Lucy and Sarah sat down at the breakfast table.

"Good God, Winnie," Lucy said. "You look like ya were run over by a hoss cart. Is this all because of a little bite?"

Winnie raised her head and looked at Lucy through bloodshot eyes. "I practically bit it off. When this gets around, my business will dry up completely." Winnie put her head back in her hands.

"Well, darlin', drownin' your sorrows in a bottle won't get 'em bangin' on ya again."

"Bugger off, Sarah. It's none of your fuckin' business what I do when I'm off duty."

The room fell silent, but after a moment Lucy shifted in her chair and changed the subject. "That's a pretty good shiner ya got there, Seamus. Who's doing this to ya?"

"He's not telling," Ray said.

"Well, what's he mad at you for?" Lucy asked, leaning over so Seamus could not avoid looking at her.

"There's two of them, actually," Seamus said softly. "They don't seem to like where I live."

"Well, as your aunt Winnie here says, just tell 'em to bugger off. It's none of their business where you live. Tell them it's a free country, and they should just bugger off."

"I try to be friendly, but they're always mad at me." Seamus returned to the punching bag.

After breakfast, Maggie stopped by Winnie's room. She was back in bed, her makeup and hair still in the same unkempt state. Maggie pulled the plush red chair close to the bed and sat down. A shot glass half full of whiskey sat on a small table nearby. Maggie looked at it, and Winnie noticed her glance.

"I heard you were in pretty bad shape this morning."

"I been better," Winnie responded sarcastically

Maggie walked over to the trash can and pulled out an empty whiskey bottle. "How much o' this did you drink *before* you bit into Angus?"

"That's none a' your business."

"It's me business when you almost bite the johnson off one o' me customers." Maggie's voice was louder than she intended. She could feel her heart starting to race.

"*Your* customers! You were a prissy little Irish schoolgirl when I started fuckin' Angus Cahill. It's me that's kept him happy all these years, not you. No, not you, you're too good to do the dirty work that pays the bills around here." Winnie reached for the shot glass and downed its contents in one swallow. Then she slammed the glass back down on the table.

"Goddamn it, Winnie, you're plastered every night, and now you're drinking in the morning too. You're off the payroll as o' right now. You've got one week to sober up and stay sobered up — otherwise you're out on the street!" Maggie was red in the face.

"You can't do that to me!" Winnie yelled.

"I just did!" Maggie left Winnie's room, slamming the door behind her.

Maggie sent no customers to Winnie the next week. Winnie kept her door closed most of the time and came down for food only when she knew she wouldn't bump into Maggie. The next Friday, with the week almost up, Winnie came to Maggie's office after breakfast when, as usual, she was doing the books. The air was a blue haze — Maggie had taken up smoking. Winnie was in her most conservative dress, with makeup on and hair pinned up.

She sat down across from Maggie. "I'm forty years old, and I been here over twenty years. I earned my place." She was slurring her words slightly.

Maggie set her pipe in a half-full ashtray. "I can't have you working drunk…. How much have you had this morning?"

"Just a shot to steady my nerves, that's all."

"Pack your bags, Winnie."

"After all we been through? I stood up for ya…." Winnie's lips quivered.

"I'm sorry, but this is a business," Maggie said evenly. "We all have to play our part. I can't have a drunk working for me. I gave you your chance. Now you have to go."

"I don't have anywhere to go," Winnie pleaded. "My only friends are here. This is the only work I know."

"You've saved up some money. Get yourself a room. Get yourself sober. You'll be all right," Maggie said, tensing her jaw muscles and trying to keep her emotions under control.

Winnie stared at her, but Maggie didn't budge. Finally, Winnie got up and left.

Maybe she'll sober up and come back, Maggie thought. But as soon as the thought jelled, she realized she did not want that to happen. Winnie was too old. It would be best if she just melted away and found a life elsewhere. But still, she had been good to Seamus all these years, and now she might be in serious trouble…. But there was no sense in brooding over it.

Maggie filled her pipe with the finest Virginia tobacco, tamped it down, and fired the bowl with a wooden match taken from a brass matchbox. Then she called Mildred in and promoted her to Winnie's room upstairs. She leaned back, taking a deep drag on her pipe, and smiled. *Mildred will be a good one*, she thought.

Three days later, Maggie came down to breakfast to find Sarah and Lucy sitting quietly with their mugs of coffee. The new maid, Jean, was making breakfast. "How's Mildred's training going?" Maggie asked cheerfully.

"She's doin' all right," Sarah said without enthusiasm. "So are we next? Are we the next ones gettin' the boot?"

Maggie's smile evaporated. "Winnie refused to quit drinking. She couldn't function anymore. Neither of you has a problem with booze."

"Jesus, Maggie; it's old age that did her in. I'm a year older than she is, and Sarah here ain't far behind. I've wrinkles around my eyes, my arms are flabby, and my bubbies are hangin'. Just be straight with me. How long have I got?"

Maggie didn't answer, but Lucy kept staring at her until she couldn't sit still any longer. "Change is going to happen. If you look around town, you don't see ladies working into their forties anywhere. If it were just up to me, I'd keep you here forever, but . . . but it's the fishermen who make the decision. It's who they spend their dollars on."

"So it all just comes down to cold cash, does it?"

"I'm sorry, Lucy. I don't know what else to say." Maggie returned to her office without eating breakfast.

The next Sunday Maggie walked Seamus up to Elizabeth's house; then, in what had become a routine, she stayed and prepared dinner while Elizabeth took him to church. Emily joined them whenever Enoch was at sea, and Ray joined them when he was ashore — but just for dinner. He had vowed not to walk through those church doors again until Maggie could walk through with him.

On this Sunday, Louisa May Alcott was the subject of the dinner conversation. The author of *Little Women* had given a talk at the Universalist the previous evening. Maggie couldn't go, of course, but Emily had, and she described the event. Miss Alcott spent most of the hour talking about her sisters, who had been the inspiration for *Little Women.* She also talked of her service as a nurse in the war, but of most interest to Emily was that she talked about women's suffrage. Now that slavery was outlawed and Negro men had the right to vote, women's suffrage was the great civil rights issue of the time, she said. After the lecture, she had invited Emily to come to Concord for a suffrage meeting. Emily asked Maggie to come along with her.

A few days later, Emily and Maggie boarded the early-morning train to Boston. The railroad car was one

343

of the hand-me-downs that served the Gloucester line. The varnished wood paneling had darkened with age, and the ceiling was smudged with years of soot from the kerosene lamps that lit the railcar. The cabin was too warm from the well-stoked coal stove, and it was filled with a faint odor of sulfur and stale tobacco. Maggie and Emily sat on cracked green leather seats worn thin by the trousers and skirts of countless passengers.

After struggling with a sticky bronze latch, Maggie opened the window to let in the early-fall air. With five sharp blasts from the steam whistle, they were on their way. Soon they crossed the Annisquam River on the wooden drawbridge that had made train service to Gloucester possible a decade earlier.

"Do you think we're ever going to get the vote?" Emily had to speak up to be heard over the rhythmic sound of steel wheels rolling over poorly joined rails.

"Women will win this battle one day, Em, but I'm not sure either of us will be alive to see it." Maggie reached up and closed the window, making conversation easier.

"The trouble is that we have to get men to vote in favor of the idea, and they don't want to give up the sweet deal they have now. Enoch won't vote with us, and I doubt Ray will either."

"Oh, I can bring Ray around," Maggie responded cheerfully.

"I don't know, Maggie. Yesterday I found an article written by Judith Sargent Murray that my mother gave me when I was still a girl. Mother actually knew her." Emily took a yellowed pamphlet out of her bag and held it out gingerly for Maggie to see.

"I read about her in Babson's *History*," Maggie said. "Wasn't she married to the founder of the Universalist Church?"

"She was indeed. John Murray was actually her second husband. Her first was a shirttail relative of Ray's family, although they never talk about him. He fled to the West Indies to avoid debtor's prison and died down there. Libby's ashamed of him even now, all these years later, and they're only related by marriage. I don't understand her sometimes.

"Anyway, Judith Murray was a remarkable woman, mostly self-educated, had to be — girls didn't go to school much back then. But she became an accomplished writer anyway. In 1790 she published an essay called 'On the Equality of the Sexes.' She used an assumed name, of course. She said women's problems could be traced to the denial of an equal education, which leaves us unfit for most intellectual pursuits and for most good jobs."

"She could be writing about Ireland, Em. The girls in me village weren't given any schooling after the monthlies started."

"You're better educated than most, Maggie. You're a lot like her. But most of us don't have your spunk, that drive that helped you get an education on your own. Men don't have to be self-starters; they get all the advantages as soon as they put on their first pair of short pants. Then, once they're grown, they justify holding us down by saying we don't have the knowledge to do the things they can do."

Maggie gave an understanding nod. "My ladies work for me because being a prostitute's the only decent-paying job they can get."

The two men in the seats in front of them jerked their heads in surprise. They turned their heads to look at Maggie and Emily, as if they had never heard the word "prostitute" before.

"Something we can help you with, gentlemen?" Maggie asked sweetly.

"We thought we heard one of you saying you had a prostitute working for you," the younger man stammered.

"That's right. Me place is called Fannies, and I've got six ladies working for me. We're on Duncan Street in Gloucester, right near the waterfront. Come on in some night, and I'll see that you have a good time."

"Good God! We would never do such a thing," the older one sputtered, turning brusquely to face forward.

"Maggie, that's scandalous," Emily whispered. But she was obviously thrilled by Maggie's boldness.

"I'm sorry if I embarrassed you, Em. Like it or not, me work has become part o' who I am. I'm beyond apologizing for it, and I'm fed up with people's hypocrisy. There are more than a few of our so-called upstanding citizens, people who cross the street rather than speak with me, who sneak up Fannies' back stairs for secret relief."

"I wish I had your courage," Emily said, mostly to herself. "Aren't you afraid of, well, of being judged by God one day?"

"Em, I was raised Catholic. We're supposed to feel guilty most o' the time, and I've felt plenty guilty for years, believe me. But I've come to realize that the Church doesn't understand sex at all. The priests taught us that sex was sinful, but what do they know? I think they have it all wrong. Sex is a natural part o' life, like eating or breathing or using the privy. Cows have sex, horses have sex, and so do chickens. Do you think a chicken and a rooster feel guilty about it? If you want to know about sex, don't ask a priest. The ladies who work at Fannies are the ones to teach that subject.

"No, it just isn't enough to scare me anymore when some man says God doesn't approve o' what I do. What if he said God doesn't approve of eating apples because Adam and Eve ate one when they weren't supposed to? Would you feel guilty about eating an apple? Not me, not anymore. I don't believe the priests know what God wants any better than I do."

"That's blasphemy!" the older man in the seat ahead of them roared, loudly enough to startle a passenger dozing across the aisle. He had turned his head toward them. "You are going to rot in hell," he muttered.

The older man turned to face his companion. "It's blasphemy, Bill, wicked blasphemy. That woman should be whipped in the public square. That's what we would have done in your grandfather's day."

"Em, I'm afraid you're not going to want to ever ride anywhere with me again," Maggie said apologetically.

"On the contrary, my dear," Emily said. "This has been the most interesting train ride I've ever had. So let me ask you this." She leaned close to Maggie, so the men in front of them couldn't hear. "What if it isn't between a man and a woman?" She almost couldn't get it out. "What if it's between two women?"

Maggie looked into Emily's eyes and saw the vulnerability there. She finally understood why Emily and Elizabeth had a special bond.

"Em," Maggie said in a low and measured tone, "I've come to realize that love between women is more common than most people know. I think it's a wonderful thing when two people love each other, no matter who they are."

Emily's eyes were wide with astonishment. "You know of others?" she whispered excitedly.

"Several o' the ladies at Fannies. I'd have to ask them, o' course, but I think they would be willing to talk . . . to talk with you about it . . . if you'd like . . . if that would help." Maggie shivered as she thought of her moment in Winnie's arms.

"Oh, Maggie!" Emily whispered with excitement. "I thought we were all alone in the world. I've been tormented for decades, like Reverend Dimmesdale . . . just riddled with guilt. . . . Oh, we must keep quiet about this. Oh, but to know there are others like us in this world! How glorious!

"Elizabeth is going to be very cross with me for saying anything to you. I shouldn't have. She wouldn't want Ray to know. I wouldn't want Jane to know — or Enoch, by God, not Enoch. It would be a disaster if anyone found out."

"I won't say anything about it to anyone, not even to Ray. Frankly, I'm not sure how he would react."

"Thank you," Emily said. She relaxed in her chair. "My goodness!" she said to no one in particular.

A few minutes later, the train pulled into the North Boston station. Emily and Maggie took the horse-drawn omnibus through town to where the Boston, Clinton and Fitchburg Railroad departed for Concord. The streets were dirtier than Maggie remembered; a pungent odor of manure filled the air.

They got to the station just in time to catch the Concord train. This car seemed as if it had just come out of the carriage shop that day; the padding under the supple leather seat covers was ample, and the car was spotless inside and out. Most passengers were well dressed, the men in hats and suit coats, the women in bonnets and long, full dresses. Their conversations were reserved and polite.

Once the train pulled out of the station, Emily opened the basket she had packed, and they each ate a muffin and an apple, accompanied by fresh milk. As the train lurched around a bend, Emily spilled her milk, then wiped a drip off her chin with her handkerchief.

"Oh m'God! That reminds me of a story, and you don't know the half of it," Maggie chuckled. She told Emily just how John Pitt had been convinced to pay Elizabeth her share of the insurance from the *Raiatea Sunrise*. Soon they were being stared at by another carful of passengers, this time because they were howling with laughter as Maggie described Winnie wiping milk off Pitt's chin and Pitt standing at her dressing table writing Elizabeth's check while Timkins stared at his shriveled buttocks.

"They're going to throw us off the train if we keep this up," Emily said with undisguised delight. "How I wish I could have been there to see that! John Pitt got his comeuppance that night."

"Isn't it ironic that he's the church elder, and I'm the one who is banned?"

"It is so unfair, my dear. I was thinking about your troubles with the church after Miss Alcott's lecture the other day. May I tell you a story? It may suggest a solution."

"Of course," Maggie said.

"Long ago, one of Papa's fishermen fell off the main gaff. Papa did what he could, but the man couldn't be saved; his neck was broken. The fisherman was a hard-drinking man, like so many of them are, and he'd not set foot in a church for years. His mother was a good Congregationalist, though, and she wanted her boy to have a decent funeral and a proper burial.

"Well, old Amos Billcock, the Congregational minister back then, refused her flat. 'The boy was wicked and ungodly,' he said. But my papa showed Reverend Billcock the way in the form of a fifty-dollar gold coin, enough to keep him in whale oil and firewood all winter long. And that fisherman got a church funeral and was buried in the church cemetery — in a pretty good spot too, under the shade of that big elm just off Prospect Street. A few years later his mother died, and now she rests right next to her boy, just where she wanted to be.

"Now, every week for the last few months, Reverend Smithson has made a special appeal from the pulpit. The Universalist needs a new roof, and that's expensive. Many of us have made contributions, but the fund is still well short of what's needed, and the reverend's getting pretty anxious about it. The roof leaks like a sieve, the plaster on the west wall is always damp, and now it's turning black with mold. I wonder, if you made a hefty contribution to the roof fund, might Reverend Smithson see the light just like old Billcock did?"

"Em, me da used to say there were two roads to heaven," Maggie said. "You could live a kind and godly life and confess all your sins on your deathbed, or you could lead whatever life you wanted, die rich, and leave your estate to the parish priest. Da said we'd always be poor, so we had to take the high road, but he never imagined I'd end up running a . . . a successful business. . . . Oh, I remember how Ma would get on him when he talked like that. She prayed every day. Da bowed his head only on Sundays, and then only when he was in church and Ma had her eye on him. . . . I miss them, Em."

"You should bring them here for a visit. It's high time they met your husband and your son."

"For sure 'tis that, but I'm not that brave. Oh, I'm plenty bold when it comes to telling two strangers to come on down to me brothel for a good time, but I don't want Ma and Da to know what I do. I'm a big talker, but I still live with the shame."

"They love you," Emily said. "That will see you through."

Maggie nodded politely, but she was unconvinced.

Eventually the train pulled into Concord, stopping with the screech of locked wheels skidding on steel rails. The two women tightened the sashes of their bonnets and stepped out of the train to the hiss of vented steam. The train's fireman, his hairy chest black from coal dust and wet from sweat, leaned out an open window and tipped his cap politely as they walked down the platform into the station.

The midday heat was moderated by a light breeze that replaced the steam and the coal smoke with the fragrance of fresh-cut hay. Maggie and Emily walked the ten blocks to the Unitarian church where Miss Alcott's meeting was to be held. The streets were lined with American chestnuts, English elms, and sugar maples, their leaves brilliant with the reds, yellows, and oranges of the New England autumn.

They walked up the steps past Doric columns into the First Parish church, one of the oldest churches in America. The pews were half full, mostly with well-to-do middle-aged and older women. Maggie led Emily to the front, and they sat down between two women from Newburyport and an older gentleman, one of the few men in the church.

Emily chatted with the women, while Maggie greeted the man politely. He was in his sixties. Underneath his hat, his hair was streaked with gray, and once-stylish sideburns framed his large, hooked nose. He was conservatively dressed in a dark wool suit that was well kept but had seen many years of service. He told Maggie he was a friend of Miss Alcott's and was here to support her and the noble cause of women's rights. Before he could say more, the meeting started.

Miss Alcott took the stage with confidence. She had a special guest who would speak for a few minutes, she said. "He is a man who truly needs no introduction, and since we have much to do, I will not waste your time telling you of his many accomplishments. He is a great friend to our movement and to me personally, and we are privileged to have him here to speak to us today. Please welcome Ralph Waldo Emerson."

The man next to Maggie stood and walked slowly to the podium as polite applause built to a standing ovation. "Oh m'God!" Maggie exclaimed as she rose to her feet. She remembered reading Emerson's essay "Nature" years before. She had been drawn then to his advice to find God within, and she found it even more important now that the Church had rejected her.

Emerson spoke for only a few minutes, but the last sentences of his speech filled Maggie with hope:

> It is certain that what is not given today will be given tomorrow, and what is asked for this year shall be given in the next year; if not in the next year, then in the next lustrum. The claim now pressed by woman is a claim for nothing less than all, than her share in all. She asks for her property; she asks for her rights, for her vote; she asks for her share in education, for her share in all the institutions of society, for her half of the whole world; and to this she is entitled.

Everyone stood and applauded again, this time for nearly as long as the whole of Emerson's short speech. When the applause died down, Miss Alcott announced that he was afflicted with the ague and had exerted an unusual effort to join them this day. He would now retire to his bed and leave the business at hand to the rest of them. He left through the vestry door as applause rang out a third time.

The meeting went on for three hours. Miss Alcott moderated as group after group spoke of the work being done across the state. The strategy was to organize for women's right to vote in school board elections. Once the camel's nose was under the tent, they would press for the right to vote in general elections. Emily was excited by what she learned and eager to get back home and start organizing.

Maggie was enthused as well, but her short exchange with Emerson had been the highlight of the day for her. Before they returned to Gloucester, she took Emily to the same bookstore she had visited years before, and bought up every work of Emerson and Alcott they had. *Maybe*, she said to herself, *it isn't too late to become a writer.*

The day after they returned home, Emily, Maggie, and Elizabeth planned their Gloucester suffrage campaign. It would only hurt the campaign for Maggie to be a visible part of it, so her role would be limited to drafting letters, inviting speakers, and financing posters, banners, and buttons. It fell to Emily and Elizabeth to be the public face of the campaign. Emily dug into her role with relish and soon became known as Gloucester's suffragist leader, while Elizabeth fell naturally into a supporting role. Maggie, as she often did, turned to reading, this time on Emerson and the American Transcendentalist movement.

A week after Maggie had spoken to Emily about love between women, she and Elizabeth hosted a late-afternoon tea party at Middle Street. Elizabeth made scones and hard cookies, and served her homemade jam and her precious Chinese tea. Lucy and Sarah were the guests.

It was an odd party. That it happened at all was surprising: Elizabeth could not previously have imagined any circumstances under which she would invite a pair of prostitutes into her home. The conversation was strained most of the time. The women had so little in common except for one thing, and none of them knew quite how to discuss it.

But as strained as it was, all four were intrigued in one way or another: Lucy and Sarah, because they had never before been entertained in such a genteel way, and Elizabeth and Emily, because they could finally see a tiny crack in the isolation they had thought would be their fate forever.

A month later, Ray returned from a salt cod fishing trip to Browns Bank that had been hard and only marginally profitable. After a month they were still less than half full of fish when they were caught in a late-fall storm that cracked their foremast and forced their return.

He was more exhausted than Maggie had ever seen him. But she managed to cheer him up with her enthusiasm for Emerson and with the news that Seamus wasn't getting beaten up anymore. Ray was sure it was his boxing lessons that had done the trick, enabling the boy to give his tormentors a good whipping. Maggie could sense there was more to it, but Seamus wasn't talking.

Once Ray had had a day or two at home to relax, he visited his friend Spashy McCloud. Spashy had recently been made a deacon at the Universalist, and Ray wanted the deacons to reconsider their decision to bar Maggie. Spashy knew Seamus, of course; escorted by Elizabeth, the boy had been going to the Universalist regularly for years. Spashy agreed with Ray that it was unnatural to admit the child but bar the mother, especially now that the mother was Ray's wife. He was eager to get his boyhood friend back to church too. The Stevens were one of the church's original families. He promised to make a plea to admit Maggie to the church.

Meanwhile, Emily and Elizabeth made the rounds of the other deacons. The women had known them all for many years, of course. They assured the deacons that Maggie would not be coming to church to recruit new girls or customers. They made no attempt to defend her profession, but pleaded sincerely that she had a good heart and a deep interest in the spiritual life. With a light and diplomatic touch, Elizabeth made it known to the reverend that if the whole Stevens family could be reunited under one church roof, they would find the means to repair that roof.

John Pitt was not approached. He was quite surprised on the day Spashy made his move, and more surprised still when everyone — even Sergeant Smith — supported Spashy. Maggie returned to church with her family the following Sunday, and when the weather improved in the spring, the Universalist got its much-needed new roof.

Chapter 30

Gloucester — March 1871

Two years went by. Early one morning, Ray and Maggie were sipping their coffee when Anne came downstairs with her baby, Holly, cradled in her arms. She sat down next to Ray and started to nurse while he tried to look the other way. "Maggie, I'm gonna take Sylvie up on her offer to adopt Holly," Anne said.

Maggie smiled. "Sylvie will be delighted, but are you sure it's right for you?"

"I've given it a lotta thought. I looked into gettin' work that was . . . well . . . work that normal folk would consider respectable. There's the mills up in Lowell; I had a cousin doin' that. She made six dollars a week, workin' twelve hours a day. Lived in a room owned by the mill and bunked with three other girls. Then one day she comes home in a box. Hair got caught in one a' them big machines. She had beautiful long black hair. Pulled right in headfirst, she was. No thanks. Not for me.

"So I thought 'bout workin' in one a' them taverns in the West End. The Bowsprit was hirin', so I went up there and asked Charlie what the deal was. You remember Charlie, always asks for me when he comes in — bless his heart. He'd hire me all right, he says, six nights a week for five dollars. Hell — he pays four dollars now for twenty minutes a' my time. So I asked him if that's what the men made and he said no, he started 'em at six dollars a week 'til they learned the trade, and then he moved 'em up to eight. I asked if I could move up to eight when I had some experience and he said no — the job for women pays five. Men have to support their families, he said. He must be blind to think women don't support their families here in Gloucester.

"He told me Helene Wicks works for him and does all right by takin' in the wash for some a' the fishermen. So I talked to Helene. On a good week she makes two bucks doin' the wash, and along with the five bucks Charlie pays her she makes ends meet, but she spends every wakin' hour workin'. That's no kinda life. I might as well be dead if I gotta work all the time. So I figured I'd just keep this job. I can support myself and Ma, and have money left over for some frills."

Maggie scratched her chin. "How much can a good hand make on a schooner, Ray?"

"Well, it's all done on shares, like it works here at Fannies. It depends a lot on the boat and the skipper and your luck. But a good hand can make six to eight hundred a year."

"Well, how 'bout takin' me on when ya got an openin'?" Anne asked. "That's better than I could make at a factory or in a tavern — a lot better."

Ray chuckled. "You're not serious . . . oh!" Anne had shifted Holly from right to left, momentarily exposing both breasts.

"Why can't Anne be on your crew, Ray?" Maggie knew what his reaction would be.

Ray stammered: "It . . . it just isn't done. You have to be strong to be a fisherman. And . . . and . . . and there's no privy, and everyone sleeps in the same room." Holly was full, so she let go, exposing a wet nipple. "Ah . . . ," Ray breathed, turning away. "It just isn't done; it wouldn't work." He was almost facing the wall now.

Maggie laughed. "You're so easy to tease, darling." She turned to Anne. "You don't have to give Holly up. I'm raising Seamus here, and we can work out a way to raise Holly here too, if that's what you want to do."

"That's decent a' ya, Maggie. Ain't no other house in town that lets a woman keep her baby. But I don't want my daughter to say she was reared in a whorehouse. I want her to have a normal life, marry a nice man, and settle down and have him support her. It didn't work out that way for me, and that's all right. I like to please 'em and then shoo 'em out the door. But I don't want that for Holly."

"I understand, Anne. Seamus has been beaten up more than a few times because o' where he lives. It would be worse for a girl."

Sylvie came in. "Anne, have you told Maggie?" Anne nodded.

"We're gonna buy a house and Robby's gonna support us, just like we were normal folks. We got our eye on a place on Fremont Street, over on Rocky Neck. I'll be a real mother . . . I'll stay on here 'til ya train someone to take my place. I won't let ya down."

"You're a good woman, Sylvie," Maggie said. "I'll miss you."

"Maybe you could bring Winnie back to take over the bartendin' job," Sylvie suggested cautiously. "I hear she ain't doin' too well."

"I'll need to think that over," Maggie said, although in truth she didn't need to think about it at all. She was not going to make an alcoholic her bartender.

Later that morning, Maggie knocked on Lucy's door. Lucy and Sarah were playing cards. "Have you heard Sylvie is leaving?" Maggie asked.

"Yup," Sarah responded, "we heard."

"I came to offer Lucy the bartender job. If you don't want it, Lucy, I'd be happy for you to have it, Sarah."

"It's been a tough coupla years," Lucy said, looking down at her cards. "It's not easy watchin' your

362

business drift away, seein' your customers visitin' younger ladies . . . but we thought you'd offer the job to Winnie. She needs it more than we do."

"I'm offering it to you, if you'll have it."

Lucy looked at Sarah, who nodded. "How 'bout we both take it? You don't need to pay us both. We'll split one share between us and switch off on the job."

"And we won't need two rooms anymore," Sarah added. "I'll move the rest of my things in here; I spend most a' my time here anyway. You can give my room to a new girl."

"All right," Maggie replied. "That will work just fine."

Maggie started to leave, but Lucy stopped her. "I been scared," she said, tears welling in her eyes, "worried sick that we'd wind up like Winnie."

Sarah caught Maggie's eye and mouthed, "Me too."

That night, Maggie gave Colleen a permanent position. She was a slender seventeen-year-old who had been working Anne's bed since Anne had started showing. Maggie also promoted Jean, Colleen's sixteen-year-old cousin. Jean had been the maid since Mildred had moved up. At first she was reluctant to take a bed upstairs, but once Maggie explained how much Colleen was making, she came around, and she turned out to be a good one. Lydia was now the only veteran in the house, and she was just over thirty. With all the young talent, Fannies was about to become more profitable than it had ever been before.

The next morning after breakfast, Maggie walked down to the Fort to find Winnie. The Fort was on the southwest end of town, where until recently Fort Defiance had guarded the entrance to the inner harbor. Now it was filling up with small businesses and tenements.

Winnie lived in an attic above a rigger's loft. Maggie walked up two flights of wooden stairs and knocked hard on her door for many minutes before she answered. It had been two years since Maggie had let her go, but Winnie looked ten years older. She had lost twenty pounds, and like an apple that had started to dry out, her skin was bunching up in wrinkles. Her cotton dress was stained, and her once beautiful black hair was now dyed a garish shade of yellow-blonde. Her eyes were bloodshot, her breath was bad, and one of her upper front teeth was missing. "I never expected to see you here," she said. "Come on in and see my palace."

Winnie's palace was a single room. She could stand upright only in the center of it; near the walls, the ceiling came down almost to the floor. A double bed filled one end of the room, its bedclothes bunched up. Maggie did not want to get close to it; it looked like a haven for lice. The two windows, one at each end, were shaded with dingy yellow curtains, ensuring that it would never be bright in that loft, no matter the weather. An unemptied chamber pot sat near the bed, its odor filling the room.

"So what brings ya down to the ghetto?" Winnie sneered.

"I heard it's been hard for you. I came down to see how you were doing."

"How does it look like I'm doin'? I'm still workin', but not for two dollars a pop. Hell, I'm lucky to get four bits. Old men and curious fourteen-year-olds, that's what I get these days, and all I can afford is rotgut gin made by some third-rate moonshiner up in Dogtown. . . .

"How am I doin'? Never better, just like the good ol' days when Pitt was milkin' me five days a week. . . ." Winnie's voice trailed off, as if she had forgotten what she was saying. "Just like that," she said, almost in a whisper. She sat down on the bed, head in her hands.

"Do you want me to send Doc Gray down here to take a look at you?"

Winnie perked up and threw her head back. "I don't need a damn doctor. What I need's a drink a' some real booze. You wanna help me? Get me some first-class whiskey, or some a' that Salem rum."

Maggie said nothing, and Winnie started talking again. "Oh yes, how *could* I forget? You don't approve a' my drinkin'. Well, why don't ya just go back to your fancy whorehouse and count your damn money?"

She flopped onto her back, her face contorted in pain; she groaned, and the bedsprings squeaked.

Maggie stood and waited, but Winnie just lay on the bed, staring at the ceiling. Finally, Maggie turned toward the door. She placed a twenty-dollar gold coin next to the washbasin and stepped out into the bright sunlight.

Two nights later, Winnie died of acute alcohol poisoning. Maggie buried her next to Skip after a short graveside ceremony. She said a few words, and Seamus placed a bouquet of flowers on his aunt Winnie's casket.

Maggie didn't sleep that night, but the next morning she was back at work. She had a business to run.

Chapter 31

Gloucester — March 1871

The morning after Winnie's funeral, a banging was heard on the red door. Everyone except Maggie was upstairs, so she answered.

There stood Seward Buckley, William Hudson's coachman, wearing a crisply pressed uniform, with his hat tucked neatly under his arm. "Good morning, Mrs. Stevens. I have a note for you." With a white-gloved hand, he gave Maggie a small buff-colored envelope on heavy stock.

Inside, on an embossed card, was an invitation to dine with William at the Pavilion Beach Hotel. "I am instructed to await your reply and, if it is favorable, to offer you a ride in the master's carriage." Maggie now noticed the horse and carriage tethered across the intersection on Locust Street.

"It's been a long time, Seward. How have you been?"

He hesitated. "Well enough, I suppose . . . Mrs. Stevens."

"It's Maggie, Seward — just Maggie. We haven't changed that much, now have we?" Her words transported her back to the time long ago when William had asked her to use his first name.

"I don't suppose we have . . . Maggie."

Maggie shook herself back to the present. "Good. Come on in and have a seat, Seward. I'll dine with William, but I'll need a few minutes to get ready."

"Thank you. But I'd better stay with Betsy — that's my horse — my job, you know."

"Very well." Maggie changed into one of her going-to-church dresses and rode with Seward to the hotel.

On arrival, she was escorted into a small private dining room overlooking the beach. A table in the middle of a threadbare Persian rug was set for two. Small paintings of fishing schooners hung on two of the walls, and a varnished half model of a schooner hull adorned a third.

William was standing by the window, hands clasped behind his back, staring out at Gloucester Harbor. It had been six years since she'd seen him at Elizabeth's house. He had a corpulent look about him now: a distinct belly and the start of a double chin. His hairline had receded a few more inches, further exposing his broad, pale forehead. He looked older than his thirty-seven years, but he was impeccably dressed, as always — at least that had not changed.

The conversation was polite. They decided early on to return to first names — "More appropriate when the lawyers are not present," William said. Inquiries were made about the health of Ray and Victoria, and the state of the fishing business. The three-course meal was fancy by Maggie's standards, but plain by William's — no eateries in Gloucester could match the elegance of the Union Club of Boston, where he usually dined. The old-fashioned Indian pudding was on the table before he finally got to the point.

"Seamus must be ten now. How is he getting along?"

"He's quite well, William. He excels in school."

"That does not surprise me, given the intelligence of his parents." Maggie had to smile. No wink came with this statement, no tongue-in-cheek humor. He'd meant to flatter her, but his pomposity killed the flattery.

"Maggie, I shall be frank. I have no children with Victoria, and it is not likely I ever will."

"I'm sorry for you, William."

"Does Seamus know I am his father?"

"I told him that his father died on the boat from Ireland." William looked pained, and Maggie could feel his sadness. "William," she said, not unkindly, "I couldn't rightly tell him what had happened, now could I? He's just a boy."

"No, quite right. But still, I long to be a part of my son's life. That summer eleven years ago . . . it . . . it was the best time of my life." Maggie was stunned at this revelation and didn't know what to say.

"I could not own up to what I had done then. You see . . ." He clenched his jaw in a failed attempt to keep his emotions in check. "My father would have disowned me, disinherited me, removed me from the company. I would have been left poorer than my coachman." Choked up, he stopped speaking.

"I know what I should have done. I knew it then too. But to renounce all the wealth, the prestige, everything I had and knew, to renounce it all for the love of a woman — I do not have that kind of courage. 'It is easier for a camel to go through the eye of a needle than for a rich man to enter the kingdom of God.' Jesus said that, and it is true enough. And now, what have I? A loveless marriage — I rarely ever see the woman. And under the law, I am childless. But I want to leave my legacy; I want to pass on to my son what it is to be a Hudson. No matter what the law says, he is still my flesh and blood."

He looked into her eyes. "Maggie, let me atone for the past. The boy could be rich; he could have all the advantages of a great family. I will not take him from you, and I shall do this in whatever way you ask, but please let me into my son's life." William had risen up out of his chair; now he sat back down and looked across the table, pleading with moist eyes.

Despite all the years that had passed and all that had happened, Maggie felt for William, sitting there, as vulnerable as he was. It would have been hard for any human being to not have sympathy for him. But she knew what answer she must give. She delayed now only because she wanted to say it in the least hurtful way. But there was no good way to say it.

"I'm not going to let you see Seamus. It's not fair to Ray. He's truly been a father to the boy: he's given him love and affection all these years, and he's teaching him to be a man. And it's not fair to Seamus. It's been hard on him, being raised as he has, but things are going well for him now, and I won't upset that.

"And finally, William, what you're asking is not fair to me." Now it was time for her voice to waver. "I loved you once, and when I most needed you, you failed me. I can forgive you, but I can't forget. Me family has no place in it for you. I appreciate your candor, but telling me you dumped me penniless in a whorehouse because you loved money more than you loved me doesn't make me want to turn me family inside out to suit you."

Maggie stood up. "I'm sorry, William. I'd like Seward to take me home now." Her words had all come out more stridently than she'd intended when she'd started to speak. She left him staring out at the harbor, shoulders drooping, alone.

While Maggie was meeting with William, Ray and Robby were examining every inch of the mainsheet

371

on the *Benjamin Parsons*. The previous fall Tobey had replaced the standing rigging — the hemp lines that braced the masts and held them in place against the strains of the wind and the rolling and pitching moments generated in a seaway. The other lines — the anchor line, the mainsheet, and the lines that hauled the sails in and out, as well as the halyards and topping lifts that raised and lowered the sails and the gaffs — had been inspected at the same time but not replaced.

But now, two hard winter trips to Georges later, Ray had his doubts, so he had asked Robby to look it all over with him. They pulled the strands apart at the worst-looking spots and found the unmistakable signs of rot. Manila, like hemp, could act like a wick — water could seep into it; a line could look dry and sound on the outside but be rotting from within. They didn't find much rot, just a few strands in the center. Robby thought the line would pass the inspection of most, but it didn't pass Ray's.

"Robby, I'm going to McCloud's and have new line delivered first thing in the morning. We'll replace all the line we didn't replace at the start of the season. Let the crew know I want everyone down here first thing tomorrow to run the new lines."

"That's a lotta money, Ray. Is Tobey gonna be all right with this?"

"Long ago he told me to be careful. He'll back me up."

Two days later the *Parsons* set sail for Georges Bank. The north wind was brisk and the sky was deep blue, but thin, high-level cirrus warned of unsettled weather in the offing. With the wind behind her, she sailed easily out of the harbor. Fifteen hours later, she reached Georges at dawn and anchored a cable length to the north of the *Abigail,* Tobey's new schooner. Three dozen other boats were in plain sight. As soon as the anchor flukes bit the sand, they had lines over the side and began to fish. It was April Fool's Day, 1871.

By sunset the wind had veered around to the east and the glass was dropping. Like the other skippers, Ray noticed these signs, but assumed from the gradual nature of the changes that the approaching storm would be a mild one. He could not have known that they were about to endure the worst April blow in decades. At dawn on April 2, the wind had veered more and was blowing at gale force. It built to near hurricane strength that afternoon, creating steep, closely spaced seas.

The men who tried to sleep up forward were momentarily weightless as the schooner leapt off the wave crests and fell through thin air. Then they were pressed hard into their bunks as the boat bottomed out in the troughs. Each wave enveloped the bow in solid water, throwing the *Parsons* hard back against its anchor line. Then, as the boat surfed down the back of the wave face, the stretched anchor line recoiled like a spring, pulling the boat forward into the next wave to repeat the cycle. The stress on the ground tackle was extraordinary, and the anchor line was let out a little every thirty minutes to save it from chafing through. This work had to be done at the bow, where icy waist-deep water washed over the deck with each wave.

Late in the afternoon, a schooner to their west broke her anchor line and went flying downwind, mercifully missing all the boats moored to leeward. Then it happened. The *North Wind*, one of Pitt's boats moored dead to windward of the *Parsons,* broke her anchor line. Ray did not wait; he yelled to the crew forward to cut their anchor line, and in two desperate chops it parted. Having seen the *North Wind* veer off to port, he threw the wheel to starboard, and the *Parsons* backed off in that direction. As she came broadside to the sea, she was rolled hard onto her port side. The gunnels submerged, and the mast tops almost hit the water. Ray wrapped his arms around the wheel and held on; the two men forward somehow held on too, and then she rolled back level.

Ray yelled to raise the storm stays'l they had bent on hours ago in anticipation of this need, and the two men forward moved back to the foremast to grab the halyard as others struggled up on deck to help. Before the sail was up, another wave laid the schooner on her port side again. This time the *Parsons* stayed down on her beam ends for one whole wave cycle before slowly righting herself. They all knew the next time might be the end of her, but as she rolled level Ray saw the storm stays'l fly up the stay, and in the same instant the two men who had clawed their way onto the deck sheeted it home.

The sixty-knot wind grabbed the sail, and its immense leverage pulled the bow to leeward as the *Parsons* was lifting to the next wave. Now, rather than rolling onto her side, her stern was lifted up and she accelerated away from the oncoming wall of water, but she was not yet moving fast enough to escape. The wave broke over her stern, pouring a hundred thousand pounds of frigid salt water onto her deck. The *Parsons* groaned, but the deck beams held. Torrents poured over the gunnels back into the sea just as her stern was lifted up by the next wave. But now the power of the stays'l was pushing her forward fast enough to lift her stern up and over this wave, so she avoided getting pooped a second time.

Having successfully turned downwind without capsizing, Ray faced the next threat: the *Abigail* was a mere two wave crests away, and he was pointing directly at her. He spun the wheel to starboard, and the *Parsons* responded with enough agility to avoid a collision. As he raced by the *Abigail,* Ray saw two men standing over her anchor line with axes at the ready. In another second he was looking directly across at Tobey, who was at the wheel. The captain raised his arm in salute.

Behind the *Parsons*, the *North Wind,* still out of control and rolling wildly, was coming down fast on the

Abigail. Tobey gave the order and the axes were swung, but he had waited too long. Propelled by a breaking wave even bigger than the rest, the *North Wind* came crashing into the *Abigail*'s starboard side. The wave washed over both boats, leaving two keels pointing into the angry gray sky. The schooners started to roll back, but they were held together in a death grip of tangled rigging. The next three waves broke clean over them, as if they were large rocks newly planted on Georges Bank.

Then they were gone.

The *Parsons* ran south all night, driven by the hurricane-strength winds. Ray dared not risk turning broadside to the sea to head home; the danger of rolling over was too great. By dawn the fast-moving storm had abated, and he was able to reverse course and steer to the north, back toward Gloucester. Thirty-six hours later they arrived home in the midst of a brilliant spring sunset, but the mood of the town was black as the darkest night. Four schooners had sunk on Georges; forty-three men, including Paul Tobey, were never coming home. Maggie and Sylvie were relieved to have Ray and Robby back safe, but no celebration honored their return.

Two weeks later, Abigail Tobey sold the *Benjamin Parsons* to Ray. He paid her more than a fair price. It was his last thank-you to Tobey for all his old skipper had done for him. The widow also collected the insurance on the much newer *Abigail*. She got most, but not quite all, of what she had coming. William Hudson had been running the insurance business for over a decade now, and he knew exactly what he could get away with.

It took a week to repair the storm damage to the *Parsons*. The Franklin stove that broke loose from its moorings and smashed through a bulkhead caused the worst of it. Despite their harrowing experience, the crew was eager to get back at it. They had bills to pay.

Before Ray returned to sea, he took Maggie out to a West End tavern. They talked about Seamus and his progress at school, the new challenges boat ownership would bring, and how Maggie could help by handling the boat's accounting. They talked about the house on Rocky Neck that Sylvie and Robby were buying and how they might get one themselves one day. They talked about everything but what was really on Maggie's mind — her fear that Ray was going to die at sea. That evening they made love, and then she spent the rest of the night staring at the ceiling, wondering whether this time was the last time, while Ray slept peacefully by her side.

Chapter 32

Gloucester — June 1877

Six years passed. The losses in the Gloucester fleet were staggering — ten boats and sixty-eight men lost in the best year, twenty-seven boats and two hundred twelve men lost in the worst — but each season Ray went to sea and safely returned. Maggie heard nothing more from William. At Fannies, business was booming and Maggie was becoming a wealthy woman. Seamus continued to excel in school, and now he looked much as William had when Maggie first met him — but Seamus had the deep tan of someone who enjoyed life outdoors.

On one fine day in June, the Stevens family went for a Saturday sail. The temperature was already in the eighties, and it would hit ninety before the afternoon was out, but a quarter of a mile off Niles Beach a ten-knot sea breeze cooled the air. Seamus was at the tiller of the twenty-four-foot sloop that Ray had given him for his sixteenth birthday. He had named the little boat the *Cobbler* in honor of his grandmother, Elizabeth, and the dessert she so loved baking.

At noon they hove to, and Maggie brought out the picnic basket of ham and cheese slices on fresh bread paired with mild homemade applejack that Eunice, Fannies' new maid, had put together that morning. Eunice had auburn hair and lots of freckles. She was the same age as Seamus, but had been raised by hermits in a shack in Essex and had never attended school. Seamus had taken on the task of teaching her to read.

After the picnic, Seamus gave Maggie her first sailing lesson. For the next two hours she handled the tiller while he explained the careful balance needed to go upwind, how the sails had to be let out to go downwind, and the proper procedure for tacking the boat. At the end of the sail, Seamus took the tiller to guide the little boat to her mooring in Smith Cove. They furled the sails and stepped off the *Cobbler* into the old dory that once had belonged to Augie and Ray, and Seamus rowed them back to the Harbor Cove dock.

"Father," Seamus said over the rhythmic creak of pine oars in bronze oarlocks, "I'm sixteen now. I've got all summer before I start at Bowdoin. Couldn't I go out in the *Parsons* for a trip or two?"

Ray wanted to show Seamus the fishing life, but he knew Maggie's wishes and had agreed to honor them. "Remember what President Chamberlain said when we visited the college last month?" Ray said. "He told you to read the great books. You're starting college younger than most, so you need to work extra hard to get ready. You've no time for fishing this summer."

"Books! I've read book after book about adventure, but I've never had an adventure — nothing like the ones you and Grandpa have had."

"Go to college, get your degree, and then if you still want to go to sea, I'll take you," Ray said. "I started fishing because I had to support your grandmother. But you won't be forced down that path."

"Besides, Seamus, I want to read those books along with you," Maggie chimed in. "I couldn't go to college, so this will be the next best thing for me. We'll read together, and you can teach me to sail. When you come home from school, maybe your father will take us *both* to sea." Maggie looked over at Ray and chuckled when she saw his disapproving frown. But the frown quickly dissolved into a smile at what had long ago become a running joke between them.

"All right, Ma," Seamus said. "I'll study this summer, and I'll teach you to sail. But keep that job open for me, Father. Someday, I'm going fishing."

"In the meantime, Seamus," Ray said, "Bowdoin has a fine boxing team. Maybe you'd enjoy some competitive fisticuffs."

"I was never any good at boxing. It's not my cup of tea."

"You were good enough to take care of those bullies back in fourth grade."

Seamus grinned.

"What's so funny?" Maggie asked.

"Well, it was a long time ago. Despite the boxing lessons, I was still getting beat up. Then one day Sergeant Smith showed up at just the right time. He handcuffed my two tormentors and told them they'd do three months for assault. One started crying, and they both begged to be let go. Sergeant Smith made them promise to never lay a hand on me again, or he'd toss them right into the jailhouse.

"I had no trouble after that. Sergeant Smith asked me not to tell anyone, and except for thanking Aunt Sarah, I've kept my mouth shut ever since."

"Sarah?" Ray asked.

"Well, yes. I knew how things worked, even then. I had told Aunt Sarah they usually got me right after school, just as I turned the corner onto Eastern Avenue. Next day, there was Sergeant Smith. He never said so, but I know Aunt Sarah put him up to it. She used to treat him real well . . . everyone said Aunt Sarah was a magician with that tongue of hers."

"Seamus!" Maggie exclaimed.

Now smiling broadly, Seamus neatly shipped the oars at the last minute and slid the dory in parallel to the dock. Ray stepped off to secure the painter, and Seamus held the boat steady while Maggie stepped gingerly onto the dock. She looked at Ray as Seamus started up the dock ahead of them. He shrugged his shoulders and mouthed, "So are you." Maggie smiled and shook her head.

A cold front had come through, and the next morning felt like fall even though the fragrances of spring filled the air. Seamus wore the new suit Maggie had bought him in Boston at the same Essex Street tailor the Hudsons had used for decades. He looked good in a vest and tie, and unlike Ray, he enjoyed dressing up. Ray wore the suit he'd been married in. It still fit him well enough, but it was worn and no one would call it stylish. He was quick to throw off his jacket, loosen his tie, and roll up his sleeves whenever he thought he could get away with it.

Maggie wore a bonnet and a yellow and white summer dress with far less bulk than was fashionable. She had argued long and hard with her Newbury Street dressmaker to convince her to make the dress, and the result was remarkably successful.

The trio walked up to Middle Street, where they picked up Elizabeth and Emily, and then continued on to the Universalist. Sergeant Smith and William Sewall were at the door as usual. Ray extended his hand to Smith. "Wonderful to see you, Sergeant," he said. "Thank you for protecting our town."

Bewildered, the sergeant shook Ray's hand.

Emily's daughter, Jane, along with her husband and her six-year-old daughter, Rebecca, were already seated. Rebecca waved and said, "Hello, Gram," when

Emily walked by, but Jane stared straight ahead, as she always did when her mother was in Maggie's company.

They sat in their usual pew. Robby, Sylvie, and their daughter, Holly, were seated next to Spashy McCloud, his wife, and his two daughters, the youngest of whom had just started school with Holly. Spashy was now running the family cordage business, and he was trying to convince Robby to come work for him, but Robby was having none of it. "I was born a fisherman and I'll die a fisherman," he told Spashy.

Soon the service began. Reverend Smithson based his sermon on a reading from the Gospel according to Luke:

> And it came to pass the day after, that he went into a city called Nain. . . .
> Now when he came nigh to the gate of the city, behold, there was a dead man carried out, the only son of his mother, and she was a widow. . . .
> And when the Lord saw her, he had compassion on her, and said unto her, "Weep not."
> And he came and touched the bier: and they that bare [him] stood still. And he said, "Young man, I say unto thee, 'Arise.'"

And he that was dead sat up, and began
to speak. And he delivered him to his
mother.

After the service, the Stevens family walked
back to Middle Street for Sunday dinner. On the way
Maggie struck up a conversation about the reading: "So
Seamus, what is it you learned today from the reading
of the Gospel?"

"Well, Ma, Reverend Smithson says the story
shows God's compassion. He felt for the widow, and
that is why he told her to weep not. I suppose the
purpose of the story is to reassure us that God cares
about us."

"What do you think, Ray?" Maggie asked.

"Uh . . . I agree with Seamus," Ray said, giving
his son an appreciative pat on the back and Maggie a
wink. She was unable to suppress a smile.

"Seamus," she said, "I have to confess the story
bothers me. The widow is taken care of because Jesus
takes pity on her. In the world I know, women who are
alone have to take care o' themselves. Telling 'em to
wait around for God to help sends the wrong message,
for sure."

"Amen to that," Emily said. "Girls need to go to
school, graduate with the boys, and be smart enough to
solve their own problems."

They were back at Elizabeth's now. Lucy and
Sarah had cooked the dinner and set the dining table,

and all seven of them sat down to eat roast chicken, mashed potatoes, and spring peas. The cousins had become regulars at Sunday dinner. They would come up in the morning, and while everyone else went to church, they would do the cooking — except for making the dessert, a job Elizabeth insisted on retaining.

"The more I think about that sermon, the less I like it," Emily said as she passed the potatoes to Sarah. "We've been working for a decade now trying to get the good people of Gloucester interested in women's suffrage. We aren't having much luck, and I think sermons like this are part of the problem."

"I don't know, Em," Elizabeth said. "I agree with Seamus; this lesson is about compassion. Jesus is telling us that God loves us."

"Oh, Libby, you're so naive sometimes. The Bible was written by men, and this is just one more example of men telling women to wait around for them to solve our problems. Whenever an enterprising woman wants to make it on her own, she's ridiculed or worse, and then stories like this one are offered up as proof that it's God's will that women be helpless and weak. Please pass the chicken, Maggie."

Seamus enjoyed this discussion; he and his mother had been debating every subject under the sun for years. They had only one rule — they had to be scrupulously honest with each other. Opinions could be withheld, but the truth had to be told. Now they were

385

embarking on their greatest intellectual adventure — reading the great books on President Chamberlain's list together and discussing them every day.

Ray didn't share this part of Maggie and Seamus' life. He was just dismayed that the treatment of women was coming up again, as it always seemed to when they were eating.

"I'm with Em," Lucy said. "What's so terrible 'bout women gettin' an education? Look at Sarah and me, stuck usin' our bodies to make a livin'. A' course, most a' the fishermen are no better off." She separated a drumstick from the thighbone before continuing. As she paused, Ray considered saying something in defense of fishing, but he thought better of contradicting Lucy in this crowd.

She continued, gesturing with her drumstick to make her point. "As a matter a' fact, what we do's a lot safer than fishin'. Think of all our customers who've died at sea over the years. But fishin's still an honorable profession. Yet everyone looks down their noses at us. Damn hypocrites — we'd be runnin' this world if sex was recognized for the wonderful thing it is."

This was too much for Elizabeth. "But selling it is wrong. It ruins so many young girls."

"It ruins 'em because they're told from when they're little that enjoyin' sex is sinful," Sarah chimed in. "If ya ask me, they're ruined by the guilt, not the sex. If we got rid a' the guilt, we'd get rid a' the hurt,

386

and then bein' a prostitute would be honorable, just like bein' a doctor."

"*Doctor* Sarah, please pass the peas," Seamus said, with just the right emphasis on the word to get everyone laughing.

"I don't know," Elizabeth said. "I just don't know."

"I've come to think the answers to the important questions are found out there in nature and in here, inside our own hearts," Maggie said. "I used to think I'd find the meaning to life if I understood the mystery of the Trinity, and if I truly believed in the resurrection. Now I look to the majesty o' the stars on a moonless night, to the annual miracle o' new leaves on a chestnut tree and, most importantly, to the purity o' the love between one human being and another. Me ministers these days are right around this table, and me bishop is the beautiful bearded child o' nature sitting right across from me."

The conversation stopped, and everyone looked at Ray. He put down the wing he'd been gnawing on, and used his napkin to wipe the grease off his fingers and out of his beard. "I'll tell you what being a good Christian is," he said, looking back at Maggie and shifting in his chair. "It's just being kind, that's all."

Everyone stayed silent and kept looking at Ray, waiting for him to say more. But he picked up his wing and resumed gnawing on the bone. After a while, conversation again filled the room.

Chapter 33

Gloucester — May 1880

Three years later, Maggie bought a home on Clarendon Street on Rocky Neck. It was a proper sea captain's house with tall ceilings, a slate-covered mansard roof, a cupola, and a widow's walk. The first thing Maggie did on taking possession was plant a chestnut sprout in the backyard and lilacs out front. She wanted to make this place feel as much like her old home in Enniskerry as she could. From the backyard she could see Fannies, barely a quarter mile away across the inner harbor. Ray promised to build a small dock down in front so she could row to work.

Now that she had a home away from Fannies, she invited her brother and his wife to visit, and soon Seth and Louisa arrived on the train from Boston. Maggie promptly took Seth out for a sail on the *Cobbler*. Louisa did not fancy a sail on so small a boat, so she stayed behind. Seamus had taught Maggie well, and she could now easily handle the boat by herself.

The family still kept the *Cobbler* on a mooring in Smith Cove, but now that they had moved to Rocky Neck, they kept Ray's old dory there too, at Bickford's wharf, just two blocks from their new home.

Maggie and Seth walked to Bickford's down Terrace Lane, passing several art studios that looked out over the cove. The uneven ground of the gravelly lane meant slow going for Seth, who leaned heavily on his cane, but it wasn't far. At the end of the wharf a small, pitched roof shaded a man with leathery skin who was splicing line for a new mooring. Below him, two Friendship sloops were tied next to Ray's dory on the floating part of the dock, their sails flapping lazily in the breeze.

Seth insisted on rowing, but he knew little of boats and soon had rowed them in a half circle, then run aground on the mud flat next to the Rocky Neck causeway. He fumed on hearing the guffaws of a man rigging a trawl in another dory, but he was helpless. Maggie took over and rowed the hundred yards to the *Cobbler*'s mooring.

She rigged the sails, and in a few minutes they were close-hauled in the gentle southwesterly breeze. Seth knew even less about sailing than he did about rowing, so he had no choice but to let his little sister take charge. Soon the *Cobbler* was heeling to the breeze and kicking a foamy white bow wave off to leeward. They passed abeam of Maggie's house, and under the bright yellow porch awning they saw Louisa in her broad red bonnet waving down at them. They waved back.

After a circuit around the outer harbor, they hove to off Ten Pound Island and ate a picnic that Seth had prepared — smoked salmon and strong cheese, fresh strawberries and beer. The wake of a passing schooner slapped the topsides of the *Cobbler* and kicked up a spray that got them both wet. They laughed, and for a moment they were boy and girl again, frolicking much as they had around that big old chestnut tree in Enniskerry. Seth poured more beer, and Maggie asked him how his tavern was doing.

"I'm getting by, Maggie, but 'tis a struggle. I do the cooking, Louisa does some o' the serving, and I have me kits helping out with the cleaning and the odd jobs. We're not getting rich, but we're making it, and it's entirely mine. Nobody can fire me, and that's important to me, as you can well imagine. But what about you? Your man certainly has made a big success o' himself. That's quite a mansion you live in, surely 'tis."

"Ray's a big success." Maggie thought about leaving well enough alone but, exhilarated by the beautiful day and the beer, she continued. "'Tis more to it than that . . . there's something . . . something else . . . I don't know whether I can ever tell Ma and Da this, but I want to be square with you."

"What is it, Maggie O? You can tell me anything," Seth said with convincing sincerity.

"I hope so." Maggie took a deep breath. "Ray makes a fine living with the schooner, now. But it's just one boat, and this house was frightfully expensive — truth is, I bought it with me own money."

"Your own money! Oh m'God, Maggie, where did you get that kind o' gold?"

"Twenty years ago, after William Hudson put me in a family way, he shipped me to . . . to a brothel."

"That bastard."

"Now, I'm not finished. That's water long gone o'er the weir. I got me Seamus as a result o' me summer with William, and for that I'm grateful, I surely am. The madam o' the brothel took care o' me for a while. That's what William paid her to do. After a bit she wanted me to work as a prostitute, but I wouldn't — no, I would not do that. Eventually though, I took over and ran the brothel for her. When she died, I bought it, and I'm still running it today. That's where the money came from to buy our beautiful house."

Seth stared at the bottom of the boat while Maggie held her breath. "I don't know what to say." He fidgeted in silence, and finally he started in with determination. "You can never tell Ma and Da. Never. They'd be ashamed, and they'd think your sins were their fault. It would be cruel to put them through that."

Maggie winced. "What about you?"

"Louisa and I go to St. Leonard's in the North End. It's Italian Catholic, pretty strict. Her uncle is the monsignor there. She has a good Catholic family; her ma, Rose, is especially devout. I don't want 'em to know me sister runs a bawdy house. I don't want me kits to know either. I'm not a saint, for sure, but I've done nothing like what you're doing. . . . I've tried to live the Christian life. . . . You must stop, Maggie. For the sake of your eternal soul, you must stop. What's to become of you?"

"I've asked meself that question many times," Maggie said, calmly and carefully. "I don't need more money, and if I did, I've got a good husband who will support me. But I never wanted to just be someone's wife. I'm running a successful business, for sure. Not everyone can do that. And I'm running it the right way. I treat the ladies right. . . ." She stumbled, but continued on. "I never planned to be in this business, that's for sure. But I'm proud o' what I've built. Does that make any sense to you?"

"No. It makes no sense at all," Seth said sternly. "It's all right for a woman to help her husband out in a business, like Louisa helps me. But running a business is a job for a man, and running that business of yours is a job for the devil. What you're doing is not right," Seth said emphatically. "Have you been to confession?"

"No," Maggie said with profound sadness. "We've been going to a Universalist church. I haven't been to a Catholic church in a long time."

"You should go to confession. You should stop this business right now and confess your sins. You'll be going straight to hell if you don't."

They sailed back to Smith Cove in silence. Maggie skillfully guided the *Cobbler* up to her mooring, gliding to a stop at just the right time. When the boat was secure and the sails furled, Seth climbed down into the dory and sat in the stern, arms folded, while Maggie glumly rowed them back to Bickford's wharf.

Seth and Louisa took the train back to Boston that evening. Maggie didn't know what excuse her brother gave his wife for cutting the visit short, but she was sure he didn't tell her the real reason they were leaving.

After they left, Maggie walked down to Sylvie and Robby's place on Fremont Street. It was a small white clapboard house just three blocks away, set atop a little hill with a view of Smith Cove and the Railways. Sylvie and Holly were at a birthday party for one of Holly's friends, but Robby was in the backyard, sipping whiskey. He poured Maggie two fingers, and they sat in cedar chairs that had weathered gray over the years.

"I'm glad you're home," Maggie said. "I need to talk, and with Ray and Seamus gone, it's pretty lonely up on Clarendon Street."

"Always nice to gab with ya, Maggie," Robby said cheerfully. "I'm out here enjoyin' the last a' the day. I head out on the *Julia Gorton* day after tomorrow."

An awkward silence followed the mention of the *Gorton*. Ray and Robby had had a big row that resulted in Robby quitting the crew of the *Parsons,* but neither of them would talk about it. "So how's the visit with that brother a' yours coming?" he asked. "I'd like to meet him before I sail."

"He's already gone, Robby. He and Louisa just got on the train back to Boston," Maggie said grimly.

Robby put his whiskey glass down on the grass and leaned forward. "What happened?"

"I told him about Fannies. I've wanted to tell him for years, but I should have kept me mouth shut. He said I was a sinner and Ma and Da would be ashamed o' me." Maggie took a deep breath. "I don't think I'll ever see him again. . . . I'm completely cut off from me family. 'Tis a dreadful feeling." Maggie's voice wavered.

"Oh, Maggie. He just doesn't know. You're not alone. You've lotsa friends, ya know."

"This hurts — it really hurts. We were so close in the old days; I thought he would understand."

Robby jumped up and went inside, returning with a small kitchen towel. "Here," he said, "this is the closest to a hankie I could find. I don't know where Sylvie keeps 'em."

Maggie took the towel and dried her eyes. "I'm better now, Robby. Thank you."

"When I was little, right before I went to sea, I cut school one day and snuck home to get my fishin' pole. I was gonna head down to one a' those piers near the Fort. I knew Mother was outta the house at a bake sale, so I thought I could sneak in and out quick-like and nobody would be the wiser. I got my pole, then heard this commotion in my folks' room. I took a peek, and there was Papa doin' Cousin Sybil. First time I ever seen that sorta thing goin' on, but I sure knew it was serious wrong for him to be with Sybil like that."

Robby paused and reached down for his whiskey, but he didn't drink before continuing. "I was surprised as hell. 'Jesus Christ,' I said, pretty loud too. Papa pulled out and turned around. I never seen him lookin' like *that* before. 'Robby!' he shouts. That's all he said. I grabbed my fishin' pole and ran." He gulped down the rest of his whiskey.

"I never told a soul. Never talked to Papa 'bout it, never told Ma. Papa never said a word to me either. He was betrayin' Ma, though, and I hated him for it. Well, we hardly said two words the next month. Then we went to sea. It was my first fishin' trip; it was his last." Robby sighed. "So now he's been dead all these years."

Maggie silently handed him back the towel. "Papa died thinkin' I hated him," Robby said, burying his face in it. "Jesus Christ, I was tryin' to make you feel better, and look what a mess I made of it."

Maggie took his hand. "You're a dear one. You've not made a mess of anything, now. For sure, your da knew you loved him."

"We all make mistakes, Lord knows." Robby exhaled deeply. "But we're all entitled to forgiveness

395

too," he said, looking back up. "Your brother's gonna be mighty sorry one day."

The next morning, Maggie was sipping her second mug of coffee when she heard a knock at the back door. It was nine-year-old Holly Sprague, blonde hair tied back in a ponytail under a bonnet, holding a basket decorated with a yellow ribbon. She was in the midst of a growth spurt and had become tall and gangly, as her bones had grown too fast for the fat and muscle to keep up.

"Ma asked me to bring this to you, Mrs. Stevens."

"How nice," Maggie said. "Come in, Holly. Would you like a glass o' milk? I've got some in the icebox."

"Thank you, ma'am, I would."

Maggie poured the milk and they moved into the dining room, where Maggie opened the checkerboard cloth in the basket to uncover freshly baked oatmeal cookies still warm from the oven. "These smell lovely. Did you help make them?"

"Yes, ma'am."

"Would you like one?"

"Yes," she said, reaching in and grabbing an especially fat cookie.

"You'll be starting school again soon, won't you? What grade will you be in?"

"I'll be in the fourth grade, Mrs. Stevens."

"Do you like school?"

"Yes, ma'am. I like to read, and my teacher says I'm lightning fast with figures."

"That's good, Holly. It's good for a girl to be smart. Do you have any favorite books?"

"I like *The Tales of Peter Parley About America*. Ma and I just read it together. I like the part where Peter goes with Wampum to Vermont. It's scary; Wampum's an Indian. He's friendly, but some of the other Indians are mean."

"There aren't any Indians left around here."

"There are still lots out west, Mrs. Stevens. I'm going to take a train out there when I get older. I want to go all the way to Oregon. I'm not afraid."

Holly finished her cookie and milk. After she left, Maggie retrieved her old copy of Anna Jameson's *Winter Studies and Summer Rambles in Canada* from her bookshelves and spent the rest of the afternoon re-reading Jameson's tales of her travels in the American West. Maybe on Holly's next visit, they would read them together.

Seamus took the train home from Bowdoin, where he'd been working for the summer, to visit for a few days before his classes started in the fall. On his first full day home, he took Elizabeth, Emily, and Maggie out for a sail. That night he took a friend to a tavern downtown and stayed over in his old room at Fannies.

The next day he was back on Rocky Neck for a farewell Sunday dinner with his mother before returning to Brunswick. It was a beautiful late-summer afternoon, so Maggie set a table on the porch and they ate dinner overlooking the inner harbor. She boiled lobsters and served them with melted butter, thin pan-fried potato slices, and a shredded cabbage salad dressed with malt vinegar and mayonnaise.

As they had hundreds of times before, they removed the lobster meat from the tails, the claws, and the knuckles, and dipped them in the butter before downing them. Then they forced the meat out of the legs by pulling them through their clenched teeth. Seamus didn't bother with the hard-to-get little bits of meat in the body; consistent with family tradition, he gave that part of his lobster to Maggie. She was picking over the two carcasses with a tiny fork when she finally got to what was on her mind. "So who was the friend you went out with last night?"

"No one special, Ma."

"Seamus, I wasn't born yesterday. You were out with Eunice." Maggie had promoted Eunice the previous winter to take Lydia's place. It was the same old story — Lydia had aged and the fishermen had stopped asking for her, so Maggie had to let her go.

"I took her to that nice tavern next to the Pavilion Beach Hotel. We had a fine time," Seamus said matter-of-factly.

"Why didn't you tell me you were dating her?" Maggie asked.

"Dating? I just took an old friend to a tavern. I don't tell you every detail of what I do. I'm nearly twenty."

"Don't you think your mother would want to know if you're seeing a . . . a professional woman?"

"Is there something wrong with that?" he asked, feigning innocence.

"It's not something most mothers would be happy about."

"But you're not 'most mothers,' are you?"

"Whose bed did you sleep in last night?"

Seamus hesitated, then said, "I'd rather not answer that question."

"I'm your mother. I'm entitled to know."

"I'm grown now; this is not a subject I wish to discuss. Please don't push, Mother; you don't want me to lie, do you?"

"Of course not. We always tell each other the truth — always. But Seamus, you shouldn't go to bed with . . . with a woman who sleeps with men for a living. You shouldn't go to bed with anyone before you're married, for that matter. What would Reverend Smithson say?"

Seamus smiled. "Mother, that bridge was crossed long ago. Given where I grew up, how could you expect anything else?"

Maggie let out a deep sigh. She'd been worried about this happening ever since Seamus hit puberty. Goodness knows, he saw enough of women's bodies and heard enough sexually charged talk, but she thought he'd made it through without actually losing his virginity. Who had it been, she wondered.

She could see he was eagerly awaiting her response, looking forward to taking the debate to the next level. But it was obvious this conversation wasn't going to get her anywhere. She longed to have the name of the lady, or ladies, who had laid hands on her boy, but she had no chance of getting that information out of him today. She would just have to be content that he was heading back to school, where in time he might give up any entanglement with Eunice.

"All right, dear. I was afraid something like this would happen. What's done is done. Just please remember that other women are going to have a rather different reaction to your entreaties than the ladies at Fannies. I don't want some outraged father coming at you with a gun."

That night they set up Ray's telescope on a flat spot at the top of the mansard roof, inside the small fenced enclosure named for the wives who watched in vain, waiting for their husbands to come home from the sea. The moon was down, and it was clear; the stars were brilliant. As always when they were visible, Maggie wanted to see the moons of Jupiter. She aligned the equatorial mount, pointed the telescope at the planet, and kept it focused by slowly rotating the drive wheel at just the right speed to counter the earth's rotation. "There they are: Europa, Ganymede, and

Callisto, just where the almanac says they should be. Io is behind Jupiter now."

"I love looking at the planets with you," Seamus said. "I've missed this."

They were quiet as he looked through the telescope and she looked at him. She was proud of him, and of herself. He'd had an unusual upbringing, but he was turning into a capable, hardworking, and kind man. She'd done well with the most important task entrusted to her. She looked up at the grandness of the Milky Way, then around at the darkened harbor, and beyond it at the lighted steeple of the Universalist. This felt like home now.

"Ma, what was my da like? My natural father."

Maggie frowned, but in the dark Seamus couldn't see her expression. "He was handsome; he looked very much like you. Same round forehead and sparkling eyes. He was a few inches taller, though, and your hair has more of an auburn tint than his did. You get that from me, I guess. And like you, he was very smart." She almost went on to say how educated he was, but she caught herself in time.

"It must have been hard on you to lose him. Where did you bury him?"

"At sea. . . . He was buried at sea. . . . Look, dear, a shooting star."

"Was there a service?"

"Not much. The captain said a few words."

"I wish I could have met him. I'd like to visit Ireland someday. Are my grandparents still alive?"

"My ma and da are, so I suppose his are . . . I've lost track."

To Maggie's great relief, Seamus dropped the subject. But she was left with an all-too-familiar discomfort. This wasn't the first time she had lied to him about who his father was.

Maggie recovered over the next two hours as mother and son looked through the telescope, sometimes not saying a word to each other, other times discussing a wide variety of subjects. She was delighted to hear he was planning a future that had nothing to do with fishing. His studies were focused on government and history, and his favorite professor was urging him to consider becoming a lawyer. Maggie said she knew an excellent lawyer in Salem; maybe Seamus could apprentice with him. They agreed to visit David West when Seamus came home for Thanksgiving.

Chapter 34

Anchored on Georges Bank

February 1885, Again

Five more years went by. The morning watch on the *Julia Gorton* had just ended. Soaked to the bone by the wave that had almost carried them overboard, Joey Amero and Robby Sprague made their way down the foc's'le companionway. The bow was rising and falling nearly twenty feet from crest to trough, forcing them to hold on tight with their mittened hands. Each step was a triumph of strength and balance over violent movement and profound fatigue.

Below it was cold and dark. The stove had been smothered and the kerosene lamps shuttered long ago. The crew quarters were dimly illuminated by what little winter sunlight found its way through the thick deck prisms, and by the faint yellow rays of a flickering candle housed in glass thickly coated with splattered wax.

They braced against a bulkhead and grabbed a handhold so they wouldn't be tossed about as the boat repeatedly launched itself off one wave and into the next. With their free hands they slowly removed oilskins, boots, and layers of wet wool, hanging their oilskins near the companionway and shoving their boots and clothes under their bunks, where they could find them quickly in the dark. Then they put on nightclothes not so wet — Robby long johns and wool socks hand-knitted by Sylvie, Joey a sleeping smock made by his wife, Esmeralda. Finally they were almost dry, and newly warmed by the energy exerted in the usually simple tasks of dressing and undressing.

Robby grabbed a hardtack biscuit and a piece of jerky from a bag the cook had tied above the stove. He rolled into his bunk and raised the lee cloth that would keep him from being thrown onto the floorboards as he slept. Only after settling in did he smell the vomit ejected earlier that evening by other stomachs too abused to hold food down.

He finished his cold meal and huddled under a heavy wool blanket. His body was pressed first against the cold fir of the inner hull, then against the lee cloth, and then back and forth with the violent rhythm of the sea. Exhausted, he at last drifted off to sleep.

Twelve hours later, he and Joey were back on deck. The snow had stopped, and when not obscured behind racing clouds, a sliver of moon illuminated the deck. But the wind was still blowing a full gale, and the waves were immense. They had just finished letting out the anchor line and moving the chafe mat back into position, and were making their way back to the center of the boat, when the bow slewed hard to starboard off a large wave, and the anchor line snapped.

Suddenly the *Gorton* was broadside to the sea. She rolled to port as she descended into a trough, and then to starboard as the next crest approached. The process repeated, but the third wave was another giant and its crest was breaking. As the *Gorton* moved up the wave face, the deck rolled to sixty degrees, then to eighty degrees, then past ninety degrees.

Robby didn't see the leeward rail go by, but he felt the numbing effect of the cold water pressing in on his head as he plunged into the frigid sea. In the blackness he couldn't tell which way was up. The next wave spit him out, and he could breathe again. He struggled to stay afloat, dragged down by oilskins, boots, and water-soaked wool. When he floated up on a wave crest, he saw the *Gorton* right herself. She was drifting away, still broadside to the wind. When the next crest lifted him up, he was a hundred yards upwind of her. Paradoxically, he felt warmer as his body grew numb to the deadly cold. Atop the next crest he could no longer see the boat, but he saw Joey floating away in the silvery moonlight. Joey waved goodbye.

Robby drifted. He'd enjoyed thirty years of life since watching Tommy slide down that deck — or was it thirty-three? What year was it now? He had a wife and a daughter who was fast becoming a woman. Tommy had died too young for any of that. A wife: "Sylvie," he murmured. "Oh, Sylvie." He was so tired, but he wasn't cold anymore. Maybe he was in a Gulf Stream eddy. Maybe he would stay warm until he could be picked up. Did he still have his boots on? He couldn't feel his feet. And now his hands were numb.

"I'm sorry," he murmured.

Forty-eight hours later, the *Julia Gorton* sailed into Gloucester Harbor with her flag at half-mast. Maggie saw the schooner come in and noticed the flag right off, as any fisherman's wife would. She walked fearfully to Fremont Street to get Sylvie, and then they walked together to Pitt's dock. Ray saw the *Gorton* go by from the deck of the *Parsons* moored in Harbor Cove, and he hitched a ride to Pitt's on the harbor tug.

By the time Maggie and Sylvie arrived, Ray and Sandy Brown, the *Gorton*'s captain, were talking privately. Maggie could see their somber faces as she approached. Ray delivered the bad news. "Sylvie, it's Robby. I'm so sorry. He didn't make it."

Sylvie collapsed in Maggie's arms. Maggie led her into Pitt's fish-drying shed, where they found a bench.

Sandy took Ray aside. "Come on board, Ray. Let me show you something." They went down to Sandy's cabin, where a three-foot section of anchor line lay on the navigation table. "The worst of the storm was over when it happened. We lost our anchor, and she came broadside to the sea and rolled her mastheads into the water. Robby and Joey were swept off during one of the rolls; they were gone by the time I got on deck. We got her going downwind, and when we had her squared away, we saw that this line was still over the side. It didn't chafe through; it parted about eighty feet down."

"I don't understand," Ray said. "What would make it do that?"

"Look here," Sandy said, showing Ray the frayed end of the thick line. "Look at the middle strands," he said as he peeled back the outer layers.

"Rot!" Ray exclaimed.

"This is the original anchor line, Ray. It was put on twelve years ago, when the *Gorton* was first outfitted. Here, look at the clean end." One end had been neatly cut and whipped, It was easy to see that the core of each twist of the three-strand line, fully half of the line's diameter, was rotten.

"Twelve years is a long time to expect an anchor line to last," Ray said gravely.

"Don't I know it. We re-rigged last fall. I told Pitt we needed a new anchor line too, but he was already spending three hundred dollars, and he said that was enough for one boat. So I put out to sea with this line, and now two good men are dead. I didn't know it was rotten. But twelve years — nobody should let an anchor line go that long."

"What are you going to do now?"

"What can I do? Robby and Joey are gone."

"Well, what are you going to do with that piece of rotten line?"

"Throw it away, I guess."

"Why don't you give it to me? My boy's a lawyer now; maybe he can do something for Sylvie. Did Joey have a wife?"

"Yeah, and three kids too; the oldest one's ten. They live up on Portagee Hill," Sandy said. "You can have the line, but get it off the boat before Pitt gets wind of what you're thinking."

"Loan me a bag, will you? I'll take it away right now."

Robby's funeral was held at the Universalist. Reverend Smithson presided, and the service drew a big crowd of fishermen, professional women, and regular parishioners. For the past few years Sylvie and Holly had sung in the choir, and Robby's easy way had made him many friends in the congregation. After the service his name was chiseled on his family's monument at the Mount Pleasant Cemetery, next to those of his father and his two brothers. As was often the case in Gloucester, there were no bodies buried beneath the granite.

On the way home from the funeral, Maggie asked a question she had been curious about for a long time. "Now that Robby's gone, will you please tell me what went on between the two of you? Why was he on the *Gorton* instead of on the *Parsons* with you?"

Ray shook his head. "Five or six years ago, I was down in the foc's'le having my mug up. Robby and Pat McCurdy were lying in their bunks. They hadn't heard me come down, I guess, and they were talking to each other. Pat says, well, he says — Maggie, I know you've heard it all — he tells Robby he's 'horny as hell,' and asks him where he might — 'get some good twat' was the way he put it. These aren't my words, Maggie; I'm just saying what I heard."

"Yes, darling. I understand, go on."

"So Robby says Betty's running a two-for-one special featuring these cute little sixteen-year-old twins. 'Best arse I've ever had,' he says.

"Well, Maggie, I'm no prude, but Robby was dishonoring Sylvie. I asked him what the hell he was doing screwing around behind Sylvie's back. He told me I was out of line — it was none of my business, he said. He didn't use words as nice as that. . . . It came to blows between us.

"It's a good thing we were out for three more weeks, because it took that long for the bruises to heal. We pretty much beat the stuffing out of each other. At the end of that trip, Robby put his duffel bag over his shoulder and walked up the dock. We never sailed together again. It's too damn bad; he . . . he was my best friend . . . and now he's gone."

Maggie stood on her tiptoes and kissed Ray on the forehead. They walked silently, hand in hand, the rest of the way home.

Chapter 35

Salem — May 1885

Seamus looked out the tall office window onto Federal Street, where David West was emerging from between the granite columns of the Essex County Superior Court building. West was sixty-one now; age had rounded his shoulders and thrown a curve into his spine, and he had a noticeable limp.

Seamus looked around the office. West's bar certificate and a copy of the first judgment he had won, both yellowed with age, still hung behind the desk. A photograph of his mother hung on the opposite wall. And now a new photograph, of Seamus and West on the day Seamus was admitted to the bar, hung next to his mother.

The office door opened. "You're looking well, Seamus. How is your mother?"

"She's fine, David, thank you. She's spending more time at the house and less at Fannies since Lucy took over the day-to-day operations. Father has started calling her the Lady of Clarendon Street."

"And a lady she is. Please, sit down," West said, seating himself behind his desk. "So what brings you to beautiful downtown Salem?"

"It's a case I'd like your advice on — and your help, if you're interested. I have two widows, one with three small children and the other with a fourteen-year-old daughter. The husbands were fishermen killed at sea last winter. I've got good evidence of unseaworthiness."

"Who's on the other side?"

"John Pitt. He's insured by the N.S. Hudson Company."

"Well, Pitt's an old reprobate. He'll hold a grudge, so you need to consider that if you're going to build your practice in Gloucester. And William Hudson never pays on injury claims unless he's forced to. The way he sees it, the workingman ought to be glad to be of service for as long as he can, then go to a gracious, uncomplaining death.

"That brings us to the toughest part of your case. It's a wrongful death claim. Since before the founding of the Commonwealth, the common law we inherited from medieval England has refused to allow widows a claim for the wrongful death of their husbands. I can hear the judge ruling even now: 'The plaintiffs' claims died with the plaintiffs. Case dismissed!' How do you plan on dealing with that?"

"The law is changing," Seamus said. "It makes no sense to allow a claim for injuries caused by negligence but deny it when the negligence is serious enough to cause death. There are half a dozen new cases holding that the wrongful death rule is an outmoded relic of English feudal law. Have you read Chief Justice Chase's decision in *The Seagull*? It was a Maryland case, and he ruled that the survivors of men killed at sea could claim damages for the negligence that caused the deaths."

"No, but we'd have to bring your case here in Massachusetts, and getting our state's judges to follow some Maryland case when they know damn well that common law doesn't allow wrongful death claims — well, that's a tall order."

"You've always advised me to file my cases in state court and avoid federal court like the plague. But maybe this case is the exception," Seamus mused. "As you point out, all the state court judges have grown up with the wrongful death rule, and to win we'd need to convince them the rule doesn't apply at sea. But the federal judges are the experts in admiralty law, and the best case we've got was authored by a federal judge. So might we have a better chance in federal court?"

"Not likely. We'd have to bring the case in Boston," West said. "The federal judges who rule the courtrooms there come from the best families and marry well-bred girls who come out in the grandest cotillions. They go to the finest schools and clerk for the most prestigious judges. Naturally enough, they identify with their own tribe. And that tribe runs the banks, the businesses, and the insurance companies that humble barristers like you and me must sue to get justice for our clients."

"People like William Hudson," Seamus said.

"Exactly, my young protégé," West said. "The plight of a fisherman's destitute widow and her children may be something a federal judge can appreciate intellectually, like Newton's calculus or Kant's transcendental idealism, but emotionally, our clients would be as foreign to him as if they came from the aboriginal hinterlands of Australia."

"But the law is critical here. Don't I have the best chance of beating back the wrongful death rule if I'm in federal court?"

"My boy, the law is only a part of what determines whether you win a case. The facts are usually more important than the law, and finding the right judge to decide your case is more important than both. In federal court, maritime cases are tried in admiralty court without a jury — so one judge determines your client's fate. In Boston you're almost certain to be before old Josiah G. Roberts Jr., for he fancies himself the master of all things watery. He is the son and namesake of one of the Commonwealth's first federal judges, and he was born with a silver spoon in his mouth and a stone where his heart should be.

You'd be wasting your time if you take any case other than a sure winner before him."

Seamus thought for a moment. "Do you think I'd have a chance in Superior Court?"

"Maybe — if you've got a compelling case. If you can tug at their hearts, the best of those judges will find a way to work with you on the law. So what have you got?" he asked, rubbing his hands together in anticipation.

"It was that big storm last February. Four Gloucester schooners sank. One of Pitt's schooners, the *Julia Gorton*, was anchored on Georges Bank. Robby Sprague and Joey Amero were on night watch. The schooner was hit by a big wave that snapped her anchor line and then another wave that knocked her down, dumping Robby and Joey into the sea. The rest of the crew got on deck and were able to save the ship, but by then Robby and Joey were gone."

"What's the basis for the lawsuit?"

Seamus pulled the line out of a bag by his feet. "This is a piece of the anchor line. It didn't chafe through at the deck. That's usually how they let go. This one broke about eighty feet down, because the line was rotten. Look here." Seamus showed West the rot. "Once the anchor was lost, the boat turned broadside to the wind. Robby and Joey died because the anchor line was no good."

"That may be enough to establish unseaworthiness, but how was the captain, let alone the owner, to know the inside of this rope was bad?"

"The line was twelve years old. I can get a dozen experienced fishermen to say a line that old should have been replaced years earlier. But I have more. Last fall, the *Gorton* was having her rigging replaced. Her captain told Pitt the anchor line needed to be replaced. Pitt refused — 'Too expensive,' he said."

"That's pretty good. How solid is the captain as a witness? Will he go against Pitt in court?"

"I think so. He gave us the line, and he's a friend of my father's. He's a good man."

"Well, this might work. You set up a meeting down in Gloucester. I want to talk to the widows, the children, and this captain. And get me a copy of this case you like — *The Heron,* is it?"

"*The Seagull.* I took the liberty of checking it out of the library across the street while you were arguing your larceny case this morning." Seamus couldn't suppress his grin as he pulled the leather-bound volume out of his briefcase.

"You're well prepared. You must have had a good teacher," West said with a smile of his own as he put his arm around Seamus' shoulder.

"I've learned from a master."

Chapter 36

Gloucester — June 1885

As the June meeting of the Gloucestermen's Association was breaking up, Henry Wonson found Ray and asked him to stay and discuss a matter with a few of the other owners. He led Ray into his office, just off the main floor of his fish-packing shed.

Two men were already there. John Pitt sat behind Wonson's small desk, and a middle-aged man in a three-piece suit stood in front of it. Pitt swung his chair around to face the window behind the desk, leaving the cracked and stained back of the old leather chair facing Ray. The other man extended his hand and introduced himself as Stuart Bishop, a lawyer retained by the N.S. Hudson Insurance Company to represent Mr. Pitt.

"I see," Ray said as he shook hands with Bishop. "So what is it you want to talk to me about?"

"Mr. Stevens," Bishop said, "it has come to our attention that you have something from the *Julia*

Gorton that belongs to Mr. Pitt, namely a small section of anchor line. Mr. Pitt would like it back. He insists on having it back, in fact."

Pitt swung his chair around to face Ray. "I thought ya were above stealin', Stevens."

"John, that's not a proper way to talk to Ray," Wonson said. "We don't know all the facts."

Ray looked from one to the other, then focused on Pitt. "I don't have it. Robby's widow, Sylvie, does, or I should say her lawyer does."

"And you gave it to her, *didn't ya?*" Pitt said, practically spitting out the last words.

Ray put his hands on the desk and leaned forward, his face not eighteen inches from Pitt's. "Damn right I did!"

Wonson and Bishop now spoke at once, both anxious to avert a fight in the office. "Hold on now, wait a minute!" — "Calm down, you're too old to start swinging at each other!"

Ray leaned back and took his hands off the desk.

"Mr. Stevens," Bishop said, "would you be so kind as to tell us how you got this line?"

"No, I'd rather not."

"You don't have to protect Sandy Brown — I fired his arse this morning!" Pitt roared.

Bishop spoke again. "Mr. Stevens, won't you sit down?"

417

"No, I don't think I will. Is there anything else you want to talk about?"

"Mr. Stevens, as a boat owner, you are in this together with Mr. Pitt," Bishop said. "Sometimes fishermen die at sea; it is the price paid for putting food on America's table. This sordid business of bringing claims against upstanding boat owners just pushes up the cost of insurance. In the end, it is the fishermen who suffer. An owner with large insurance bills cannot afford to pay his fishermen generously."

"Mr. Bishop, you don't know your client very well. That man," Ray said, pointing toward Pitt, "wouldn't pay his fishermen another dime if you gave him a million dollars. He just wants that line back so he can get away with sending two good men to their deaths. The bastard!"

"Mr. Stevens, we had hoped you would see our common interest here and cooperate. I must tell you that absent your cooperation, it may be very difficult for the company to justify continuing to insure your boat — the *Benjamin Parsons,* is it?"

"Mr. Bishop, you go back to that self-righteous prig William Hudson, and you tell him Ray Stevens says, 'No deal, not now, not ever!'" He turned to Wonson. "I wouldn't have hit that shriveled-up excuse for a man, but thanks for cooling things down. Good night."

Ray nodded to Bishop and turned toward Pitt, who had swung his chair around so its back was to Ray again. Ray shook his head in uncloaked disgust, then stomped out the office door into the cool night air. It stung his flushed cheeks.

Chapter 37

Boston — October 1886

Stuart Bishop sat on the brown leather Chesterfield couch in the waiting room of the N.S. Hudson Insurance Company. He wore a gray three-piece suit, as he always did during the business day, and a tasteful crimson tie in tribute to his alma mater. The walls of the waiting room were paneled in cherry, and polished bronze oil lamps sparkled in the sunlight streaming through the large bay window. In a glass cabinet opposite the couch sat a beautifully detailed model of the *USS Constitution* with her guns run out, as if about to fire a broadside.

Bishop recalled his first meeting with William, some twenty years earlier. He had been the newest lawyer at the venerable Hughes and Black firm. A young woman and her brother had tried to blackmail William with photographs of an affair he'd had with the woman, and Bishop had acted as the go-between. Rennyson Hughes, then a senior partner in the firm, had arranged a payment of a thousand dollars to keep them quiet.

But Mr. Hughes knew money alone would not silence them forever, so he arranged for the blackmailers to be quietly arrested as they accepted the payoff. The police were well briefed and naturally were on William's side. They could have sent the blackmailers to jail for a decade, but that would have kicked off a horrible scandal. Instead, with the brother and sister safely in custody, private detectives hired by Mr. Hughes had searched their rooms and retrieved all the photographs. Bishop had never seen photographs like those, before or since. What the newspapers would have done had they gotten hold of them!

With the destructive evidence safely in hand, Mr. Hughes had cut the deal. William would still give them a thousand dollars, but they were to board a boat for New Zealand forthwith. They would use the money to start a new life halfway around the world, but if word of this ever leaked out, they would be brought back to America and jailed. The plan had worked well; not a peep had been heard from them in all these years, and William had remained properly married.

Bishop's attention turned to the attractive young woman with auburn hair who sat behind the small desk outside William's office. She had introduced herself as Miss Martin, Mr. Hudson's personal secretary. She was studiously copying a document, so she did not notice Bishop looking intently at her smooth complexion, her perfectly upturned nose, and her lightly painted lips. He thought again of those salacious photographs. A bell called her into William's office, and she returned a moment later to usher him in. He brushed closely by her as she held open the door, and caught a hint of ambergris — a rare fragrance his wife wore, but only on very special occasions.

"Stuart, thank you for coming. How is the wife?" William asked as the door closed behind him. In the last few years his waist had continued to expand, and now his face was reddish and puffy, no longer defined by the sharp angles of his youth. He was as impeccably and conservatively dressed as ever, though. He ushered Bishop to a stuffed leather chair by the fireplace and sat down next to him.

"Fine, sir, and I trust Mrs. Hudson is well."

"Victoria is wintering in Venice again this year with her beloved mother; the Lowell women live longer than Methuselah." He opened an elegantly carved wooden box. "May I offer you a cigar?"

They each took a cigar from the box and rolled the soft, dark tobacco between their fingers while inhaling its musky aroma. William produced a bronze cigar punch trimmed in varnished maple. They prepared their cigars, then lit them with wooden matches from a silver matchbox.

"I am always surprised at how good these Havanas are," William said. "The dagoes have mismanaged everything else in Cuba, but they do make fine cigars." He leaned back in his chair, inhaled deeply, and exhaled a cloud of smoke. Bishop knew from experience that he was expected to enjoy his cigar for a moment before the business discussion could begin.

He took in the familiar surroundings. A large portrait of Nathaniel Hudson as a young man, one of the last painted by Gilbert Stuart, hung directly behind William's desk. The other walls were mostly covered with paintings of clipper ships, barks, and even a few fishing schooners.

On the wall opposite the Hudson portrait, where it would be hidden when the door was open, was an incongruous painting Bishop had not noticed before: a portrait of a redhead in a homemade dress — a peasant girl from the old country perhaps, shapely and alluring. Before he could linger long on the young lass, William spoke, and Bishop turned to face his client.

"I want you to brief me on the trial starting next week in Salem — two widows claiming damages for their husbands who died at sea. I thought wrongful death claims were not recognized in the law. What the hell is this all about?"

"Well, sir, you are quite right. For many hundreds of years, common law has denied claims for wrongful death. This sensible rule has eliminated many trumped-up charges. But, sir, in the last twenty years or so, there have been a few isolated cases — none of them well reasoned, of course — that have refused to apply the rule in a maritime setting. In most cases the boat owners found other ways to dispose of the claims, but I am afraid I cannot tell you a win is certain."

"Why are we down in Salem anyway? You never know how some yokel from the country might rule. I would like to get this case before Josie Roberts. I got to know him across the whist table when we prepped at Exeter. He could play trumps like no other man I have ever seen. Have you explored getting this transferred to Boston so Josie can decide it for us?"

"I am afraid that is not possible, sir. The plaintiffs have the right to choose whether they go to federal or state court, and we cannot override their choice."

"All right, I am sure you have done your best. Your dear departed mentor, Renny, loved Josie as much as I do. Did you know the Hughes and Roberts families summered in Kittery when Josie was young? He grew up calling your senior partner Uncle Renny. Where have the years gone?

"Those must have been the days, sir," Bishop said.

"Renny was a good man; he saved my bacon more than once," William said. "But enough nostalgia — tell me more about this case, Stuart. It was one of John Pitt's boats, I remember, but I do not know much more. Is there anything I should be worrying about?"

"These two fishermen died when they were swept off the boat after the anchor line broke. The line

424

was old and rotten, and before the season started, Pitt had refused the captain's request to replace it. It might well look to a jury as if Pitt valued saving the relatively modest expense of a new line more highly than he valued the lives of his crew."

"Damn that Pitt! If the boat had sunk, I would have been out five thousand dollars for the hull. I have bought too damn many new boats for him as it is. I want to talk to him about this. He shall see I mean business when he gets a look at the rates he will be paying next year." William exhaled a cloud of smoke in disgust.

"The lawyers up against us are an interesting pair. One is a young man, almost a boy actually, out of Gloucester by the name of Seamus Stevens. . . ."

"Seamus Stevens! How old is he?"

"Quite young, sir — only in his mid-twenties," Bishop replied, somewhat taken aback by William's abrupt tone. "He just passed the bar last year and has no trial experience. He would not be much of a threat, except he has teamed up with an old warhorse named David West."

"West, by God! That man has no morals."

"Are you . . . acquainted with these gentlemen, sir?"

"I do know West — all too well, but we do not have to talk about that now. You should watch your back; that is all I have to say. Now, is there any good news you can give me about this case?"

"Absolutely, sir. It is not all bad, not by a long shot. The plaintiffs' damage claim is weak. You are not going to believe this, but one of the poor suffering widows is an ex-prostitute. Word is she met her dear departed husband in a brothel. No jury will give her much of anything."

"Good. What about the other widow? Anything there?"

"Almost as good, sir. She is Portuguese and dark-skinned to boot, as are her three children, and she hardly speaks any English. She will not make a good impression before a jury full of old Yankees."

"It sounds like we may get justice in the end after all. It is high time I saw you in action, Stuart. I will come to Salem and attend this trial. It will be a good time to lay down the law to Pitt too. Will he be there?"

"Oh, yes. I need him to counter the testimony I expect from that captain."

"Thank you, Stuart, for this encouraging briefing." William reached for a decanter on the side table and poured brandy into two small cut-glass snifters. Handing one glass to Bishop, he said, "Let us toast to our success in Salem."

Chapter 38

Salem — November 1886

Two weeks later, Maggie sat in the front row of the courtroom watching Seamus and thinking of poor old Rufus Harrison. Her boy was about to do what Rufus had been too scared to do. He was going up against the fancy Boston lawyers in a court of law, and he was doing it for a righteous cause.

She could see some of her brother Seth in the way Seamus walked and in his auburn hair, but it was William she saw there the most — the angular Hudson jaw, the round forehead, and the perfect posture. Strangely, though, he had the same nervous tic she had noticed in Ray — he would grab the bottom of his jacket with his left hand and rub it between his thumb and fingers.

Ray was supposed to be sitting beside her now, but the *Parsons* hadn't returned from sea yet. It had been stormy a week earlier, not an epic nor'easter but enough to knock down an old poplar tree that had taken root along the tiny stream at the head of Rocky Neck. She could not help but worry that something had gone wrong.

The gavel banged three times. "All rise," the clerk said. "Hear ye, hear ye, hear ye! The Superior Court in and for Essex County is now in session, the Honorable Epes Ellery presiding." A door to the left of the oak bench opened, and in walked a corpulent man wearing a long black robe. His jowly face was red, and bright white hair stood away from his head at random angles. With an audible groan, he climbed the three steps to his perch and plopped into his chair. He told everyone they could be seated. "Counsel, please make your appearances."

"Your Honor," West said as he and Seamus stood, "David West and Seamus Stevens for the plaintiffs."

"Stuart Bishop for the defendants," Bishop said after standing. "And if it would please the court, the defendants have a motion we would like to bring before the jury is impaneled."

"Why am I not surprised?" the judge said sarcastically. Bishop didn't move a muscle. "Every time I have a Boston lawyer in my courtroom, he wants to make a motion. Don't you big-city barristers ever let juries decide things? . . . All right then, go ahead."

"Thank you, Your Honor. As the court is probably aware, this case is brought by the widows and children of two fishermen who tragically died at sea last

428

year during a violent storm," Bishop said. "The plaintiffs allege that the vessel was unseaworthy and that this condition was the cause of death. We are prepared to show the jury that the defendants were not at fault in these deaths. But, Your Honor, a trial here is unnecessary. As I will explain, it is clear the law does not recognize a claim for wrongful death — a plaintiff's claims for negligence die with the plaintiff."

"Mr. Bishop, I have reviewed the statement of authorities that you provided to me," the judge said, "and I can assure you that here in Essex County, we are familiar with the wrongful death rule. Now, I understand that in a minute Mr. West is going to stand up and tell me it is all different when the death happens at sea. Please direct your argument to any special circumstances applicable to claims arising out of negligence on the high seas. I don't see many such claims here in Superior Court; matters of admiralty law are usually decided by my betters on the federal bench in your hometown."

"Of course, Your Honor," Bishop said. "I have tried many cases before the District Court sitting in admiralty, and I can assure you that the wrongful death rule is much respected in maritime matters. In the statement of authorities, I have identified many maritime cases throughout our federal system where claims for wrongful death were disallowed.

"However, I would like to draw the court's particular attention to *Insurance Company v. Brame,* a recent case in the U.S. Supreme Court. Now, that case is not a maritime case, Your Honor, but there the wrongful death rule was challenged on the same basis that the plaintiffs challenge it here, and the court flatly rejected the challenge, holding 'that by common law no civil action lies for an injury that results in death.' There is no aspect of maritime law that warrants any different result, and I am sure the Supreme Court will so rule the first chance it gets."

"Thank you, Mr. Bishop. Mr. West, what do you have to say?"

"Your Honor," West said as he stood, "Mr. Stevens will respond to the motion." Seamus stood up, but before he could begin, the judge spoke again.

"What's the matter, Mr. West? Did the big-city barrister use too many polysyllabic words for you?" The judge chuckled contentedly, then continued. "Very well, Mr. Stevens, I'll hear from you."

"Thank you, Your Honor." Seamus started with just a slight tremble in his voice. "The wrongful death rule is an antiquated, unfair rule that is criticized everywhere. It is being rapidly phased out of the common law and has never been a part of maritime law. Your Honor, maritime law was a distinct branch of the law in England, based not on common law, but rather on civil law. Its foundational codes are the Laws of Oleron, of Hanse-towns, and of Wisby. . . ."

"Oleron! Hanse-towns!" the judge exclaimed. "I've never heard of such places. What does this have to do with a drowning on Georges Bank?" He frowned down at Seamus from his high perch.

Obviously flustered, the young lawyer said nothing for what seemed like a very long time. Bishop smiled, while Pitt smirked. Maggie wanted to run up and wrap her protective arms around her son, but then the judge spoke again, this time in a soothing tone. "Son," he said, "when you encounter an irascible judge, you just have to soldier on." He glanced fleetingly at West.

Seamus took a deep breath and resumed his tale. "Your Honor, these are European seafaring towns that have had maritime codes since the Middle Ages."

"Counsel, I don't want a course in world history. Just tell me why you think Mr. . . . uh, Mr. . . . uh, the fine gentleman from Boston here — tell me why he is all wet." The judge chuckled.

"Your Honor, the best case I have is *The Seagull*. I included it in my pretrial materials. Perhaps you've seen it?"

"Young man, I have. Despite what Mr. West has undoubtedly told you, I can read." West smiled.

"Then Your Honor knows that Chief Justice Chase ruled that the survivors of those killed on the high seas do have a cause of action for negligence that causes death. He said the wrongful death rule was outmoded and unfair. A number of other good judges have followed *The Seagull* — most recently last year, when a Pennsylvania court awarded damages to the widow of Silas Rickards, who died in a schooner rammed by the steamer *Harrisburg* off Martha's Vineyard."

"Mr. Stevens, it seems to me there are cases going both ways. Can you tell me why this rule got started in the first place, and whether the reasons for it warrant its continued application in modern times?"

"Yes, Your Honor, I was getting to that."

"Well, now's the time, son. It's close to noon, and as Mr. West will tell you, I never miss my lunch."

"Your Honor, in feudal England, negligence that resulted in death was a crime punished by death, an eye for an eye. But more significant for our purposes today, it was also punished by the forfeiture of the defendant's property to the king. Wrongful death claims were a waste of time because the defendant was not only dead but destitute."

"I see. That makes sense," the judge mused. Seamus looked encouraged. "If the negligence merely injured someone, the injured party had a claim because the defendant still had property from which to pay a judgment. But if the negligence caused death, there was no point in a lawsuit because the king would take all the defendant's property, so there would be nothing left for the poor widow.

"And I suppose you'd argue that those reasons no longer apply today," the judge continued. "As we can plainly see, Mr. Pitt has not been executed by the Commonwealth, and we can infer from his ability to hire such distinguished and expensive counsel that he is well-heeled and ready to answer any judgment."

"Precisely, Your Honor," Seamus said.

"Very well. I understand your argument. Any reply, Mr. . . . uh, Mr. . . ."

"*Bishop*, Your Honor," Bishop said with an annoyance he was unable to conceal completely.

"Ah, yes, Mr. Bishop. What do you have to say in defense of the ancient rule? Do you disagree that it has its origins in the crown's confiscation of the defendant's property?"

"I am not sure we will ever know its origins with precision, Your Honor. But we do know with certainty that it has been followed for hundreds of years. Legal traditions should not be trampled upon lightly, as the doctrine of *stare decisis* tells us. Changing well-understood law that businessmen rely on always leads to unfairness."

"Mr. Bishop, your Latin is impressive. I'm always delighted to have a Latin scholar before me; it is *such* a refreshing change." The judge looked toward West with a broad smile on his face; when he looked back toward Bishop, the smile evaporated. "But are you telling me that your client arranged his affairs in the expectation of being able to kill his fishermen and escape responsibility for the loss? What if he miscalculated and maimed these two instead of killing them? Would the extra expense of two large damage claims have put him out of business?"

"Your Honor, my client never planned on killing the fishermen who work for him. He is deeply saddened by the loss," Bishop said somberly.

"Good. I was posing the question rhetorically, of course. But the point is that your client did not plan his affairs in reliance on the continuation of this rule. I am convinced that the ancient wrongful death rule has long outlived its usefulness and, indeed, that there hasn't been any real reason behind it for hundreds of years. The defendants' motion to dismiss is denied."

"Your Honor," Bishop continued, "if I may say one more thing? One of the cases Mr. Stevens referred to, the case involving the steamer *Harrisburg,* was appealed, and it was argued before the U.S. Supreme Court last April. The precise issue raised by my motion will be decided once and for all in that court some time soon. May I suggest that judicial economy would be well served if we were to continue this trial until after the Supreme Court rules in *The Harrisburg?*"

"Mr. Bishop, we have all the parties here, and everyone is prepared. If you had made your motion for a continuance a month ago, I might have been more interested. We will impanel a jury and move forward with this case. But first, lunch. Court is adjourned until one-thirty."

Maggie wanted to run forward and hug Seamus, but that would have been undignified, and besides, he was too busy to deal with the distraction of a jubilant mother. They were all to meet during the break in the back room of The Tavern at Pickering Wharf, a place West knew well. As Maggie got up to make sure the arrangements were properly made, she saw William staring at her from two rows back. She willed herself to start toward the exit, and as she neared him, she said simply, "Hello, William."

"Hello, Maggie," he replied. "Seamus was nervous, but he did a fine job."

She nodded. "Yes, he did — a very fine job, for sure."

Maggie could see sadness in his eyes. "Well, I should be going," she said. "I want to be back by one-thirty."

"Yes, of course," William responded. He walked to the front of the courtroom to join Pitt and Bishop.

Maggie watched him as he conversed with Bishop, then walked over to Seamus and shook his hand. It looked innocent, but it was more than enough to stir up her old fears. Despite the pounds William had put on and the hair he'd lost, the resemblance between father and son was strong. *Will Seamus notice?* she wondered. *How will he react if he realizes I've lied to him all these years?*

After the break, the lawyers and the judge questioned prospective jurors, and by midafternoon twelve men had been selected to serve. Then West gave the opening statement for the plaintiffs. He outlined a simple case. Pitt had sent the *Julia Gorton* to sea with a rotten anchor line. He had been warned that it needed to be replaced, but he refused to spend the small sum needed to do so. In the midst of a storm it snapped, and as a result Robby and Joey were swept away to their deaths, leaving behind two widows and four fatherless children. The tragedy deprived the families of the wages that Robby and Joey would have earned between now and when they retired, the value of which the plaintiffs would prove with particularity.

When West finished, Bishop gave his opening statement.

The line was not perfect, but it was still strong and the boat was seaworthy. Robby and Joey were negligent in not having tethered themselves to the ship; if they had exercised reasonable caution, they would be alive today. And even if the owner bore some small responsibility, the amounts sought were grossly distorted by the unfortunate greed that sometimes followed a tragic accident. The two widows, one a woman of questionable morals, the other a Moorish woman not even a citizen of this country, were seeking an unjust windfall at the expense of an upstanding Essex County businessman, a man whose family had been in America for generations, a man who employed hundreds and was a pillar of his church.

The two opening statements consumed the remaining hours of the first day, and the court adjourned until the following morning. Seamus spent the evening with Esmeralda and her son, Joey Jr., who translated. She would testify the next day, and Seamus would conduct the examination.

Maggie went to the tavern that night with Holly, Sylvie, and West. From their table they could see the masts of Salem's few remaining merchant vessels. The air smelled of salt and pine tar, more pleasant than the odor of fish that permeated the Gloucester docks. The interior of the tavern was a monument to the merchant trade. Brass, oak, and hemp hung from the ceilings and walls.

Maggie and Sylvie ordered the locally made Witches' Brew rum, neat for Sylvie, with water and lime for Maggie. Holly, although fast developing into a woman as beguiling as her birth mother, Anne, was still only fifteen, so she drank sarsaparilla. West ordered a beer that was the specialty of an old Marblehead brewery.

Sylvie took a swig of her rum. "I been so scared. But Seamus said the hardest part was to convince the judge that we had the right to bring the case at all. We done that now — smooth sailin' from here, right?"

West sipped from his mug. "It did go well today. And we've got an advantage with the judge. He appears to be a disagreeable old sot, but he's fair, and he's not afraid to do the right thing. But we're not out of the woods yet, not by a long shot. What you need to prepare yourself for are Bishop's claims that you have questionable morals and are greedy.

"Insurance companies think anyone who wants their money is greedy; nothing unusual there. But you have a special issue to deal with. That fellow Bishop is going to turn himself inside out to make the jury understand that you used to be a . . ." West stopped in midsentence as he realized that Holly was sitting quietly by his side, sipping her sarsaparilla.

"You can say it, Mr. West. Holly knows I used to work in a brothel. It's the way things are for us — there's no hidin' it."

"Good, then. When you're asked, just own up to it, but tell the jury that it's in your past."

Maggie walked Holly to the courtroom the next morning. As they were waiting for the trial to start, the girl pulled Dickens' *Bleak House* out of her bag and started to read. Maggie couldn't help but notice. "That's an interesting book to be reading. Do you like Dickens?"

"Not so much. I had a terrible time getting through *David Copperfield.* But I thought *Bleak House* was especially appropriate. I hope this court is better than Chancery Court in England. I don't think Jarndyce and Jarndyce is ever going to end."

"Yes, that's the point, I suppose. Who's your favorite author?"

Holly put her book down and cocked her head thoughtfully. "If you'd asked me a month ago I would have said Daniel Defoe, and maybe he still is — I love *Robinson Crusoe.* But I just finished reading Mark

Twain's new book, *The Adventures of Huckleberry Finn*. It's a great story, even though the dialect's hard to follow. I love an adventure. Twain's my favorite now, I guess. . . . Mrs. Stevens, Mother's very nervous. She can't afford to make a mistake. We're almost out of money. I've been doing some sewing, but it doesn't pay much. It'll kill Mother if we lose our house. What do you *really* think? Are we gonna win?"

Before Maggie could answer, the gavel came down and the trial resumed.

Captain Sandy Brown was the first witness. He testified that he was from Lunenburg, Nova Scotia, and had started lobstering with his father when he was a boy. Twenty years ago, at seventeen, he'd hired on to a Gloucesterman that had been fishing the Grand Banks when she came to Lunenburg to buy herring for bait. He had been fishing out of Gloucester ever since, and Pitt had made him captain of the *Gorton* five years earlier. West continued the direct examination.

"Now, Captain Brown, you commanded the *Gorton* in February 1885?"

"That's right."

"You had Robert Sprague and Jose Amero on board?"

"Yes. I knew them as Robby and Joey, but yes, they were on board, or I should say they were on board at the start of the trip. They didn't make it home."

"What happened?"

439

"It was a bad storm, one of the worst I've ever seen. It had been howling for twenty-four hours, and in the early evening Robby and Joey were on anchor watch. Well, the anchor line broke, and without the anchor to hold her bow into the wind the *Gorton* went broadside to the sea. A big wave rolled her over onto her beam-ends. I was down below and was thrown across the cabin. After a while — it seemed like a long while to me — she rolled back upright. I got on deck as fast as I could, and so did the rest of my crew. Robby and Joey were gone, washed overboard."

"Did you try to find them?"

"You must understand . . . we were still broadside to the waves when I reached the deck. It was blowing fifty knots, and she was rolling violently from side to side. Eventually we hoisted the stays'l in reefs, and that stopped the rolling. But by then twenty minutes had gone by, and we'd been blown a mile downwind. A man can't live for long in water that cold, and we couldn't sail back upwind in that sea anyway. Robby and Joey couldn't be saved; it just wasn't possible. We never saw them again."

"Captain Brown, I'm handing you the section of line that the clerk has marked as Exhibit 1. Can you tell me what this is?"

"That's a piece of the anchor line from the *Gorton*. After we got her squared away, we found about eighty feet of line still hanging off the bow. We reeled it in, and this was the last three feet of it. I cut it off myself."

"Your Honor," West said, "the plaintiffs offer Exhibit 1 into evidence."

Bishop stood. "Your Honor, the defendants would like to *voir dire*."

"You may proceed," the judge said to Bishop.

"Has this line been in your possession ever since — how did you put it — you 'cut it off'?"

"No."

"When you got back into port, did you give it to Mr. Pitt, your employer?"

"No."

"You gave it to Ray Stevens, a friend of Mrs. Sprague, didn't you?"

"Yes."

"The same Ray Stevens who's the father of Seamus Stevens, one of the plaintiffs' lawyers?" Bishop asked, pointing to Seamus.

"Yes."

"You don't know what's been done with this rope in the last year and a half, do you?"

"I — I guess not, no."

"Your Honor," Bishop said, "we object to the admission of this exhibit. The plaintiffs have failed to establish a proper chain of custody."

"I'll sustain the objection," the judge ruled.

"Captain Brown," West continued. "How do you know this is the same line you gave to Mr. Stevens?"

"I whipped the end myself. I recognize the whipping; it's done the way my papa taught me. See the five loops circling around the main part of the whip? That's the way we do it in Lunenburg. Most of you Yanks use just three loops. And I sure remember the rot in the middle here. That's why I saved it in the first place."

"Is this line in the same condition now as it was when you gave it to Mr. Stevens?"

"Yes."

"Your Honor, the plaintiffs reoffer Exhibit 1."

"Same objection," Bishop said.

"I'll admit the exhibit. I'm convinced the plaintiffs have adequately identified the line."

West continued, "Captain, could you explain to the jury where the rot is that you mentioned?"

Brown held up the line for the jury, pointing out the soft and flaky strands that were darker than the surrounding fibers. The jurors leaned forward to get a good look. Several nodded sagely.

"Captain, how did you happen to go to sea with a rotten anchor line?"

"The *Gorton* was twelve years old, and this was the original line. That's a long time to expect a line to last. I didn't know for sure that it was bad, but it really was too long to expect it to last."

"Why didn't you just replace it?"

"The anchor line is three hundred fathoms; that's a third of a mile. It costs over a hundred dollars — no small expense. I have to get the owner's permission to spend that kind of money."

"Who's the owner?"

"John Pitt."

"That's the man sitting there next to Mr. Bishop," West said as he turned and pointed to Pitt.

"Yes."

"Did you ask him if you could replace the line before the 1885 season?"

"Yes."

"What did he say?"

"He said, 'Money don't grow on trees.'"

"Was that a no?"

"It certainly was a no. There's no arguing with John when he says something like that."

West let that answer linger. Then he turned to Bishop. "Your witness."

"Captain, is every piece of gear on an older fishing schooner always in perfect shape?"

"No, it's not. Not every piece of gear on a brand-new boat is in perfect shape either."

"It's not unusual for gear to break in the middle of a violent storm?"

"Gear breaks; it's part of fishing."

"As captain, you are primarily responsible for the safety of your crew?"

"I am."

"Are you in the habit of taking your boat out in an unsafe condition?"

"No."

"When you left port in February 1885, you didn't think the *Gorton* was unsafe, did you?"

Brown looked to West, who seemed not to notice. He turned back to Bishop. "No."

"You thought that anchor line was good enough to go to sea one more time."

"I would have felt better if I could have replaced it."

"Well, it looked all right, didn't it?"

"Yes, you couldn't tell from the outside."

"And to break it took, how did you put it?" Bishop looked down at his notes and quoted from them. "'A storm that was one of the worst I've ever seen.'"

The captain shifted positions in the chair before answering. "That's right."

"Captain, have you ever heard of men wearing tethers — that is, tying themselves to the ship in bad weather?"

"I've heard of it."

"Neither Mr. Sprague nor Mr. Amero was tethered to the *Gorton,* is that correct?"

"That's correct. Neither was tethered."

"You wouldn't have objected if they'd said they wanted to be tethered, would you?"

"No, I wouldn't have."

"Your Honor, no more questions," Bishop said.

"Captain Brown, did you order any of your crew to be tethered to the boat in that storm?" West asked.

"No."

"Did you ever suggest that they be tethered?"

"No."

"How many boats does Mr. Pitt own?"

"About twenty, I think."

"Does he have any policy requiring men to be tethered during a storm?"

"Not that I'm aware of."

"Captain, why didn't you order your crew to be tethered to the boat in this storm?"

"The way I've heard of it being done is to tie a line around the man's waist and tie the other end to a mast. It's cumbersome, and it slows you down. Most of the men take their chances because they need to move quickly around the boat. If a tether slows a man down too much, he can be a danger to the boat and to his mates. He can't react fast enough to do what needs to be done. That goes double in a storm."

"When you were on deck in this storm last year, did you tether yourself?"

"No, I wouldn't do that. The men would think I was scared."

"No more questions, Your Honor."

"Very well," the judge said. "We will take our morning break."

After the break, Esmeralda took the stand. Joey had been thirty when he died. They had known each other since they were very young and had married when she was only sixteen. They had three children: Joey Jr. was eleven now, and the girls were eight and four. They had moved to Gloucester six years ago, and they regularly attended services at Our Lady of Good Voyage Church.

Esmeralda took care of the children, and Joey had been their sole provider. He earned about six hundred fifty dollars a year. Joey spent fifty dollars on his clothes and fishing gear, leaving six hundred dollars to support her and their children. It was Joey's dream to have a boat of his own one day, and they saved a little whenever they could. At this point, Esmeralda could no longer hold back the tears. Seamus decided that was enough.

Bishop started his cross-examination. "Mrs. Amero, do you and your children live in your own house?"

After a pause as the interpreter and Esmeralda spoke in Portuguese, the answer came back from the interpreter. "No, we live with Joey's mother and father and one of his cousins."

"Do you pay rent?"

"We all help out with the expenses."

"Is it less expensive to live in the Azores than in America?"

"Oh yes, much less. Half, maybe."

"Do you still have relatives back there?"

"Two uncles, an aunt, and many cousins."

"Thank you," Bishop said. "I have no more questions."

They took their lunch break, and when they came back, West put Sylvie on the stand. "Mrs. Sprague, how long had you and Robby been married?"

"We were married on August 23, 1865. I had twenty wonderful years married to Robby."

"And you have a daughter?"

"Yup, Holly's sittin' right there in the second row." Most of the jurors looked over at Holly. Several kept looking at her as Sylvie's examination continued.

"How did you and Robby meet?"

"Mr. West, I had a very hard start to life. Papa was a fisherman, and when I was fourteen his boat sank off Newfoundland. They never found his body. Ma couldn't stand the pain. I came home from school one day, and — "

"Excuse me, objection," Bishop broke in. "Your Honor, the question was how she met her husband."

"Mrs. Sprague, Mr. Bishop is correct. Would you please tell us how you met your husband?"

"Your Honor, I was workin' in a brothel when I met Robby." There was a gasp from several of the jurors. "I was explainin' how I came to be in the brothel."

"Thank you, Mrs. Sprague," the judge said without showing surprise. "Mr. West, you may continue."

"Mrs. Sprague, please tell us how you came to be working in a brothel."

"Objection. Irrelevant."

"Overruled. I think some explanation is required, to be fair, but it is a bit far afield. You may answer, Mrs. Sprague, but please don't drag it out. Let's just hit the highlights."

"Well, like I was startin' to say, I came home a few weeks after Papa died to find Ma had hung herself. She was danglin' from the banister on the second floor of the house we shared with my uncle. Her face was all purple and . . . After that my uncle looked after me, but he, well, he took liberties. So I ran away and lived on the street 'til I got real hungry, and then I found my way to the brothel."

"And you met Robby there?" West asked.

"Yup, Robby was my best customer. Eventually we married, and I had a normal life. I took care a' Holly and did the household chores. Robby supported us with his fishin'."

"How old was Robby when he passed away?"

"He was forty-five."

"How much did he make?"

"'Bout the same as Joey, around six, seven hundred a year. It varied some. The fishermen don't get regular pay."

"Where do you live?"

"We have a small house on Rocky Neck."

"How much of Robby's earnings were required to pay the expenses for you and Holly and your home?"

"Most of it, I'd say. We could never save much."

"Thank you. No further questions."

Bishop stood up from behind the counsel table. "Mrs. Sprague, how old was Mr. Sprague when he started fishing?"

"He was only thirteen."

"How old was he when you met him in the brothel?"

"'Bout sixteen, I guess."

"When Mr. Sprague was your favorite customer, how much of his paycheck did he spend at the brothel?"

"Back in those days, he gave half his paycheck to his mother. She was a fishin' widow too, and he lived with her and his sister. I'd say he spent most a' the other half at the brothel."

"Were you the only one he visited there?"

Sylvie shifted in her seat before answering. "No."

"After you married, he kept going to the brothel, did he not?"

"He did not!" Sylvie said indignantly.

"You do not really know, do you? You did not follow him around all the time."

"I didn't follow him around, but I know my Robby."

"You and lots of other ladies, apparently."

"Objection!" West exclaimed.

"Sustained!" the judge bellowed, banging his gavel for emphasis.

Bishop sat down, shook his head with a disapproving frown, and said with theatrical disgust. "No more questions of this witness."

"Your Honor, the plaintiffs rest," Seamus said.

Bishop stood up. "Your Honor, the defendants move to dismiss. The plaintiffs have failed to put on a *prima facie* case of unseaworthiness."

The judge ruled almost before Bishop stopped talking. "Motion denied. Put on your case, Counsel," he said.

"The defendants call John Pitt to the stand." Pitt walked slowly to the witness chair. He was wearing a wool suit that was too small. Once on the stand, he focused intently on Bishop.

"Mr. Pitt, please tell us about your business."

"I been in the fishin' business my whole life. Started out just like Robby Sprague." Pitt looked at the jury and then back at Bishop. "I worked my way up to captain. Bought my first boat when I was thirty. After that the business grew and grew. Today I own twenty-two fishin' schooners and the John Pitt Fish Packin' Company. We sell Gloucester's fish all over the country."

"Do you keep all those boats in good shape?"

"A fishin' schooner ain't a yacht, ya know. They're workin' boats, no varnish or polished brass, and the paint ain't shiny. But I take care a' my boats. If I didn't, I'd a' been outta business years ago."

"The *Gorton* is one of your boats?"

"Yup."

"Yesterday, Captain Brown testified that you refused to replace an anchor line. What do *you* recall?"

"I never refused any request to replace gear that was unsafe. Before the *Gorton* went to sea that year, we did a lotta work on her. Just to be on the safe side, we replaced every bit a' riggin' — cost over three hundred dollars. I don't remember Brown sayin' anythin' 'bout the anchor line, but if he'd told me it was rotten I woulda told him to get a new one. Boats can sink when an anchor line breaks. I seen it happen. I gotta bundle invested in every one a' my boats. I'd never chance a five-thousand-dollar schooner just to save a hundred on an anchor line."

Bishop walked over to the clerk's table and picked up the anchor line. "Mr. Pitt, I am handing you Exhibit 1. Is that anchor line unsafe?"

"Well, there's some rot in here, more than I like to see. If I'd a' known the line was like this, I'd a' replaced it. But like I said, a fishin' boat ain't a yacht; it's not kept perfect. Look at any boat out there that's more than a few years old, and you'll find rotten wood, corroded metal, and weak line, if you look hard enough.

This here rope was strong enough to handle everythin' but one of the worst storms a' the decade. Four boats sank in that storm. There's only so much you can do."

"Your witness," Bishop said.

West got up and walked over to Pitt's right, forcing him to turn away from the jury to answer. "Mr. Pitt, how many of your boats have been lost at sea over the years?"

Pitt looked at Bishop, who gave an almost imperceptible nod of the head. "Eight. I lost eight a' my boats."

"How many men have been lost on your boats?"

"I don't know."

"Did any men survive the sinking of those eight boats?"

"All but one off the *Sadie May* got saved."

"Any others saved?"

"Not that I remember."

"So you lost all the crew on seven boats?"

"Yup."

"Average crew about ten?"

"That's normal."

"So you lost about seventy men on those boats, and one on the *Sadie May,* and Robby and Joey. Were there others?"

"Yup, there's been a few others washed overboard here and there. Fishin's a dangerous job."

"You're getting close to a hundred dead?"

"No-o-o," he said, dragging out the word. "Not more than eighty-five, I'd say."

"Now, eight boats lost. You said a little earlier that the *Gorton* was worth about five thousand dollars. Is that about average?"

"Pretty close."

"But you had insurance on those boats, didn't you?"

"Objection, Your Honor," Bishop said indignantly. "May we approach the bench?"

"Yes," the judge said. Bishop and West had a hushed conversation with him at the bench, then resumed their places. "The objection is overruled."

"Mr. Pitt, I'd asked whether you had insurance on those boats that were lost."

"Yup, I did."

"So the insurance money paid for their replacement."

"Not all of it."

"Most of it?"

"Yup, I suppose.

"Have you replaced anchor lines on any of those boats?"

"Sure, you bet I have, lotsa times," Pitt said eagerly.

"Insurance never paid for that cost, did it?"

"No-o-o," he said slowly. "Insurance don't cover that kinda thing."

"You had to pay that expense out of your *own* pocket."

"Yup."

"No more questions."

"The defense calls Dr. Albert Hanson," Bishop said.

Dr. Hanson took the witness stand. He was a slight man in his mid-forties with light brown hair in need of trimming. He wore a tweed jacket with leather elbow patches and a crimson bow tie.

"Dr. Hanson, what do you do?"

"I am a professor of mathematics at Harvard College."

"What did I ask you to do in connection with this case?"

"You hired me to look at the fishing industry in Gloucester and make some calculations regarding the mortality and likely lifespan of men engaged in that fishery."

"How did you go about it?"

"First, I gathered the data. The local newspaper in Gloucester has reported extensively on the fishing industry over the years. It is a remarkably good source of information on how many boats sail out of that port and how many boats and men are lost at sea each year. After I compiled the data, I calculated the likelihood of fishermen dying at sea. Then I applied the calculation to the situation of Mr. Sprague and Mr. Amero."

"What did you find?"

"I looked at the twenty-five-year period from 1860 to 1885. During this time, three hundred sixty-four Gloucester fishing schooners sank, and two thousand four hundred twenty-two Gloucester fishermen were lost at sea." Half a dozen people in the courtroom gasped.

Hanson seemed startled. He looked up at the judge, who nodded, and continued. "I estimate that in an average year, about four hundred schooners were fishing out of Gloucester, each with an average crew of ten, so there were, on average, four thousand men employed in the fishery at any one time."

"Over twenty-four hundred died, you say?"

"That's right. By simple division, I calculate that ninety-three men of the four thousand who were fishing were lost in the average year, which is a mortality rate of two point three percent. But that is not accurate for Mr. Sprague and Mr. Amero, for they were engaged in the Georges Bank fishery, which the records show is far and away the most dangerous of the Gloucester fisheries. I estimate mortality in the Georges fishery is, conservatively, fifty percent higher than average, or three point four five percent."

"What conclusions relative to our case did you reach?"

"Well, first off, I conclude that Mr. Sprague was a lucky man. He fished for thirty-two years, from age thirteen to age forty-five, before being killed at sea. A man has only a thirty-three percent chance of living that long in the Georges Bank fishery. The average lifespan of a fisherman on Georges Bank is twenty years. A boy who starts fishing at age thirteen can expect to live to age thirty-three; any longer, and he is living on borrowed time."

"Mr. West is claiming that these fishermen would have worked until they reached age sixty-five if they had not perished in the 1885 storm, and that their widows were denied the benefit of their wages for all that time. What do your calculations say about that?"

"That is unlikely. It is more likely than not that both fishermen would have died from some other accident in the next twenty years if this calamity had not done them in. I do not see how you could justify concluding that Mr. Amero would live beyond age fifty. While it is possible Mr. Sprague could live to sixty-five, if he did, he would be a very rare man indeed. Only sixteen percent of Georges Bank fishermen will be lucky enough to survive a fifty-two-year career without dying at sea."

"Thank you, Dr. Hanson. Your witness."

Seamus stood up to cross-examine. "Dr. Hanson, how many of those three hundred sixty-four schooners sank because the equipment on them was not properly maintained?"

"I have no way of knowing that."

"Surely some of those boats sank because they were not well maintained?"

"They might have. I really do not know."

"How many of those twenty-four hundred men were lost because the captain or a crew member was careless?"

"I do not know that either."

"Some of them were lost due to carelessness, weren't they?"

"That is reasonable to assume, I suppose."

"Are the eighty-five men who died on John Pitt's boats included in your statistics?"

"Yes, if they died between 1860 and 1885."

"How many of them died due to Mr. Pitt's failure to properly maintain his boats?"

"Objection. Speculation," Bishop broke in loudly.

Everyone looked at the judge. He paused, then said. "Well, speculation is what experts do. I'll let him answer."

"I do not know," the professor said.

"No further questions." Seamus sat down.

"Your Honor," Bishop rose. "The defense rests."

The judge looked to West. "Any rebuttal case, Counsel?"

"One witness, Your Honor."

"Proceed."

"The plaintiffs call Mr. William Hudson."

Bishop stood and looked confused. "Your Honor, this is irregular and improper."

The judge looked at his pocket watch. "We will send the jury on their break a little early, and then counsel may address the bench." The bailiff escorted the jury out through the door to the jury room, and at the same time Seamus left quietly through the main door. Once the jury had left, the judge spoke again. "Am I correct that Mr. Hudson is of the Boston Hudsons? Mr. West, how is his testimony relevant here?"

"Your Honor," West responded, "Mr. Hudson is the president of the insurance company that insures Mr. Pitt's fishing boats. I believe he will testify that Mr. Pitt has not been adequately maintaining his fleet."

"This is ridiculous, Your Honor," Bishop said. "It is exceedingly improper for the subject of insurance to even be mentioned in the presence of the jury. And it is certainly improper for Mr. Hudson to be testifying about how Mr. Pitt maintains his boats. He has no firsthand knowledge on that subject."

"Mr. Bishop," the judge said, "as I ruled earlier today, you opened the door on insurance when Mr. Pitt testified that he would not risk a five-thousand-dollar boat to save the expense of a hundred-dollar line. However, I take your second point. Mr. West, can you lay a foundation as to Mr. Hudson's knowledge of Mr. Pitt's maintenance practices?"

"Your Honor, Mr. Hudson is an expert on the causes of fishing boat accidents. His company insures most of the fleet, and he closely watches accident statistics. I do not plan to elicit his personal knowledge of the facts, but rather his opinions as an expert."

"All right, Mr. West. I'll let you question this witness. I'm curious to see how you intend to make this man your expert. But I warn you, no empty theatrics, or you'll regret it."

The court adjourned for its afternoon break, but Maggie remained seated. She had known it all along, she supposed — year after year, all the boats that went to sea and didn't come back — but twenty-four hundred dead! Gloucester, a town that had never been home to more than twenty thousand, was flushing its men into the sea.

Twenty years — an average lifespan of twenty years. Ray had been fishing for twenty-six years now. And where was he? He should have been back days ago.

Maggie looked over at Pitt, sitting at the counsel table. He had sent eighty-five men to their deaths. But then she thought of Winnie as she had looked that last day, in her stained cotton dress, lying on her unwashed bedsheets in that smelly loft after Maggie had let her go. And then Anne, the most sensuous woman she'd ever met and the best she'd ever seen at her profession — but last year she had turned forty. Twenty-four years in the business had taken its toll, and the men had stopped asking for her. Maggie had to let her go. Twenty-four years, just about as long as a fisherman lasts. *Am I any better than Pitt*, she wondered.

The jury was brought back, and William was called to the stand. As he took the oath, he cocked his head arrogantly, but he fidgeted when West began his questioning.

"How long have you been president of the N.S. Hudson Insurance Company?"

"Twenty-seven years."

"We heard Mr. Pitt testify that he has lost eight boats at sea. How many of those boats did the N.S. Hudson Company insure?"

"All of them."

"Were you personally involved in the decision to pay the insurance on Pitt's losses?"

"Yes. I'm the president of the company. That is my job."

"Have you formed an opinion as to whether Mr. Pitt failed to adequately maintain his boats?"

"No, Mr. West. No, I have *not*." Now he was defiant, and angry.

"Mr. West," the judge said sternly, "is there some reason we should continue with this witness?"

"Your Honor, if you will bear with me, I will need to cross-examine Mr. Hudson. I realize I called him, but I think his hostility is self-evident."

"All right, Mr. West, but it had better pan out."

"Mr. Hudson," West continued, "you supped at the Harbor Club last night with Mr. Pitt?"

William clenched and then relaxed his jaw. "Yes," he said.

"You got into an argument with Mr. Pitt during the second course?" Two of the jurors leaned forward so they could hear better.

"I would not say that. No, Mr. Pitt and I had a business discussion, that is all."

"You don't recall smashing your fist into the table and breaking your plate?"

"I . . . I am not sure."

"You don't recall Mr. Pitt calling you a pompous blowhard and throwing a glass over your shoulder?"

At this, one of the jurors in the second row smiled. Then, with perfect timing, the courtroom door opened and in walked Seamus, followed by a man wearing a white server's apron. All eyes were on them as they walked silently down the aisle. When they reached the front row, Seamus seated the man next to Maggie and took his own seat at the counsel table.

"Mr. Hudson, do you recognize Francis Sable, your waiter from the Harbor Club last night?" West asked as he turned and gestured with open palm toward the man in the apron.

"I do not know this man's name, but . . . but yes, that is the waiter," William said weakly, his chest deflating.

"Let me ask you one more time. Did you argue with Mr. Pitt last night?"

"Perhaps you could call it an argument."

"Did you say," West looked down at his notepad and put on his reading glasses, "'Pitt, you are not maintaining your boats, goddamn it! Your neglect is costing me money'?" West looked up from his pad and removed his glasses.

William looked at his lawyer, but Bishop could do no more than shrug his shoulders. William looked at the waiter, who was staring straight ahead, pretending he didn't notice his gaze. "I may have said that," he finally answered, almost without opening his mouth.

"Your *neglect* — is costing *me* — *money*," West repeated deliberately, and the courtroom was silent. Before the silence became unbearable, West said, "Your witness."

William's face was drained of all color, and he was looking down at the floor. Bishop started to ask something, then changed his mind and said simply, "No questions."

"Your Honor, that concludes our rebuttal," West said.

The judge cocked his head and looked at Bishop with a smile. "Any surrebuttal, Counsel?"

"No, Your Honor."

Maggie watched William descend from the witness stand. Bishop put a hand on his shoulder and started to say something to console him, but William was having none of it. He turned and walked silently out of the courtroom, passing Maggie with his head down so as not to meet her gaze. She couldn't help but feel for him. A remnant of long-lost love came to the surface, just for that moment.

The next morning they reconvened for closing arguments. West addressed the jury first. "As is plain to you all, I am not a young man." With a slight limp, he walked from the counsel table to stand directly in front of the jury box. "I have had the privilege of standing here, in this room, on this very spot, to argue my clients' causes for thirty-four years. Mine has been a charmed life, for I have done what I love doing.

"Robby Sprague and Joey Amero lived charmed lives, for a while. They loved their wives, they loved their children, and perhaps they loved going to sea as much as I love lawyering. But you and I shall never know them, because their voices have been silenced, forever muted by the frigid sea, their bodies sunk into oblivion to lie alongside twenty-four hundred other men of Gloucester, men who were brave enough to face dangers that this old barrister can barely imagine.

"It falls to you to judge the seaworthiness of their vessel." West walked to the clerk's desk and picked up Exhibit 1. "The anchor line was rotten at its core." He took hold of one of the inner strands, and it disintegrated as he gave it a tug. "This line was twelve years old in February 1885, when Captain Sandy Brown told Mr. Pitt he should replace it. Twelve years is too old, Captain Brown testified. It was Mr. Pitt's refusal to pay for a replacement that drowned Robby and Joey.

"So what does Mr. Pitt say in his defense? Well, he told Captain Brown that 'money don't grow on trees,' remember that? Mr. Pitt doesn't remember saying it now, but when he took the stand, he didn't deny it. And remember what else Mr. Pitt said when he was trying to convince you he did the right thing: 'I wouldn't risk my five-thousand-dollar boat to save the hundred dollars a new anchor line would cost.'" West slowly shook his head. "Even now, a year and a half after this tragic accident, Mr. Pitt still doesn't understand the enormity of what he did. He didn't just risk money, he gambled with the lives of the *Gorton*'s crew when he refused to replace that line — a hundred dollars against the lives of ten men. Robby and Joey were the losers — this time. But they are just the most recent of the eighty-five men who have died while sailing for John Pitt. How many of them perished because that man," West turned and pointed to Pitt, "wouldn't spend a few dollars on maintenance?

"And then we learned that the five thousand dollars Mr. Pitt was so concerned about wasn't even his. His boats are insured, so when they sink, the insurance company pays the loss. Is Mr. Pitt willing to pay even a hundred dollars to protect the *insurance company* from a five-thousand-dollar loss? We know the answer that Mr. Hudson gives to that question — he believes Mr. Pitt *neglects* his boats, and damn the consequences in dollars, and in *lives*, as long as they're not his dollars or, heaven forbid, his life.

"The judge told you that all you need to do to find for the plaintiffs is to find that the *Gorton* was unseaworthy, which in this case means that this rotten anchor line was not as strong as it should have been. You don't have to find that it was Mr. Pitt's fault for the plaintiffs to win, although I would submit to you that his fault is obvious.

"The defense suggested that Robby and Joey should have been tethered to the boat. But they produced no evidence that this was the practice anywhere in the industry. It certainly is not the practice on any of Mr. Pitt's boats. If this is an important safety issue, then Mr. Pitt should have insisted on it. It's not fair to blame Robby and Joey for not doing what no other fisherman does.

"If you find that the *Gorton*'s rotten anchor line made her unseaworthy, then you must determine the loss to the widows and the children. We know from the testimony that each widow received about six hundred dollars per year from the fishing efforts of her husband. Dr. Hanson told you that you should award no more than twenty years of those wages, but you can find that both Robby and Joey would have worked until they were sixty-five. They have demonstrated with their long careers that they were each good enough to beat the odds, as long as they were given a seaworthy boat to work on.

"Finally, you should not succumb to Mr. Bishop's invitation to cruel bigotry. Mrs. Sprague does not deserve to be punished because she had a rough start to life. If anything, she should be praised for turning her life around and for raising a fine daughter.

"And Mrs. Amero does not deserve less because she is a recent immigrant. We are a nation of immigrants, and we know that someone who comes from another place, speaks another language, or has darker skin than we do is no less human for it, and no less deserving of justice. It was not that long ago that we suffered through a great war to prove this point. Shame on the defense for suggesting that Mrs. Amero is not entitled to fair compensation.

"A weighty burden has been placed on your shoulders. Today you are the arbiters of justice. We have been told by the defense that Georges Bank fishermen cannot expect to live beyond the age of thirty-three years. Think of how young that is, of how much of life they never live. Men asked to work in an environment that dangerous deserve the best we can give them, and when they don't get it, they deserve to have their widows and children taken care of. Their fate is in your hands now." West turned and walked slowly to the counsel table without looking back. He sat down.

Bishop stood and walked briskly to the jury box. "I will be brief, because this is a simple case." He spoke a little too quickly, as if he were in a hurry to get his argument over with. "Fishing boats are never perfect. The law does not require them to be perfect, just reasonably fit for the task. The first witness called by the plaintiffs was Captain Brown, an obvious friend of theirs, who helped their case as much as he could by saving that piece of anchor line and giving it to them instead of to his employer.

"But he gave the most important testimony of the whole case. Captain Brown admitted that the *Gorton* was safe when it left port. Brown would have helped the plaintiffs more if he could have, but he is an honest man, so he had to admit what is true: the *Gorton* was not in perfect shape — but she *was* seaworthy. If you agree with Captain Brown, and I submit to you that no one knew the condition of that boat better than he did, you *must* find for the defendants.

"Now, I am very reluctant to speak ill of the dead, but it is my duty to point out that Mr. Sprague and Mr. Amero are as much at fault as anyone. They would be at home with their families tonight if only they had bothered to tether themselves to the boat. It was the worst storm of the decade, and they were strolling about the deck without a safety line. They should have known better.

"Even though you should find for the defendants and thus never consider this issue at all, I am compelled to discuss the enormous sums requested in damages. Mrs. Amero wants thirty-five years of wages at six hundred dollars a year — that is over twenty thousand dollars. She testified that she and Mr. Amero were saving for a boat they hoped to buy one day; well, with this sum she could buy four boats right now. Or she could take this fortune back to the Azores, build a castle, and live like a queen. She is not entitled to such a windfall.

"Mrs. Sprague has lived a hard life, no doubt, and Mr. West is correct that her hard times are not relevant here. But Mr. West would have her move to Easy Street: twenty years at six hundred dollars per year — that is twelve thousand dollars. She could buy a couple of her own brothels with that kind of money. We all know that if Mr. Sprague were alive today and given twelve thousand dollars, he would go out and spend most of it in pursuit of his own pleasure. A leopard does not change his spots, gentlemen, and the part of Mr. Sprague's wages that he would have squandered at a brothel should not be given instead to Mrs. Sprague. But you really do not need to sort this out. Mr. Sprague was living on borrowed time — there are very few fifty-year-old fishermen. You can easily conclude he would have worked no more than another year or two. In any event, Mrs. Sprague should not get more than the thousand dollars or so that he would have earned in that time.

"Gentlemen of the jury, thank you for your attention. I ask that you give this case the sober evaluation that it deserves and that you render your verdict for the defendants."

The bailiff ushered the jury out so they could begin their deliberations, and Maggie, West, Seamus, and the plaintiffs withdrew to the tavern. As their meal was being served, Bishop arrived and asked to have a word with West and Seamus. The three stepped out onto the wharf, where young Joey Amero Jr. was playing jacks with his oldest sister.

"Mr. Hudson would like to discuss settling the case before the jury returns a verdict. Are you interested in talking?" Bishop asked. West said they would be willing to entertain an offer. William had a condition, however: he wanted to meet alone with Seamus. After a brief discussion West and Seamus agreed, and Bishop walked Seamus across the street to the Harbor Club. Bishop ushered Seamus into a private sitting room, then left him alone with William.

William motioned Seamus over to two overstuffed leather chairs that faced a red brick fireplace. A decanter and two small snifters had been placed on a small cherry end table between the chairs. William poured brandy into the snifters and handed one to Seamus: "Let us toast to the conclusion of a difficult trial." He raised the glass to his nose, and after swirling the brown liquid and inhaling the vapors, he took a sip.

Seamus had learned to drink rum and whiskey at Fannies years ago, but brandy was new to him. He imitated William as best he could, but he downed the full glass in one swallow. His eyes watered as he tried in vain to hold back a cough.

William poured him another glass, then leaned back in his chair and confidently draped one leg over the other. "Young man, I thought you did a splendid job this week. Was this your first trial?"

"Thank you." Seamus coughed and tried to clear his throat. He shifted uneasily in his chair. "Yes, it was." He draped his own leg over the other, mimicking William.

"You have a fine future ahead of you. When this is all over, I would like to discuss retaining you on a regular basis. The N.S. Hudson Insurance Company gets into legal scraps from time to time. I could use an enthusiastic young man like you."

Seamus' practice had been hand to mouth. He was making ends meet only because his mother was paying the rent for his office above the savings bank. Having a client like Hudson would ensure his success. But this offer seemed too good to be true. Why would Hudson want a brand-new sole practitioner from Gloucester when he could, and did, employ the likes of the Hughes and Black firm?

But there would be enough time to ponder that later. "Mr. Hudson, I do have time for a new client or two, and would be delighted to discuss the subject with you in due course, but perhaps now we should focus our attentions on the business at hand."

"Of course, quite right, first things first. Stuart tells me I should not offer you much; truth is, he does not approve of me even talking to you, but it is my money, after all. He thinks we are even-money with the jury, but if we lose, he is very confident of our chances on appeal. He has a classmate on the Supreme Court, and he is sure the court will go our way in that case where the steamship ran down the schooner. The . . . uh . . . uh, I am getting old; what is the name of the case?"

"I believe you are referring to *The Harrisburg.*"

"Yes, *The Harrisburg,* quite right. Stuart says it will come down our way before you can get through an appeal, so we should just wait for that to happen. What do you think?"

"Sir, I think our case went quite well before the jury. As for the Supreme Court, there really is no reason for the old rule. I think they will see that."

"Oh, I love the innocence of youth. I used to have it myself. Seamus — may I call you Seamus?"

Seamus nodded.

"Those men on the Supreme Court are like me. They are my age, they went to my kind of school, and like me, they know it is commerce that makes the world go round. The reason the wrongful death rule has lasted all these years has nothing to do with medieval murders; it's still around because it's good for business, and good for people like Pitt and me.

"You can see that plain enough from the case we have right here. Give twenty thousand dollars to that little Portagee firecracker, and she and her whole family will sit on their broad derrieres drinking Madeira all day. But give it to that crude old bastard Pitt, and he will buy four more fishing boats, employ thirty people,

471

and feed a small city. The men on the Supreme Court understand this."

William sat back and nodded, as if agreeing with himself. As West had instructed, Seamus did not respond. He waited.

William eventually filled the void. "Well, let us get down to brass tacks. Since the jury could come back at any moment, I will lay it all on the line. No negotiating — this is my first and final offer. I will pay each of your widows one thousand dollars. It is a generous offer, and it is one thousand dollars more than they will get if we play this out to the end. What do you say? Do we have a deal?"

Seamus hesitated, but he knew what he had to do. "I appreciate the offer, Mr. Hudson. I will have to discuss it with my clients."

"All right, but do not delay. The money is off the table if the jury comes back before you accept. And as soon as we take care of this case, let us discuss your coming to work for me."

They shook hands, and Seamus returned to the tavern. He had high hopes for more than a thousand each. Rickard's widow had gotten fifty-one hundred in *The Harrisburg*, but Rickard had been the first officer of the schooner. What if Hudson was right, and the Supreme Court took it all away? He was unsure what was best, but he didn't need to agonize over it. Sylvie and Esmeralda dismissed the offer out of hand, as if they were insulted Hudson had made it.

472

Seamus wasn't so sure that rejecting the offer was the right thing to do. Maybe they should at least test Hudson with a counteroffer. But he was uncertain of his own motives. He did not want to tell his clients, or West, about everything Hudson had said to him, and that made him feel dirty. He ordered a shot of rum, and then another, and then he began to feel better.

West and Sylvie were whooping it up now, as if they had already won and pocketed the money. Esmeralda was part of the celebration too, even though she didn't understand most of what was being said.

Maggie sat across the table from Seamus, quietly sipping a rum and lime. She could feel her son's distress, and she was worrying herself sick over what William might have told her boy. She ordered another round.

That night she gently asked Seamus to tell her everything William had said. He responded that it was all business: they discussed the case, and William made his offer. Maggie sensed he was holding something back, but her fear that William had told Seamus that he was his father subsided. *For sure, Seamus would have mentioned that once we were alone*, she thought.

It was midafternoon the next day when they were summoned to the courtroom. The jury foreman was an old farmer from Ipswich whom they had not been able to read. He had seemed unhappy with everyone's testimony, and now he was to deliver the verdict.

"Has the jury reached a verdict?" the judge asked.

"Yes, Judge," the farmer said.

"In February 1885, was the vessel *Julia Gorton* seaworthy or unseaworthy?"

"The jury finds the vessel unseaworthy."

The courtroom was silent. The judge's chair creaked as he leaned forward to ask the next question.

"What damages do you find were incurred by Sylvie Sprague and her daughter?"

"Nine thousand dollars, Judge."

Sylvie started to cry.

"What damages do you find were incurred by Esmeralda Amero and her children?"

"Twelve thousand dollars, Judge."

Joey Jr. translated for his mother, and she let out a yelp and jumped out of her seat. Seamus popped up, grabbed her, and sat her back down as the judge banged his gavel. She looked up at him and mouthed an apology. The judge's frown turned into a smile, and he nodded to her that it was all right.

"Mr. Foreman, is this the unanimous verdict of the jury?"

"It is, Judge."

"Do any of the jurors disagree?"

All the heads in the jury box shook from side to side.

"Very well," the judge said. "The jury is dismissed. Thank you for your service. Counsel for the plaintiffs shall prepare a form of judgment. You may present it at two o'clock one week from today. Court is adjourned."

Sylvie hugged Seamus as if she never wanted to let him go. Esmeralda said thank you to West and thank you to Seamus, and then again and again to each. Maggie held back, watching her son bask in the moment. She was happy for him, of course, but there was no joy in her heart. Last night she'd dreamt of an underwater cemetery filled with barnacle-encrusted tombstones that stretched in front of her as far as she could see. She had willed herself awake before she got close enough to read the names, afraid that one of them was Ray's.

Pitt had slammed his fist down on the counsel table when the foreman announced the verdict. He stormed out of the courtroom under cover of the commotion as Seamus was getting control of Esmeralda. After adjournment Bishop packed his briefcase, and when things simmered down, he stepped over and congratulated West and Seamus on their victory. Then they all went home.

Two nights later, Fannies held its grandest party. The crowd overflowed the bar into the cellar. The fishermen were there in force, and Esmeralda, her family, and many of her friends overcame their reluctance to come to this place and joined in the party. Seamus was the beau of the ball. The truest native son of Fannies, he was now the hero to the Gloucester fishermen that he had been all along to the ladies. Photographs of Robby and Joey were hung above the bar, and garlands and ribbons were laid around them.

When it seemed the place couldn't hold another soul, the red door opened and in walked ten more men, led by Ray. They had tied up less than an hour earlier, and as soon as they heard the news, the whole unwashed crew walked up Duncan Street to join in the celebration. The fishing had been slow and they were two days late leaving the grounds, but what had truly held them up was a profound lack of wind: five days of drifting with sails and booms slapping back and forth as the *Parsons* rolled helpless in the swells, five days to cover the one hundred twenty miles back to Gloucester.

After the party finally wound down, Ray and Maggie rowed back across the harbor to Rocky Neck. While they were getting ready for bed, Maggie confessed how scared she had been. "I've had nightmares, Ray."

"I couldn't help the lack of wind."

"Of course not, darling." They slid between the bedsheets, and she put her arms around him. "A mathematics professor testified at trial. He said twenty-four hundred Gloucester fishermen have died in the last twenty-five years. Think of it, Ray: twenty-four hundred in just about the time you've been fishing."

"It's a dangerous job. But it provides a good living."

"Not for long. This professor said the average fisherman lives only twenty years before the odds catch up with him. You've been fishing twenty-six years now." She kissed him gently on the lips. "Maybe it's time you gave it up."

"Oh, Maggie, after all these years, I still love it. Last night we were over Stellwagen, just drifting. I took the midnight watch — I could have assigned it to one of the men — but I wanted to be out on deck. The days without wind had flattened the sea; it was like time itself had stopped.

"Then I heard a pop, then another and another and another, like four rocks bouncing off the hull. I looked over the side and saw them. Red and purple tubes shot at the port quarter and disappeared under us — two, then three, then four. Dolphins made them as they darted just under the surface — brilliant tubes of phosphorescence, Maggie! They circled around and shot back from bow to stern, crisscrossing up and over each other. They kept at it for a whole hour! I've seen them play a thousand times, but it was magic last night, just like the first time. Those dolphins love life, and they remind me that I love it too."

"But I love *you* — and I'm so afraid you'll head out to sea and never come back. I'm afraid the last image I'll ever have of you will be with your right hand on the wheel and your left hand waving goodbye to me."

Ray looked out the bay window across the inner harbor. Fannies was visible in the dim light of the moon, but his gaze was not focused on it or anything else. "I was on night watch with Robby one time when I first started fishing. He told me about this horrible storm that killed his father and his two brothers, and that almost killed him when he was only thirteen.

"I asked him why he kept on going to sea. He needed to support his mother and his sister, to be sure. But there was more. He said he was lucky to have been born a fisherman, and he was proud to do what his father had done. He knew death would come to him one day, but fishing was his calling, his destiny. I didn't understand back then, but I do now. Maybe it's because my own father and brother have died at sea since then.

"I don't know whether God ever visits that Universalist church we go to. Sometimes when I'm sitting in church, I don't even know whether God exists. But when I'm at sea, I feel connected to everything around me — to the men, the boat, and the sea itself. It's like I'm part of it all, and all of it is part of me. If God lives, I think he must be a sailor, or a dolphin, or a violent squall, or maybe all those things. I know little of God, but I do know where he lives — he lives at sea."

"Ray, you have to promise me to be as careful as you can be."

"I always am. I was foolish when I was first starting out, but Paul Tobey straightened me out. I'm a cautious captain. Some of my men think I'm too cautious."

Maggie knew caution had not kept Tobey alive, or Ray's own father, Gus, but she would take what she could get. "I know you will be, darling. Do you know about tethers?"

"I've heard about them. They restrict your movement quite a bit."

"Please learn more about them. Will you do that for me?"

"Of course, my love, I'll do anything for you."

A week later, Seamus and West had been at the counsel table for half an hour when at two-fifteen the courtroom door flew open and Bishop entered with uncharacteristic haste. Beads of sweat had formed on his forehead, and his bow tie was askew — all very much out of character for the proper Boston lawyer.

He had barely reached the counsel table and was doffing his hat and coat when the clerk boomed out, "All rise," and the door to the chambers was flung open. Judge Ellery took the bench and, without even calling the calendar, lit into Bishop. "Counsel, when this court sets a time for a hearing, it expects Counsel to be in the courtroom and seated at the appointed hour. No excuses are adequate for such a delay."

"I beg the court's pardon," Bishop said, still out of breath. "But I knew the court would want to consider this, and I was not able to put my hands on it until the very last moment." Bishop pulled his briefcase onto the counsel table and extracted papers. He handed a small bound document to the clerk for the judge and a second to Seamus. Seamus looked down at it and felt dread well up inside him.

"Your Honor," Bishop continued, "this is Chief Justice Waite's opinion in *The Harrisburg*. It was published just yesterday and rushed to Boston on the overnight train. The decision of the court is found on the last page. He writes:

> The argument everywhere in support of wrongful death suits in admiralty has not been that the maritime law is different from the common law, but that the common law is not founded on good reason and is contrary to "natural equity and the general principles of law." Since, however, it is established that no action at law can be maintained for such wrong, we are forced to the conclusion that no such action will lie in the courts of the United States under the general maritime law.

Bishop stopped reading and looked to the judge, who had been following along.

Judge Ellery took his eyes off the page and looked sadly at Seamus. "Mr. Stevens, it appears it is not enough for the Supreme Court that the rule has no reason. All the esteemed court seems to care about is that it has always been the rule."

Seamus could not think of anything to say. The pause was filled by Bishop. "Your Honor, the defense moves for judgment *non obstante veredicto*. This decision makes clear that there is no cause of action for wrongful death on the high seas."

Judge Ellery was so dispirited that he didn't comment on Bishop's use of Latin. "Young man," he said gently to Seamus, "this is a court of law today, not a court of justice. As much as I would like to ignore what I think is a cruel and unfair decision, if I do, the supreme judicial court of our fair Commonwealth will strike me down. Since there is no good reason for delaying the inevitable, I grant the defense motion and dismiss the plaintiffs' case. I wish I could do otherwise." He turned to Bishop. "Counsel, it won't be necessary for me to hear an application for a cost bill, will it?"

Bishop knew when enough was enough. "No, Your Honor. The defendants waive costs."

After the judge retired, Bishop turned to West and Seamus. "Gentlemen, you should have taken Mr. Hudson's offer." Seamus watched in a stupor as West shook hands with Bishop and congratulated him on his victory. Somehow, Seamus summoned the willpower to do the same.

Chapter 39

Gloucester — November 1886

Ten days later, on a cold November morning, Maggie sat facing the harbor in the dining room of her Clarendon Street home. Her scrambled eggs were half-eaten, and her coffee was now cold. By her right hand sat a yellow-stained clay pipe next to an ashtray full of burnt tobacco remnants; by her left hand was the tattered copy of *Winter Studies and Summer Rambles in Canada* that she had pulled off the shelf in a fit of wakefulness during the night. She stared at it now with bloodshot eyes.

Holly Sprague had started work at Fannies. She was just the maid, nothing wrong with that, Maggie had assured Sylvie. Lucy would take care of her. But they both knew. The familiar reality was as cold and hard as it ever was in this town. Sylvie needed the money to hold on to her house, and that brutal fact was the foundation on which Holly would have to build her life.

Maggie watched two herring gulls soar on an updraft. For the thousandth time she replayed the tumultuous meeting she'd had days earlier with Seamus. She had been doing the books at Fannies when he dropped by. William Hudson had sent a telegram asking him to come to Boston to discuss taking a case for his insurance company. "What do you think I should do?" Seamus had asked her.

Two weeks earlier, flush with excitement over the victory the jury had handed him, Seamus had been looking forward to a fulfilling career representing the widows of drowned Gloucester fishermen, but the Supreme Court had taken away that dream. Now he had the opportunity for good, steady, paying work. He could learn his trade while earning his keep. But he would be joining the opposition. West, Ray, and maybe even his mother would think he was being disloyal to side with Hudson. What should he do?

She had to tell him, of course; she couldn't let him make this decision without knowing. She confessed. His father hadn't died on the way to the New World. She had worked as a maid in William's house. She had been so very young.

Seamus was speechless with anger. She'd lied to him about who his father was, and then made up a story when he started asking questions. Honesty was the foundation for everything; she'd told him that time and again, all the while lying to him about who he was and where he'd come from, questions he had asked a dozen times. She had let him go through that trial and negotiate with Hudson, not knowing the truth. She had played him for the fool — Hudson had to think him a fool.

Seamus had stomped out and slammed the door behind him. She couldn't blame him. She had broken the cardinal rule she had recited to him his whole life. She had lost his respect.

She knew he had taken the train to Boston to talk to William. He would work for William; she knew that now too. Seamus would move to Boston. Father and son would become close. She had asked him to stop by Fannies when he returned, but it had been two days now and he hadn't come. He had been so mad when he stormed out of her office; he was in a righteous rage. She was afraid she had lost him forever.

Maggie pushed the eggs away and looked down at her beat-up copy of Jameson's book, the sorrowful symbol of her broken dreams. Then she looked back up and saw that familiar old schooner, working its way south in the moderate breeze under a blue sky that was starting to fill with horsetails.

The *Benjamin Parsons* had been tied up at the Railways overnight, and now, in winter trim, she was headed out to Ipswich Bay on a halibut trip. She was hugging the Rocky Neck shore and would pass not more than a hundred feet away. Maggie forced herself to rise, open the door to the porch, and step out into the cold, where she could be seen. A young boy was sitting with legs spread on the bowsprit, delighting in watching the *Parsons* push aside the small waves that had made it this far into the harbor. She could not make out his face, but she knew who he was. Ray had taken on eleven-year-old Joey Amero Jr., who was going to sea to support his family, just as his father had done in his time.

Now the quarterdeck pulled abreast of the porch, and there he was. Right hand on the wheel, he gave a big wave with his left. He was smiling broadly, his white teeth plainly visible amid his dark beard. She leaned against the porch rail with the cold westerly in her face and waved for all she was worth.

The *Parsons* was moving fast, and in minutes she was behind the paint factory. Maggie watched the bubbles dissipate in her wake. Soon all traces of her passing were gone, leaving behind just the sea and the vision of Ray waving goodbye that was burned into her brain.

Maggie walked back to the dining room and shut the door against the cold. She slumped in her chair and buried her face in her hands. She was alone, so very alone.

She'd remained that way for a while when a hand was laid on her shoulder. Startled, she bolted upright. Seamus had let himself in when she was out on the porch, and she hadn't heard him. He pulled up a dining room chair and sat down next to her. Her face was wet with tears, and her hair was tangled and windblown.

"How long have you been watching me?" she asked.

"A wee while, Ma."

"Did you see your father?" She was barely able to get the words out.

"No." Seamus pulled out a handkerchief and handed it to his mother. "I saw William Hudson, and he offered me a job as his general counsel, and told me I would be president of the company one day."

"What did you tell him?" Maggie asked, almost inaudibly.

"I told him I was needed back in Gloucester," Seamus said, taking his mother's hand, "where my father and a few thousand other brave men risk their lives every day to put food on the table, and where a courageous woman raised me in a brothel and made me the man I am today. I told him no, Ma. I told him no."

Epilogue

2018

The extraordinary loss of life in the Gloucester fishery continued unabated during the remainder of the age of sail. By the end of the nineteenth century, primitive internal combustion engines had been added to a few schooners. At first these were deck engines called "donkeys" that provided power to raise the anchor and the sails. Then larger engines facilitated docking and propelled the schooners when the wind failed. Finally, newly constructed mechanically powered vessels replaced the sailing schooners altogether.

Radio communication, weather forecasting, and the diesel engine eventually made offshore fishing much safer than it was in Ray's time, but even today, fishing remains the most dangerous job in America. In 1923, on the three hundredth anniversary of the town's founding, its iconic Gloucester Fishermen's Memorial statue was dedicated to the thousands upon thousands of local fishermen who lost their lives at sea.

The business of fishing has evolved since Ray's day. Many fishermen now work in the bowels of factory trawlers, where they operate machines that head, gut, fillet, freeze, and pack the catch at sea. These ships are operated by large corporations that own quotas given them by the federal government, granting them the exclusive right to catch hundreds of thousands of tons of fish every year. By and large, Congress has attached no strings to this gift.

Like the mills of nineteenth-century Lowell, Massachusetts, most of today's floating factories are exempt from laws mandating minimum wages and overtime pay and from much of the workplace-safety regulation that is routine in factories ashore. As a result, the Pitts of today can and do require workdays of twelve to sixteen hours or even more, and workweeks seven days long are the norm. And since they toil far below deck, many of today's fishermen never see the Milky Way, the Summer Triangle, or the cavorting dolphins that so lifted Ray's spirits.

It was not until 1920, when Congress passed the Death on the High Seas Act, that the widows and children of fishermen and other working seamen who were killed on the high seas could recover anything for their loss. Fifty years after that, in 1970, the Supreme Court finally overruled Justice Waite's decision in *The Harrisburg*, allowing for the first time a general maritime claim for wrongful death occurring on inshore waters.

Even today, however, the surviving spouses and children of fishermen killed at sea are treated as second-class citizens by the law. Unlike survivors of those wrongfully killed ashore, they are not entitled to compensation for their loss of comfort and affection, or for the pain and suffering endured by their departed loved ones, no matter how careless or reckless the conduct that caused their suffering. To that extent, the medieval wrongful death rule lives on today in our courts of law.

Today's women have many more options than they did in Maggie's time, of course. The professions and the avenues of commerce have opened up to women to an extent that would have pleased and astonished Maggie and Em.

Prostitutes have it better today in some important ways — contraception is inexpensive and effective, safe and legal abortions are available in most places, and antibiotics have revolutionized the treatment of venereal disease. But the law has not been kind to the practitioners of the oldest profession. Prostitution became illegal in most states in the first decades of the twentieth century, forcing brothels like Fannies out of business. Pimps have replaced the madams, and seedy motels, back seats, and dark alleys have replaced the brothels. It's still a hard, harsh, all-too-short life for the ladies of the night.

Disclaimer

This is a work of fiction. A few peripheral characters, the ones found in history books, lived real lives, but none of the others have ever existed outside of the imagination of the author. To give the story the right tone, some surnames common to the time and place were used, but any resemblance to people who actually existed is unintended and coincidental. So to any Hudsons, O'Gradys, Pitts, Stevens, Wonsons, or others, be assured that this novel is not about your ancestors; these characters are entirely fictional.

The carnage that was the Georges Bank fishery, however, was all too real. Between 1860 and 1885, three hundred sixty-four Gloucester fishing schooners did sink, and two thousand four hundred twenty-two Gloucester fishermen did die at sea.

Acknowledgments

I am grateful for the many volunteers who were kind enough to read drafts of this work and who have provided invaluable feedback. Thank you to Bob Alsdorf, Caroline Becker, David Brewster, Ralph Brindley, Sandy Brown, Joleen Burgess, Joanne Burt, Heidi Dahmen, Jan Eckman, Barbara Geisler, Leslie George, Connie Haslam, Ben Harer, Robert Hauck, Karen Gates Hildt (who waded through two versions!), Fred Huebner, Karen Hust, David Jurca, Andy Kinstler, Eric Laschever, Benjamin Nivision, Linda Robinson, Tony Robinson, Andy Ross, Gail van Norman, Richard White, Craig Wright, Christopher Wronsky, Patricia Wronsky, and no doubt others I've lost track of. Special thanks to Helen Ross, whose infectious enthusiasm spurred me on. Very special thanks to David Weber, who many decades ago taught me to write, and who more recently devoted countless hours to editing multiple drafts and who provided many insightful suggestions.

I am also grateful to my editor, Sherri Schultz, a true professional, for her dedication, hard work, and expertise. She has taught me much, and her efforts have made this manuscript far better than it otherwise would have been. Thanks also to my publisher, Greg Shaw for his faith in me and my work, and to Barbara Geisler for her excellent work on the cover design.

Finally, last but by no means least, thank you Sally Bagshaw for reading, re-reading, and reading again the many drafts of this work, and for your inspiration and ceaseless encouragement, without which this book never would have been written.

About the Author

Bradley Bagshaw grew up in Gloucester and has lived with the sea since exploring Gloucester Harbor in a beat-up dory at age ten. Sailing instructor was his first job at sixteen, which was followed by work on the docks as a stevedore and a forklift driver. Then he was off to Exeter, Bowdoin, MIT, and Harvard Law School, and to a career as a lawyer suing fishing companies for mistreating their fishermen. Starting in 2007, Bradley and his wife sailed eleven thousand miles from Seattle to Tahiti and back on a thirty-nine-foot cutter. On that trip he conceived the idea for *Georges Bank*, his first novel.

CPSIA information can be obtained
at www.ICGtesting.com
Printed in the USA
LVOW13s2250080618
580108LV00010B/850/P